ORIGIN

DOCTOR WHO – THE NEW ADVENTURES

Also available:

THE NEW

Doctor WHO

ADVENTURES

ORIGINAL SIN

Andy Lane

First published in Great Britain in 1995 by
Doctor Who Books
an imprint of Virgin Publishing Ltd
332 Ladbroke Grove
London W10 5AH

Cover illustration and internal illustrations by Tony Masero

ISBN 0 426 20444 1

Phototypeset by Intype, London
Printed and bound in Great Britain
by Cox & Wyman Ltd, Reading, Berks.

To the Fictionmeet crew, especially Ian Atkins, Alan Barnes, Ian Barnwell, David Bartlett, Paul Cornell, Andy Cowper, Val Douglas, Robert Francis, Jackie Marshall, Keith Topping, David Tulley and Mark Wyman.

Acknowledgements

Round up the usual suspects – Chris, Tina, Molly, Craig, Liz, Ben, Jim, Justin and Gus, with special mentions to Mark ('An excellent read... a real contrast to *All-Consuming Fire*') Benoy, Sarah L. ('Have you considered seeking professional, medical, chemical or other help?') Winters and Andrew ('Don't quibble grammar with a psycho') Martin. And to Rebecca Levene, for trusting me enough to let me abandon the plot and make this book up as I was going along. I promise it won't happen again.

'Things fall apart; the centre cannot hold;
Mere anarchy is loosed upon the world,
The blood-dimmed tide is loosed, and everywhere
The ceremony of innocence is drowned [...]
And what rough beast, its hour come round at last,
Slouches towards Bethlehem to be born?'
                              W. B. Yeats, *The Second Coming*

'We will sing of great crowds excited by work, by
pleasure and by riot; we will sing of the multicoloured, polyphonic tides of revolution in the
modern capitals; we will sing of the vibrant nightly
fervour of arsenals and shipyards blazing with violent electric moons ...'
Emilio Filippo Tommaso Marinetti, *The Manifesto
of Futurism*

Prologue

A cold wind blew orange dust across the landing strip and into Homeless Forsaken's stalked eyes. He blinked slowly.

'I'm dying,' he hissed, surprised.

'Not if I can help it,' Bernice said, but she knew that it was too late. His sluglike Hith body was turning grey and the mucus that coated his skin was drying out as she watched. The laser blast had caught him just above the base of the vestigial shell on his tail, damaging him beyond even the legendary Hith capacity for survival.

'I'm dying,' Homeless Forsaken repeated, this time in resignation. 'Bernice, there's something I need to ask you . . .'

Bernice knelt beside him, listening to him talk. He spoke for a few minutes, then his voice abruptly stopped. Bernice ran a hand over the moist skin between his eye-stalks, checking for a pulse, but it was too late.

She heard tracks churning up the plastic surface of the strip behind her.

If there was one thing that Bernice had learned about during her time with the Doctor, it was death. She had seen too much of it. She had come to recognize the cold brush of its wing as it passed her by and selected some friend, colleague or innocent bystander. This time it had taken Homeless Forsaken Betrayed And Alone, but it could so easily have been her.

Next time, perhaps.

She ran a finger around the base of one of his stalked eyes. Apart from a bubble of blue blood at the corner of his mouth he could have been asleep.

1

'Don't move!'

She flinched at the harsh, amplified Oolian voice.

'Get up slowly, hands behind your head.'

'You didn't have to kill him,' she shouted, obeying the shouted instructions. Her voice echoed off the hangars and the slab sides of rusted manipulator robots.

'Take five steps backwards.'

'I said you didn't – '

'*Do it!*'

She stumbled over the uneven plastic as she backed away. With a rush of feet, two winged and mech-suited Oolians rushed past her and grabbed the Hith warrior's head.

'Turn around!'

She stayed where she was, watching as the Oolians hauled her friend away. His columnar body left a single furrow in the dust. The sight looked strangely like two sparrows fighting over a worm, and she laughed a short, harsh laugh.

'I *said* – '

'Yeah. I heard.'

She turned slowly, and found herself face to face with Karvellis. The Oolian militia commander had thrown her helmet back across her shoulders, and she was carrying a weapon whose barrel still glowed red from the single shot that had brought Homeless Forsaken down. Her beaked face reminded Bernice of a dodo.

The tracked militia tank behind her had clipped part of a hangar on its way round the corner. She gestured towards it with one suited wing. 'In the back,' she snarled. 'Now!'

Bernice gazed levelly at her, and nodded towards the weapon. 'If you didn't outnumber and outgun me,' she said quietly, 'I'd make you eat that thing.'

'Yeah,' Karvellis sneered, 'and humans might learn to fly like us, rather than slink through the dust like the Hith.' She gestured to one of her troops. 'Throw her inside and drive her back to town.'

The Oolian pushed Bernice towards the back of the

tank and threw her into a darkened holding cell which smelled of alien sweat, alien dirt and alien things she didn't even want to think about.

'That's you crossed off my Christmas card list!' Bernice yelled as the hatch slammed shut. Score one for the birds. It wasn't going to be easy, getting out of a metal box on tracks while driving through a desert. She couldn't even rely on the Doctor to help; when the warehouse exploded, he'd been inside. She'd seen him escape from tighter corners before, but one day his luck was going to run out. Perhaps it already had.

Light from outside shone through a grille high up in the wall, casting a patchwork glow across the ceiling but illuminating nothing of the cell. She climbed to her feet and began running her hands along the metal walls, searching for seams, hatches or weak spots.

The floor vibrated as the tank's gravimetric engines revved up. A sudden lurch threw her sideways. She stumbled, trying to regain her footing, but the vehicle shifted into gear and moved off, causing her to fall. What with the smell, the motion and the darkness, Bernice began to feel queasy.

The tank turned a corner and, with a metallic grinding sound, a hatch in the front of the cell slid open. A familiar gnomish face looked at her.

'What's a nice girl like you doing in a place like this?' asked the Doctor.

Bernice bounded to her feet, relief and happiness flooding through her, dissolving the little knots of tension and fear that she had not even acknowledged were there. 'Doctor? I thought you might be – '

'Yes, so did I,' he said.

'How did you – '

'Find you? The usual method. I just followed the militia.'

'Er . . . Doctor?'

'Hmm?'

'Who's driving?'

He looked hurt. 'I am,' he said.

3

'But you're talking to me,' she said.

With a terrible grinding sound the tank lurched sideways and stopped dead, sending Bernice sprawling into the metal bulkhead. The gravimetric engines whined, setting her teeth on edge, then cut out altogether. She waited for an explosion that never came.

Deprived of power to its magnetic locks, the hatch at the back swung open. Bernice scrambled out and took great whooping gulps of fresh, clean air.

She looked around, still breathing heavily. They were in the middle of a stretch of desert. The churned-up tracks led back across the orange dust to where the neglected manipulator robots reared like giant insects above the hangars, silhouetted against the eye-searing purple of the sky. Ahead, their path was blocked by the comforting blue shape of the TARDIS. It appeared to be intact, which was more than could be said for the tank, which had crashed into it. Apart from the tank, the TARDIS and the buildings and cranes behind it, the landscape was empty.

One of the doors at the front of the tank fell to the ground with a loud metallic clatter. The Doctor stepped carefully out, using his umbrella for support. He was still wearing the Oolian mech-suit, and his arms fitted badly into the wing-slots.

'Typical,' Bernice said, shaking her head. 'The only obstacle between us and freedom and you have to run straight into it. Bloody typical!'

'You wouldn't have me any other way,' he said with a twinkle in his eye.

'Just make sure you never give me the choice,' she said.

He gazed out towards the warehouses. 'They'll soon spot the guard whose suit I'm wearing,' he said, shading his eyes. 'I left him my scarf, but it clashes with his plumage.'

'We'd better get a move on then.' She glanced at him with tears in her eyes. 'They killed Homeless Forsaken, you know?'

'I know.' He nodded. 'I saw it. What was the reason? I

know Oolians aren't the friendliest of races, but that was uncalled for.'

She shrugged. 'I don't know. He wasn't even armed.'

'Well, there's nothing to keep us here now. Unless, of course, you fancy a little sightseeing?'

She surveyed the flat landscape. A small cloud of dust appeared to be racing towards them from the distant strip.

'The only sight I want to see at the moment is the inside of a tumbler of whisky. Let's go.'

Within seconds, they had left the planet entirely and entered the dimensionally ambiguous interior of the TARDIS. In a few seconds more, even the TARDIS's outer plasmic shell had dispersed upon the dry Oolian wind.

Chapter 1

'Good morning. I'm Evan Claple and this is The Empire Today, *on the spot, on and off Earth. Today's headlines: the Imperial Landsknechte should be scrapped, claims Duke Marmion, Lord Protector of the Solar System and its Environs, in an exclusive interview on this programme. And off-world: twenty-nine alien races file claims for reparation from the Imperial Court for damages during the Wars of Acquisition. We ask whether these alien scum should ever have been left alive to complain...'*

The sun was rising across the towers of the Overcity.

The flitter rose from the pad on top of the Central Adjudication Lodge like a leaf trying to reverse the passage of autumn. Chris Cwej watched from the passenger seat as the shadows of the shrubs and trees extended like clutching fingers across the parkland. The greenery stretched as far as he could see: individual squares of green and brown on top of each tower, separated by the black gaps and linked together by a web of bridges and walkways. It was said that a man could start walking in Spaceport One and end up back where he started without changing direction. It wasn't true, of course – the Seacities weren't continuous across the ocean floor for a start – but it was a romantic notion, and Cwej wished that it were true.

Cwej's golden fur glowed in the rosy light. He ran a proud hand up and down his forearm, feeling the luxuriant growth bend and spring back beneath the pressure. The body-bepple had been worth every penny. Every single penny.

People were moving in the park, even this early in the day. Some were running, some were walking hand in hand, while others were standing by the edges of the buildings, gazing into the gaps. In every open space, groups of elderly people were practising some form of slow martial art akin to a solo dance. Cwej found it all fascinating. His family lived down in one of the lower levels, and it wasn't often that he got the chance to see the top of the city, especially at sunrise. He wanted to make the most of it.

A couple were kissing over by an Arcturan sheckt bush. The sun backlit them with a golden glow, casting their shadows across the lush grass. Cwej felt a pang of envy, and looked away. Far below, the shadow of the flitter rushed between patches of darkness like an animal occasionally breaking cover.

The pilot glanced over at him. Cwej could see his own bearlike face reflected in the man's eyes. The sight still brought him up with a slight shock of pleasure and surprise. He gave a thumbs-up.

'Great view,' he shouted.

The pilot's expression didn't change. Cwej smiled. Pilots belonging to the Order of Adjudicators were notoriously juvenile. Cwej had been one himself, not too long ago. He knew the tricks of the trade. The guy would probably dive the flitter towards one of the gaps at any moment, expecting him to scream or something. Like all hell he would.

As the sun crawled upwards, the shadows contracted. The pilot's hand suddenly moved sideways. The flitter banked, and dropped towards a narrow gap between the green tops of two towers.

Cwej smiled. Knew it, he thought, as the shadow of the flitter rose up to meet them. The pilot's gaze slid sideways. Cwej yawned ostentatiously.

The edge of the gap flashed past. A row of faces along the rim watched open-mouthed as they plunged between the buildings. Darkness suddenly engulfed them . . .

8

. . . and then the flitter was descending on a spiral path, with the slab sides of the buildings looming like cliffs all around them. Cwej craned his neck, but all he could see of the sky above them was a rose-tinted slit. The buildings themselves were dark, unbroken cones, towers and inverted pyramids, dimly illuminated by the light from above, dripping with condensation.

Far below, Cwej could just about make out the dim glow of firelight glittering on water.

'Welcome to Spaceport Five Undertown,' said the pilot.

The walls of the TARDIS were closing in on her.

That's what it felt like, at least. Bernice lay back upon her bed and put her clenched fists over her eyes, pressing her knuckles hard against the lids until fireworks began to explode on the inside of her head.

Damn it, she'd liked the stupid slug. Why did he have to die?

She threw herself off the bed and looked around her room. Piles of clothes and junk collected from half a hundred worlds littered the floor. On a whim she picked an object up: a spiky ball made of soft, red metal. What the hell was it? Where had she found it? She threw it to one side and picked up another memento: a translucent blue seashell with the image of her face etched into its surface. It triggered a vague flash of memory, but nothing more. She'd been to too many planets in too short a time. Living with the Doctor was like living in a huge restaurant full of the finest food and wine in the universe. For a while it was fun, but after a while you craved bacon and eggs and a cup of tea.

She threw the shell aside and marched out of her room, kicking a pile of dirty laundry to one side as she went. With an incensed 'Meow', Wolsey the cat shot out of the pile and past her into the corridor.

The white walls and enigmatic roundels of the corridor walls mocked her. Wherever she went in the TARDIS, the view was always the same. The swimming pool, the golf course, the rose garden, the art gallery . . . White walls

9

and enigmatic bloody roundels. The outside was supposed to be infinitely reconfigurable – at least, it had been until the Doctor sabotaged the chameleon circuit – but the inside never changed its appearance.

It was always the way. You spent a couple of days being chased around some alien planet or robot battleship in fear of your life, desperate to get back to the TARDIS, and five minutes after you did you were climbing the walls to get out again. Frying pan to fire to frying pan in one easy lesson.

She chose a direction at random, and began to walk. The image of Homeless Forsaken's moist flesh flaring as Karvellis's blaster beam ate through it followed her. The stink of burning flesh remained in her nostrils. Another friend gone. How old was she? Thirty-three now. Wasn't it time she did something with her life? Something more than rushing around after the Doctor?

She smiled briefly at the memory of her short sabbatical at the archaeological dig on Menaxus, but scowled as she remembered how the Doctor had managed to poke his sticky little Time Lord fingers into even that.

Pulling herself back from the brink of anger, Bernice found herself outside a door that she didn't recognize. Intrigued, she pushed it open and poked her head into the shadows within.

And couldn't believe what she saw.

The dream clung to Roz Forrester even after she was awake and staring at the ceiling.

It was the usual dream. Martle was standing in the empty doorway of the hotel room, half turned towards her. 'There's nobody here, Roz,' he said in his soft and deceptively casual voice. 'Let's get a coffee and call it a day.' As he spoke, Forrester could see the glint of a claw in the shadowed interior, but she couldn't open her mouth to warn him. The brutal thunk as it carved its way up his spine would echo in her ears forever.

Eventually she crawled out of bed and staggered to the wall-wide simcord screen. It was displaying one of the oscillating deserts of Gallipoli V: a newly colonized world out in the Quirillis Sector. A very popular image, apparently. Very exclusive. Very expensive. Very nauseating.

She reset the screen to its default blankness, and peered at her dim reflection, trying to tell whether she looked as bad as she felt. She sighed as she realized that she did. Worse, if anything. Her dark, grey-speckled hair hung limply, her eyes were bloodshot and her face looked puffy. Hardly surprising: she'd spent the previous night curled up with a three-pack of cheap Martian ale, and felt as if the top of her head had been screwed tighter on while she'd been asleep.

She tapped out the code for the Spaceport Five Undertown Lodge. The screen flickered for a moment before Lodge Warden Lubineki's face appeared. The lodge's simcord had been playing up for some time: the 3D effect was exaggerated, thrusting his moustache out at her and pulling the rest of his face back into a streamlined cone.

'Justice by your side,' she croaked in the ritual greeting.

'And fairness be your friend,' he said, frowning out of the simcord screen at her. 'Forrester. You're not looking too good. Calling in sick?'

'The Adjudicator Secular would never forgive me,' she said, trying not to flinch as his moustache waggled in her face. 'Tell her I'll be in late this morning.'

'Will do. She's been looking for you.'

Forrester groaned. 'Just my luck. She forgets about me for months on end, then the one morning I'm going to be late, she wants me. Any particular reason?'

'Dunno.' He frowned. 'Some new guy's turned up, though. Name of Cwej. Perhaps he's waiting for you.'

'Cwej?' That was a new one on her. 'How do you spell that?'

He consulted a screen out of the range of the simcord. 'Uh . . . C-W-E-J, Cwej.'

The name seemed familiar. She'd seen his file recently. Or talked to somebody about him. 'Any idea who he is?'

'Transferred across from the Spaceport Nine Overcity

Lodge, traffic detail. Rumour says he might be a replacement for Martle.'

A chill ran through her. Remnants of the dream were still floating through her head. Thunk, as the claw ripped his life from him.

'Nobody can replace Martle,' she said.

'Hey, I didn't mean – '

'Forget it,' she said dismissively. A memory bobbed to the surface of her mind: Adjudicator Secular Rashid's bloated face, and a discussion about who she wanted to work with next.

'It's not pronounced "Cwej",' she said, remembering, 'it's pronounced "Shvey".'

'Says "Cwej" here,' Lubineki said, frowning.

'Yeah, but – oh, never mind.' It was none of her business what the new guy got called, so long as he wasn't called her squire.

Lubineki's gaze had shifted past her to her apartment. 'Nice place,' he said appreciatively. 'What level you on?'

She shifted her body to block his view. The apartment didn't look *that* expensive – she was too much of a slob for that – but the size alone would be enough to make Lubineki think. The last thing she needed was rumours spreading about her lifestyle.

'Five-oh-five,' she said.

He tried to look unimpressed, but the distortion of the simcord emphasized the envious twitch of his mouth. 'Five-oh-five, eh? Got a rich boyfriend?'

'If only,' she muttered, deflecting the query. 'See you soon.'

He flipped a sketchy salute. 'Have a good trip.'

She closed down the simcord and shut her eyes. Her head ached. Her head ached fit to burst, but still not enough to drown out the images. Jeez, Martle, why you? Why you?

Ahead of District Inspector Artik Glebe, the walkway slowed to a halt as it approached the door to the warehouse block. Two conspicuously armed security bots stood waiting for him, weapon arms extended.

'My name's Glebe,' he said. 'Imperial Food Administration Office. We're doing a check on the animeats.'

There was a pause, as the bots checked with centcomp that Glebe was expected, and he still had to submit to gene-testing before he was allowed inside. For a few moments after the door opened and the walkway started up again, Glebe was disoriented. He had expected shadows, echoes and oppressive heat. What he found was a cool, bright space where the far walls vanished in a distant haze, and only the faintest hint of a roof could be made out. It was like standing in a meadow on a summer's day.

The walkway deposited him at the edge of a springy floor. Somewhere out in the centre of space, shimmering in and out of the haze like a mirage, Glebe could make out huge but vague shapes. He walked closer. A cool breeze caressed his face, and he had to force himself to remember he was inside, not out. Gradually the haze pulled back to reveal the animeats.

Glebe stood entranced. He'd heard descriptions, of course, but even so . . .

The closest animeat was so large that its back was lost in the haze hiding the ceiling. Huge rolls of flesh lapped around it like waves. Spade-shaped flippers the size of flitters ringed its grey, pebbled body. It had no eyes, no mouth, nothing but flesh.

Behind it, like a range of foothills, Glebe could make out other animeats.

'They come from a gas giant out on the Rim,' said a voice behind him. 'They float through the high density atmosphere, absorbing nutrients.'

Glebe turned. A woman in a seamless foil coverall stood behind him. She was in her forties, striking rather than attractive, with close-cropped grey hair and green eyes. In her hand she held a small control unit.

'I'm impressed,' he said. 'My name's Glebe. I'm the new Inspector from – '

13

'The IFAO, I guess. Thanks for coming.'

He smiled. 'No problem. If it wasn't for ElleryCorp, Earth's billions would starve to death. I'm just here to do the regular check for toxins, mutagens and suchlike. Shouldn't take long.'

She nodded. 'Appreciate it,' she said. 'I'm Anna Taverjl, by the way. I'm ElleryCorp's representative for this sector of the Empire.'

'Pleasure.' He extended his hand, and Taverjl shook it.

'No problem. You've arrived during feeding time, though. Mind if I get on with it?'

Glebe shook his head, and Taverjl fed commands into her control unit. As Glebe watched, jointed mechanical arms descended from the clouds, trailing cables and pipes behind them. They oriented themselves to face the animeats. Simultaneously, sprays of liquid gushed from nozzles on each arm, soaking into the cliffs of flesh and vanishing almost immediately.

'The "food" is just a hydrocarbon mix,' Taverjl said, and started walking towards the animeats. 'We use waste products from refineries and sewage stations. Cheap, and the animeats just lap it up.'

'You don't slaughter the things outright and cut them up?' Glebe said as they walked.

'No, of course not. Terribly wasteful. We harvest them on a continual basis. The vast majority of their flesh is completely useless to them, of course; they've been engineered that way. We can remove the excess with impunity. Keep watching.'

Glebe glanced up at the approaching wall of animeat. The feeding arms had withdrawn into the ceiling, and were being replaced with others. Only the colour of the cables was different. A sudden flare of light made Glebe avert his eyes. He looked back, more carefully. The arms were travelling across the surface of the animeat, slicing off fragments of flesh with knives of laser light. Other arms came after them, scavenging the scraps through some kind of vacuum hose.

'Very neat,' was all Glebe could think of to say.

14

They reached the base of the nearest animeat, and Glebe reached out a hand to touch its skin. The surface was cool to the touch, spongy, with nodules the size of his head distorting the surface.

Scraps of flesh were falling all around them as the robot butchers did their work high above. Taverjl reached down and picked up a piece. She offered it to Glebe. He waved it away.

'Thanks,' he said, 'but no thanks.'

'Your loss,' she said, biting a chunk out of it and swallowing. The exposed flesh of the fragment was greenish, and seeped a pale fluid. Threadlike vessels hung from it, twitching. Glebe looked up again at the harvesting.

'Doesn't it hurt?' he asked.

Taverjl looked confused for a moment, then realized what he was asking. 'No,' she said. 'They don't feel any pain.'

One of the mechanical waldoes appeared from around the side of the animeat, sucking raw meat up from the floor into its maw. A deactivated laser cutter was attached to the jointed arm. Glebe hadn't realized quite how big they were. The vacuum pipe itself was as thick as his entire body.

The arm paused in front of Glebe. Some sort of optical sensor scanned his face.

'I hope the safeguards work,' he said, laughing nervously.

'So long as nobody interferes with the software,' Taverjl said, with a tone in her voice that Glebe didn't like. He turned to face her. She was inputting commands into her control unit whilst watching him with a level, cool gaze.

'What do you mean?' he asked, very aware of the arm stationary behind him.

'I mean,' she suddenly snarled, 'that interfering minor officials who have nothing better to do than recycle paperwork aren't covered by the safeguards.'

She pressed a button, and something went fizz in Glebe's mind. Pins and needles shot through his nerves. An impossibly thin line of bright green light seemed to be emerging from a hot spot in the centre of his forehead and plunging into the distance. It looked like one of the laser beams that the cutters had used to harvest the animeats, but it couldn't have been. He would have been dead if it was. Wouldn't he?

He turned, trying to see where the light was coming from, but he only succeeded in cutting the top of his head neatly off.

As he fell limply to the floor, the last thing he saw was Taverjl's previously impassive face.

Smiling.

Adjudicator Roz Forrester left her apartment and went down twenty levels in the null-grav shaft to where a walkway crossed her block. Given her position on level 505, her biochip implant would allow her access to all of the lower levels, and none of the ones above. That gave her a lot more choice than the people who lived lower down. They could only use the walkways on the levels below theirs. As an Adjudicator she could, in theory, access any level she liked, but she wasn't on duty yet, and it wouldn't have been fair. And if there was one thing that Roz Forrester was hot on, it was fairness.

Five minutes on the crowded moving belt got her to Block Eighty-Nine. Another null-grav shaft took her downwards, past level after level, towards the bottom of the building. There was nobody about: the lowest levels were reserved for the environmental controls and the massive null-grav engines.

As Forrester approached the end of the shaft, she pressed the override button on her comm-unit. The bottom of the shaft opened like a flower, and she slowly dropped out of the building entirely.

The old and mouldy carpet of Spaceport Five Undertown spread out a kilometre or so beneath her, illuminated only by the light filtering down from between the towers. As usual, the stench of rot and decay rising from moss-strewn buildings, fungus-coated walls and water-filled alleys made her eyes itch and her stomach heave.

Moisture dripped constantly from the bottoms of the buildings. Fires burned in the distance, as did strings of fluorescent lamps, bio-lights and rad-globes. Anything that the underdwellers could beg, steal or borrow. Especially steal.

Tiny rafts and boats navigated the canals that once, before the Overcity was built, had been broad thoroughfares and ornately decorated streets. Their navigators punted past gaping windows and carved ledges, past the walkways that had been strung alongside the canals and the precarious bridges that linked rooftops and windows, past the heads of drowned statues and the ruined architecture of a once proud city. How quickly things could change. Forrester had been a child when the most recent Wars of Acquisition started and the first of the floating buildings was constructed above the battle-torn cities of the Earth. Within ten years, the battle lines had been pushed so far away from Earth that humanity had almost forgotten the Wars were still taking place, and half the population lived in the Overcities, heedless of the havoc they were wreaking on the climate. Now, twenty years further down the line, the surface was neglected. Except by the underdwellers.

The underdwellers: a fermenting scum of outcasts, criminals, malcontents and off-worlders. Forrester shivered just thinking about the off-worlders. Despite the fact that the Earth Empire extended its welcoming arms to beings of all races so long as they abandoned their off-world ways and lived in a civilized manner, with only the minimum amount of paperwork between them and a position as a second-class subject of the Empress, most immigrants seemed to end up down in the Undertown. As far as Forrester was concerned, they were untrustworthy and unsanitary, and deserved everything that happened to them.

Forrester cast her eyes heavenward as she descended. A thick miasma hid all but the lowest levels of the towers. Supported by intangible beams of gravity, they hovered like regular, pendulous clouds over the water-sodden landscape beneath. Somewhere, thousands of feet above her head, there were parks and playgrounds, and a rose-hued sky. Down here it was always dark and it was always raining.

She could feel a dull pressure building up behind her eyes. All Adjudicators in the Undertown lodges got it. Presumably the underdwellers did too, except that nobody had ever bothered asking them. The medics suggested that it was something to do with the harmonics of the null-grav units that kept the Overcity up where it belonged, but they couldn't find anything physical to treat. Wasn't it always the way?

The null-grav beam deposited her on the roof of an irregular complex of plasticrete buildings. Off-world scavengers moved among piles of rubbish and puddles of brackish water. She pulled her neuronic whip out, just in case any of the underdwellers were around, but the place was silent apart from the hiss of the rain and the very faint, teeth-jarring whine of the null-grav generators.

She unclipped the centcomp glove and glasses from her belt and slipped them on. The heat of her hand activated the system, and a glowing yellow menu appeared in the air before her. She reached out and pressed a virtual button. Feedback mechanisms in the glove gave her the sensation of having actually pressed something physical. Within a few seconds she had progressed through a series of different menus and discovered where her lodge was based today. Centcomp put a map up, and Forrester knew enough about the area to find the quickest and, more importantly, safest way along the walkways, ladders, roofs and bridges of the Undertown. Nowhere was there a line of sight that ran for more than a few metres. No path could be walked for more than a minute before there was a corner, a set of steps or a ladder.

She found the lodge in the centre of a flooded plaza. Having cordoned off all the canals leading into the plaza with floating security fencing and illuminated the surrounding area with hoverlights, the Adjudicator Secular had obviously felt safe enough to relax security.

Officers were walking freely across the catwalks between the rafts with their robes hanging loose. Securitybots lumbered to and fro. Flitters were lined up along the primary raft like an armoured Imperial Landsknecht division ready to roll into some small off-world city and impose the will of the Empress.

She found her way down to water level and strode out along the single floating catwalk that led to the rafts.

'Justice . . .' said Lubineki as he held out the gene-tester. 'Adjudicator Forrester, good to see you.' He was sweating freely in the heat. Forrester shoved her hand into the device's opening. 'How're you feeling?'

'Fairness . . .' she said wearily, wincing as the device removed the standard cell sample from her finger tip. The gene-tester was clumsy, but more reliable at proving identity than the ubiquitous biochips, which could be surgically removed and reimplanted, if the price was right. Even body-bepple couldn't faze it. 'I'm feeling like shit. What have they moved the raft down here for? I thought we were still anchored over beneath the Eastern Towers.'

'Didn't you read the memo yesterday?' Lubineki seemed genuinely surprised. 'Big case going on: some guy had his head cut off. They wanted the lodge close at hand so they moved the whole shebang down here.' He looked around, and sniffed. 'Least they could do is issue us with masks,' he said. 'That water smells like puke.'

The gene-tester buzzed. Lubineki studied the display carefully. 'You're the real Forrester,' he said finally, and grinned.

After leaving the shower and locker raft with her black robes flowing around her, and after the minimum amount of meditation on and recitation of the Adjudicator's Creed in the Shrine of Justice that she could get away with, Forrester diverged off to one side and stood on the edge of the catwalk. Beneath her feet the dark water lapped sluggishly at the plastic, depositing a thin film wherever it touched.

'Excuse me?'

Forrester turned, then wished she hadn't when the

inside of her skull failed to move as quickly as the outside. The man behind her looked as if he had just climbed out of a body-bepple tank. His golden fur glowed, his small black nose was moist and shiny and his little button-eyes shone with health and vitality. He was so muscular that his robes were tight around his chest, and bulged at the seams. For a moment, Forrester hated him.

'Who the hell are you?' she said.

'Cwej. Chris Cwej.' His eyes scanned her in the usual way that people did when they were looking for examples of body-bepple. He'd have to look a lot closer than that if he wanted to see how she'd changed herself.

'Isn't it pronounced "Shvey"?' she asked.

'Nope.' He shook his head. 'Too many people got confused. I stick to "Cwej": it's easier.' He smiled. 'I'm supposed to report to Adjudicator Secular Rashid. Can you point me in his direction?'

Forrester sighed. '*Her* direction. Fresh out of the Academy?'

Cwej's smile widened. Forrester felt nauseous. Nobody had a right to be that cheerful.

'No, I graduated last year. I've been on traffic patrol over in Spaceport Nine Overcity ever since.'

'Of course you have,' Forrester said, looking around for Rashid's raft. 'I've got to see the Adjudicator Secular myself. Follow me.'

'Thanks. 'Preciate it.'

'Don't mention it,' Forrester snarled. This boy was going to get on her nerves pretty damn fast.

Bernice was sitting on the floor of the TARDIS boot cupboard when the Doctor found her. From the doorway, all he could see was her cross-legged form in the far distance, illuminated by a single beam of light. As he stepped inside the room, however, he realized that the shadows around her were filled with row upon row of shoes and boots, arranged in concentric circles, like a waiting audience. Burnished highlights shone back from cracked leather.

Bernice did not appear to have noticed him.

He picked his way cautiously through the boots, noticing step by step old friends whom he had thought lost for ever. There were the elastic-sided pair inside which he had hidden the TARDIS key when he was in the Ashbridge Cottage Hospital. Next to them were the green rubber waders that he'd splashed about the marshes of Delta III in. Over to one side he saw the brogues that he'd been wearing when Kellman had electrified the floor of his room on Nerva Beacon. The heels were still charred. He smiled. Portrait of the Doctor as a collector of shoes. Time considered as a collection of worn-out footwear.

Clearing a space, he sat beside Bernice. She was holding a tumbler of some amber fluid and gazing out across the sea of attentive boots. She had an old rag across her lap and a pair of Roman sandals beside her.

'Some people might think,' she said suddenly, startling him, 'that possessing several thousand pairs of shoes, boots and sandals indicated an obsessive personality.'

'Nonsense,' he replied. 'Do you know how long I've lived? Over a millennium. Do you know how much footwear I've got through in that time? A lot. A lot more than a lot.'

'A mega-lot,' Bernice muttered.

'Yes, a mega – '

The Doctor trailed off into silence. Mega. A word he had not thought about for some time. Quite deliberately.

'Quite a few,' he finished lamely.

'They don't look worn out to me,' Bernice said.

'Fashions change. Opinions alter. Location must be taken into account. What looks good in the light of a red giant sun can cause severe embarrassment on a planet circling a white dwarf. What one race might consider to be footwear fit for the gods might cause another to call for the fashion police.'

He reached out and snared a pair of bright green shoes with orange spats. Bernice winced when she saw them.

'Take these . . .' the Doctor started.

'No thanks!'

'I used to love these, once upon a body. Nowadays I wouldn't be seen dead in them.'

He caught Bernice's sideways glance at the brushed suede shoes that he was wearing, and shifted his position slightly so that he was sitting on them. They sat in silence for a few moments, gazing out towards the sketchy shapes of the roundels in the shadows. Eventually, more to break the silence than for any other reason, the Doctor reached out and took the tumbler from Bernice's hand. '*Lch'thy-li*!' he said, and gulped the liquid down.

' "*Lch'thy-li*"?' She looked at him strangely.

'Berberese for "Here's blood on your horns".'

'Oh.' She shrugged, still eyeing him as if he had done something completely bizarre. 'Well, the feeling's mutual, I'm sure.'

The Doctor knew that human emotions weren't his strong point, but he took the plunge anyway. 'There's something wrong, isn't there?' he said.

'And they said you were insensitive,' she murmured.

'Who said?'

'Nobody. I was joking.'

'Would a holiday help?' His eyes gleamed.

'No thanks! Your holidays are more dangerous than your deliberate adventures.'

He smiled, remembering some of his holidays. 'Did I ever tell you about the time I had a tooth removed in the Old West?'

'Yes,' Bernice said levelly.

'Oh. What about the effervescent oceans of Florana?'

'Yes.'

'Oh. What about – ' He saw her face, and stopped.

'Doctor,' she blurted suddenly, 'Homeless Forsaken told me something just before he died – something that's been worrying me. He said I shouldn't go back to Earth for the next few years. He said it wasn't safe – that something terrible was going to happen and he didn't want it to happen to me.' She sighed. 'He said even though the Hith are notorious for being loners, he liked me too much to want to see me die.'

'Earth,' the Doctor mused. 'Thirtieth century in Homeless Forsaken's time. A time of peace and prosperity: well, for the peaceful and prosperous, at least. Run by the full panoply of an Imperial Court – earls, viscounts and the rest – and divided up into areas called spaceports. Just like the old countries, except that they better reflect the socio-economic realities of life in the future. Not a pleasant place, as places go, but I wouldn't want to lose it just yet.' He was silent for a moment. 'Does this have anything to do with our adventures on Oolis?' he said finally.

'No.' She shook her head. 'That was something else that he had got mixed up in.'

The Doctor was silent for a few moments, remembering their time on Oolis. Homeless Forsaken, Hith warrior, had been a drifter: a rootless, homeless member of a downtrodden race. He hadn't talked about himself very much, but he had a sense of honour, and the Doctor had not known him to lie.

'The Hith,' he mused. 'As I recall, they lost a short but very nasty war with the Earth Empire – ' He took his gold hunter watch out of his pocket and consulted it. ' – four years or so ago. Their home world was terraformed, and the remnants of the Hith were left wandering around the galaxy in whatever spaceships they could beg, borrow or run off with without paying spaceport fees. I wouldn't be surprised if they were intending to take some terrible revenge.'

Bernice nodded. 'I'll never forget what Homeless Forsaken said about the despair of knowing that somebody had taken your planet away and wouldn't give it back. Did he tell you about his name? Apparently all of the Hith have renounced their original names and taken new ones to remind them and the rest of the galaxy what happened to them. His full name was Homeless Forsaken Betrayed And Alone.'

'You can imagine it, can't you?' the Doctor said. 'Some human security guard asks him who he is. "I'm Homeless Forsaken Betrayed And Alone," he replies. Passive resistance. Gandhi would have been proud.' He sighed, gazing out across the sea of shoes. 'But getting back to this threat, we haven't got much to go on. Is that all he said?'

'That's it. Oh, he mentioned somewhere called Space-port Five Overcity. He said that if I ever did go to Earth, to avoid going there.'

The Doctor handed the tumbler back to her and stood up, feeling suddenly shaky. That amber liquid certainly packed a punch. 'Then that's where we go,' he said. 'My interest has been piqued.'

Bernice sighed. 'Yeah, that's what I thought. I wasn't sure whether to tell you or not, but I guess I had to in the end. I'd have felt guilty as hell if we'd pitched up in thirtieth-century Earth in a few years' time, only to find it wasn't there any more.'

'Coming?'

She looked into the tumbler, and rolled the last few drops of amber fluid around. 'Why not?' she said, frowning.

'Moping in the dark is a fruitless occupation, Bernice.' He nodded towards the tumbler. 'And besides, you drink too much already.'

'Er, Doctor,' she said carefully, 'I think I should break some bad news to you. I was looking for something to do, and I found this place, so I decided to clean some of your shoes. Trouble is, you've gone and drunk the polish.'

Waiting For Justice And Dreaming Of Home slithered through the waist-high canal, dreaming of past glories.

The dank, mossy walls of the Undertown rose on either side of him, but in his drunken stupor Waiting For Justice was gliding past the soft, warm bulkheads of a Hith battle cruiser, dressed not in rags and tatters but the black and silver body-sleeve of a navigator.

The bottle clenched in his pseudo-limb dribbled a milky liquid into the canal. Attracted by the unfamiliar taste something broke the surface for a brief moment and brushed against his thigh, but to him it was the slap of a holstered blaster.

He staggered sideways, and paused for a moment, resting against a wall. Water cascaded down the brickwork, soaking his already moist body. He rotated his eye-stalks unsteadily, and saw a faint image of the present overlaid on the past. Somewhere in the recesses of his mind a decision was made. He would head for home.

Laboriously he pulled himself up out of the water and sprawled headlong upon the narrow wooden walkway. Eventually, he surged up until his body was balanced on his muscular basal foot, and took a long swig from the bottle.

Something moved in the shadows.

'At last,' a voice said. 'The prodigal returns.'

'Whassat?' he cried. He saw the blade as it arced through the air towards him, and was still trying to fit it into his fantasies when it slashed through his neck. As his lifeblood ebbed into the canal, and the blade cut away at him, he dreamed of battle in space, and glory, and death.

The TARDIS materialized beside a moving walkway at the point where it passed through the three hundred and first level of a residential tower in the Overcity.

Bernice stepped out of the time vessel, and was immediately carried away by the walkway. She gazed around, too surprised to cry out. The walkway was moving through an open plaza, around which shops and restaurants were clustered to attract passing trade. It seemed to be early in the morning: most of the premises were either closed or were just opening up, and the walkway was almost deserted.

Bernice turned to look back at the TARDIS. The Doctor had placed his key in the TARDIS lock before stepping outside, and was hanging onto it like grim death. He was having to run backwards just to keep himself in the one spot.

As Bernice watched, he managed to lock the door and let go. The walkway carried him away from the TARDIS. He watched it recede with a forlorn expression upon his face, clutching his multicoloured umbrella for comfort.

Turning away with a resigned shrug, he raised his hat to an old couple who passed by. They smiled, and waved back. A robot valet by their side waved as well.

'Do you think anybody will notice it there?' she called.

'I wouldn't have thought so,' the Doctor replied, walking along the strip towards her. 'The TARDIS has an amazing capacity for being overlooked. So long as we remember where she is, we'll be all right.'

'I hope you're right,' Bernice said.

Ahead of them, the walkway plunged out of the tower entirely, spanning the space across a rosy sky to a hole in the side of its nearest neighbour. Judging by the position of the sun, it was early morning. Looking ahead, she could see a number of towers strung along their path like stations on a monorail line. She took a deep breath, and felt something inside her chest relax. There was something about the smell of Earth that couldn't be duplicated.

The Doctor smiled as he joined her. 'Aren't I always?'

'I refuse to answer that question, on the grounds that it may incriminate you.'

It suddenly occurred to Bernice that the Doctor was further away than he had been a few moments before. She looked down at the walkway. It was continuous between the two of them, but he was definitely moving slightly faster than she was.

'Doctor,' she said, 'we're drifting apart.'

'Don't say that,' he cried, shaking his head. 'I know we've had our tiffs, but fundamentally we're still friends!'

'No,' she said, exasperated, 'I mean, we're *physically* drifting apart. This stuff we're standing on isn't solid. It's more like a very thick liquid.'

He looked around, then down at his feet. 'You may be right.'

He bent down to examine the material of the walkway: pressing it with his fingers, sniffing it and, to Bernice's embarrassment, licking it. She looked away, desperately hoping that nobody was watching, and cringed as she saw a group of people stepping on the edge of the walkway, where it appeared to be travelling extremely slowly.

'Interesting,' he said, rising. 'A single crystal exhibiting a high degree of thixotropic behaviour in a unilateral direction under the influence of an electromagnetic current.'

'What does that mean?' she asked, watching as the people walked closer to the centre of the strip and immediately began to accelerate.

'It means that this stuff that we're standing on isn't solid. It's more like a very thick liquid.'

'Fine. Thank you. That makes it all perfectly clear.'

The walkway was filling up slowly, and Bernice noticed a number of off-worlders amid the throng – Arcturans, Alpha Centaurans, Thrillp and Foamasi. Oddly, they were getting some dark looks from the humans, although there were a few races who were intermingling quite happily with the humans, including one with a blue warty skin, four blank orbs that might have been eyes and a ruff of coarse red hair around the neck.

'What race is that?' she said, nodding towards the alien.

The Doctor followed her gaze, and frowned. 'I'm not sure,' he admitted, squinting at the being as it passed them by. 'I don't recognize it at all.' His face suddenly cleared, and he cried: 'Of course! It's not an alien at all. It's human!'

'Human?' Bernice wasn't sure that she had heard correctly. 'What is it, Mardi Gras?'

'No.' The Doctor watched the alien's receding form. 'Genetic alteration. I think the trade name is "body-bepple". Quite easy, if you know what you're doing.'

'But why would you want to?'

'Why would you want to wear high heels?'

'I don't.'

'No, but if you did.'

'Haven't got a clue. Fashion, I guess.'

The Doctor nodded. 'Exactly. Fashion.'

'So how does it work?'

'Well,' he mused, 'on the basis that all cells in the human body except for brain cells are replaced every three months or so, if you can stick a specific mutagen onto a targeted virus, you can alter your body quite significantly. Within the general design limitations of the human body, of course. Interesting: I hadn't expected humanity to be quite this far advanced. Probably the Wars.'

'The Wars?' Bernice asked as the walkway took them out of the tower and into the open air.

'Indeed. Earth is in an expanding Empire phase at the moment. The Wars of Acquisition only ended a few years ago, when the Sense-Sphere finally capitulated. After a few years of austerity, there was an economic and technological upsurge. The current era is characterized by an intense hatred of aliens in person exceeded in intensity only by a desire for anything actually alien – food, artwork, fashion, et cetera. It's a common pattern. Impose sanctions and restraints on a growing culture for a few years, then suddenly take them away and watch the culture expand rapidly. Bacteria do the same.'

Bernice looked around at the forest of elegant, needle-like buildings sprouting from a dark jumble of shadows and cloud. 'Yes, but bacteria don't build floating skyscrapers and moving walkways,' she said.

'Ah, well, the Minorith of Barrab Major – '

'Doctor?'

'Yes, Bernice?'

'Shut up.'

Adjudicator Secular Rashid's office occupied the whole of one raft. Never one to ignore the opportunities offered by technology, she had perfected the twin arts of computerization and delegation to such a degree that her job involved no physical paperwork at all, freeing her to plan her office for comfort rather than efficiency. In her current form – one beppled to resemble a classical musician named Elvis Presley – she seemed to spend most of her time striking poses and waxing her quiff.

When Forrester and Cwej entered, she was standing beside the sofa, blowing up a small inflatable ring. With no noticeable embarrassment she sat down gingerly, shoving the cushion beneath her robes. She curled her lip with pleasure.

'Justice . . .' she said in greeting. 'Piles are giving me gyp. Must be the heat. You wouldn't believe.' She looked Forrester and Cwej over. 'You're late.'

'And fairness be your friend. They moved the – ' Forrester started to say.

'Don't want to know.' Rashid gave Cwej another glance, and frowned. He smiled sunnily back. 'Who's this?'

'This is Cwej.'

'Reporting for duty, sir!' Cwej said cheerily.

Rashid and Forrester exchanged glances.

'Keen, isn't he?' Rashid said.

Forrester decided to get out while the going was good. 'Adjudicator Secular, if there's nothing you want to see me for, I'll mosey across and grab some breakfast – '

Rashid smiled. 'Not so fast. Glad you're here. Saved me calling for you.'

Forrester felt a sinking sensation in the pit of her stomach.

'Cwej here is your new squire,' Rashid continued.

Forrester glanced across at Cwej. To give the guy his due, his expression fell slightly at the news. Just slightly, but it made Forrester feel a lot better.

'Oh good,' she said.

'Nice to know you,' Cwej said, recovering his sunny smile and holding out a hand. Forrester looked at it for a long moment, then shook it.

'Now that the pleasantries are over,' said Rashid, 'get your arses across to District Five. Been a murder. Only an off-worlder, but we've got to go through the formalities. Securitybot happened to be passing by on patrol just after it happened. Suspect's being held.'

Forrester frowned. 'Another one? What's going on?'

'Just get over there. Centcomp'll have the details.'

'Adjudicator Secular, we must be batting *way* over the stats here. How many murders have we had this month? Fifty? Sixty? We usually average ten a month, max. Something's going down.'

29

'All solved, though. Even the off-worlders.'

'That's not the point.'

'Tell me about it,' Rashid grumbled, shifting position on the cushion. 'Ulcers are playing merry hell. Not just the Undertown, either. Lodges up top are reporting an increase in crimes of violence. Had another one this morning: some company executive cut a guy's head off with a laser. The killer's hysterical now: claims she doesn't know why she did it. Centcomp says we're dead on the percentages, though. Nothing unusual. Probably a freak statistical spike. Just get out there and pull in the suspect.'

They got.

The room was dark, apart from the glow of a desk-screen. A pair of fat hands was clasped across the surface of the desk, appearing to hover above the stream of images and data that spurted, too fast for the human eye to follow, within its crystalline depths.

The hands suddenly jerked, the fingers separating convulsively. Slowly they caressed the surface of the desk.

'So,' a voice crooned smugly in the darkness, 'you return again to our little planet, Doctor, with a new face and a new friend. You must find us very interesting indeed. Almost as interesting, perhaps, as I find you. You and your fascinating and, I must say, refreshingly anachronistic craft.'

The voice's owner chuckled.

'After all,' it continued, 'I must be the only man alive who still remembers police boxes.'

Chapter 2

'I'm Evan Claple and this is The Empire Today, *on the spot, on and off the Earth. Today's news: Imperial fleets devastate the planet Jallafillia, bringing the insurrection to a close. We have live footage of the execution of the alien ringleaders. Also: controversy as a leaked Imperial report recommends that the Undertowns be razed to the ground, and their inhabitants with them . . .'*

While Cwej powered up the least battered flitter on the raft, Forrester accessed centcomp for the location of the murder and programmed their destination into the vehicle's navicomp.

'Roz Forrester . . .' Cwej mused as they lifted off and skimmed close to the scummy surface of the water. His furry, snub-nosed face was screwed up into a caricature snarl. 'I know that name. I *know* that name.' His face suddenly brightened. 'Hey,' he said, 'you're not the Roz Forrester who eats idents, are you?'

Here we go, Forrester thought. They'll never let me forget it. 'Yeah. The same.'

'Wow!' It's one of the stories they tell us about at the Academy. I couldn't believe it when I first heard. Is it true? Did you really eat a guy's ident?'

'Yeah.'

Cwej brought the flitter round in a tight curve, his paw-like hands easily handling the controls. The gravitational stabilizers sent spray arcing in a rainbow to one side, catching the light of the fires. The old, stained walls of the

31

buildings surrounding the plaza zipped past, dark windows gaping at them. Faces watched them go, most of them with more or less eyes than the norm, all of them ducking out of sight if they thought they had been spotted.

'Would you tell me about it? Please?'

He sounded so eager that Forrester didn't have the heart to refuse. Besides, she'd told the story so many times that she could remember it word for word. 'It was just after the Hith Pacification,' she said. 'I was squired to Fenn Martle. We must have spent fifteen years together. Good years. Anyway, we were on traffic duty one day, up in the Overcity. We were trolling along in a flitter, just like we are now, and Mart spotted a guy throw a ditz off a walkway.'

'A ditz?'

'Yeah. Centauran animal. Like a bee, only it's the size of a poodle. 'Bout as intelligent as a three-year-old. Expensive to keep as well: they need some special kind of food from their home world. Buzzing's supposed to be soothing. Anyway, this guy threw it off the walkway, thirty floors up. Ditzes can't fly on Earth, something to do with the gravity, or something. This one just dropped like a stone. Mart swore he could hear the thing's frantic buzzing through the flitter canopy till it was out of sight. We landed by the guy and Mart gave him an earful, but he denied it. Said he didn't own a ditz, and even if he did, why would he throw it off a walkway? Well, we knew what we'd seen, but it was our word against his.'

'Didn't you have the cameras on?'

'By the time we realized what was happening, it was too late. And we'd never have recovered the body. Even if anything survived the drop down to the Undertown, the underdwellers would have had it barbecued by the time we got there. So, the guy's got bored with his pet, and throws it away, and we can't do anything about it. Except that I like animals, and I don't feel like letting him get away with it.'

A large building with a gaping hole in its wall was coming up on them fast. Forrester winced as Cwej aimed them straight for an alley between it and its neighbour and notched the speed up from FAST to TOO FAST.

'Shouldn't you leave that to the navicomp?' she hissed between clenched teeth.

'More fun flying by hand,' Cwej said, his eyes shining with exhilaration. 'So what did you do?'

'About what?'

'About this guy and his ditz?'

'I asked for his ident, but he was one of these wackos that didn't believe in the biochips. Some kind of religious problem. Had special dispensation from the Empress to carry a plastic ident. When he handed it to me, I ate it. And then I busted him for not possessing any identification.'

Cwej laughed. 'Didn't he tell anyone?' he asked.

'Of course he did, but who's going to believe that an Adjudicator goes around eating IDs? Centcomp fined him once for not having any valid ident and again for perjury.'

'Brilliant!'

'You're new to this. Tell me again in a month that it's brilliant and I'll buy you a drink.'

'You're on.'

Cwej swung the flitter through narrow gaps and skimmed close to the blank faces of decaying houses and crumbling office blocks. Glancing to her left as a wall loomed large in her field of vision, Forrester caught sight of her own reflection in the shattered remains of a window. She looked nervous. She felt nervous. Goddess save her from rookies.

'So what happened to Mart?' Cwej asked. Forrester wished that he hadn't.

'He died,' she said, the words like ashes in her mouth.

'How?'

No tact. Didn't they teach them tact at the Academy?

'Badly,' she said with enough bite in her voice to shut even Cwej up.

The flitter began to lose height, looping around a topless church spire and descending towards the dank alleys and festering slums at its base. The sun couldn't penetrate that deeply, and so Cwej switched the simcord screen to infrared and aimed the vehicle towards a glowing shape. Flurries of dust were kicked up as they came in to land on a low roof next to a sluggish canal. An armoured form lumbered over towards them, shielding its sensors. It was clutching a woman in its restraining arm. She was just hanging there as if unconscious.

'You discovered the body?' Forrester said to the bot as she clambered out of the flitter.

The bot swung to examine her. It was one of the latest INITEC models: humanoid, four-armed and eight feet tall. The company logo – an eye in the palm of an open hand – was embossed discreetly upon its carapace. 'Ident?' it asked in its uninterested voice.

She held her arm out. A low-intensity laser flicked across her wrist.

'Ident confirmed,' the bot continued. 'Forrester, Roslyn Sarah. Adjudicator, Spaceport Five Undertown Lodge.' It turned to Cwej. 'Ident?'

Cwej glanced at Forrester, innocent puzzlement upon his face. She mimed holding her arm out. He followed suit, and laughed as the laser played across his fur.

'It tickles!' he said.

'Ident confirmed,' the bot said. 'Cwej, Christopher Rodonanté. Assigned to traffic squad, Spaceport Nine Overcity Lodge.'

'Yeah, transferred to Spaceport Five Undertown,' Forrester snapped. 'Keep up with the news. Where's the body?'

The bot swung one of its four arms – the one equipped with the blaster – towards a damp grey mass about eight feet long. She strode over. Cwej followed. Forrester bent down beside the body.

'Hith,' she said. 'Don't find many of them on Earth since we terraformed their planet.' The off-worlder's chest was a mess. It looked as if it'd been carved like a turkey, and its eye-stalks had been severed close to the head. Forrester looked back to the woman in the grip of the robot. She was so bundled up against the rain and the cold that she could hardly bend her limbs. Her face peered out from a beehive of towels and scarves like a monkey from a forest, and her eyes had a dull, unfocused look, as if she had been drugged. A sharp spike of metal dangled loosely from her left hand.

'What happened?' Cwej asked the bot.

'Start report. Body was discovered during routine patrol. Suspect was standing over body. Suspect was apprehended. Suspect offered no resistance. Suspect identified as Falvoriss, Annie Thelma, based upon subdermal biochip. Victim unidentified. Local station supervisor was notified. End report.'

Forrester glanced across at Cwej. He shrugged.

'Record,' she said to the securitybot, then, to the woman: 'I am obliged to inform you that your words, gestures and postures are being recorded and may form part of any legal action taken against you. Under the terms of the data protection act 2820, as amended 2945, I am also obliged to inform you that you and any appointed legal representative will be able to purchase a copy of all recordings upon payment of the standard fee.'

The woman just stared at her. A thin string of drool hung from her lower lip.

'Drugs?' Cwej ventured uncertainly.

'Not now,' said Forrester. 'I'm on duty.'

Cwej's pointed ears pricked up.

'Joke,' she added. He smiled uncertainly, revealing small, pointed teeth. 'Okay,' she said to the robot. 'Disarm her, tag the weapon and put her in the back. Then notify the clear-up squad.'

It was just an accident.

Archer McElwee was practising his t'ai chi in the park. Every morning, as soon as the sun rose, he took the null-grav shaft up from his apartment to the roof of the tower and went through the whole set of exercises in the warm, golden glow. Repulsing the Monkey. The Heron Flying West. The Crane at Sunset. One hundred and thirty-five, he was, and he still felt like a ninety-year-old!

He took a deep breath and gazed around the park. The azaleas and sheckt bushes were in full bloom and, close by, a number of friends from the tower were also practising their exercises. It all looked so beautiful. He was a lucky man.

Beside him, Kari Nbaro turned to smile. She was a hundred and ten, and beautiful with it. He waved back. Perhaps after they finished, he could offer her a cup of coffee.

He raised his hands above his head in the Crane position and turned slowly to one side. His hand brushed accidentally against hers.

He caught her eye again, but she was frowning.

'What the hell do you think you're doing?' she snapped.

'I'm . . . I'm sorry,' he stammered, shocked. 'I didn't – '

'Pervert!'

Her hand lashed out, catching him across the nose. He fell backwards, hot blood gushing into his mouth. He tried to apologize, cry out, anything, but her hands were flailing at him, scratching his cheeks and neck, catching at his forehead. His arms were trapped beneath her knees as she straddled his chest, her fingers gouging into his eyes.

Warm, salty blood bubbling in the back of his throat.

Obscenities screamed in his ear.

Fingers thrust deep into his eyes.

It was just an accident.

Powerless Friendless And Scattered Through Space woke up shivering as a pang of pain shot through his tail. Absently, he scratched the old scar just beneath the vestigial shell at the base of his tail, taking stock of the situation. His battered fedora hat had slipped off and he had managed to shrug off the monofil thermo-blankets in his sleep. He pulled his eyes back inside his body, extruded a pseudo-limb to pull the hat back over his head, rolled himself up in the blankets and settled back to sleep.

His basal foot was cold. He tried to shift himself so that the blankets wrapped around his column-like body, but by the time he'd done that a stone was pressing into his back. He wriggled sideways, but the blankets rucked up around him.

Every morning this happened. He hated it. He hated it all.

As his mind gradually crept back to consciousness, he became more aware of his surroundings. Bright light. Lapping water. Hard floor.

Earth.

He extended his eye-stalks, and withdrew them quickly, wincing at the weak sunlight that filtered down from between the towers of the Overcity, reflected from the water outside the window and made patterns on the ceiling.

The ceiling was low and cracked. Fungus had crept across it, one step behind the patches of damp. Once it had been an office, before the Overcity had been built. He had been living there for a few months now, and he was beginning to get twitchy. More and more people knew where he was. He didn't know why, but that made him nervous. Jumpy. Perhaps it was time to be moving on.

His back and his joints protested as he climbed laboriously to his feet. He couldn't see Krohg, but that wasn't unusual. The little *glih* would be around somewhere.

He knew that he had to find somewhere to wash the mucus from his body before he wandered up to the lower levels of the Overcity and started work. It would leave his skin dry and sore, but it was worth the sacrifice. The bulk of the workers would be heading for their offices in an hour or so. Like all Hith he hated crowds, but they were used to seeing him hunched over his old, battered Earth Reptile *hag'jat*, same spot every day, performing rock 'n' roll classics or some of the more playable Martian and Earth Reptile pieces. A few regulars always shelled out for him, probably more because of the incongruity of a Hith playing an Earth tune than because he was any good, but if he didn't wash some of the mucus off his body then the day's take would be down. He knew: he'd tried it before. Humans were intolerant of alien beauty. Humans were intolerant of anything that wasn't human.

He thought for a moment. At this time in the morning it was just possible that the sports facilities and showers in the basement of the INITEC tower would be open. It was worth a try. The worst that would happen was that he'd get a little more exercise than usual.

With his backpack full, no longer fulfilling the role of pillow, he extended a pseudo-limb to swing it over his shoulder and bent down again to retrieve his *hag'jat* case. For a moment the moist skin of his pseudo-limb looked strange to him – gnarled, grey and twisted, like an old tree root, instead of young and smooth. Sighing, he placed the fedora over his head, poking his eye-stalks through the holes, and set off.

As he walked, he scratched at his skin. There were new cracks there alongside the old scars – the ones that he couldn't remember ever getting, but which covered his body – and he could feel the bites over his tail and mid-torso. Pests, creeping in from the spaceport. Terrestrial pests were like humans themselves; they tended to avoid coming into contact with off-world flesh. Unfortunately it seemed to him that, ever since the end of the Wars of Acquisition, during which the Earth Empire had grabbed whatever it wanted as quickly as it could, there were more and more multi-legged, multicoloured things taking up residence in his skin, and he was spending more and more of his hard-earned money at the autodoc trying to get rid of them. He knew of one old woman who dossed down a few streets away, and who'd been infested with some sort of protoplasmic parasite picked up from a passing alien tourist. By the time she'd got to old Doc Dantalion – well, by the time Powerless Friendless had taken her to him – it was too late. The things had been radioactive, and she only had a few weeks left.

Powerless Friendless had never asked what happened to the body. With Doc Dantalion, you never could tell.

The rest of the underdwellers had looked upon Powerless Friendless with some sort of respect after that. Looking after their own, that was the first rule of the streets, off-world or not. He hadn't liked to say that he'd been worried about her ruining his trade with her weeping sores and her moaning. If he'd known the things were radioactive he'd have been halfway across the city.

So preoccupied was he with his usual early morning litany of complaints that he hardly noticed the journey across the roofs and along ledges, alongside the flooded alleys and the sunken squares with the heavy weight of the Overcity forever pressing down. It was only when an Adjudication flitter droned across the sky above him, angling for a landing on the roof of a nearby building, that he realized where he was. Humans! He slid quickly into the lee of a tumbledown shack. He mustn't let them see him! He wasn't entirely sure why they mustn't see him, but he hid anyway.

Powerless Friendless extended his eye-stalks around the edge of the shack. The flitter had landed next to a group of street life, and two black-robed Adjudicators had got out. One of them was a short-haired, sour-faced woman; the other was a tall, furry creature that moved like a human, not an off-worlder. There was a securitybot as well. He cursed. How could he have been so careless? He had almost walked into them!

The bot was holding a woman he'd seen around in its metal paw. Annie. She usually slept over beneath the INITEC Building, in the remains of a crashed Scumble ship. It was a well known doss – Powerless Friendless had used it himself, once upon a time. She was looking dazed, and she held a metal spike in her hand. There was blood on the spike, and . . .

Oh.

Powerless Friendless poked his head out, risking detection. He had to be sure.

It was Waiting For Justice. Waiting For Justice And Dreaming of Home, who, despite the notorious Hith dislike of company, he had sat up with on occasion, drinking voxnik they'd stolen from the warehouses at the spaceport. Waiting For Justice, who had served on the *Gex*, flagship of the Hith Navy, during the Great Patriotic War against the Humans, and lived now amongst their filth in the Undertown. Waiting For Justice, who had earned the Red Stripe of Courage during the defence of Hithis. Waiting For Justice, the only other Hith that Powerless Friendless knew on Earth.

Dead.

Ripped to shreds.

The bot was leading Annie towards the flitter. The two Adjudicators were looking around for witnesses. Powerless Friendless slipped back into the shadow of the shack.

Perhaps it *was* time to be moving on again.

In the darkened room, a plump hand slowly passed across a desktop. Lights glowed deep within its translucent surface, responding to the touch. Money moved from one non-existent place to another, growing as it did so. Policies changed, jobs were created and destroyed, planets changed ownership.

Something was wrong.

The man behind the desk didn't believe in coincidence, and that meant that the sudden reappearance of both the long-lost Hith navigator and the Doctor must be regarded as probable enemy action. The Doctor was notoriously devious: this had the appearance of a classic opening gambit. However, the opportunity to obtain the Doctor's time and space machine and rip it apart for its technological secrets was one that could not be missed.

The man thought for a moment, and smiled slightly. He didn't need the Doctor, after all. The time machine's secrets should be easy enough to crack. Having the Doctor around might only prove embarrassing later on, given the man's propensity for sudden escapes and amazing reversals of fortune.

The hands moved rapidly across the desk. His safest course of action would be to get the Doctor and his companion arrested on some trumped-up charge on the basis of faked evidence. That way his tame Adjudicator could safely brainwipe the two of them. The records would be straight, and there would be nothing to point the finger of blame on him. Not that he was worried, but it was best to be sure.

And he was always sure.

Some sort of scuffle appeared to be going on in the distance; a crowd was gathering around a fight. After a cautious initial look – life with the Doctor had taught her to be wary of anything out of the ordinary – Bernice ignored it. Instead, she let the walkway carry her to a point midway between two buildings, then walked across to its stationary edge and leaned against the semi-transparent bulwark.

'Progress moves fast,' she said as the Doctor caught up with her. 'How do they keep it all up in the air?'

He took his hat off and fanned at his face with it.

'Cheap and effective null gravity. One of the key discoveries that keeps the Earth Empire ahead of the opposition. Null-grav had been around for centuries, of course, but this particular variant was based on a completely novel principle. It caused a minor technological revolution, and a major demographic one.'

He flipped the hat back up his arm and onto his head.

'Everybody lives in the towers of the Overcity now,' he continued. 'Well, everybody who is anybody. Some levels are accommodation, some are shops, some offices and some are a mixture. Status depends on how high up you live. Implanted identification chips limit access to the levels you are allowed to visit, and no others.'

Bernice craned her neck and gazed down towards the ground and the shadows too deep for the sun to penetrate. Tiny lights seemed to flicker within the darkness.

'Are those fires?' she said.

'Hmm? Yes, indeed. That will be the Undertown.'

'The what?'

'The slum area. The bit that got left behind when all this – ' He waved a hand at the surrounding towers. ' – was built.'

'Slums?' she asked, disbelievingly. 'Haven't they done away with slums by now?'

41

'It's always like this,' rejoined the Doctor. 'The rich build upon the backs of the poor.'

He peered over the edge. 'No doubt Ace would have said it was like Hong Kong hanging over Venice,' he added. 'Very pithy, was Ace.'

The Doctor broke off as a deep rumble shook the walkway. Looking up, Bernice saw the dark, irregular shape of a spacecraft descending through the atmosphere.

'Is there a spaceport around here?' she asked.

The Doctor grimaced. 'There's a spaceport everywhere,' he said. 'Hundreds of thousands of spaceships dock here every day. Trade and transport are so important to the Empire that the cities have been renamed for the spaceports. This, for instance, is Spaceport Five Overcity, although it used to be known as Central City, and before that as London. According to your friend Homeless Forsaken, this is where the danger will start. Any ideas as to how we go about identifying it?'

Bernice puffed her cheeks out. 'Nothing springs to mind,' she murmured. 'Unless . . .'

The Doctor's face was expectant. 'Yes?'

'Unless we find another Hith on Earth who can tell us what's going on.'

The Doctor's face fell again. 'It's a long shot,' he said.

'But it might just work,' Bernice replied.

An Eirtj Knight asked the way to the market as Terg McConnel walked into the alley. It was crouching in the shadows, mist swirling around its sleek body, eyes glinting faintly in the twilight. He ignored it. The Eirtj probably knew the Undertown better than he did; they only requested directions in order to start a conversation, but once you'd spoken to one of them for any length of time you'd exhausted all possible topics of conversation with the entire race. And besides, aliens made his skin crawl. Goddess alone knew why he'd agreed to head the research team. He should have stayed back in his comfortable office in the university block, up in the Overcity. Amongst his fellow humans.

McConnel headed down the alley, water sleeting down from the half-hidden bases of the Towers that hung high above the Undertown. Behind him he heard the Knight sigh faintly, and stalk off in search of somebody more garrulous.

A warning notice hung in the air a few feet into the alley. Static blurred the faint red letters. DANGER, it said, DO NOT PASS: RADIATION HAZARD. McConnel walked through the notice, raising a hand to brush at his forehead as the letters curved around him with a brief caress of light, and halted as he came to the end of the alley. The scanners were still there, attached to the stonework like little metal snails. The radiation leak story wasn't true, of course, but it was the only way to keep the damned underdwellers from removing the scanners and selling the parts as scrap. A sign saying PLEASE DO NOT PASS: SCIENTIFIC MEASUREMENTS IN PROGRESS just didn't carry the same weight. The fact that McConnel's team of students were trying to help the ungrateful scum by measuring the effects on the Undertown of the Overcity's null-grav generators wouldn't cut any ice at all.

The devices were damp with condensing mist. His fingers slipped as he checked them, and he grazed his knuckles upon the rough stonework. The water stung in the wound. He cursed and held his wrist up to the scanners, waiting for the information to download into his processor. When he got the readings back to the university he would pore over them for hours, pulling every morsel he could out of them, but he could already see from the figures scrolling across the screen that the levels of ultrasonic vibration were well above safe limits.

He turned away and headed back towards the mouth of the alley. The restaurant where he had arranged to meet the team was nearby, according to the centcomp map, but 'nearby' was a flexible concept in the Undertown. It took McConnel fifteen minutes to get there through alleys and streets thronged with stinking aliens and degenerate humans. He made sure that his stunner was visible to all as he walked. He had to double back on himself five times, and twice miscalculated and found himself in blind alleys or up against the banks of one of the infinity of canals that were the arteries of the Undertown. His path took him across bridges, through dog-leg bends, down narrow alleys, up corkscrew stairways and through concealed entrances. Finally he recognized a flight of stone steps which had been smoothed into curves by generations of feet. Bodies sprawled on the steps, some of them asleep, others muttering obscurely to themselves. Humans with heavily lined faces and long, matted hair were side by side with various alien races whose features were combinations of beaks, antennae, horns, eyes hooded, stalked and slitted, ears small and pointed or large and leathery, and whose arms ended in claws, or tentacles, or strange mixtures of flesh and bone like surgical instruments.

The restaurant was basic: a stone-clad room with a canal cutting off one corner, near to the toilets, forming an entrance for the various amphibian races that patronized it. The ambience made his skin crawl. He'd made the mistake of leaving it up to the students to find a place to eat. He should have guessed that they would choose an alien restaurant in the Undertown instead of heading back up to the Overcity, and some decent human food.

McConnel's team was already waiting: a mismatched group of eager young people drawn together by the excitement of research. He pulled up an empty chair, squeezing in between two postgrads. His head was beginning to throb. This hadn't been a good idea.

'Look!' Lymaner was saying. He was dark, intense, and slightly pudgy. 'We have a responsibility to the underdwellers. We can't dump our crap on them, take their sky away and make it rain all the time and expect them to like it. I tell you, there's going to be big trouble one day if we don't do something.'

The meagre light was gleaming off the blade of a knife on the table. McConnel couldn't drag his gaze away from it.

'We are doing something,' a blonde named Dara said. 'That's why we're here.'

With a slight jolt of surprise, McConnel realized that he had picked up the knife.

'We're here to come up with a report that absolves the Empire of all responsibility,' Lymaner snorted, casting a wary glance at McConnel. 'That's our job, isn't it, Professor?'

The heat was conspiring with the smell of the food and the crush of the crowd to make McConnel feel nauseous.

'Damn the stinking underdwellers,' he whispered. The students gazed uneasily at him. 'Damn the stinking under-life and damn you all for caring more about them than about your fellow humans.'

McConnel glanced up at Lymaner.

And plunged the knife into the boy's eye.

The flitter was still powering down when Forrester jumped out onto the raft. The smell inside was getting to be unbearable, despite the air-conditioning, but at least the woman had kept quiet for the journey, staring blankly out of the window without moving.

At least the station was still where they had left it. That was one small bonus.

'Shove her in a holding cell,' Forrester barked at Cwej, gesturing to one of the Adjudication securitybots to come over to help him.

'Why, where are you going?'

'May as well get this over with quickly. I'll break out a portable mindprobe from stores. If we can retrieve the killing from her recent memories for centcomp, we can get her convicted and sentenced before lunch. Since the victim's only an off-worlder, there's no point dragging it out.'

'If she's guilty.'

Forrester turned to look at Cwej. He was gazing at her in all seriousness, his button-bright eyes gleaming, his fur bristling.

'If?'

'We can't assume anything until we've seen the scan.'

'Yeah. Right. Dream on, kid.'

She strode off to the equipment truck and signed out a battered mind probe. Lugging the machine over to the holding truck, she wondered how long Cwej's innocence was going to last.

The inside of the truck was small and bare of anything except a table and three plastic chairs. Cwej had sprayed a restraining suit over the woman. The flexible foam encased her completely apart from her little, wizened face, making it impossible for her to hurt herself or her captors, or to move faster than a waddle. She looked to Forrester like a child's toy: soft, pliant and blank.

Forrester threw the mindprobe upon the table, folded up the screen and plugged the input contact and the hand-scanner into the jack-points.

The securitybot was standing beside Cwej. Coincident-ally, it was another INITEC model. The RECORD light was flashing on its chest.

'Did you switch it on?' she asked Cwej, nodding towards the bot. He shook his head.

'No. Is it recording? Must have been left on by the last guys.'

'Slobs.' Forrester sat down. 'May as well start afresh,' she said, turning to the bot. 'Stop record.'

'Recording stopped,' the bot said.

The light remained winking.

'Stop record,' she repeated, louder.

'Recording stopped,' the bot repeated.

The light went out.

'Must be a malfunction,' she muttered. 'That's all we need.'

'These things aren't supposed to break down,' Cwej said. 'Mean time between failures is ten thousand years, according to the manuals.'

'Yeah, right. And Father Christmas lives on the fiftieth floor of my block.' She raised her voice. 'Start record.'

The light began to flash again.

'Recording started,' said the bot.

'Have you got the spike?' she continued, turning to Cwej.

46

'The what?'

'The murder weapon?'

Cwej reached beneath his seat and retrieved a vacuum-sealed bag with the bloodied spike inside.

'Here.'

Forrester placed it on the table and waved the mind-probe's sensor over it, registering the item in its memory.

'All right, bring her over.'

While Cwej had manoeuvred the uncooperative but unresisting woman into one of the chairs, her arms and legs sticking out stiffly in the foam suit, Forrester attached the metal mindprobe contact to the centre of the woman's forehead.

'Ever used one of these?' she asked Cwej.

'Saw one in a lecture once,' he said.

'They always work perfectly in lectures, and never in real life. The early models needed so much power to read anything through the skull that they sometimes screwed around with the memories they were trying to read. These new ones are magic. Perfectly safe. Would you like to try it?'

He shook his head.

'Fine,' she continued, 'just asking. Now, I've scanned the murder weapon into the mindprobe. We should now be able to peel back her recent memories, looking for the last time she remembers seeing it.'

'Won't that be just now, when I pulled it out from beneath the seat?'

'Well done. Glad to see you're paying attention. I can then go back to the time before that – '

'Just after we first arrived.'

'And scroll slowly backwards until we find the murder.'

'If she committed it.'

'Have it your own way, Academy boy. It's just a for-mality. We know she did it.'

Forrester's fingers danced across the controls. She had operated mindprobes so many times that the procedure was instinctive, automatic. If she had stopped to think what she was doing, she would have lost it.

47

'Okay,' she said. 'Let's boogie.'

She pressed the button marked ENGAGE PROBE. Lights flashed on the body of the machine, and the woman's face creased into a slight frown.

The screen sprang to life with a fuzzy, distorted picture of the table and an empty chair. The mindprobe was on the table: Forrester was standing by the chair. From one side, Cwej's hand could just be seen holding the vacuum-sealed bag with the spike inside.

'That's the most recent occurrence,' Forrester said. 'Let's go back one.'

Her fingers danced again across the controls. The screen washed with static, then cleared to show a picture of the area where they had found the body. The body itself was off to one side, out of sight. The woman had been looking at the ground, down the smooth, metallic length of the bot as it restrained her. The spike was held loosely in her hand.

'Let's skip back ten minutes,' Forrester said, holding down a button. The picture jumped, and settled down to the same state.

'And again.'

The same.

'And again.'

Different. The hand holding the knife was slashing down again and again at a sluglike off-worlder with a moist, grey body. Its thin, flexible limbs were raised to protect its face. A thin blue fluid was spurting from gashes in its limbs, its face, its body. The knife suddenly changed direction, coming in from the side and catching the victim unprepared. The blade cut right through its eye-stalks. Blue fluid fountained down its body. Its tentacular fingers flailed briefly, uselessly, and it sank slowly to the ground.

'Goddess!' Cwej exclaimed. 'That's gross.'

'That's life,' Forrester said. 'It's all recorded here. Soon as we feed the info into centcomp, this lady'll be for the chop.'

'What do you reckon she'll get?'

Forrester reached out towards the mindprobe. 'Murder?

Mandatory brainwipe and indenture to a corporation for ten years.'

'Yeah, but look at her,' he protested. 'She's juiced up on something. Got to be: just look at her eyes.'

Her finger rested on the DISENGAGE PROBE button.

'No excuse. Didn't they teach you anything in the Academy?' She looked at the underdweller's blank eyes. 'Strange, there's a lot of them around like this at the moment.'

'Like the Adjudicator Secular was saying?'

'Yeah. Been involved with quite a few myself. Ordinary people suddenly turning violent and killing friends, family, even total strangers. They all have that look. Like they just switched off. Sign of the times, I think.'

She pressed the button.

The suspect suddenly jerked in her seat as if she was having a fit. One flailing padded arm caught Cwej across the cheek and sent him sprawling. Forrester dived across the table, trying to tear the contact from the suspect's forehead, but the woman had toppled backwards in her chair, still thrashing her arms and legs. Cwej pulled himself up by the table leg. He and Forrester reached the suspect's side at the same time. Forrester went to pull the contact off, but her hand hesitated before it touched the wire. The suspect's eyes bulged slightly, then half closed. She sighed: a long final exhalation.

And died.

'Shit,' Cwej breathed. 'That never happened in the lectures.'

Chapter 3

'I'm Evan Claple and this is The Empire Today, *on the spot, on and off the Earth. Today's headlines: drama during the investiture of a new baron at the Imperial Court orbiting Saturn as a courtier starts firing a plasma rifle towards the throne. Imperial Landsknechte killed the courtier within moments, but have themselves since been executed for their lapse on the direct orders of the Empress. The question remains: how did the rifle get into the throne room? And today's weather...'*

The end of the rope-ladder swept across the roof, blown by the wind.

Powerless Friendless gazed up at its length to the point where it vanished into the clouds. It was a long climb, especially for a gastropod, but he'd done it every day for five years. The ladder connected the wasteland where the old Scumble ship had crashed – a waterlogged marsh now – with the base of the INITEC building. It was one of the many ways that the underdwellers used to gain access to the riches of the promised land.

Powerless Friendless's acquaintances – he didn't have friends because Hith didn't like company – covered a range of professions. Some were thieves, some were beggars and some even had real jobs to which they commuted every day. There was always a call for cheap labour, even in a robot-rich economy. The standing joke in the undertown was that even bots had more rights than the underdwellers.

Powerless Friendless's position was somewhere between beggar and worker. He busked in a plaza just outside the entrance to the off-world zoo. Always the same place. Force of habit. People still paid to hear live music.

Quickly Powerless Friendless swarmed up the rope, using the muscles in his basal foot and the adhesive properties of the mucus secreted by his skin to pull himself up. He tried not to look down at the receding marsh and the wreckage of the Scumble ship, but he couldn't help being aware of the irregular buildings and canals of the Undertown appearing in wider and wider circles as he climbed. Tendrils of mist encircled his body. The weight of the *hag'jat* and rucksack slung across his back pulled him down, but he struggled on. His pseudo-limbs were tiring, his lymph pump was beating fast, but he kept on going. The wind tugged at his fedora, but he kinked his eye-stalks to hold it more firmly on.

His mind began to wander. With a sudden shock, he found himself thinking about Waiting For Justice's bloodied body. He tried to pull his thoughts away, but the vision of his agonized face, not seen, but imagined, hung in front of Powerless Friendless as he climbed. Death was nothing new in the Undertown, but Powerless Friendless hated it when someone he knew was killed. It reminded him of –

No. Don't think about that. Anything but that.

He looked around in an effort to distract himself, and became aware that he had climbed up into the clouds without realizing. The rope ladder was suspended in nothingness. How long had he been going? Minutes? Hours? Days, perhaps? Above him, the curved undersides of the null-grav field generators appeared through the mist. Not far to go now. He counted off the rungs, one by one, as he laboured upwards and the hexagonal base of the tower came into view.

With a deep sigh, he heaved himself onto the ledge that ran around the bottom of the INITEC building and lay there, panting. He could feel his lymph pump thumping against his gut and, a fraction of a second later, the thud of his pulse in his eye-stalks. He was getting too old for this game. He'd once been a lot fitter than he was now. Hadn't he?

Gradually his pulse returned to normal. He climbed to his foot, his muscles protesting, and slid around the ledge, looking for an open ventilation hatch. It was common knowledge amongst the underdwellers that one of the robot caretakers took its cleanliness programming a little more seriously than its security programming, and regularly left a hatch open to air the place out.

He rounded a corner, and saw, a little distance ahead, a sliver of light. He was in luck! Shuffling forward, he bent down beside it. The hatch was open just a crack, but it wouldn't budge when he pulled it and the control panel was on a wall inside. He put his ear to the crack – there was no noise from inside, no people, no robots, no showers running. If he could only reach in and hit the controls . . .

He lay down and extruded a pseudo-limb through the gap. The tentacles on the end of his pseudo-limb waggled in the air. He could sense the controls just out of reach. The cold, smooth metal taunted him. The edge of the hatch bit sharply into his flesh. Tingles edged down his tentacles, and his tendons strained until he thought that they would snap.

Powerless Friendless sighed and pulled his limb back into his body. He was going to have to ask Krohg to do it. He didn't want to, but it was the only chance he had.

'Krohg?'

Nothing. He tried again.

'Krohg? Please?'

Something stirred deep in a pocket of his rucksack. Careful not to touch Krohg's skin – it was always a bit on the snappy side when woken up – he slid a pseudo-limb into the pocket and waited until it had nestled moistly in his curled-up pseudo-palm.

'Sorry about this,' he said, pulling the limb out, 'but I need your help.'

Krohg stared malevolently up at him. As usual, he couldn't help wondering why he'd kept the creature. Not that he could remember how he had come by it; his memories became fragmented and diffused the further back he tried to push them. It was too ugly to evoke sympathy in the heart of any passing human. Most of them found its slimy orange skin and fringe of cilia repellent, and the gleam of nastiness in its three eyes didn't help. Neither did its mouth. Those cog-wheel-like teeth had even given *him* a couple of nasty rasps. No, it had to be said that Krohg didn't have many redeeming features. Occasionally, when it could be bothered, Krohg would help Powerless Friendless with fiddly things like half-open hatches and wallets in pockets. That was about it.

He pointed it at the crack between the hatch and the frame.

'Good thing,' he muttered. 'Open the hatch for me.'

With a wriggle, Krohg eased itself onto the hatch frame and through the crack. A few moments later he heard the click of a magnetic catch, and the hatch sighed open. He found Krohg inside, curled up around the OPEN button. He picked it up and slipped it back in his rucksack with a murmured. 'Thanks.'

He slid through the hatch into the sports facility and slithered towards the showers, where he let the fingers of ultrasound caress his body and ease the ingrained dirt from his flesh. Shame it took all that lovely, protective mucus with it, but he was used to the sacrifice by now. After fifteen minutes he stepped out and slithered back into the dressing room. There was a full-length mirror field across one wall, and for a moment he stopped and stared at himself. He didn't like what he saw. His skin was greyer than he would have liked, the fringe of cilia around his mouth trembled slightly and his body was so thin that his basal foot was wider than his waist. The nubs of his withdrawn pseudo-limbs were withered and mis-shapen, and a band of scarring extended down his flanks, but his mind shied away from thinking about that.

And there was a number burned into the flesh of his tail.

Something cried out in the back of his mind. His head suddenly jerked away so that he couldn't see it.

There was a number.

He tried to turn his head back, but it fought him. Something deep inside him didn't want to look.

A number.

He didn't recognize his body; it didn't match with his memories. The scarring, the nu– the nu– the thing on his tail: it wasn't the way he remembered himself. What had happened to him? There had been better days, days when he had been handsome, and respected, and well fed, but there was a gap, and now there was here, and he didn't know how to bridge that gap. He didn't like to dwell on the memories. There were other things lurking down there, and it was best not to expose them to the light.

He was just about to leave when he heard someone coming down the stairs. Quickly he bundled all his things into a cubicle and slid halfway up the wall before the robot janitor entered and began to wash the floor. Powerless Friendless listened for the tell-tale series of clicks and whirs as the mop and bucket appendages disappeared back into the robot's body, then gave it another few minutes to leave.

Time to hit the walkways.

Fillip almost gave up when she told him that her name was Laverne, but she had curly blonde hair and legs that rose, stockinged and impossibly long, into tight black shorts, so he kept at it. She'd been working a twelve-hour shift in a bar in Spaceport Eight Seacity. She told him that she came from the Helvetian colony, and was slogging her way through a degree in Artistic Terraforming. Fillip hadn't known that anybody could *do* degrees in Artistic Terraforming. Things had changed since his day.

It was the noise of several of the regular Earth Reptile bands who played there that had first attracted Fillip. He'd been sitting at his desk in the Transit Authority Tower, processing the paperwork for a party of Hith ambassadors

54

who had been granted an audience with the Empress, when the sounds of loud music and people having fun had drifted through the suppressor field of his window. He felt he deserved a drink: he hated aliens at the best of times, and this particular group of slugs seemed to be going out of their way to be irritating. They were all travelling to the Imperial Palace in orbit around Saturn from different planets, for a start, meaning that he had to complete a different set of forms for each one, and they insisted on putting their home world as Hithis, even though everybody knew that Hithis was occupied entirely by humans. They all wanted separate rooms, preferably on separate levels, and he'd never come across a set of names as stupid in his life! Working late to impress the boss was one thing, but this was carrying dedication too far. He saved the forms in centcomp's memory under a TRANSIT AUTHORITY ONLY password and followed the noise.

The bouncers were exchanging banter with their counterparts across the plaza when he arrived. He told them that he wanted a bar where he could sit and drink without having a menu thrust in front of him. Rather than lead him through the maze of corridors and stairways one of them took him round the side of the building, unlocked a door and gestured him in. He walked uncertainly up three flights of stairs and found a half-empty bar waiting for him. And Laverne.

There were two young Earth Reptiles squeezed into a corner of the room, each one wielding a *hag'jat* and trying to sing further off-key than the other. They weren't really aliens; in fact, some of his best friends were Earth Reptiles. Fillip talked to Laverne, he talked to the Reptiles during their breaks, they all drank Martian ale out of huge bowls that looked like space helmets, and pretty soon they were all squeezed in the corner trying to sing 'You Can't Always Get What You Want' by The Rolling Stones. The Reptiles with the *hag'jats* only had an approximate idea of the lyrics but they made up what they didn't know, and it sounded fine. As they talked, and drank, and sang, the bar ebbed and flowed like a tidal pool – some local customers, some tourists and some uniformed military personnel, all friendly and fun.

Eventually the Reptiles packed up their instruments and bade Fillip a long farewell that involved many bowls of ale and proclamations of friendship. He asked Laverne if she would consider spending the night with a balding, middle-aged paper-pusher, and to his astonishment, she said yes.

Laverne drove her flitter too fast through still-busy air-spaces to her apartment, where they snapped laces and broke buttons in a race to see who could get the other's clothes off faster. The Hith diplomatic mission was about as far from his mind as it was possible to get.

And while Fillip was asleep, Laverne poured most of a bottle of Arcturan brandy over the bed and set fire to him.

Despite the crowds, Powerless Friendless spent about half an hour slinking around one of the plazas, loitering at the entrances to the restaurants and trying to identify everything that he could smell before a securitybot moved him on. He didn't mind; they turned a blind sensor most of the time. Occasionally one of them got a bit heavy-handed, but it was rare. Anyway, with the change he hoped to pick up that morning, he should have enough to buy something decent to eat.

But he had to earn the money before he could spend it.

He made his way along the nearest walkway to the tower on top of which he usually played, and went up in the null-grav shaft. Without a biochip, there was no way for centcomp to know that he was even there. Five levels of the tower were occupied by the off-world zoo, and he timed his arrival to coincide with its opening for the day. He wasn't sure why, but something still drew him to it: the feeling that he had some kind of connection with it. People did their best to ignore him as they entered. He didn't mind. He preferred being ignored. He had dedicated a number of years to being ignored. It was safer that way.

Once he had emerged in the plaza and spent a few moments taking in the vivid greens of the grass and the vibrant hues of the flowers, setting up was easy. Powerless Friendless slumped with his back against the rim wall, his *hag'jat* cradled in his lap. If it hadn't been for his case acting as a collecting plate, he would have looked as if he were meditating.

As people passed by on their way to work, he played, and to avoid having to think about the press of other beings around him, the claustrophobic presence of so many other living creatures, he let his mind float amongst half-formed dreams of his home planet, Hithis, and of the wide blue sward where a Hith could slither for days without having to see another Hith.

After a while he pulled himself back and paused for a moment to empty out his hat and look around. Fortunately, the crowds had thinned out now, and his gaze was attracted by a human woman who stood a full head above the rest of the workers. She was wearing a baggy overall of some sort, with a brightly patterned waistcoat over the top, and she was carrying a carton of take-away food from one of the stalls that lined the plaza. A man was with her – a small man who scurried along as if he might trip over his feet at any moment. They were both looking at him, almost as if they were looking *for* him.

He tensed, ready to flee. He didn't know why – who on Earth would be after him? – but it was an instinctive reaction and he could not fight it.

Too late: she stopped by his side. He let the last few chords die away, then looked warily up at her.

'Hi,' she said. 'My name's Bernice. What's yours?'

'Powerless Friendless,' he said hesitantly.

'This is my friend, the Doctor,' she said. 'We're friends of another member of your race: Homeless Forsaken Betrayed And Alone. Do you know him?'

Powerless Friendless felt a shudder run through him. The rooftop blurred around him, and he tried to quell the rapid pit-pat of his lymph pump. Homeless Forsaken. He hadn't heard that name for years. He'd been doing his best to forget it.

'Don't know him,' he said. 'Never heard of him.'

'Are you sure?' she persisted.

'I've never even heard the name before,' he shouted.

The woman looked at him in some concern, her gaze travelling across his dry, cracked skin, his painfully thin and scarred body. 'Here,' she said, passing him the container of food. 'Have some of this.'

The Doctor leaned forward towards Powerless Friendless. 'May I ask a question?' he said.

Powerless Friendless retracted his eye-stalks slightly. 'What sort of question?' he asked.

'Those scars,' the Doctor began, indicating the gnarled, twisted flesh of Powerless Friendless's upper torso and the nubs of his retracted pseudo-limbs. Powerless Friendless flinched. He didn't like being reminded of – of his scars. They made him think about . . .

'Scars?' he asked, trying to quell the seething unease in his mind.

'Do you mind telling me where you got them from?'

Powerless Friendless opened and closed his mouth, trying to find the right words, but they were gone, gone wherever the memories had gone. 'I – I don't remember,' he said finally.

The Doctor frowned. 'It looks to me,' he said slowly, 'as if you have been tortured. Quite comprehensively tortured. I would be surprised if you could forget something like that.'

Powerless Friendless extruded a pseudo-limb and ran it over the twisted flesh as if he had never really seen it before.

'And that number burned into your tail,' the Doctor continued remorselessly. 'Where did it come from? Who did it to you?'

The knife flashed in the half-light of his cell, drawing a line of agony across his flesh.

'An old-fashioned device,' a human voice said, 'but then,

I am an old-fashioned man. You may find this difficult to believe, but I am over a thousand years old.'

Powerless Friendless screamed.

Springing up, he backed away from them, pseudo-limbs held up as if to ward them off. Before they could stop him, he had turned and slithered out of the plaza, leaving his *hag'jat* behind, trying to block the words, the memories from his mind. A spindly bot with an emblem on its chest tried to stop him, but he slithered under its four outstretched arms and across the plaza. It grabbed for him, its metal feet thumping the ground as it ran, but it only succeeded in grabbing the fedora from his head. The hat caught at his eye-stalks, but he pulled away, panic-stricken.

Homeless Forsaken Betrayed And Alone. A name that held associations for him. Unpleasant associations. Things he had done his best to forget. Things that he had paid people to help him forget.

Things that seemed to be bobbing to the surface, whether he wanted them to or not. Ghosts from the past.

The bot was following him. Perhaps the Doctor and Bernice had sent it after him. Or perhaps . . .

No. Not that thought. Not now. He dived into the nearest null-grav shaft, then out at the next junction. Using guile, skill and his knowledge of the myriad levels of the Overcity, he began to make his way towards the best access point to the Undertown. Within moments, the bot was out of sight.

Memories flitted through his mind. Faces and places that he thought had been buried. Old times. Painful times. As he exited the shaft and transferred onto a walkway, he tried to suppress them, but they were too strong. His old life was breaking through the patina of conditioning that had formed over it, and there was nothing he could do about it.

It was as if he had two parallel sets of memories: two identities. There was Powerless Friendless the anonymous musician and down-and-out whose body was covered in odd scars and who lived in the Undertown. And there was the other, the space pilot who appeared to him in dreams. The hero. The one who went away.

He made his way back towards the Undertown. It may not have been home, but it was the best he had.

Cwej was still shaking when Forrester led him into the refectory raft. The place was crowded with off-duty and resting Adjudicators. A scent of coffee and frying soy-bacon hung in the air. Simcords of alien forests and seas hung on the walls, making the place look tawdry rather than exotic.

'Hey, Forrester,' yelled a small man with a large moustache, 'who's your friend?'

'He's no friend, Susko,' Forrester shouted back, 'he's a rookie!'

'An' he's shakin' cos he's squired to Forrester,' another voice bellowed.

'Nah, it's the thought of working out of the same station as you, Lubineki,' Susko rejoined.

The room erupted in laughter. Forrester left them to it. Finding an unoccupied table for two, she sat Cwej down.

'How are you feeling?' she asked.

'I can't believe it,' he said. He'd been repeating the same words ever since they left the interrogation truck. While he had stood by the door, looking back inside with a dazed expression on his golden-furred face, Forrester had called a bot over to guard the truck and sent another one to Adjudicator Secular Rashid with a message.

'Brain embolism,' she said calmly. The best way to bring him out of it was to be calm. 'It happens.'

His face was etched with lines of worry. 'But . . . a suspect, dying in custody. We'll be slaughtered! The Adjudicator Secular will hang us out to dry!'

'I doubt it,' she said, punching an order for coffee into the tablecomp. 'We've still got the probe evidence. She was guilty, there's no denying that. All we've done is anticipate the sentence.'

'That's not the point! We –'

She banged the table, shutting him up and sending a

tiny ripple of tension around the room. 'That's the way centcomp will see it,' she insisted, holding his gaze. 'We're good cops. We've got good records. The underdweller was a murderer. Case closed.'

He seemed to relax slightly. 'Are you sure?'

'Sure? Of course I'm sure.'

A multi-armed bot passed by and deposited two steaming coffees on the table. Forrester sipped at hers and put it down again, grimacing at the heat. Cwej swigged his without apparently noticing. 'I wonder . . .' he said.

'What? What do you wonder?'

'Well, no. It was probably nothing.'

'If you want.'

'Like you said, I'm not familiar with the equipment.'

'You don't sound convinced.'

He caught his lower lip between sharp little teeth.

'Don't do that,' she added. 'It makes you look like a kid.'

'Sorry.'

'Now, what is it?'

'Well, it was the spike. The murder weapon.'

'What about it?'

'Well, when I bagged it, I noticed that it had a scratch on it.'

Forrester thought back. 'Yes, I remember. So what?'

'Well, I couldn't help noticing that on the probe, it didn't. Not when she was committing the murder.'

She tried to remember the picture on the screen. 'It was very fuzzy,' she said dubiously. 'You couldn't possibly tell.'

'But I could!' he said excitedly. 'You could see it from all angles on the probe screen. Nothing. Not a scratch anywhere.'

'So – so what are you saying?'

He looked down at the table. 'I'm saying that the spike we bagged is a real one, and the one on the record is a simulated one. I'm saying that the real one has a scratch but the simulated one is perfect. Too perfect.'

'Let me get this right. You're saying – '

'I'm saying that I think the mind probe record was faked,' he muttered, too low for the rest of the Adjudicators to hear.

'You *what*? Are you mad?'

'Mind probe records can be faked. You know that.'

Forrester couldn't believe what she was hearing. 'Yeah, but do you know what sort of technology is needed? Do you know how much it costs?'

He nodded mutely.

'And you think anybody is going to go to all that trouble for an underdweller?' she added. She was lacing her words with as much sarcasm as she could possibly muster, and Cwej was wilting under it. 'So who's responsible, then?'

He shook his head silently. It looked to her like he was on the verge of tears. Goddess, what *were* they teaching the kids at the Academy these days?'

'Fine,' she said, quieter. 'Let's hear no more about it then.'

'I know what I saw,' he insisted stubbornly, not meeting her eyes.

'Yeah, I know what you saw too. An illusion. Something that wasn't there.'

'Easy way to check.'

'Yeah?'

'Go back through the mind probe record.'

'No,' she shouted. 'I am not pandering to your sense of the dramatic. The woman is the killer. I'm sorry if the tidiness of the thing offends you, but it's true. The simplest solution is usually the true one.'

'That's not true,' he said mulishly.

'It's street-true,' she snapped, 'and that's what counts.'

The walkway carried them back towards where they had left the TARDIS. Bernice was quiet as she watched the towers slip past. What on Earth were they doing there?

'Odd,' the Doctor said from beside her, 'I don't usually have that effect on the people I talk to.'

'Perhaps,' Bernice said, 'we should try another approach. Any ideas?'

'The Imperial Landsknechte,' the Doctor replied. 'The champions of Earth, scourge of off-worlders, defenders of the Empire.'

'Landsknechte? What, like marines? How do you work that one out?' she asked sceptically.

'The number burned into that poor Hith's tail. It's an Imperial Landsknechte identification number. They use them for prisoners of war. I noticed back on Oolis that Homeless Forsaken had one as well.

'And where are these records?'

'Er . . . not on Earth.'

'No,' she sighed. 'No, nothing's that simple, is it?'

'It's the only lead we have,' he replied, and scurried out to the centre of the walkway. 'We'll have to use the TARDIS to get to the planet Purgatory. That's where the records are kept.'

A thought struck Bernice with some force. 'Er, Doctor?'

'Hmm?' he said, glancing up at her.

'Haven't we gone past the tower where we left the TARDIS?'

He gazed around. 'I don't remember seeing it,' he said with some foreboding.

Bernice felt a sinking sensation in the pit of her stomach. 'Neither do I,' she said.

'Oh dear,' he said. 'Oh double dear. Oh double dear with whipped cream and a cherry on top.'

'You can say that again.'

Chapter 4

'I'm Evan Claple and this is The Empire Today, *on the spot, on and off the Earth. Today's headlines: in Spaceport Seventeen Overcity a woman crashes a flitter into an office block after seeing her lover with another man; in Spaceport Two Overcity twenty-five are killed when a restaurant owner laces meals with zeelan toxin; in Spaceport Nine Undertown riots result in over three hundred dead. In a special report tonight, we ask: what is happening to the heartland of the Empire?'*

'So where now?' Bernice said.

They were standing by the walkway at the point where the TARDIS had been, and where it wasn't any longer. For a while they had thought that they were in the wrong tower, but the square imprint of the TARDIS's weight was evident in the plastic. All around them, people passed by without giving them a second glance, some of them waving their gloved hands in mid-air as they interacted with centcomp.

The Doctor had a haunted expression on his face.

'I don't know,' he whispered. 'I really don't know. I can't sense where she is.'

Bernice took a deep breath. She couldn't remember seeing the Doctor quite this het up before, and for no reason. Galactic crises, near-death experiences, hair-raising risks, all of these things she had seen him shrug off with a smile and a merry quip. Take his TARDIS away, however, and he went to pieces. It was as if he couldn't function properly without it.

'Okay, let's go through the alternatives,' she said, trying to be practical. 'What could have happened to it?'

The Doctor shrugged. 'Well,' he said hesitantly, 'there's the HADS.'

'HADS?'

'Hostile Action Displacement System,' he explained. 'It's a defensive mode that the TARDIS slips into if threatened.'

'I didn't know the TARDIS had any defences.'

'Not defences in the death ray sense.' He seemed rather put out that she should even think of it. 'Defences in the sense that the old girl vanishes if she's attacked.'

Bernice nodded. 'Sounds sensible. But who would attack a large blue box?'

'Somebody who knew who it belonged to,' he said darkly.

'That's a bit paranoid, isn't it?'

'Paranoia is just another word for a heightened appreciation of how badly the universe wants to get you.'

'Yes, very deep. However, in your case, I wouldn't be surprised. What else?'

'Well, it could have just been taken,' he said in a way that made it clear that he didn't believe it.

'Taken?'

'Cleared away. Moved.'

'So we check the lost property office,' Bernice suggested.

'I doubt somehow that it will be so simple.'

'Then what do you suggest?'

He gazed suspiciously around at the crowd. 'Does it strike you as coincidental that the TARDIS vanishes at the same time that we begin to investigate a mystery concerning the fate of the Earth?'

'To be frank, yes it does.'

'I sense the machinations of the cosmos at work. The ineluctable clockwork of fate. Jung would have agreed with me. Dear old Jung. Never believed in coincidence, you know. Synchronicity, that's what he called it.'

'So you think this Jung has stolen your TARDIS?'

'No, no, no. Jung was a psychologist. He was a student of Freud, but they fell out.'

'Fell out of what?'

'Never mind. He liked beetles.'

'Who doesn't? Look, why can't you accept that this is probably a misunderstanding?'

'Because there is a connection. Believe me, Bernice, I've been involved in more conspiracies than you've had double scotches. Something is going on.'

She snorted. 'If you've been involved in that many conspiracies, someone ought to ask you where you were on November 22nd, 1963.'

He delved in his pocket.

'I'm sure something important was happening around then,' he muttered. 'Let me check my five-hundred-year diary.'

'Do the words "grassy knoll" mean anything to you?'

'No, although I once met a ghastly Kroll. Why do you ask?'

'Never mind,' she sighed. 'I was only joking. Where do we go from here?'

The Doctor rubbed a hand across his face. 'Purgatory,' he said finally. 'There's a trail pointing towards the Imperial Landsknechte records. If we follow it, we may find the TARDIS at the end of it.'

'May?' Bernice asked.

'Nothing in the universe is certain except death and taxes,' the Doctor replied, and walked away.

'What do you mean, you're pulling the plug?' Forrester shouted.

Rashid just sat sprawled behind her desk, the light gleaming off her oiled quiff, and stared at Forrester. 'I mean what I say,' she drawled. 'I'm pulling the plug. You got a result. That's what counts. Good work.'

'But . . ?'

66

Forrester glanced sideways at Cwej for backup. He was studiously examining a spot on the wall just above Rashid's head. Never trust a rookie for support.

'No buts, Forrester. What do you want, a commendation? Only an underdweller, for Goddess' sake.'

Forrester shook her head. 'But what about the death?' she said. 'I mean, a death in custody? Like, I don't want an investigation or anything, but aren't you even going to check the mind probe for faults?'

Rashid shook her head. 'No point. Centcomp's happy with the way you handled the case. I'm happy. The whole Empire's happy, apart from you two.'

Forrester kicked surreptitiously at Cwej's ankle, but he didn't react. 'We felt, ah, that is, Cwej here felt that there was some kind of irregularity in the mind probe readings,' she ventured.

'Rookies,' Rashid sighed. 'Look, if it makes you happier, I'll review the mind probe evidence myself. Now get.'

Forrester opened her mouth to protest, but Cwej snapped, 'Yes, sir!' and turned smartly on his heel. She had no choice but to follow, cursing beneath her breath as she did so.

'What the hell was all that about?' she snapped as soon as they left the office. 'I thought you were on my side.'

'I am,' he said. 'Didn't you notice?'

'Notice what?'

'The Adjudicator Secular's simcord was on all the time. She'd turned the picture off to make it look like the whole thing was inactive, but the commlight was green. Everything we said was being heard by someone else. That's why I had to get us out before you said too much.'

Forrester frowned, opened her mouth to say something, then slowly closed it as the implications hit home.

'You mean . . ?'

'I mean that the Adjudicator Secular's being leaned on. Someone's told her to close this case down.'

Bernice had spent long enough aboard spaceships to be able to feel and understand the subtle vibrations of warp engines. The Imperial Landsknechte shuttle *Arachnae* was no exception. After all, Bernice had spent the formative years of her adolescence drifting around the universe in a clapped-out trader, swapping transuranic elements for alien art on one planet and alien art for transuranics on another, but always managing to shave a little profit off the top. She still remembered McFee, the trader's bluff Irish engineer. He'd taken a shine to her, and she had spent hours by his side while he coaxed another few light years out of the old, battered engines. She could read those sounds in her sleep now. For that reason she was already waiting in the main viewing gallery when the communication system chimed twice.

'Gentlebeings,' it said in a comforting artificial voice, 'the *Arachnae* is about to leave hyperspace and enter orbit around the planet Purgatory, home of the Imperial Landsknechte. Please do not eat or drink anything in the next ten minutes, and secure all loose articles. Any passengers who wish to observe the event, please be advised that the main viewing gallery is now open. For human passengers of a nervous disposition, medication is available by pressing button A on your autodoc. Any – ' A slight but noticeable hesitation. ' – *off world* passengers wishing medication should contact the medical orderly. Will those passengers who wish to disembark please ensure that their documentation is valid. Thank you.'

Within moments, a number of passengers had scuttled into the viewing gallery, ready to *oh!* and *ah!* and take simcords of the entire event. The wide-eyed, eager ones in the lead were tourists, taking in a quick tour of the Imperial Landsknechte facilities. Purgatory was, after all, one of the Eight Wonders of the Universe. The majority of the funding for the Imperial Landsknechte came from tourism; that and the taxes paid by the worlds that they had conquered during the Wars of Acquisition. It kept the tax burden on humanity down, and helped the Empire to grow in power and prestige. That was what the guide-books said, anyway.

The dead-eyed, crew-cut ones with the matt-black,

shell-like skins sauntering on behind the tourists were Landsknechte returning from furlough. Although the journey had only lasted a few hours, Bernice had already had to lay three of them out in the bar. The rest had left her alone after that.

The tourists were taken aback to find Bernice in the best position. She could hear them, murmuring and muttering as they jostled for position, but her attention was absorbed by the spectacle.

The viewing window was twenty metres long and ten high. It wasn't a real window, of course, just a virtual screen, but the effect was the same. From where Bernice was standing, she couldn't see the edges. it was as if she was standing in hyperspace itself.

Hyperspace was a blur, a blind spot that covered her entire vision. Tendrils of grey writhed against a grey background, but out of the corners of her eyes Bernice could see colours flashing and spiralling everywhere apart from where she was looking. The minute she turned her head, the colours vanished. The longer she looked, the deeper she could see into the unreality, and the more hints of colours she thought she could make out. It was hypnotic.

'Impressive, isn't it?'

She turned her head. The ship's purser was standing beside her: a bot of relatively advanced design, slim and elegant, with an unobtrusive logo embossed upon its carapace. Bernice tried to recall which company used the logo – a hand with an eye in the centre – but there were so many of them around that she couldn't distinguish one from another any more.

'Is it?' she responded, surprised at its forwardness. Bots didn't usually initiate polite conversation.

'It always fascinates me. You know the mathematics behind it, I presume?'

Its voice struck her as being oddly rich in tone: plummy, rather overbearing, slightly old-fashioned. Bad choice for a bot whose main duty was reassuring hysterical tourists who'd left Earth for the first time.

'A multi-dimensional realm of which our ordinary

three-dimensional space is only a part,' it continued. 'A space bigger than space through which we take our short cuts, ignorant of what else might be there.'

'Very poetic.'

The constant thrum of the engines altered in pitch. Bernice could tell to the nearest millisecond when they would break through into reality.

'We're leaving hyperspace,' it said. 'Should you not tell your companion? He might wish to see the sight for himself.'

'He's off in the bar with a group of high-powered Lands-knechte on their way to a conference. I'm sure he's seen it all before.'

The bot nodded. 'Perhaps he has,' it mused. 'Perhaps he has. Have you been travelling with him long?'

Something was wrong. Bernice could feel a chill run up her back. The bot was too familiar, too chummy. If she didn't know better, she would swear that she was being patronized.

It gazed at her for a long moment. She could feel the tension building up.

Before Bernice could reply, stars were twinkling through the grey nothingness. She watched as the tentacles of chaos withdrew, retreating before the advance of the material universe.

'You ask a lot of odd questions for a purser,' she challenged.

Although nothing about the bot changed, it gave Bernice the impression of amusement. 'Knowledge is power.'

Before she could respond, the ship turned slightly around its primary axis, and Purgatory spun into view. Bernice couldn't help blinking. Surely no planet could look like that. It just wasn't . . . natural.

Purgatory's surface was a patchwork of hexagons, each hundreds of kilometres across. The ochre of a scorching desert and the lush green of forest were separated by straight boundaries. The blue depths of an ocean and the glowing white of an icebound landscape sat beside each other, ignorant of the incongruity. Towering mountains and level plateaus, urban wastelands and jumbles of volcanic rock, glittering cities and cultivated fields: a disparate assortment of landscapes set randomly together.

'And that's Purgatory?' she said.

'That's Purgatory,' it confirmed. 'One step away from hell.'

The bot suddenly twitched as if a short circuit had momentarily overridden its balance sensors. It gazed around in what looked suspiciously like panic.

'Dear me,' it said in a high-pitched, fussy voice. 'Dear me, so near to disembarkation, and I have passengers to attend to. If you will excuse me . . ?'

It scurried off, its posture radically different from moments before. Bernice watched it, amazed. 'They didn't tell me that the tickets included a cabaret as well.'

The rain hammered steadily down upon the armoured roof of the Adjudication Chapel. It was getting on Forrester's nerves. It reminded her of the time when she'd been caught in a projectile weapon shoot-out. She'd thought that they were an historical anachronism, but the Therenids still used them, and when a group of mercenaries from a Therenid hive-ship went off the deep end in one of the entertainment towers, a lot of damage had been done. Blasters and lasers cauterized where they didn't kill. Projectile weapons caused a lot of messy and unpredictable collateral damage.

She opened her mouth to tell Cwej the story, but one look at his face persuaded her otherwise. He was slumped morosely in a form-fitting seat, pushing its adjustability to the limit, hands clenched around a cup of coffee. She'd offered him scotch, but he didn't drink on duty. Of course he didn't drink on duty; what had she been thinking of? He didn't do anything else against the rules, after all. Why should he drink on duty?

Forrester knew that she was getting more and more wound up. She'd already snapped Cwej's head off a couple of times. It wasn't his fault – well, all right, it *was* his fault;

71

after all, he did play the 'wide-eyed and innocent' card too often – but she didn't want to hurt his feelings. Not too much, anyway.

In a vain effort to distract herself, Forrester looked around the ready room. It was late in the afternoon, and the place was almost empty. Most of the other Adjudicators were out on patrol.

The rain was getting to her. She had to say something, even if it did get up the kid's nose. 'I can't believe it,' she snapped. Cwej flinched, startled. His chair tried to adjust, overcompensated, and ended up almost folding in two.

'I know I'm new here,' he said, switching the chair off in disgust, 'but does this sort of thing happen on a regular basis, or am I just privileged?'

Forrester remembered the times when Rashid had supported her, despite the innumerable rules and regulations of Adjudicator life. The times when Forrester had shot first and asked questions afterwards, used the mind probe a bit too freely or arrested innocent citizens by mistake. The sorts of thing that any eager young Adjudicator did.

'I've never known Rashid to back down under pressure,' she said finally, shaking her head in disbelief. 'She's always supported her people before. Goddess, this one must be really important.'

Cwej nodded. 'I've had a thought,' he said. 'If the mind probe record has been faked, then the old bird we pulled in is innocent.'

'The old bird?' Forrester had the impression that a blush was spreading beneath the golden pelt.

'The lady. The underdweller.'

'Hah! We'll make an opinionated, bigoted Adjudicator of you yet!' He just looked at her, and smiled slightly. She found herself smiling back. 'So, how do you work out that she's innocent, then?'

'It stands to reason. If somebody wants us to believe that she's guilty, she must be innocent.'

'Philosophically flawed . . .'

'. . . But street-true.'

She raised her eyebrows at him. That kid was getting to be a smart-arse.

'So what are we saying?' she said. 'That every one of these spur-of-the-moment murders is actually an assassination in disguise, covered up by the Order of Adjudicators?'

He shook his head uncertainly. The way the light caught his golden fur distracted her momentarily. 'No,' he said. 'Too many people involved for that. For some reason, it's just this murder. Just this one murder.'

'So why was the low-life bumped off?' she challenged.

Cwej leaned forward insistently. 'To prevent us questioning her any further. Somewhere inside her underdweller skull, she knew who drugged her and who carried out the murder. She saw them. The chances are we could have dug a clue out of her mind. With her dead, and the mind probe record faked, we were supposed to accept the whole thing, fins, fuselage and retro-tubes.'

'But you spotted that the record was faked . . .'

His gaze was sombre. 'Yeah, and got us thrown off the case.'

Forrester pounded the desk again. 'It's so damned unfair!'

Cwej winced. 'Unfair?'

Something in his tone made her look up. 'You think it's more than that?'

'Think about it,' he said. 'Doesn't it strike you as a little bit suspicious that somebody tries to sell us a set-up and then, when we look like penetrating their little game, they pull us off the case?'

Forrester felt a tiny cold bud begin to flower in her gut. 'Paranoia,' she said dismissively, but even she could tell that she was unconvinced.

'Is it?' he asked. 'When we brought the body in, I asked for a tissue-type check to be run.'

'Tissue-type?' She tried to read his fresh, innocent face for clues, but it was like reading a blank sheet of paper. 'But the bot said that the mollusc was unidentified. No biochip.'

Cwej grinned.

'Wrong murderer . . .' he said.

'. . . And wrong victim,' Forrester finished. She felt a sudden desire to forget everything, to get up and walk over to the refectory raft and have a couple of beers with the guys.

No, she thought. That's not the way Martle would have played it.

'Let's check,' she said. 'The results might be in by now.'

Cwej grinned.

It only took a few moments for Cwej to link with centcomp and type in the query. Forrester watched impatiently as he ran his finger down a list of information that only he could see.

'We're in luck,' he breathed. 'The tests are complete.'

'And?' Forrester didn't know why she was holding her breath, but she was.

'And we've got an ID for the victim.'

'How can you do that without a biochip?'

'He had a biochip.' Cwej quickly scanned through the information. 'The genetic code matches one Waiting For Justice And Dreaming Of Home. Record as long as your arm and most of your leg as well. Mainly petty thievery, assault and begging.'

'Address?'

'The Undertown. That's all it says.'

Forrester looked grim. 'That's all there is,' she said. 'You should have learned that by now. Question is, why did the bot tell us that the victim didn't have a biochip when he did?'

Cwej's face was serious. 'Because the bot didn't bother checking. Because the bot wasn't expecting the victim to have a biochip. Because the bot got the wrong off-worlder.'

'What do you mean, "got"?' Forrester asked.

'What do you think?'

'You can't mean . . ?'

'That the bot killed the off-worlder thinking it was another off-worlder?' His face was set. 'Yes, I do.'

'Well,' she said, leaning back in her chair and sighing, 'I guess they all look the same. So, we've got a murderer who isn't a murderer and a victim who isn't a victim. What else can go wrong?'

'You've forgotten one thing.'

'Oh yeah? What's that?'

'Two investigators who aren't investigating.'

She looked meaningfully over at him.

'Let's rectify that, at least.'

'You mean . . ?'

'I mean, college boy, that we're going to solve this case despite all the shit they can throw at us.'

He stared back. 'What's with this "we"?'

She raised an eyebrow. 'Requesting a new partner this soon could look real bad on your report.'

He grinned. 'And besides,' he said, getting to his feet, 'where could they find someone else stupid enough to work with you?'

'That,' murmured Forrester as she followed him from the room, 'is *my* line.'

The hands on the desk suddenly jerked into life as the fastline link to the *Arachnae* was severed.

'So, Doctor,' a voice murmured, 'you're getting away from the trap I laid for you on Earth. You think that you can escape me? Think again. I have tame Landsknechte as well as tame Adjudicators. If you don't wish to be brainwiped on Earth, perhaps it's best to have you killed on Purgatory.'

Quivering for a moment, like insects surprised by a light, the hands gradually began to scuttle across the surface of the desk, sending a message along the fastline towards a planet named Purgatory and a man named Provost-Major Beltempest. That done, the hands paused as their owner digested events that had occurred in his absence. The hands requested more data from centcomp records cross-referenced to an Adjudication lodge. The hands clasped like lonely animals and began softly to caress each other.

'And you, my friend,' the voice said. 'I thought that I had killed you, but I see I made a mistake. Not something that I am prone to do, and not something that remains unaddressed.'

The hands rested. Their owner waited.

In the privacy of his office on Purgatory, Provost-Major Montmorency Beltempest ran the tip of his trunk over the now-darkened viewscreen. The blue tip of his very expensively beppled trunk, he reminded himself. Money could buy an awful lot, and over the past few years he'd managed to indulge a number of tastes that he hadn't even realized he possessed. He'd got used to having lots of money to play with, and he wasn't about to give it up. Not for anything.

But still . . . murder? That wasn't really his line. Information, yes. He would pass on secret information with no qualms. Nobody could trace the leaks back to him, he was certain of that. And contracts. Assigning new weapons development contracts to a specific firm was piss easy. No risk there. Even that business with the Hith ship and its crew hadn't bothered him overly. But murder?

He eased himself out of his chair and crossed to the window. With one massive blue paw he moved the lace curtains aside. It was night, and Purgatory's one scarred moon was casting its reflected light upon the buildings of the Imperial Landsknechte HQ. The albino lawn trembled gently to itself and, high above, particle beams glowed as a mock battle was fought.

Beltempest sighed. He had no choice, of course. Even if he wanted to give up on his regular second income, he wouldn't be allowed to. Nobody ever resigned and lived, anyway.

The door chimed softly. He didn't jump, because what was left of his conscience was inured to deceit by now, but his mind quickly ran over prepared explanations, excuses and lies. Just in case.

'Come,' he said. The door slid open. Two silhouetted figures were stood just outside it. 'Yes? What is it, man?'

The figures raised their hands, revealing stunners. They wanted him alive, then. 'Provost-Major Beltempest?' one of them asked calmly.

So. The time had come. So soon. They must have intercepted the fastline call.

Beltempest stepped sideways and reached for the blaster at his side. His hand moved so slowly that it was as if he were standing up to his neck in one of the swampy Landsknechte training grounds, or moving through an alien atmosphere thick enough to cut with a knife. One of the Landsknechte at the door fired, but Beltempest hadn't just spent his money on fripperies. The stun beam reflected from the wire sheathing he'd had implanted beneath his skin, catching both of them. They slumped to the floor, dropping their weapons. They could have tried anything up to plasma rifles, and he would still have been standing. Money could buy anything.

He fried both men with two careful bursts from his blaster. Beltempest was nothing if not careful. With luck, a gun and sufficient bribes, he could get to his private ship and off-planet within an hour. He took two steps towards the door . . .

And stopped. Cursing, he tried to force his legs to move, but they wouldn't obey him. What was this, some kind of new weapon? He slapped his thighs desperately. He could feel the impacts, but nothing was happening. It was as if someone else had taken control. Fear flooded his mind. If he couldn't get out – if he was found there, with the two bodies – then he would be finished.

Entirely without volition, the hand holding the blaster began to rise towards his face.

He didn't scream. There was a way out. There had to be a way out. Money could buy anything.

He could feel his finger tighten on the trigger as his lips kissed the hot metal of the barrel.

He tried to scream then, but it was too late. There was no time, there was no money, and there was nothing left of his head.

* * *

'Are you going to tell me how we bluff our way off the end of this ramp or not?' Bernice hissed as she and the Doctor made their way, ahead of the tourists and the Landsknechte, down the ramp of the *Arachnae* onto Purgatory. Her breath billowed out before her in the cold, thin atmosphere.

The spaceport was a huge plasticrete plain: one of the many and various hexagon-bounded areas that made up the planet's surface. As the ship descended towards it, Bernice had tried counting the number of lighters, corvettes, frigates, cruisers, Dalekbusters and battleships that sat divided into squadrons, flights and wings, on the hard pink surface. Some were gleaming and pristine in the hard, cold light of Purgatory's sun, sitting alertly upon insectile legs, but the majority were scarred and singed, old and tired.

'Well, I haven't quite sorted out the details yet,' the Doctor said, not meeting Benny's gaze.

Blaster batteries in fortified pits had tracked the *Arachnae* as it descended, and were still trained upon it. The burnt expanse of plasticrete stretched to the horizon, and beyond. A squad of Imperial Landsknechte, immaculate in black and orange dress uniforms, waited at the bottom of the ramp, holding their plasma rifles at the ready.

'What do you mean, "haven't quite sorted out the details yet"?'

'They look very fierce, don't they?' he said, indicating the Landsknechte guard.

Bernice felt a rising hysteria. 'I'd hoped that you might have come up with some sort of plan during the journey,' she snapped.

'Of course, you know what they say.'

'I mean, it's not like we can just wander in and ask to look at their records, is it?'

'If it's a yellow alert, they issue them with plasma rifles . . .'

'Some sort of cover story is probably required, and I'd like to know what it is!'

'. . . And if it's a red alert, they give them the power packs as well.'

'*Now!*'

He sighed. 'Yes, yes, I know all that,' he scolded, as if he had suddenly heard what she was saying. As they reached the bottom of the ramp, the Landsknechte came to attention. A man in a captain's uniform stepped forward, holding a gene-tester. He was tall and dark-haired, and his skin was a dull, hard shell, like a beetle's carapace.

'Identification?' he said.

The Doctor proffered his right hand. 'I am a plainclothes Landsknechte agent, here on official business,' he said calmly.

The captain ran the gene-tester over the Doctor's hand and glanced at its tiny simcord screen. The tester buzzed faintly. 'It will take a few seconds to check your identity,' he said. 'I apologize for the – ah yes, that seems to be in order, sir.' His attitude changed markedly. 'If I can be of any assistance . . .'

'We wish to consult your records,' the Doctor announced. 'Judicial investigation, you know.'

'Of course, sir. And the lady?'

'My companion.'

'And her identification?'

The Doctor glanced at Bernice. 'She's nervous of those machines,' he said. 'Can you not take my word for it? I can vouch for her.'

'I'm sorry, sir,' the captain insisted, 'but regulations state . . .'

'Of course,' the Doctor said. 'Bernice . . ?' He indicated that she hold out her hand.

The captain reached out towards her with the genetester. Bernice felt the muscles in her back go tense.

'Oh look,' the Doctor said, gazing upwards and shading his eyes, 'is that a flock of macrobiotic dodos?' The captain glanced involuntarily upwards, and the Doctor quickly shoved his left hand into the gene-tester and out again. 'My mistake,' he said, unabashed, as the captain frowned at him. 'They're extinct, of course.'

The gene-tester buzzed. The captain gazed suspiciously at it, then at Bernice. After a few seconds, his face cleared. 'Thank you,' he said, gesturing to one of the hard-faced Landsknechte. 'This man will fly you to the officers' mess. Please accept our hospitality while your investigations continue.'

'Thank you,' said the Doctor.

'You can't resist a touch of the dramatic, can you?' Bernice hissed as they walked away from the *Arachnae* and towards an armoured hovercar that sat like a fat ladybird near the ship. She was conscious from the stares of the tourists and the Landsknechte that this VIP treatment had raised some eyebrows.

'A little foible I have.' The Doctor's face was strained, and a fine sheen of sweat covered his forehead. 'Ostentation is my middle name.'

'A big foible, Doctor, one that's going to get us into trouble, one of these days.' She frowned. 'How did you do that?'

The Doctor looked a little sheepish. 'A trick I learned from the Master,' he admitted. 'He frequently used regeneration as a means of disguise. My friend Romana – you remember her? – did a similar thing during her first regeneration: trying out various genetic configurations before she settled on one. It occurred to me that I could temporarily shift my genetic make-up enough to mimic somebody else, just for a few seconds. Two somebodies else, to be precise. Or do I mean "two somebody elses"? Whatever. It saps the energy, but it's an effective disguise.'

The Landsknechte dilated an iris door in the side of the hovercar and gestured for them to enter.

'*That's* why you were so chummy with that group of Landsknechte of the *Arachnae*,' Bernice said as they sat in the spartan interior. 'You were trying to pick up their genetic make-up!'

'They were nice people,' he protested.

'Then you should be ashamed of yourself.'

He squirmed in his seat as the hovercar took off in a cloud of dust. 'Time Lords don't get ashamed.'

80

'What, never?'

'No.' He sighed. 'We had our shame psycho-surgically removed a great many generations ago.'

The rain joined heaven and hell with a myriad threadlike silver lines, and the hiss as it hit the water of the square reminded Powerless Friendless of static, although he couldn't remember ever hearing static. Just another orphaned memory. He should put them all in a box and shake them up in the hope that they might reassemble and tell him who he was, or rather, who he had been.

Clouds curdled, high above the Undertown. Through them, Powerless Friendless could just make out the bases of the ever-present towers, looming like gods over the broken remains of their domain. As he looked at the crumbled stone buildings surrounding the crowded square, their massive columns now fallen, and their arched porticos rotted with the passing of the centuries, Powerless Friendless could see why, if they were gods, they chose to remain so aloof. It wasn't much of a world for a deity.

He shivered as the constant rain pricked at his exposed eyeballs and trickled down his too-moist skin. Usually he tried not to think about gods. Religion was a tricky business – every race had a pantheon that was incompatible with every other race – but that didn't stop the worship, or the arguments. The Hith were no exception.

His eye-stalks twitched in a smile. Perhaps there was a Hith deity who watched over those whose memories had been taken away, but if there was then Powerless Friendless couldn't remember its name.

Reluctantly, he lowered his gaze to the crowd of under-dwellers that filled the square. He felt his skin crawl at the presence of so many other living beings. He shouldn't have come. A lonely Hith is a happy Hith, isn't that what they said back on Hithis?

He'd been fine, slinking alone through the alleys and bridges of the Undertown. After the Doctor and Bernice had shaken up his memory he had started to believe that everybody was watching him, following him, talking about him. After a few hours of aimless wandering, he had decided that he was overreacting. Warily, he had returned to what he laughingly called his home. As time passed he had relaxed. He was safe.

In contrast to the narrow alleys and rotting walkways that characterized the worldwide Undertown, the square was the largest open space for miles. The moss-covered flagstones suggested that it had once been submerged – a nexus for various main canals, perhaps – but dams now blocked off each entrance, and a clever series of run-off channels and wind-driven pumps kept it clear of rainwater. It was a meeting place: the only one the local Underdwellers had. He didn't usually go there, but this was a special occasion.

He hoped that Olias would get a move on. He felt exposed, standing there. Anybody looking for him – if anybody was looking for him – wouldn't get a better chance than this. Anybody who knew anything about the Undertown would know it was Waiting For Justice's and Annie's funeral, and Waiting For Justice had been an associate of his.

Olias stood atop an island of stone in the centre of the square, flanked by four metal statues and seven brutal Ogron bodyguards. Legend had it that the statues represented long-extinct animals, but Powerless Friendless had always thought that their regal bearing and calm and benign expressions marked them out as superior life forms, perhaps the original inhabitants of the Earth, once powerful but now overthrown by vicious, squabbling humanity. There had been a column, midway between the statues, but it had fallen in some natural or wartime disaster, and the rubble still littered the square.

'Gentlebeings,' Olias rasped, her voice echoing from the distant ruins, 'we have gathered together to honour, in our respective ways, two of our own. Friends who lived life without hurting others. Friends who were generous. Friends who were kind. Friends who took nothing from those who could not afford it.'

Olias was a Sunhillowan: race whose body chemistry

was based upon germanium rather than the more usual carbon or silicon. Her skin glittered constantly, and shifted upon her etiolated frame as if smaller animals were running up and down beneath it. She was also the most powerful crime boss in the local Undertown area, a position she had held onto by an odd but effective combination of viciousness and benevolence. It was said that she knew everybody within her area of the Undertown by name.

A movement behind her attracted Powerless Friendless's attention. It was old Doc Dantalion: the arachnid Birastrop who tended to the Underdwellers if they got sick. His fees were high, but he had no compunction about accepting stolen goods, and those underdwellers who couldn't or wouldn't steal could always give him something else. Limbs or organs were preferred.

Doc Dantalion. Something scratched away at the back of Powerless Friendless's mind, something about his past. Somehow, Doc Dantalion was involved.

'Gentlebeings,' Olias said, 'I ask you to call upon your deities, if you have any, to mark the passing in whatever way you choose of Waiting For Justice and Dreaming Of Home of the Hith race and Annie Thelma Falvoriss of the human race. They will be missed.'

As she spoke these words, some freak effect of the weather opened a channel through the clouds to the rose-tinted sky beyond. For the first time Powerless Friendless could remember, a shaft of sunlight shone down upon them like a benediction, filling the air with a golden haze. A rainbow glimmered in the distance, and the crowd of humans and aliens drew in their breath in wonder.

All except Powerless Friendless.

He was more concerned with the way the light glittered on the metal shell of a bot on the fringes of the crowd.

The same bot that had tried to grab him as he slithered out of the plaza in the Overcity.

Chapter 5

'I'm Evan Claple, and this is The Empire Today Update, *broadcasting from the heart of the Empire. Tonight's special report: are the Overcities safe for humanity? As the latest figures show a disturbing five thousand per cent increase in violent crimes, we talk to Adjudicator Spiritual Nbomo of the Church of Adjudication and Vice-Admiral O'Gottif of the Imperial Landsknechte. All that and more, after this message . . . '*

'Unknown.'

The word hung in mid-air, mocking them both.

Bernice leaned back in the chair and glanced around the cubicle. Nobody was watching. The muscles across the back of her neck were knotted with tension, and she dug her fingers into them, pressing until it hurt, trying to force them to relax. It was no good. Impersonating a Landsknecht on a planet run entirely by the Imperial Landsknechte was not a situation designed to induce comfort.

She gazed past the Doctor and out of the crystal window instead. At least the view was tranquil. A few minutes after take-off, the hovercar had crossed an invisible boundary between two of the hexagons she had spotted from orbit, passing with an almost imperceptible tremor from the bleak, mechanistic spaceport to a lush, landscaped area of trembling white lawns and low buildings: the central administration area for the planet and, presumably, the Landsknecht fleet.

The Imperial Landsknecht Archive was a large building of rose-tinted marble set in the middle of an albino lawn. The next section of Purgatory was visible as a huge wall of water that rose up and vanished in the blue of the sky. With Bernice's fingers firmly crossed behind her back, they had been escorted to a tiny cubicle with a desk and one chair. After a certain amount of 'After you', 'No, after *you*' which culminated with both she and the Doctor trying to sit down at the same time, Bernice entered into a meaningful dialogue with the computer. She told it what she wanted, it told her what it could do for her, and etched the word into the air in several languages just to make sure that she understood. She'd been doing fine, up to the point when she asked it about Homeless Forsaken Betrayed And Alone.

'Fine,' she said, looking away from the window, 'let's make the inquiry a little more general. Computer, search all public records for mentions of the Hith race.'

'All records concerning individual members of the Hith race, the Hith race itself, the Hith Pacification and all subsidiary subjects are classified,' the computer said primly.

'Hmm,' the Doctor said, leaning forward with interest. 'The war's been over for four years. You'd think that they could declassify something.' He thought for a moment. 'Let me try.' He cleared his throat. 'Computer, search all public records for Imperial Landsknecht prisoner of war identification numbers.'

'Searched and found.'

'Display all data on subject with Imperial Landsknecht prisoner of war identification number five zero three three nine one zero two.'

A pause.

'I know what it's going to say,' Bernice whispered.

'Information concerning the prisoner of war identified by that number is classified.'

Bernice sighed. The Doctor smiled. 'We're on a trail,' he said.

'Yeah, but the trail's blocked.'

85

'Then we'll walk along the grass verge to the side,' the Doctor said. Bernice was still trying to work out exactly what he meant by that when he said: 'Computer, how many Imperial Landsknecht prisoner – oh, this is stupid.' He thought for a moment. 'Computer, for the duration of this access session, please regard the phrase ILPIN as being equivalent to the phrase Imperial Landsknecht prisoner of war identification number.'

'Acknowledged.'

'Nice to know you speaka da lingo,' Bernice murmured.

The Doctor continued. 'Computer, how many ILPINs are classified?'

'Two,' it said.

The Doctor turned to Bernice and said: 'Interesting. Our quarry is so important that he is one of two records that have not been declassified.' Turning back to the desk, he said, 'Computer, please give the date at which ILPIN five zero three three nine one zero two was issued.'

'That information is – '

'Classified,' he chorused with it. 'Very well, please – and this is the clever bit – please give the date on which ILPIN five zero three three nine one zero *one* was issued.'

'That information is – '

'Shut up!' the Doctor barked, then grimaced. 'Oh, of course. Computer, please give the date at which ILPIN five zero three three nine one zero *zero* was issued.'

'Tuesday the fifth of June in the year two thousand nine hundred and fifty-five.'

The Doctor clapped his hands together in joy. 'Smack in the middle of the Hith Pacification. Computer, please give the date on which ILPIN five zero three three nine one zero *three* was issued.'

'Tuesday the fifth of June in the year two thousand nine hundred and fifty-five.'

Bernice, who had been following this with interest, was lost. 'And this means .. ?' she asked.

'It means that, of all the prisoners of war who were given numbers during the Hith offensive, only two were so important that all records of them are still classified four years later. And we were having dinner with one of them a few days ago.'

'Homeless Forsaken Betrayed And Alone?'

'I think that we can safely assume so.'

'Something of an ironic joke,' Bernice said.

'I hope the joke consoles you during your incarceration,' a deep voice said from behind them. They turned, to find two Landsknechte pointing guns at them. Big guns, bristling with matt-black attachments. Beside them stood a portly Landsknecht in a provost-major's uniform, his hands behind his back. His skin was blue and wrinkled, his ears were huge flapping sheets and his nose had been elongated into a flexible tube that dangled down across his ample belly. An expensive body-bepple, for sure. He reminded Bernice of something, but she couldn't remember what.

He smiled at Bernice.

'I apologize for the inconvenience,' he said pleasantly. 'I'm Provost-Major Beltempest, and you're under arrest for impersonating Landsknecht officers.'

He took his hands from behind his back, and Bernice was oddly unsurprised to find that he had four arms. 'I hope you enjoy your stay,' he said. 'It's liable to be a long one.'

The sound of metal sliding against wood was almost drowned by the soft hiss of rain against the surface of the canal.

Powerless Friendless took a deep, silent breath, and tried to squeeze himself closer to the side of the building. He was standing on a wooden walkway which dangled unsteadily from lengths of rope, wire and discarded fibre-optic cable. As with all the walkways in the Undertown, the cables were attached to the roof of the building above. The wall beside him, and the one across the canal, were sheer faces of polycarbide-reinforced plastic. The rain poured down in a steady, monotonous rhythm. High above, the massive towers of the Overcity loomed impassively over the Undertown like stone clouds.

Metal again, scraping against the walkway. Powerless Friendless tried to locate it, but the hiss of the rain made it almost impossible. He could usually tell when there was a living creature nearby – his skin crawled and his eye-stalks itched – but bots were different. They weren't alive.

He slid back a few metres.

Nothing. Perhaps it couldn't hear him. Perhaps there was nothing there.

He slid back a little more.

Still nothing. He'd been spooked by a rat, or some kind of scavenger. His nerves were all shot to hell. Not surprising he was scared. Not in a place like the Undertown.

He slid back again, more confident now.

Scrape.

He froze.

What the hell was it? The Undertown was dangerous, no mistake about that, but it was an obvious kind of danger. A danger that came at you screaming with a knife in its hand, not one that hid in shadows. There were gangs, sure – groups of underlife pulled together by hunger, oaths and the threat of violence – but they mainly stuck to raiding the lower levels of the Overcity and fighting each other over territory and imagined insults. Powerless Friendless did his best to keep out of their way as much as possible. Disorganized crime, he always called it, but not to its face. Too many acquaintances of his had laughed at the gangs, and were dead as a result. And then there were the kids who came down from the Overcity, thinking that beating up a few of the underlife was fun. But not this. Nothing like this. Nothing that skulked in shadows, watching, waiting.

Perhaps he could lure it out into the open. Find out what it was, what it wanted. He bent and ran his pseudo-limb along the rain-sodden walkway, checking for loose bits of wood or metal. Nothing. Absolutely nothing.

A stinging squall of rain lashed across Powerless Friend-less's face and slid off the water-repellent mucus that covered his body. He should have been in some dark, empty building, sleeping or practising his *hag'jat*, not out in the open, playing cat and mouse with something from a nightmare.

Another squall sent splashes skittering across the slats of the walkway. Powerless Friendless extruded his eye-stalks to their fullest extent and peered into the darkness, trying to separate black from black.

And then he noticed.

The rain was falling straight down in cold silver lines, with no breath of wind to disturb it, but some of it was bouncing in shallow curves off a tall shape in the shadows. He tried to follow the shape with his eyes, only to lose it amid the rain and the darkness. But it was there.

Cautiously he felt in his rucksack for some loose change. His hand re-emerged with a triangular coin. He hefted it for a few moments, then tossed it past where the figure was standing. The coin hit the wooden walkway with a dull thud and the figure stepped forward into the dull light that filtered down through the miasmic clouds.

It glistened in the rain. The rain rebounded hollowly from its metal skin.

A bot. A manual labour bot: the one he had seen outside the plaza and again at Waiting For Justice's funeral. It *had* been following him!

It turned its head, trying to determine what had made the noise. 'Why are you hiding from me?' the bot said in a rich, fruity voice as it looked around. 'I know you're there. Why prolong the agony?'

'Why are you following me?' Powerless Friendless yelled, trusting the rain to disguise his location.

'Ah, you wish to play the innocent lamb? It won't do you any good, you know. I still have to kill you. I'm afraid you know too much.'

'I don't know anything!'

'If only I could believe you.' The bot sounded apologetic. 'This should have been over years ago. You shouldn't have run. You shouldn't have escaped.'

Glittering scalpels, cutting his flesh: machines that buzzed

inside him, chewing their way along his nerve endings: a
sardonic metal face, sneering down at him . . .

'You tortured me!' Powerless Friendless yelled as the
images unfolded before him. They had always been there,
fermenting in a corner of his mind, but he had refused to
acknowledge them. What had those humans in the plaza
started?

'I needed information,' the bot said in a surprised voice.
'Surely you understand that? But you escaped, and I
thought I'd lost you. The Undertown is a large place to
search, but I managed to find you. And then, to kill the
wrong Hith . . .' The bot spread its hands wide in a curi-
ously human gesture of contrition. 'Still, at least I had the
good sense to know that you would attend the funeral.'

Waiting For Justice . . . Powerless Friendless felt his eyes
prickle with tears. Waiting For Justice had never said why
he was on Earth, but now he was dead. In Powerless
Friendless's place. Mistaken identity. A senseless death.

As if the bot had been listening to his thoughts, it
continued with disarming *bonhomie*: 'I was too eager. I
admit that. Time makes us all careless, my friend, and I've
had more time than most. It didn't occur to me that any
other of your race would be on Earth. We can't be your
favourite people, after all.'

If he closed his eyes, Powerless Friendless could almost
believe that he was listening to a man, not a machine. The
voice was that good.

The bot chuckled unnervingly.

'Still, he was only an alien without a home world, wasn't
he?' it continued. 'No great loss to mankind. I put him
out of his misery. Such a lot of misery, but I promise I'll
make it quick for you. It's the least I can do, after all you
did for me.'

'Murderer!' Powerless Friendless shouted into the rain,
feeling the droplets sting against his tongue.

The bot's head turned suddenly until it was staring
straight at him. Its eyes glittered with a feral green light.
'Ah, *there* you are,' it said, amused.

It walked slowly towards him.

'Don't worry, my boy,' it said. 'It'll all be over soon.'

The room was large, plain, unfurnished and locked. It had taken the Doctor all of five seconds to exhaust all its myriad possibilities. He now stood by the window – unbreakable transparisteel – looking out at Purgatory.

An Imperial Landsknecht warbot stood in the corner, looking at him.

'Stop glowering at me,' he snapped.

The warbot didn't react. It was twice as tall as he was, and three times as broad. The armoured metal of its shell was painted in yellow and red splotches – camouflage colours for some alien campaign, he assumed – and it stood on two massive legs. Two of its six arms ended in weapons, two in multi-purpose tools. The other two seemed to be designed for holding people in nasty grips, if his journey from the archives was anything to go by.

'I don't suppose your mother was a Swiss army knife?' he said.

No reaction.

He hated robots. At least Daleks and Cybermen had emotions you could play on, although both races would have denied it emphatically, had they been asked. Robots, though . . . You could go through all your best routines with them and you wouldn't even raise a giggle.

He turned his attention to the view through the window. Directly outside was a huge parade ground, miles across. As far as the eye could see, groups of Landsknechte were being marched up and down. He could see their mouths moving, but the window was hermetically sealed. He didn't need to hear, though. They would be shouting the same sort of things that young men had shouted on parade grounds since the first button was sewn on the first uniform. 'Kill a Dalek for the Empire!' 'Peace through superior firepower!'

If he craned his neck, he could just make out the corner of the archive building. Soldiers ran along paths around it, moving from one meaningless ritual to another. He was grimly amused to see that they didn't cut corners. No, that would be too simple. When they came to a corner they ran past it, halted, swivelled through ninety degrees and started running again. The military mentality. If it moves, salute it, if it doesn't move, pick it up and if you can't pick it up, paint it. At least Brigadier Alastair Gordon Lethbridge-Stewart, bless his little tartan cotton socks, had maintained a sense of humour about it all. The problem was that humans as a whole didn't laugh enough.

Still, it could be worse. They could be robots.

Talking of which . . .

The Doctor turned back to the warbot.

'Can you whisk eggs with that thing?' he said, pointing to one of its multi-function limbs. The bot swivelled its sensors to follow him as he walked closer to it.

'The prisoner is warned that approaches closer than five feet will result in a weapons discharge,' it warned – somewhat obscurely, the Doctor thought as he came to a halt.

'But I haven't got five feet,' he replied, wondering how far he could twist the conversation before the bot lost track.

It failed to go for the bait. Try something else.

'Who *is* the prisoner?' he asked, glad that Ben and Polly weren't there. They would have ribbed him about that one.

'You are the prisoner,' the bot replied.

'How do you know?' the Doctor asked. This could be a line worth pursuing.

The bot thought for a moment. 'Imperial Landsknecht records confirm that you are the prisoner.'

'And are Imperial Landsknecht records always correct?'

'Yes.'

It was the Doctor's turn to think for a moment. He had to get this right first time. If he mucked it up, the robot wouldn't give him a second chance. He could only pray that it had no formal training in philosophy.

'That archive building,' he said casually. 'Contains a lot of information, does it?'

'Approximately seven quadrillion gigabytes,' the robot responded.

'Hmm. Very impressive. And how many separate documents is that? Approximately?'

'Ten billion.'

'Broken down into various categories, I'll be bound?'

'There are fifteen thousand separate categories of document.'

Almost there. Just lead it those last few steps.

'And are there any catalogues that record the titles of all the documents in each category?'

'Each category has a category catalogue that fulfils that function.'

The Doctor's mind was racing: checking each logical step to ensure that it led to one and only one conclusion. A paradoxical one. 'And I presume that the category catalogues do not actually contain entries for themselves. That would be stupid, wouldn't it?'

The robot thought for a moment, almost as if it sensed the yawning logical trapdoor. 'No,' it said finally, 'the subject category catalogues do not list themselves as entries.'

The Doctor wiped a bead of sweat from his temple. Time to spring the trap. 'If there were to be a catalogue that listed all of the catalogues that do not list themselves,' he said carefully, 'then which catalogue would list this catalogue?'

The robot stood, and thought. And thought. And thought a bit more.

The Doctor rubbed his hands together with glee. Good old Bertrand Russell. Time to really get to work.

From orbit, the Earth seemed a lush, verdant world, ripe with promise and bereft of civilization.

Micheal van Looft, shift supervisor on the Vigilant IX orbital laser satellite, knew it wasn't true. He knew that the green of the continents were just the cultivated tops of floating buildings, and the blue of the seas was a few metres of water protecting vast algae farms, and that thirty billion or so people lived down there, loved down there and died down there.

And he knew that his boyfriend was having an affair down there.

He'd known for months. Nick had simcorded up to the satellite shortly after Micheal's three-month tour commenced and told Micheal about it, laughing as he did so. He'd enjoyed taunting Micheal with stories of how good his lover was in bed. Micheal had felt like a knife had been thrust into his guts.

After three months he thought he'd got used to the idea. Life was quiet on the Vigilant belt. Nobody really thought that any aliens were going to attack – they'd all been pacified during the Wars of Acquisition – and if they did, there would be plenty of warning. He read books, watched simcords, and thought. After three months, he'd persuaded himself that he was better off without Nick. Honestly, he was.

And then he'd woken from a tormented dream in which Nick's face was obliterated by maggots of flame, and he padded naked from his bunk to the laser battery control room, and overrode the failsafes, and turned the satellite around so that the lasers pointed at Earth, not into space.

And so he sat there, the cross-hairs slaved to track the tower that Nick lived in as the satellite transited the Earth. At that range, the beam would be five or six metres wide at the surface, and hot enough to melt rock. In five minutes the rotation of the Earth and the orbit of the satellite would carry the tower over the horizon. It was long enough. Long enough to remember the humiliation, the aching pain of betrayal, the long, sleepless, tear-stained nights.

And even as his finger circled the edge of the button, feeling its silky smooth texture, running lightly across the incised letters of the word FIRE, something inside him screamed that this was insane.

But he pressed the button anyway.

'Tisane?' Provost-Major Beltempest said.

'Bless you,' Bernice replied.

He smiled.

'No, you misunderstand. I was asking whether you wanted a tisane. It's an infusion of leaves in hot water.'

'I didn't misunderstand at all,' she sighed. 'I was making a joke. A small joke. And talking of small jokes, where is the Doctor?'

Beltempest eased his elephantine body out of his over-sized chair and walked over to a filing cabinet with an impressive security lock. Placing his palm against it, he said, 'Your friend is currently held in a secure cell. I'll deal with him in good time. First, I thought I should have a chat with you.'

'I think I should warn you, I'm not very communicative under stress.'

'You'd be surprised,' he said calmly as the cabinet opened to reveal a kettle, a tea caddy and two cups.

Bernice bit back a sarcastic response and took a moment to study the provost-major as he busied himself pouring water into the cups and adding a sprinkling of dried leaves from the caddy. He made a strange figure amid the walnut panelling and lace curtains of his office. He must have been well over six feet tall, and his stomach bulged so far that it must have been years since he last saw his feet. His skin was the colour of Earth's sky at dawn, his trunk swung back and forth as he moved and he had the sweetest, kindest eyes Bernice had ever seen.

He handed her a cup of tea and settled himself back into his seat. She sniffed the tea cautiously. Spicy, but not unpleasant.

'How did you know who we were?' she said. 'I mean, how did you know that we weren't who we *said* we were?'

He looked away, out of the window. 'Your name appeared on the *Arachnae*'s passenger manifest,' he said. 'When we cross-referenced to Imperial Landsknecht records, which we always do in order to spot potential terrorists, troublemakers and deserters, your names sprang up in glowing red letters underlined in fire. Known troublemakers.'

'You're lying.'

'Would you believe that a little bird told me?'

'No.' Bernice shook her head. 'You were tipped off, weren't you?'

Beltempest's face was the picture of innocence. 'By whom?'

'By the person who stole the TARDIS and tried to kill us.'

'That sounds like paranoia to me,' he said, leaning forward in apparent interest. 'What's the TARDIS when it's at home?'

She sighed. 'Look,' she said, 'we're getting on so well, but can I ask what's going to happen to me?'

'You'll be shot,' he said calmly, and sipped at his tisane.

'What!' Bernice exploded. 'But I thought – '

Beltempest's stare was implacable, and tinged with disdain. 'The sentence for impersonating a Landsknecht investigator is death,' he said, pressing a button on his desk. The door opened and a yellow- and red-splotched warbot strode in, weaponry bristling. 'Take her to the prep centre,' he said, and smiled. 'Don't worry, he added, 'your death will be useful to us.'

'What about an appeal?' she yelled.

'If you like,' he said, and raised a hand to his head for a minute as if he was thinking. 'I'm sorry,' he said after a moment, 'your appeal failed.'

The bot took her arm in a surprisingly gentle grip and led her towards the door. She felt her spirits sink.

'Wait,' Beltempest said calmly.

The bot stopped. Bernice turned around as far as she could in the bot's grip. Beltempest had produced a blaster from his desk drawer and was pointing it, oddly enough, not at her, but at the bot.

'Nice try, Doctor,' he said. 'But you haven't got the walk quite right.'

With a hiss of hydraulics, the top half of the robot swung open to reveal the Doctor's gnomish face.

'It's amazing what you can get in tins these days,' he said.

* * *

The flitter was already inches off the raft when Forrester jumped into the passenger seat.

'Quick, get out of here,' she said, throwing the battered mind probe unit over her shoulder and into the back.

'Already done,' Cwej said calmly. The flitter jumped into the air, pressing Forrester back in her seat.

'Head for the Overcity. Find a space in a park somewhere. We'll access the info there.'

'Any problems?' His wide toy-bear eyes never left the control panel.

'No.'

One of the simcord screens showed the raft receding into the mist. Within moments Forrester could see the whole lodge laid out beneath them, twenty rafts linked by catwalks and bridges. The Undertown encroached on the edges of the screen as they ascended.

'Sure you got the right one?'

She scowled at him.

'Of course you're sure,' he continued. 'Silly of me.'

'It was connected up to the centcomp input,' she said. 'Had to be the right one. They'd downloaded the info, but hadn't got round to flushing the buffers yet. The underlife's memories are still in there.'

'Good thing for us: it's the only evidence we have. I hope you signed it out properly.'

'Don't be stupid,' she snapped. 'This is no time for paperwork. I sneaked it out.'

The picture began to fade as the flitter entered the greasy, rolling clouds that separated the Undertown from the Overcity. The bottom levels of a block appeared in one corner.

'I feel like a kid,' he said.

'Don't worry,' she said, straight-faced, 'we'll stop and pick one up on the way.'

He laughed. 'You know what I mean. Like we're playing truant or something. Didn't you ever do that?'

'Do what?'

'Sneak out of school and go off somewhere?'

Forrester thought back to her childhood, so long ago

that it almost seemed to belong to someone else. Someone innocent. Long hours in front of a simcord screen, alone. Lessons from centcomp. No friends. No fun.

'No,' she said.

Cwej picked up on her tone of voice, and shut up. Forrester closed her eyes and let the acceleration press her back into the seat. She felt sick. She'd disobeyed orders before, but never like this. If Cwej was right – and she'd seen the evidence every step of the way – then they were really on their own. There was a cover-up going on, and the Order of Adjudicators was implicated.

She cursed under her breath. Eight hundred years of history lay behind the Adjudicators. They prided themselves on being incorruptible. They depended upon it: Adjudicators were the only means of dispensing unbiased, unarguable justice across the whole of human space. One whisper of corruption and the whole fragile edifice would come crumbling down. Planets would develop their own laws: what was legal on one would incur a death sentence on another. The economic basis of the Earth Empire would be thrown into chaos. And all because of one frigging underlife murder. It had almost happened during the Lucifer crisis and it had taken the then Adjudication Service hundreds of years, and a metamorphosis into a quasi-religious organization, to put right the damage.

The flitter lunged up from the clouds into the glittering world of the Overcity. As always, Forrester felt a flash of vertigo. The towers seemed to loom over her, crowding together at the top, threatening to fall and crush her. As always, it only lasted an instant.

Cwej skimmed close to the side of one of the towers. Mirrored glass reflected Forrester's face back at her. She felt her hands clench, and tried to relax. He was only a kid. Let him enjoy himself.

In an attempt to relax, she wondered what might be behind the mirrored surface of the glass. It could have been anything: a home, a restaurant, a brothel or a bowling alley. No way of telling. Surfaces deceived.

The top of the block was approaching fast. Cwej took

them arcing high above the rim and looped over, bringing them down softly on a stretch of grass. Forrester climbed out while he shut the systems down. The sky was a deep, glorious rose colour, dotted here and there with wisps of pure white. Sunlight glinted from an alien craft as it came in to land at Spaceport Five. Forrester couldn't tell which race it belonged to, but she felt a sliver of hatred penetrate her heart none the less.

She looked around. The park stretched on as far as she could see, broken here and there by the blue, waist-high walls that marked the edges of the towers. A small grove of aspen trees provided some convenient shade nearby. She started to walk over to them, but felt herself drawn to the nearest rim. The blue walls were merely a convenient marker: the real wall was transparent and twenty feet high. She placed her hands against its cold, slightly springy surface and looked over. The clouds rolled, far below, hiding the Undertown from the eyes of the Overcity.

'You want I should set it up?' Cwej called as he walked over, dangling the mind probe in one hand.

'Know how?' She walked over to the grove of trees, beckoning to Cwej to follow.

'Can't be that difficult,' he replied. Forrester smiled at his brashness.

She watched as he looked around for somewhere to sit. Eventually he removed his robe and laid it on the ground. His body armour was bright and unscratched, complementing rather than contrasting with his golden fur. Forrester removed her robe and threw it down next to him. As she sat, she noticed him staring at her own body armour. Compared to his it was shabby and battered. Compared to anyone's it was shabby and battered.

'Seen some action, huh?' His voice was oddly hesitant.

'I've been around,' she said neutrally.

'Looks like you've been in some dangerous situations.'

'The Undertown's a dangerous place.'

His gaze was steady, and she couldn't look away.

'Ever thought of a transfer?'

'To where? I'd be bored silly up here in the Overcity. Tried it, didn't like it.'

He smelled musky, warm, and she felt her head swim. She wanted to run her hands through his thick, silky pelt. Goddess, this was stupid! He was her squire. Her *squire*, for Goddess' sake!

Like she had been Martle's squire.

He reached out a paw and traced the path of one of the scratches across her breastplate.

'How'd you get this one?' he asked, his fingers lingering at the end of their path.

'Never mind,' she snapped. 'Get on with what we came here for.'

He pulled his hand back. She took a deep breath, hoping he hadn't noticed the shake in her voice.

'Yeah. Right.' Deftly he set up the mind probe, turned it on and angled the screen so that they could both see it. 'Here goes.' He quickly typed instructions into the probe. The screen dimmed, flickered, and went blank.

'You've broken it.'

'I have *not* broken it.'

'It never does that when I use it.'

'You never went to the lectures.'

She had no answer to that.

The screen began to strobe with scenes too brief for Forrester to identify. Faces, places, objects . . . all fuzzy and none lasting long enough for her to place them in context. 'What's going on?' she asked.

'Well, we assume she was drugged, right? So that she couldn't run away from the securitybot.'

'Yeah.'

'And that's why her memories were fuzzy when we reviewed them earlier.'

'I guess.'

'So, if we go back to the latest point where her memories are clear, that's when she was drugged.'

'Uh-huh.'

'And whoever was around at the time is our major suspect for having drugged her.'

'Seems fair. What's your sample rate?'

'I'm taking a memory every ten minutes.'

The strobing continued. Forrester was getting a headache trying to follow it. She squinted, and knelt closer to the screen.

A face, clearer than the rest.

'Stop!' she cried.

Cwej's finger hit the button. The screen froze on a close-up of a bottle gripped by a gnarled hand. The picture was crystal clear.

'Go forward,' Forrester barked, but Cwej was already feeding instructions in. More pictures, slower this time. Grimy, graffiti-laden walls of crumbling brick. Flickering firelight upon an arched roof. A group of underlife in the remains of a collapsed church, clouds rolling overhead. Two people, a man and a woman.

A fuzzy image of a securitybot.

'Got it,' Cwej murmured. 'If I increase the sample rate to a memory every ten seconds . . .'

It took five more minutes to focus down upon the last thing the old woman saw before she had been drugged.

'And there they are,' Cwej announced. 'Prime suspects one and two.'

The image was sharp. Sharper than the rest. Forrester had seen the effect before. The low-life's mind had been brought into focus by a powerful emotion. Love could do that, and hate. And fear. Especially fear.

The man in the image was small and dark-haired. He was wearing a crumpled suit and a battered hat. The woman was tall and fine-boned. Her hair was close-cropped. Her clothes were plain except for an embroidered waistcoat.

She was holding a dermal patch towards the old woman. The image was so clear that Forrester could make out the individual pores on the patch, through which the drug would be absorbed into the skin.

'So,' Forrester breathed. 'Our murderers. Run the record on in real time.'

The image jerked into life. The woman's hand disappeared out of sight. The image began to fuzz over.

'Drug's taking effect,' Cwej murmured. 'Must be a fast acting one.'

'Wait,' Forrester said, 'she's going to say something.'

On the probe screen, the woman turned to the man and mouthed something.

'Can we get audio on this thing?'

Cwej frowned. 'Audio's usually difficult. The neural pathways it's stored in are too fiddly to access from the outside. Smell's the easiest, followed by visual. Touch and sound are buggers.' He fiddled with the controls. 'However,' he said distractedly, 'the memory is so sharp that we might be in luck.'

A blare of static. He turned the volume down quickly.

'Replay,' Forrester ordered.

The picture jumped back ten seconds. The woman turned to her companion.

'She's going under, Doctor,' she said. 'Give her the spike. She can kill the slug for us.'

'Well,' the man said, 'we make a fine pair of murderers, don't we my dear?'

Chapter 6

'I'm Evan Claple and this is The Empire Today, *on the spot, on and off the Earth. Today's headlines: disaster strikes Spaceport Eighteen Overcity on Earth as an orbital laser platform malfunctions and destroys an entire accommodation block. Fifty thousand people are feared dead along with an unknown number of aliens, and damage is estimated at over one billion Imperial schillings. Earth Defence Coordinator Jim Hallis has promised a full investigation. Also, as official figures indicate that the murder rate on Earth is rising rapidly, we talk to Minister Stammatina of the Church of the Goddess. Off-world now, and latest figures from . . . '*

Wherever Bernice looked, the jungle seethed with life.

Fleshy purple leaves quivered like palsied hands at the end of branches covered in hair. Vines wound themselves tighter around the gnarled boles of trees, occasionally shifting position as if seeking the best grip to strangle them with. Flowers with vast, fleshy petals and twisted stamens seemed to distend then shrivel in a grotesque parody of respiration. Tiny animals with insane glints in their multiple eyes scurried, fought, screamed and mated their way from tree to tree and vine to vine. Through chinks in the oppressive canopy of leaves, flocks of flying reptiles with razor-edge talons wheeled through a fiery sky. The leaves were wet with condensation, which trickled down and fell to the spongy ground.

'Let me guess,' she said. 'This isn't the restaurant.'

'That depends on who's doing the eating,' Provost-Major Beltempest said pleasantly. He was standing in the centre of the clearing made by the descending flitter, his tunic open to show his huge blue paunch, a blaster rifle loosely cradled in his arms. Despite the flapping of his huge ears, he was sweating in the intense heat; dark patches had appeared at his armpits, and drops of perspiration were rolling down his trunk.

His pilot, a close-cropped young Landsknecht with metallic skin and eyes like those of a dead fish, also held a blaster. To Bernice he looked a lot more trigger-happy than his superior.

The Doctor stood beside Bernice. He was looking around with interest, fanning his face with his hat. 'Some people collect stamps,' he said brightly, 'and others collect beer-mats. You obviously collect planets.'

'Not me,' Beltempest responded, wiping the sweat from his domed forehead with the back of his hand. He seemed in no hurry to do anything. 'The Landsknechte. As you saw from the orbit, Purgatory has been terraformed into a set of different segments, each with its own ecology and climate, each separated from the others by a force wall. Some even have their own individual atmospheres. We have copies of thousands of planets here, each one presenting its own special survival problems. They're all training grounds for our Landsknechte. All apart from the administration, spaceport and the accommodation segments, of course.'

'I don't think "terraformed" is the right word,' the Doctor said quietly.

'Why not?'

'Because it means "made to look like the Earth".'

'I stand corrected. What would you prefer?'

'Distorted?' the Doctor suggested. 'Twisted? Perverted?'

'You don't appreciate what we're trying to do,' Beltempest said, gesturing carelessly to the forest with the blaster. 'This segment, for instance, is a perfect representation of

104

the jungles of Ybarraculos Epsilon. Nasty place. Wouldn't go there for a holiday, that's for sure.'

'That's all right,' the Doctor murmured, 'they wouldn't take you.'

Beltempest waved the blaster off to one side. 'Over there,' he continued, 'this segment abuts onto one representing the acid ice-cap of Throssa. You might want to avoid that one: the icefish have a particular taste for human eyes, and it's an evens bet whether their caustic flesh kills you before their teeth do.'

Bernice suppressed a shudder. 'You're enjoying this, aren't you?' she asked.

'On the other hand,' and he pointed over their shoulders, 'in that direction you will find a perfect replica of one of the ruined emerald cities of Dargol. Beautiful place. Absolutely beautiful. Don't stop moving, though, or the jewel-wraiths will melt your minds out through your ears.' He smiled. 'Or perhaps I'm lying. Who can tell? Anything could be true here. The Landsknechte set Purgatory up some years ago. We've replicated almost every environment that the Landsknechte might be called upon to fight in. We can simulate almost every type of conflict in every potential location. Very useful. Our lads leave here the best fighters in the galaxy, ready to take on any alien scum under any conditions.'

'Those that leave at all,' the Doctor murmured to Bernice.

'The strong survive,' Beltempest said, overhearing him. 'And the weak die. That's why we won the Wars of Acquisition. Superior training. Superior personnel.' He tapped his head. 'Superior intellects.'

The Doctor scratched his head. 'Now who was it who said, "We have met the enemy, and he is us"?'

'Any advice for us?' Bernice asked.

Beltempest's warm, friendly eyes suddenly weren't so warm and friendly any more. 'Run,' he said. 'Run fast. And then die.'

'This isn't fair,' she protested. 'It isn't fair and it isn't legal.'

'It's perfectly legal,' Beltempest said calmly. 'The War Act of 2825 gave the Landsknechte full powers to administer their own laws to their own personnel on their own planets and on their own space vessels, and to administer punishments as they saw fit. We're not Adjudicators. The penalty for *anything* on Landsknecht planets and vessels is death. That's how we maintain discipline.'

'But the war's over,' the Doctor said.

'Unfortunately, due to an oversight on the part of the then Imperator, the Act was never rescinded.'

'Unfortunately?'

'For you.'

'But we're not in the Landsknechte!' Bernice cried.

Beltempest smiled. 'We'll stretch a point,' he said.

The Doctor cocked his head to one side and gazed shrewdly at Beltempest. 'Whose orders are you following?' he asked.

'What?'

'Somebody has told you to get rid of us, haven't they? Somebody alerted you to the fact that we were arriving and told you to – what was that phrase they used to use back on Earth? Terminate us with extreme prejudice.'

'Interesting,' Beltempest said. 'Why should anybody want to eradicate two minor troublemakers like yourselves?' He seemed genuinely curious. 'If you can tell me that, I might be able to spare your lives.'

'If we knew that,' the Doctor murmured, 'we probably wouldn't be here in the first place.'

'In that case . . .' Beltempest looked at his watch, then stood slightly straighter and pulled his uniform into some sort of order. 'Under the powers vested in me,' he said formally, 'and in line with Landsknecht practice, you are sentenced to act as targets during a Landsknecht training session.' He relaxed. 'Start running,' he said. 'They'll be here any minute.'

'What happens if we survive?' Bernice asked. 'Do we go free?'

'No,' he replied.

'No, we don't go free?'

'No, you don't survive,' he explained. 'It's a death sentence.' He stepped into the flitter. 'I'd wish you luck,' he said, 'but you'd have no use for it. The best you can hope for is a quick shot in the back of the head.'

The flitter rose, humming, into the scarlet sky, scattering flocks of reptiles in all directions. Within seconds, it was gone. The background noises of the jungle, the hisses and clatters, the cries and the rustles, slowly filled in the silence left behind.

Spaceport Five was suspended on the tops of five huge towers. They reared above the parkland of the Overcity, casting a disc of shadow on the towers beneath that gave the Overcity dwellers a taste of what the Undertown must be like.

Cwej stood at the edge of the spaceport, watching the ships come and go. A Draconian warship was just taking off, its turquoise fins unfurling as it rose, the sun glinting from the inlaid insignia that decorated its flanks. The space that it left was only empty for a few seconds before a Thanatosian freighter lurched unsteadily in to land, venting coolant fumes from its engines. Two Antonine Assassins sat, side by side, on the edge of the field, their sharp lines and impressive armaments drawing an admiring crowd of ship-spotters. Craft of a thousand different designs and types of propulsion jostled for position in the skies above, turning the air into a rainbow haze of warped space and shifted probabilities.

'Got it!' Forrester trotted up to his side, waving a centcomp printout. 'The scheduler didn't want to give it over, so I had to threaten to fine him for being uncooperative.'

'You can't do that,' he said, wondering how she could get away with flouting the rules so flagrantly, time and time again. 'We're on leave.'

'Yeah,' she said, not in the least defensive, 'but he didn't know that.'

Cwej sighed, and ran his tongue across his sharp predator's teeth. 'So what's the story then?'

'According to centcomp, they bought tickets to Purgatory.'

He blinked in surprise. 'Purgatory? But that's – '

'The Landsknecht planet. I know.'

He gazed out across the field again. He'd always wanted to leave the Earth, but *this* . . .

'So we follow them?' he whispered.

'They're our prime suspects,' Forrester said. 'Of course we follow them. I booked two tickets on a Falardi passenger liner. They can drop us off at Goreki X. We pick up a supply shuttle from there. It's the quickest way, and its also the least likely. If Adjudicator Secular Rashid wants to recall us, she'll have to find us first, and she'll be expecting us to take the tourist shuttle.'

'She'll just ask centcomp where we are,' Cwej murmured, trying to convince himself that this was a bad idea.

'I thought of that.' Forrester was short-tempered. 'I pulled in a favour: got my sister to book the tickets. Difficult to trace.'

Cwej frowned, and ran a paw through the fur on his forehead.

'But what about the price?' he asked. 'Isn't it expensive? I'm only on a basic salary, you know?'

'Don't worry,' she said neutrally. 'It's covered.'

'But don't we . . ?'

'Look!' she snapped, 'I don't necessarily want to do this any more than you do, but we both took the Adjudicator's oath, and I still remember something about swearing to do everything in my power to uphold justice. So, like it or not, I'm getting on that Falardi ship. Coming?'

There was something about her tone of voice that caught his attention. He turned to look at her. She was looking away from the spacecraft with her arms folded across her chest. Her knuckles were white.

'What's the matter?' he asked.

'Nothing,' she snapped.

'Come on, what is it?'

She looked sideways up at him. Her lips were a thin

line, and two bright spots of colour burned in her cheeks. 'I hate aliens,' she said quietly. 'Especially the Falardi.'

He couldn't believe what he was hearing. 'But ... but they're just like you and me. I mean – '

She shook her head. 'You don't understand,' she said. 'A Falardi killed Fenn Martle, my partner. I've hated them ever since.'

Bernice's heart was pumping, and she felt faint. She didn't mind facing death; she'd done it often enough before. It was the fact that she didn't know why that hurt. It was the fact that she might die in ignorance.

'Bright ideas?' the Doctor asked.

Bernice sat down in the centre of the clearing. She could feel eyes watching her from all around. The knowledge that they were up against the armed might of an entire planet weighed her down; she felt like crawling into a ball and going to sleep. For ever, if necessary. She just didn't want to move.

'Give up?' she ventured.

'I'm over a thousand years old,' the Doctor said, looking around. 'If I'd given up, where would I be now?'

'Well,' she snapped, 'you wouldn't be standing in the middle of a killer jungle, with an expanse of acidic ice on one side and a ruined city full of mind-sucking wraiths on the other, waiting for a load of gun-toting morons to blow your head off.'

'You're being defeatist,' he chided. 'Come on.'

He held out a hand. After a few seconds, she reached out to take it.

'Never say die,' he said, pulling her to her feet.

'Even if everything inside you wants to say it?' she asked.

'Especially then,' he smiled.

She breathed deeply, then pulled the diminutive Time Lord to her and hugged him tightly. 'Doctor .. ?'

'Yes,' he said, a smile crossing his face. 'I know.'

Somewhere above them, Bernice could make out a descending whine.

'Flitter,' said the Doctor. 'That'll be the troops. There's only one chance.'

'What's that?'

'I don't know yet, but there's always one chance. Let's try and find out what it is.'

Taking her hand, he led the way into the jungle. Within moments, the fleshy foliage had closed around them. Bernice couldn't see more than a few feet in any direction. The leaves were warm to the touch, and flinched as she pushed her way past.

A sudden whine in her ear made her jerk her head away. A dartlike shape whizzed past her, so close that she could feel the breeze of its passage. The insect halted in mid-air a few feet away, eyes glittering as it studied her.

'Don't move,' the Doctor hissed.

'I wasn't intending to,' she hissed back. Not unless it comes back this way.'

'Look at that proboscis.'

'That what?'

'That – oh, never mind.'

The thing suddenly flashed towards her, too fast for her to see. She tried to duck, but knew she would be too late. Her heart seemed to stop as she waited for the impact.

Nothing came.

She opened her eyes. For a moment she thought she had gone blind, then she realized there was a dark shape blocking her vision.

The Doctor's hat.

He lowered his hand, carefully squashing the hat closed. Something within it buzzed, and the hat shook slightly.

'Fast,' he said. 'But not fast enough. Good thing this hat is made from something more than just cloth.'

'Doctor . . .' she said shakily. There was another whine nearby, and her head jerked involuntarily. Sweat prickled across her back. This place was deadly.

'We need to disguise ourselves,' he said. 'We're alien in this place. Too noticeable.' He looked around thoughtfully, brightening as his gaze fell upon a large blue flower shaped like a bucket.

110

'Is there any liquid inside that thing?'

Bernice walked carefully over to check.

'Yes. And some of those flying things. Looks like they've drowned.' She looked closer. 'And they're dissolving.'

'Thought so. Don't put your hands in the liquid.'

'I have no intention of putting my hands in the liquid. What is it?'

'Digestive fluid,' he said. 'Probably gives off a scent that the things find attractive.'

'Fine. Does this help us?'

'It does. Interesting how evolution converges on so many planets. Where you get insects, or some equivalent, there's usually some kind of plant that lures them to it somehow and kills them.'

He walked over to join her and tugged experimentally on the leaves that made up the bowl.

'Quite tough, too.'

Bernice listened, trying to block out the sound of the jungle. The flitter seemed to be circling overhead.

'They're trying to track us,' she said.

'They won't have much luck,' the Doctor murmured, still testing the strength of the plant. 'The jungle is about the same temperature as our bodies. We should be shielded.' He smiled. 'However, the military mind being what it is, they have to run through all the usual checks first. Ultra-violet, infrared, boson count, pheremonic trackers. Once they discover they don't work, they'll land and track us on foot.'

'And our one chance – do we know what it is yet?'

He smiled sunnily.

'We go on the offensive,' he said. 'Now, one of us has a little sewing to do, and the other one will have to catch some more of those flying things. Shall we toss a coin for it?'

From his elevated position, Baron Heddolli took a deep breath, and launched into another subordinate clause to a digression that he had started some twenty minutes before. Tiny camerabots with the words *The Empire*

Today on their side stalked around him on long, multi-jointed legs, desperately looking for his best side. Behind him, the shuttle that had brought the Hith ambassadors to Earth lurched from the ground, causing acrid dust to swirl around the greeting party of minor nobles and the Landsknecht Honour Guard, covering silk robes and armoured uniforms alike.

'. . . and it was Duke Marmion himself,' the baron proclaimed in his dry monotone, 'Lord Protector of the Solar System and its Environs, who, in his definitive marshalling of the sovereign degrees of honour, assigned the premier position to the *Condirotores Imperiorum*, founders of the Empire, without whose august and ever-vigilant hand . . .'

Dweller In Sorrow Abandoned And Lost ran a pseudo-limb up her eye-stalks, trying to perk them up a bit. 'How much longer is that damned human going to prattle on for?' she whispered to her aide. 'If I can't get some time alone in a mucus bath soon, I'm going to go mad, and to *Jakkat* with the diplomatic consequences!'

'He's clocked up two hours so far,' Avenging Injustice And Burning With Ire sighed, edging slightly away from his superior. 'As welcome speeches go, it's impressive. I'm not enjoying this any more than you are. Just retract your eyes and pretend you're alone.'

'Impressive my basal foot,' Dweller In Sorrow growled. 'That sun's drying my skin out like leather.'

'. . . we would be in a position diametrically opposed to the one we find ourselves in now,' Heddolli continued bathetically. 'Truly the strength of humanity is its ability to build up from the discordant elements of our nature – the passions, the interests, the opinions of the individual human, the rivalries of family, clan, tribe and caste, the influences of climate and planetary position, the accidents of peace and war accumulated for ages – to build up from those oft-times warring elements a well-compacted, prosperous and powerful empire . . .'

The two Hith stared forlornly at Baron Heddolli's plump form. In the convoluted hierarchy of ranks and positions that made up Earth's peerage he was relatively unimportant, controlling only a three-hundred-level slice of Spaceport Ten, but the Hith diplomatic mission had to be welcomed at the spaceport by him before they could see the Viscount of Spaceport Ten, and they had to see the Viscount before they could petition for a meeting with the Countess of Spaceports One to Ten, and they had to petition for a meeting with the Countess before the Marquesa of Earth would deign to receive them, and the Marquesa had to receive them before they could attend the court of the Duke of the Solar System, and they had to attend the court of the Duke before they could be granted an audience with the Divine Empress herself. And an audience with the Empress was the only way that the Hith could ever hope to regain Hithis.

Mathematics had never been Dweller In Sorrow's strong point, but she had a terrible feeling that they were trapped in an infinite regression of petty officialdom.

'. . . an empire whose benign and controlling hand extends to friend and foe alike,' the baron pressed on, regardless of the increasing restlessness of the petty nobles in the welcoming party, not to mention the two Hith dignitaries.

'To human and alien, to those who, in their turn, reach out to grasp its tender embrace and to those who spurn its overtures. And yet, were that effort to be accomplished by one effort in one generation, it would require more than . . .'

'What's that shuttle pilot doing?' Avenging Injustice murmured, extending an eye-stalk to where the spacecraft that had taken off moments ago was turning and heading back towards them.

'I don't know and I don't care!' snapped Dweller In Sorrow. 'I just want to get to a decent hotel and dive into a pool of hot mucus.'

The craft was getting nearer now, weaving erratically through the sky towards them. A number of the Landsknechte had noticed it too, and Dweller In Sorrow watched in disbelief as they reached for their weapons.

What was this: an assassination attempt? And if so, against whom?

Baron Heddolli's voice was almost drowned out by the roar of the ship's jets now. Irritated, he turned around, still talking. Dweller In Sorrow didn't know much about human body language, but even from behind she could spot the shock, outrage and fear that passed through the baron's plump frame.

Around him, the glue of tradition and custom that was holding the various minor peers and dignitaries together suddenly failed. The crowd scattered in every direction.

The shuttle was close enough that Dweller In Sorrow could see the human pilot – the woman that had brought them down from their orbiting ship. There was no expression on her face.

'Diplomacy or no diplomacy,' shouted Avenging Injustice over the roar of the engines, 'I think that we should get out of the way!' Extending a pseudo-limb, he dragged Dweller In Sorrow to one side.

He was only just in time. The shuttle ploughed into the ground some ten feet in front of the baron's podium. Tentacles of flame spread out across the spaceport, carrying with them the sweet smell of protonic fuel rods.

Dweller In Sorrow almost caused a diplomatic incident by laughing out loud, but managed to stifle her reaction before anybody saw her. After all, who would believe that the baron had still been reciting his speech when he fried?

The bot walked towards Powerless Friendless with small, precise steps. Raindrops trickled down its metal sides, pooling in its joints and waterfalling to the wooden slats of the walkway as it moved. There was something about its stance and the light that glowed in its visual sensors that made it look as if it knew something that Powerless Friendless didn't. Which, Powerless Friendless reflected, was almost certainly true.

Powerless Friendless glanced quickly round. The walkway behind him was empty. The question was, if he made

114

a slither for it, could the bot catch him? He wasn't sure. It was heavy. Probably couldn't keep up with him.

'Please don't be foolish,' the bot said. 'You may indeed be able to outpace me over a short distance, but I never tire, and I know this city like the back of my hand.'

It didn't sound like a bot. Powerless Friendless had dealt with a lot of them, over the years – most of them securitybots, admittedly – and he knew how they talked. Pedantic. Literal. Uncompromising. Not like this one.

The bot made a sudden movement towards Powerless Friendless. He flinched, but all it had done was raise its hand and look at the back of it. In some strange way, the bot's inflexible face radiated regret.

'Well,' it said, 'like the back of another hand, a long time ago.'

A metal fist lashed out, smashing into the wall and crumbling the stone to dust. Powerless Friendless's basal foot lost its grip on the wood, and he fell backwards. The bot strode forward, the walkway trembling beneath its heavy tread. A flattened hand sliced towards Powerless Friendless's face. He ducked, and the metal caught his eye-stalk, momentarily blinding him.

Blue blood was pouring into Powerless Friendless's mouth. He wiped a pseudo-limb across his face as he writhed backwards. Krohg shifted in his rucksack. Briefly he considered pulling the creature out and throwing it at the bot in an attempt to blind it or distract it, but he knew that it would only buy him a few seconds at best.

A metal foot sent him flying through the air, his torso a mass of pain. He hit the walkway, sending ripples along its length. The bot strode towards him: implacable, unstoppable. Powerless Friendless couldn't raise his head from the planks. A pseudo-limb crept up one of the cables, trying to find some purchase, some grip with which he could pull himself up, but the plastic was slippery with the rain, and his pseudo-digits just slid vainly along it.

The bot stopped beside him. A metal hand reached down.

The unyielding fingers closed around his eye-stalks.

115

Powerless Friendless could feel the pressure building up. A red haze crept across his vision. His lymph pump was beating wildly, pumping fit to break through the muscle sheath of his chest. He couldn't feel his pseudo-limbs or his basal foot. He couldn't feel anything apart from the pounding of his blood, the pressure in his head and the spikes of pain where his eye-stalks were being dragged from their roots. He could see nothing apart from the silver face that gazed impassively down at him.

With his last ounce of strength, Powerless Friendless lashed out with his basal foot, kicking not against the bot but against life itself, against every human who had ever hit him, or laughed at him, or ignored him. He felt his foot crash against something hard, something that sent shock waves rippling through his body. There was resistance for a moment, then there was nothing. The pain eased miraculously, leaving a sick residue behind. The red haze vanished.

Powerless Friendless pulled himself slowly to his foot. The bot was on the edge of the walkway, holding onto one of the thick cables that supported it with one hand while the other flailed around, searching for something to grasp. Its feet had slipped off the rain-slicked wood.

Powerless Friendless stared at it.

The bot's hand slipped a few inches down the cable.

It smiled. 'Another time,' it promised.

Something died within the bot's eyes. The hand spasmed open, and the bot dropped away, like a falling statue.

The splash when it hit the canal seemed to go on for ever.

As the purple canopy of the jungle rose up to greet them, Private Enquorian kept his eyes firmly fixed upon the kirilian scanner. A number of life-forms were registering, but two of them were larger than the rest.

'Enquorian, report,' the under-sergeant growled. The way his skull-like cybernetic face reflected the orange sky made him look as if he was aflame.

'Auras are still steady,' Enquorian said. The other nine

116

Landsknechte in the flitter were silent, but he could feel the tension as they came in to land.

'Bearing?' the under-sergeant growled. Behind him, two winged reptiles were heading for the flitter. Their heads seemed to be made almost entirely of teeth.

'Unchanged on vector five-five-niner.'

'Let me know if they move.'

The reptiles exploded into balls of flesh and flame.

'Who fired?' The under-sergeant's gravelly, part-synthesized voice hadn't changed tone.

Private Kipps, his eyes shielded by his visor, spat on the muzzle of his blaster. The spittle sizzled briefly. 'Me, sir,' he said. His voice burred with a Helvetillian accent.

'You're on report.'

'But sir,' Kipps cried. He was known for his short temper, and his stupidity.

'I didn't authorize firing.'

'But them damned reps were – '

'I know. Enquorian.'

'Sir.'

'Stun him.'

'Sir.'

Before Kipps could react, Enquorian fired from the hip, catching him high in the chest. He slumped sideways. The two men on either side slapped at their arms to minimize the splash-over pins-and-needles effect of the stun ray.

The under-sergeant leaned across and took hold of Kipps's tunic. The metal weave material bunched up in his hand. 'Lesson one about jungle warfare,' he growled. 'Jungles are full of predators.' He heaved Kipps towards the open hatch. 'If you want to keep them off your back, use some bait.'

He pushed Kipps out of the hatch. Enquorian watched the man fall. Within moments, he had vanished into the purple canopy. A series of crashes was curtailed as he hit the ground. The sounds of the jungle halted for a moment, then cautiously re-established themselves.

A flock of winged shapes in the distance began to dive towards the point where Kipps had vanished.

'That stun was sloppy, Enquorian. Should've switched to multiple shot.'

He didn't know whether to acknowledge the advice, ask why or keep silent. Eventually he settled on a non-committal 'Sir?'

'Narrower beam than single shot. Just have to snatch your finger off the trigger before you let loose a volley. For that, let's see you act as point for the landing party.'

The under-sergeant's cybernetic leg caught Enquorian beneath the chin, pitching him out of the flitter. He fell towards the canopy, tumbling through the humid air. His fingers scrabbled across his belt, looking for the repulsor switch. Leaves slapped at his face as he dropped through the canopy of vegetation. He felt a branch impact in the small of his back and snap across the body armour.

His finger brushed the repulsor stud. With a sudden jerk, he stopped falling.

After he caught his breath, he glanced around. He'd never been in the jungles of Ybarraculos Epsilon before, either for real or on Purgatory, but he'd done jungle warfare courses, and this was no different.

Kipps's body was crumpled in a heap near the bole of a nearby tree. A couple of vines were already hanging above him, vibrating slightly. Something like a flat worm with green and purple stripes slid down the bole, hissing, and the vines quickly withdrew. Enquorian watched as the worm-thing dropped the final few metres onto Kipps's head. He wondered briefly whether to fire a shot at it to warn it off, but he could just imagine the under-sergeant's reaction. No authorization to fire. Kipps would just have to resign himself to an artificial face. Or head.

The canopy crunched above him as the flitter descended. He moved out of the way, scanning the landing area for signs of trouble, descending slowly on the repulsor beams until he was hanging a few metres above the undergrowth.

As the flitter came to rest, he noticed that the worm-thing had vanished, taking Kipps's head with it. Poor guy. A number of small, multi-legged creatures with pointed heads at both ends of their bodies were already delving inside what remained.

Enquorian had never liked Kipps. Loudmouth. Deserved everything he got. Nasty way to go, but weren't they all? At least he'd been unconscious.

His feet touched the dank, mossy ground moments before the flitter came to rest.

'Trouble?' The under-sergeant was the first out.

'No, sir.'

'What about Kipps?'

'Dead, sir.'

'Still useful, though. Let that be a lesson. Which direction are the targets?'

Enquorian oriented himself. 'Assuming they haven't moved, sir – '

'They haven't.'

'Then they'll be to your right. About a hundred metres.'

'Take three of the men and come up on them from the back. You've got two minutes, then I come in from the front. And remember, I want them alive. For a while.'

'Sir.'

'All right!' The under-sergeant raised his voice. 'Disembark!'

Enquorian nodded to the three closest men. They moved to join him.

Something came arcing through a clear space in the foliage. For a moment Enquorian thought it was a creature of some kind, and tracked it with his blaster. Under-sergeant or not, he didn't want any alien creature chewing on his face. As it began to fall, he realized that it was some kind of sphere that wobbled as if filled with liquid.

The under-sergeant saw it out of the corner of his eye, and turned to face it. His blaster was only half drawn when the object burst across his chest, splattering him and the five men closest to him with a clear liquid. They brushed at it automatically, and their hands came away sticky. Enquorian took a closer look at the thing. It looked as if it had been sewn together from leaves.

'What the – ?' one of them said.

'Do you want to surrender now?' a voice yelled from the distance.

The under-sergeant's impassive metal face had the ability to reflect a range of expressions without ever moving. At the moment, he looked angry. Very angry. Enquorian didn't think much of the chances of the targets.

'Kill them,' the under-sergeant growled.

'Last chance,' the voice called from the jungle.

'Slowly,' the under-sergeant added.

Something else flew through the air towards them.

'Fire!' the under-sergeant shouted.

Enquorian's finger tightened on the trigger just as he recognized the object as another leafy bundle which had been rolled up and tied with a length of vine. The beam from his blaster painted a line of fire across the jungle. Leaves lashed backwards, screaming. The bundle exploded in flames. Cinders flew away from it. Cinders that turned in mid-air and flew straight for the under-sergeant and the four men who had been splashed with the liquid. Cinders that buzzed malevolently.

The under-sergeant screamed as the first flying creature landed on his neck. A fountain of blood sprayed into the air, turning his scream into a choked cough. The other men were screaming as well as the creatures burrowed into their flesh, lured by the sticky bait. Without thinking, Enquorian turned his blaster on them. After a moment's hesitation, so did the three Landsknechte standing beside him.

Within moments, all that was left of the under-sergeant and the four men was a charred area of ground.

'Goddess!' one of Enquorian's men breathed.

Enquorian looked round. 'There are still two targets out there,' he said, his voice shaking. 'Let's go get them.'

From their position high in the branches of a tree, Bernice and the Doctor watched as the Landsknechte fanned out and moved off through the jungle.

'We'll give them a few minutes to get going,' the Doctor said, 'and then we'll go in the opposite direction.'

'Can't we take their flitter?' Bernice asked, crushing a leaf in her hand and wiping it across her face. The Doctor had picked a number of them from a certain shrub, sniffed them and suggested that they might cover up her scent. When she had asked him why he wasn't doing the same, he had said that Time Lords didn't have a scent.

'They don't appear to have left a guard on it,' he said after a moment. 'But they *are* professionals.'

'They didn't look very professional to me.'

He tutted. 'They weren't expecting us to fight back,' he said. 'They anticipated frightened rabbits of targets who would keep running until shot. And they didn't expect us to make use of the local flora and fauna, either.'

He craned his neck to try and get a better view of the flitter. 'No,' he said finally, 'either it's booby-trapped, or it's disabled in some way. I think my plan is better.'

'All I know about your plan,' Bernice snapped, 'is that it involves us moving off in another direction. Is that all there is, or do you want to elucidate?'

'Well, it occurs to me that we're stuck on a military-controlled planet, thousands of kilometres from the nearest spaceport, with no friends and no knowledge of where the TARDIS is.'

Bernice closed her eyes and rested her head against the trunk of the tree.

'So,' he continued, regardless, 'our first priority is to get off-planet without help.'

'You make it sound so easy,' she sighed.

'So we need to confuse things enough around here that they forget about us long enough for us to steal transport of some sort.'

'Of course. How?'

'We sabotage the barrier between this segment and the next. They're bound to send out a repair team. With luck, we can hijack whatever vehicle they have.'

She opened her eyes and gazed at him in wonderment. 'Never say die?'

He grinned. 'Never say die.'

She led the way down the nearest vine towards the

ground. There was a heart-stopping moment halfway down when a moss-covered creature with a mouthful of needle-like teeth slid from a hole in the tree-trunk as she was passing by, but it ignored her and moved off up the tree.

'Can I breathe now?' she whispered.

'I told you the leaves would work,' he hissed back.

She shook her head. He was always so irritatingly sure of himself. 'You remember that restaurant on Feliss Haven?' she hissed.

'Yes. What about it.'

'You told me that the spiny hairballs in sour blood sauce were perfectly edible. I spent three days trying to bring up everything that I had ever eaten.'

There was silence for a few moments.

'I think the sauce may have been slightly undercooked,' he admitted finally.

It took ten minutes to get down to the ground. Bernice stood there for a moment, regaining her equilibrium. A dartlike predator flickered past her ear.

'How did you know about the leaves?' she said as the Doctor dropped lightly to the ground beside her.

'Experience,' he said. 'I've spent several lifetimes escaping through forests. I've learned all the tricks.'

'All of them?'

'Well, most of them.' He walked off. 'Some of them, at least,' he added.

Bernice shrugged, looked around, and followed.

His voice came floating back over his shoulder.

'All right then, one or two.'

It took them half an hour of mind-numbing, bone-wearying slog to get to the next segment of Purgatory. By the time they pushed their way past the last fleshy purple leaf and found themselves in a defoliated zone some hundred metres wide, Bernice was soaked in condensation, perspiration and the foul-smelling sap of various types of leaf. So tired was she that the sight before her failed to register for at least a minute. When it did, she suddenly forgot everything.

122

The defoliated zone ended in a straight line which continued in either direction for as far as she could see. Past the line, the translucent blue ground shone with reflected light. Deep within it, Bernice could just make out a webwork of curling white lines. Mountains rose in the distance: jagged monstrosities that loomed over the barren landscape like a whole collection of Gothic castles. The sky was a greenish-black in colour, and the stars showed up as tiny haloed points of light.

'The acid ice-cap of Throssa?' she asked, awed.

The Doctor nodded. 'Well,' he said, 'it's not the ruined emerald cities of Dargol, that's for sure.'

'How do you know?'

'Who do you think ruined them?'

She looked sideways at him, only to find that he was smiling. 'You *didn't*?'

'No, I didn't,' he said.

'Good.'

'But I know the man who did.'

'Sometimes I don't know whether you're serious or not,' she confided.

'Sometimes,' he admitted, 'neither do I.'

A flurry of activity within the ice attracted their attention.

'The acid fish?'

He nodded. 'The acid fish.'

A shoal of thin, flexible creatures was moving rapidly through the hard ground: wheeling, rising and diving almost as one. They left white lines behind them, like the contour trails of jets. Bernice realized with a slight shock that the lines were the tunnels left in the ice after the creatures had passed.

'And you want us to go in there?' she said.

'No.' The Doctor picked up a branch and threw it towards the line where the ice started. The branch never made it: rebounding instead from an invisible barrier and landing a few feet away from the Doctor.

'Force wall,' he said. 'If we can find a way of deactivating it, we'll attract quite a bit of fuss.'

'You've created quite enough fuss already,' a voice growled behind them. Bernice turned, already knowing what she would find.

The four remaining Landsknechte stood behind them, guns raised. They didn't look pleased.

Chapter 7

'I'm Evan Claple and this is The Empire Today, *on the spot, on and off the Earth. Today's headlines: controversy as the Rim World Alliance applies to leave the Empire. In a statement last night, Viscount Henson Farlander, aide-in-chief to the Empress, said that* nobody *leaves the Empire. An Imperial Landsknecht flotilla is already reported to be heading for the Rim. Also in the news today: the Tyled ambassador is murdered during an official reception at the Imperial Palace in orbit around Saturn, and fresh outbreaks of fighting on Allis Five, Heaven, Murtaugh and Riggs Alpha. Details after the break . . .'*

'So,' Cwej said with an unconvincing display of casualness, 'what's all this about hating the Falardi, then?'

They were standing at the end of the Goreki shuttle ramp, surrounded by Imperial Landsknechte whose weapons were, if not exactly trained on them, not exactly pointed harmlessly at the ground either. The shuttle itself sat forlornly upon Purgatory's plasticrete landing surface, dwarfed by the Landsknechte ships around it. Its captain glared balefully at them from the cockpit. Being a Gorekian, and having that race's characteristic three glowing eyes, he could glare balefully better than almost anybody Forrester had ever met. He also had good reason. His ship was primarily a supply vessel on a short milk run. He hadn't banked on having two extra passengers, and certainly hadn't banked on being held up pending a refusal of entry.

As soon as they had landed the Adjudicators had asked to see the local security officer. The shuttle's captain had been denied clearance to take off until Forrester and Cwej had been dealt with, and they had been refused permission to leave the shuttle. They had pushed things as far as they could by standing on the edge of the disembarkation ramp, staring at the troops surrounding them. The sun glared down as balefully as the captain, so they had removed their robes and stood there, the light shining from their armour and into the Landsknechte's eyes.

'Don't know what you mean,' Forrester retorted. They were close enough to the edge of the spaceport segment that she could see the straight line separating it from the dusty red desert of whatever environment was next door. Judging by the swirling atmosphere, it was fit only for bromine breathers. Offhand, she couldn't actually think of any races that breathed bromine, but she was sure that there must be some. Why train Landsknechte in a bromine environment otherwise?

A wry smile crossed her face. The Landsknechte didn't need reasons for anything. If it was uncomfortable and unnecessary, that was reason enough.

Cwej had been speaking while she mused.

'Sorry?' she said.

'I was just pointing out that you refused to talk to any of the Falardi on the ship. You let me do all the communicating.'

'You're so much better at it than me.'

He smiled in surprise. 'Am I? Thanks!'

Rookies were so easy to please.

A formation of fighters roared high above their heads. Cwej turned to watch them pass, admiration shining in his eyes. With his golden fur, clear blue eyes and noble stance, he reminded Forrester of some of the Landsknechte recruiting posters from the war, although the moist black nose and erect, triangular ears spoiled the comparison somewhat. He'd have been too young to fight, of course, but she was sure that he wished he had. Unfulfilled dreams of glory: always a bad thing for a young man to have.

The fighters only reminded Forrester of the terror and the tedium of the occasional off-world raids on Earth during the Wars of Acquisition. She was still slightly claustrophobic as a result of too many nights in the deep shelters, and sometimes she woke up soaked in sweat, remembering the terror, and the people who had died.

The deep shelters. Her first taste of the real world that her family's riches had managed to shield her from for all those years. Their money was old money, based on patents and stocks in the various corporations that had existed for centuries. Proud of their pure-bred African Xhosa heritage, they had refused to mix with 'inferior' humans – those whose genetic make-up was a melange of all the races of Earth. They had held themselves aloof, like gods. Until the Wars came to Earth. Until they were forced to take refuge in the deep shelters. It was there that Forrester had made friends with other children, and learned by contrast with them how barren her own life had been. Later, as she grew further apart from the lifestyle that her parents had chosen for her, Forrester had considered signing up for the Imperial Landsknechte. Either that or the Order of Adjudicators. Anything to get away from home. She had read the brochures, visited the Landsknecht information centre on Earth, even attended a week-long induction course on Purgatory itself. In the end, she had been put off by the calibre of the people she had met. Brainless morons in love with their weapons, the lot of them. The Adjudicators were a much more impressive bunch: intelligent people who cared about justice as an abstract concept. That she liked. After two years training on Ponten IV, and another five acting as squire to a roving off-world Adjudicator, she had been recalled to Earth and paired with Martle. And that's where it had all started to go wrong.

'Nice here, isn't it?' she muttered, just for something to say.

A hovercar sped towards them, kicking up a plume of dust. It stopped close to the bottom of the ramp, and a man got out: a major, judging by the discreet insignia on his battle armour. He was big in all directions, and he had been beppled to resemble a four-armed blue elephant standing on its hind legs. As he approached, Forrester tried to work out what place he held in the Landsknechte. He didn't harbour the usual uncaring, seen-it-all attitude that she had seen in Landsknechte personnel before. Instead, his expression was calm, benign and lazy. How had somebody so obviously an individual made it to the rank of colonel?

As he came to a stop before them, she re-evaluated him. Those eyes weren't calm, benign and lazy. They were shrewd. Dangerous, even.

'I am Provost-Major Beltempest,' he said, 'local security officer. Welcome to Purgatory.'

'Adjudicators Forrester and Cwej,' she said. 'And we haven't actually arrived yet.'

He smiled, and gestured them off the ramp.

'Forgive me. My underlings can sometimes be slightly too literal in their interpretation of regulations. Now, all I was told was that you are here on official business. What can we do for you?'

Forrester took a sheet of plastic from her pocket and handed it to him. He glanced at the two faces upon it. It was impossible to tell from his expression whether he recognized them or not.

'We are in pursuit of two suspects in connection with a murder on Earth,' she said, and paused, hoping that he would say something. He just handed the plastic sheet back. 'We have traced them to a craft which left Earth, bound for Purgatory,' she continued.

He didn't react. She tried again. 'There is no evidence that they left this planet.'

Still nothing. His eyes twinkled merrily, his mouth went through all the motions of smiling, but it was all faked for her benefit.

She waited. Eventually, he spoke. 'You realize,' he said, 'that the Order of Adjudicators has no jurisdiction over Landsknecht territory or property. We make and enforce our own laws.'

'We are here,' she said carefully, 'in a spirit of cooperation and mutual regard.'

'Ah,' he said. 'Of course. Two very important-sounding and completely meaningless phrases.'

'Protocol . . .' Forrester said, smiling slightly.

He smiled back. 'Might I ask what you intend doing with these suspects, should they have actually arrived?' he asked.

Forrester's heart quickened slightly at the implication that they had indeed landed on the planet. Beltempest caught her slight change of expression, and nodded slightly. There was a subtext to this conversation that would need careful monitoring.

'They will be returned to Earth for mind probing,' she said. 'If, as a result of the information retrieved, centcomp finds them guilty, they will be sentenced accordingly.'

He nodded. 'But if they have already been sentenced in accordance with Imperial Landsknechte law, then they have already been punished. Does that not satisfy your need for justice?'

'That,' Forrester said cautiously, 'would depend upon the punishment.'

He smiled. 'Rest assured,' he said, 'that it would be . . . apt.'

Cwej frowned. He was completely missing the words beneath the words. 'Look,' he said impatiently, 'are they here or not?'

Beltempest's face took on a slightly pained expression. 'If they were here,' he said, 'then I would quite happily hand them over to you so long as the Imperial Landsknechte did not have a prior claim. If I don't hand them over, it is either because they aren't here, or because we do have a prior claim.'

Cwej frowned. 'Was that a yes or a no?' he said, baffled.

Time to put on a bit of pressure.

'You mentioned jurisdiction,' Forrester said.

'Yes?'

'According to interstellar fastline records, a call was placed to you from Earth while the *Arachnae* was still in flight, following which you placed a fastline call to Spaceport Five on Earth.'

She had his attention.

'Now,' she continued relentlessly, 'the way I reconstruct the situation is: somebody here was alerted by some unknown person on Earth that these two were on their way here, and the somebody here checked back with the spaceport on Earth that they did indeed leave on the ship. As soon as the ship landed, they were arrested. Does that seem reasonable?'

'No crime there, surely?' he asked.

'Well, it all depends,' she said. 'Protocol would suggest that if you were aware of two criminals on board an Earth-registered tourist ship you should have notified the Adjudication service, rather than wait until they landed on Purgatory and arrest them yourself. It could be argued that your refusal to contact us makes you party to the crime they are suspected of committing.'

Beltempest thought for a moment. 'And if we were just about to fastline you that we had your suspects in detention, but hadn't actually got round to it?'

'Then we would be grateful.'

He nodded. 'Then we have them.'

'And we're grateful. Are they still alive?'

He checked his watch.

'I wouldn't put money on it,' he said.

Private Fazakerli watched the woman's face with feral, almost sexual pleasure. She was scared. Terrified. She wasn't showing it obviously, but he could see it in her eyes. She knew she was going to die, and he loved it.

The heat of the jungle was getting to Fazakerli. His head had started to ache, and there was something funny going on with his eyes. Everything he looked at was blurred and distorted. The fleshy leaves on the trees seemed to beckon him onwards suggestively, and the cold, blue glow of the acidic ice beyond the force wall was a purifying, purging energy, stripping him of concerns and worries.

Ever since the under-sergeant died he had been paralysed with fear, but now he was fine. Now he felt like a deity.

His finger tightened on the trigger as he waited for Enquorian to give the order to fire. Goddess, was the guy going to wait for ever? Fazakerli wanted to kill something. Anything!

'Wait,' the little man in the white suit said, stepping forward and waving his hands wildly in the air.

'Last requests?' Enquorian sneered. Fazakerli realized with disgust that Enquorian was scared. He didn't want to give the order. He wanted an excuse not to kill them.

The metal of the trigger was warm and silky against Fazakerli's skin. He could feel the sweat trickling down his spine. Goddess, he was so turned on he thought he was going to explode.

The little man's hands flapped as he tried to think up some pathetic excuse, and Fazakerli knew with certainty that Enquorian was going to buy it, whatever it was. He felt his pulse thudding in his temples and neck. He wanted to kill. He *had* to kill.

'You can't kill us because – because . . .'

'Because we've been testing you, and the test's over now,' the woman said, stepping forward. Fazakerli remembered her from the *Arachnae*; he'd been returning from leave and looking for some final action, and she'd turned him down in the bar. It hadn't bothered him that much at the time, but now . . . He kept the sights of his blaster firmly fixed upon her loins. He was going to cut her in two whatever happened.

'Test?' Enquorian queried uncertainly.

'Of course.' Her confidence fazed Enquorian, and even the little man with her looked askance, but Fazakerli could hear the shake in her voice. She was terrified. He looked sideways at his comrades. Couldn't they hear it too? Didn't they want to see her hot blood steaming in the sunshine as much as he did?

No, they were just as uncertain as Enquorian. With the under-sergeant dead, they hadn't got a clue what to do.

131

Weaklings! Why couldn't they just surrender themselves to madness?

'You don't think we could have wiped out four of you so quickly if we were just simple targets, do you?' the woman continued.

'That's right,' the man agreed, 'we're a special, ah . . .'

'Special task force,' she said.

'Yes, a special task force sent to test your reflexes.' The man pulled himself up to his full height. 'And we're not impressed, are we Provost-Major Summerfield?'

'Indeed we aren't, Provost-Major, er, Provost-Major. Not very impressed at all.'

Whatever was happening to Fazakerli was getting worse. His pulse was hammering in his ears so furiously that he had to strain to make out what was being said, and his finger kept flexing against the trigger, taking up the slack and releasing it slowly, coming within a millimetre of releasing the pent-up energy of the weapon.

'P-P-Provost-Major . . ?' Enquorian stammered. 'I . . . we . . . didn't realize . . .'

'No harm done,' the man said genially. 'Well, not to us at any rate. Least said, soonest mended. Just take us back to the spaceport and put us on the first spaceship out of here and we'll say no more about it, there's good chaps.'

Fazakerli looked around. The other guys – Enquorian, Smitts, Fellian – they were all buying it! He saw them through a red haze: blurred figures, moving in slow motion, relaxing and lowering their weapons. He wanted to scream. He wanted to rip their complacent heads from the necks and drink the spurting blood.

With a sense of vast relief, he gave in to the death-thirst.

Fazakerli raised his blaster and fired at the first target he saw. Enquorian's head exploded with a satisfying splat, spraying bone, brain and blood over everyone. The woman dived for cover as he turned the weapon on her, and all he managed to do was splash the energy harmlessly across the force wall. Grunting in frustration, he tried to burn the little man, but he seemed to have vanished into the jungle.

A blaster beam seared across his shoulder. He whirled, catching Smitts across the legs. Smitts screamed shrilly and dropped his gun, the stumps of his legs spraying blood into the air. Fazakerli laughed. Brilliant! He couldn't ever remember enjoying himself so much!

A movement to one side attracted his attention. He tracked it with his weapon. It was Fellian, trying to crawl away. Fazakerli burned through his spine, and watched him thrash around in agony on the blood-splattered ground.

Oh yes! Oh *yes*!

The thudding in his head was the beat of some primal drum, calling for sacrifice. He wanted to dance, to laugh, to scream, to fall to his knees and praise some indefinable god of pain and degradation, but most of all he wanted to bathe in the sticky rich warmth of blood.

He had never felt so alive before.

A sound behind him. He turned. The woman was crouched beside the small man, who was trying to stem the flow of blood from what was left of Smitts's legs.

'Why?' she cried. '*Why?*'

'Why not?' he giggled, and raised the blaster until she was staring down the muzzle. He didn't know whether to kill her straight away or rape her with the weapon and then kill her. Which one would be the most fun?

'There's something wrong with you,' she said. 'Look inside! Is this really what you want?'

He looked inside, and found nothing but a dark, capering figure with his face screaming, 'Kill, kill' at him.

'Yes,' he whispered. 'It's exactly what I want.'

And pulled the trigger.

Powerless Friendless stood in the shadows, opposite the building he lived in, and wondered. Did he dare go in? Something was looking for him. Something dangerous. The place was almost certainly being watched. Chances were, if he went in, the bot would be waiting for him. If it had survived the fall into the canal.

He went through the conversation with the bot again. It knew he was Powerless Friendless And Scattered Through Space, that much was certain, and it had killed Waiting For Justice by mistake, thinking Waiting For Justice was him.

He shook his head. If he shook it hard enough, he could almost hear things rattling around inside. Sometimes he couldn't remember who he was or how he'd ended up living in the Undertown. Other times he remembered with frightening detail, despite . . . despite . . .

A glowing light, and a complex mechanism unfolding from a doctor's eye socket. A wrenching pain. A voice. 'You won't feel a thing.'

Sometimes, remembering hurt.

He took a last look up at the window, and turned away. Doc Dantalion could help him. Doc Dantalion had done this to him in the first place.

Sometimes, you just had to let it hurt, and remember anyway.

Bernice closed her eyes, waiting for death.

Even through her eyelids, she could see the flash of light. She counted heartbeats. Two, three, four. She was still alive!

A feeling of relief washed over her and receded, leaving her weak and shaking. She took a deep breath, eyes still closed, and caught the tang of burning on the air. For a moment she was back on Oolis, sharp stones gouging into the flesh of her knees, watching sparks fly up from Homeless Forsaken's singed flesh. Just for a moment, but her heart cried out.

She opened her eyes, half expecting to see a purple sky and orange dust, but she was still standing on the fringes of the fleshy pink jungle of Ybarraculos Epsilon. The Landsknecht was standing in front of her, still holding the blaster with which he had killed his comrades. Smoke was

134

issuing from a small hole in the centre of his battle armour, just beneath the name tag that read FAZAKERLI.

He fell untidily to the blood-soaked ground, still grinning.

Behind him, three people were leaving the shelter of the jungle. Provost-Major Beltempest was one of them. The others – a dark-skinned woman with a lined face, and a tall teddy bear – were dressed in the blue-gold armour of Adjudicators. The teddy bear was holding a gun.

'Well,' the Doctor murmured, 'that was a close-run thing.'

'Can we leave a larger margin next time?' she asked, still not quite believing that the short explosion of violence was over.

'If the choice was up to me,' he replied, 'I would happily accede to your wishes. However . . .'

Seeing Beltempest approaching, stepping over the bodies of the Landsknechte without even a glance downwards, Bernice was suddenly filled with a rush of fury.

'Oi, four arms!' she yelled. 'Something go wrong, did it? Or were your troops supposed to shoot one another and leave the targets intact?'

Beltempest stomped over and stopped by her side. 'This wasn't supposed to happen,' he said. 'My apologies.'

'Your apologies aren't enough. What the hell happened?'

His trunk swung from side to side with barely suppressed anger. 'These are trained men,' he seethed. 'They don't fire without orders. They don't fly off the handle. They don't go off the deep end. They don't – '

'Enough with the metaphors. What *happened*?'

'I don't know!' he trumpeted.

'Would you have been so worried if he'd killed us and left them alive?'

He had no answer to that.

The female Adjudicator walked over and glanced impassively at her. Her furry companion was eyeing the bodies. He was looking a little green around the gills.

'Bernice Summerfield?'

'Who's asking?'

'The Order of Adjudicators.'

'Oh. Well, in that case, very probably. Unless I'm not. Which happens. Sometimes.'

'Whatever. You're under arrest in any case.'

Bernice groaned, and threw her arms up. 'What is this? I've been accused, tried and sentenced for this already. Look around you. The execution was just taking place!'

The Adjudicator shrugged. 'Nothing to do with us,' she said.

'Then what's the charge?'

'Murder.'

'Murder?'

'I am obliged to inform you that your words, gestures and postures are being recorded and may form part of any legal action taken against you. Under the terms of the data protection act 2820, as amended 2945, I am also obliged to inform you that you and any appointed legal representative will be able to purchase a copy of all recordings upon payment of the standard fee. I'm obliged to tell you that, but I won't bother. Just don't piss us around.'

She beckoned her companion over. He looked pleased to be dragged away from the bodies.

'Cwej,' she said, 'take them back to the shuttle.'

'Hang on!' Bernice cried. 'Just hang on a doggone minute! Who's dead? Who the hell are we supposed to have killed?'

'You'll see the charge sheet when we get you back to Earth. Cwej! Get the guy.'

'Er, boss.'

There was something in his tone of voice that attracted Bernice's attention. She turned to follow Cwej's gaze, and felt her jaw drop open at the sight that met her eyes.

The Doctor was bending over Fazakerli's body. He had opened the Landsknecht's skull with a small buzzing device and was quite calmly probing about in the man's brain. Bernice couldn't believe it. He looked as if he were searching for something, like a little kid running his hands through the Christmas pudding mix looking for the shilling. He was whistling.

Provost-Major Beltempest was crouched beside him, his trunk dangling almost to the ground. He seemed fascinated by what the Doctor was doing.

Cwej very quietly turned around and threw up against the force wall.

'Doctor . . .'

Without turning his head, he said, 'Yes, Bernice?'

'Er, Doctor, we were wondering what you were up to.'

'Looking for evidence.' He grunted with effort, and very carefully eased the two lobes of Fazakerli's brain apart.

Cwej, who had straightened up, bent over convulsively again. Steaming liquid splattered against the barrier.

'I've seen evidence hidden in a lot of places,' the female Adjudicator said almost conversationally to Bernice, 'but that's a new one on me.'

'What's your name, by the way?'

'Forrester.'

'Ah!' the Doctor exclaimed. 'Look!'

Beltempest bent closer, and gasped. Bernice and Forrester stepped forward. Cwej turned away.

Bernice craned her neck to get a better look at what the Doctor was doing, even though her stomach rebelled at the sight. The tissue of Fazakerli's brain had been prised apart by the Doctor's nimble fingers, exposing the lobes, the stringy bundle of the corpus callosum and a mess of membranes and blood.

And a vein of fire that ran through the tissue and faded as Bernice watched.

'What was that?' Beltempest asked.

'Something I've seen before. Incontrovertible evidence that this man's mind has been affected by outside influences,' the Doctor said darkly. He stood, and was just about to wipe his hands on his jacket when he realized how much blood and brain matter was on them. He held them out to Bernice.

'Tissue?' he asked hopefully.

'Bless you,' she said. 'What made you think that it had?'

'His actions.' The Doctor gazed around, and ended up wiping his hands on the force wall, leaving a reddish-grey smear that the teddy bear Adjudicator couldn't seem to take his eyes off. 'As the provost-major here said, these men are trained.'

'Trained killers!'

'Yes, but this man completely forgot all of his training. Were you watching his face? It came over him like a wave. Sheer bloodlust.'

'There's a lot of it around,' the female Adjudicator said. What was her name? Forrester?

'What do you mean?' the Doctor asked.

'Bloodlust. People suddenly going off the deep end and slicing up their nearest and dearest with the first sharp object that comes to hand. Or taking potshots at passers by. Or crashing flitters into packed restaurants.'

The Doctor's eyes took on that dreamy, misty quality that Bernice had seen so often before. It meant that he was thinking about sticking his Gallifreyan oar in.

'Just on Earth?' he said, shooting Forrester a penetrating glance.

'As far as we know,' she confirmed.

The Doctor gazed meaningfully at Bernice. 'And so it begins,' he murmured, then glanced over at Provost-Major Beltempest. 'Had this man been on Earth recently?' he asked.

Beltempest shrugged. 'Not sure,' he said. 'I could check when we get back to the admin sector.'

Bernice interrupted. 'He was on the *Arachnae* with us. I recognized him.'

'Must have just come back from leave, then,' Beltempest said thoughtfully.

'Hmm,' the Doctor mused. Everybody looked expectantly at him. He glanced up, surprised and slightly embarrassed by the attention.

'What is it?' Beltempest said. 'What exactly did we see in that man's brain?'

'Well, as far as I can make out, it was some kind of resonance effect, as if he had been subject to an extremely

138

strong – ' The Doctor paused, as if he was only just realizing what he was saying. ' – an extremely strong icaron field. Hmm.'

'Icaron field?' Forrester asked.

'Elementary particles of the tachyon family. Imaginary mass, imaginary charge . . .'

'But the effects are all too real,' Bernice said quietly.

'Indeed,' the Doctor said. 'Icarons have been known to cause paranoia and psychotic behaviour in humans under certain rare circumstances, and only to genetically susceptible individuals – those who have gone through body-bepple, I would suggest. That's why they were called icarons, I believe – because of Icarus, the legendary character whose death was a result of badly applied science. If only I knew more . . .'

'Icarons drive people mad?' Beltempest snapped, eyes wide in surprise. 'I've never seen any reports to that effect. How do you know? How can you be so sure?'

'Experience,' the Doctor said succinctly. 'Interesting that you know what icarons are.'

'Ah. I've . . . come across them,' Beltempest spluttered through his trunk.

'You suspect that there's an – what did you call them? – an icaron field affecting people on Earth?' Forrester said, frowning.

The Doctor grimaced. 'Based on other information which has reached our ears, I think it's a distinct possibility. I'd need to talk to an expert first.'

Forrester shook her head. 'Shame you're not going to get the chance.'

'But this is – '

'Don't care. You're a suspect in a murder investigation. You're both coming back to Earth with us.'

'Wait!' Beltempest's authoritative bark made the two Adjudicators freeze in their tracks. 'The Imperial Landsknechte need to know why these men died.'

'The Order of Adjudicators needs to question these two in connection with a murder,' Forrester snapped. 'That takes priority.'

'It's a matter of interstellar security – '

'Under Order regulations – '

'Wait!' The Doctor's voice cut through the babble. When everybody was staring at him, open-mouthed, he continued. 'The most important thing is to prevent any more deaths. That takes precedence over everything.'

Beltempest nodded slowly, followed by Forrester.

'So, if you have to question us over this murder on Earth, do so. But do it quickly. It's important that I get to work on whatever is causing this – this mutation in the human brain.'

'What's your suggestion?' Forrester said quietly.

'Question us here. Then, when you've cleared us, let us stay.'

Bernice shot him a baleful glance. Purgatory was the last place in the universe she wanted to be at the moment.

'No can do,' Forrester said. 'We need access to centcomp files.'

'Then take one of them back to Earth,' Beltempest suggested. 'The woman, for preference. Leave the man here to work with us. Just make sure you return the woman, if she's found innocent. We still have a use for her.' At Bernice's frown, he shrugged. 'Justice must take its course,' he added. 'Your sentence has merely been suspended, not abandoned.'

Forrester considered for a few moments, then consulted quietly with her teddy bear partner. 'Agreed,' she said finally. 'The woman comes with us. The man stays. I suggest that neither you nor we do anything . . . precipitous without consulting the other.'

'Agreed,' said Beltempest.

The Doctor sighed, and gazed sadly over at Bernice.

'Don't forget to write,' he said.

Chapter 8

'I'm Evan Claple and this is The Empire Today, *on the spot, on and off the Earth. Today's headlines: the riots that began yesterday in the Asian Undertown continue. Three battalions of Adjudicators have already been sent in to calm the situation, and the Imperial Landsknechte are reported to be standing by. Eyewitnesses claim that the riots began after an underdweller was ejected from an Overcity shop and proceeded to open fire upon shoppers. Also, as investigations continue into the tragic orbital laser cannon blast that killed sixty thousand people in the Spaceport Eighteen Overcity,* The Empire Today *has learned that the incident may not have been an accident. Details after the break . . . '*

'This is ridiculous!' the Doctor snapped, stamping his foot on the floor of Beltempest's office. The carpet of Cerumenian whispering moss absorbed the noise and transformed it into a ripple of turquoise light that raced across the room and rebounded from the walls, forming an intricate interference pattern.

Beltempest, lounging in the recliner behind his desk, tried to keep a straight face, but the slight twitch of his large ears betrayed him.

'Necessary, I'm afraid,' he said, trying to make his voice sound regretful. 'If any Imperial Landsknechte see you wandering around in your . . . habitual attire, then they'll shoot first – '

' – and ask questions afterwards,' the Doctor growled.

141

'No.' Beltempest shook his head. 'We don't encourage questions in the Landsknechte. They'll just shoot first. Security takes priority over everything.'

The Doctor looked down at the shiny black uniform that Beltempest had forced him, almost at gunpoint, to climb into. His own clothes sat in a forlorn pile beside him.

'I'm going to need a tin-opener to get out of this.'

Beltempest levered himself out from behind his desk and circled the Doctor, tugging on fastenings and checking embedded circuitry.

'Well, I've seen better, but you'll do,' he said finally.

'But my face doesn't even fit!' the Doctor wailed. 'Your Landsknechte look like somebody has lacquered their flesh. I've still got skin like a baby, and I want to keep it that way!'

'You'll get some second glances,' Beltempest said firmly, 'but the uniform should keep you alive, and there's a built-in transponder that will allow you into the labs and nowhere else.'

The Doctor's crumpled face glowered up at him. 'What about the rest rooms?' he said.

'This isn't a holiday camp,' Beltempest snapped.

The Doctor reached down and picked up his hat. 'A question,' he said, cramming the battered fedora on his head.

Beltempest briefly debated knocking it off again, but the Doctor's expression made him rethink. At least the strange little man had got into the uniform. Let him have his little victory. 'Go ahead.'

'If the mere fact that I am attired in one of these obnoxious costumes renders me safe in the eyes of your guards, and enables me to enter high security areas such as your laboratories, then what's to stop some intruder from stealing one and pretending to be a Landsknecht?'

'Didn't I mention?' Beltempest smiled, picking up a small metal box from his desk. 'The uniforms are bioengineered from an arthropod that lives on one of the moons of Threllinius Omega. Brainless, and consequently very loyal. Their nervous systems are surprisingly compatible with electronic augmentation. That's a rarity in the galaxy. We grow them into uniforms, and then key them to a particular wearer.' He pointed the box at the Doctor and pressed a recessed button. The uniform shivered slightly. 'That's your suit now. If anybody else tries to wear it, they'll set off alarms all over Purgatory.' He gestured towards the door. 'And it will rip them to shreds as well. Shall we go?'

'Oh, let's,' the Doctor muttered sourly, and preceded Beltempest out into the corridor.

The laboratory block was a short flitter ride away: a large, faceted building that shone like a jewel in the light of Purgatory's sun. The administrative sector of the Imperial Landsknecht planet was probably the most attractive of all the different environments, Beltempest thought, as the flitter spiralled down towards a landing pad on the roof. The white lawn stretched as far away as the eye could see, interrupted every few kilometres by mountainous buildings, each fashioned by a different architect, each the pinnacle of a particular school of design. It was no wonder that Purgatory was one of the chief tourist spots in the Empire.

The flitter came to a gentle rest on the top of the laboratory building, and the pilot opened the doors. Beltempest led the Doctor – who was limping in his Landsknecht boots – to the nearest null-grav lift, and down to the laboratory that had been set aside for him to work.

The Landsknechte that they passed in the lift and in the corridors saluted Beltempest, and cast odd glances at the Doctor. Still, at least they weren't firing at him.

The laboratory was hemispherical, with enhanced scanner and presentation facilities in the segments of the ceiling, capable of displaying simularities of anything in the Imperial Landsknecht computers. Beltempest had guessed that the Doctor would be requiring them. Various items of equipment scavenged from other labs or pulled out of storage sat around the edges of the room. Beltempest couldn't identify half of them. Fazakerli's body lay on a trolley in the centre, in case the Doctor wished to continue his impromptu autopsy. A medbot loomed over it, looking like an explosion of insectile arms tipped with laser scalpels, repulsor field generators, scanners and plain, old-fashioned clamps. Nobody had bothered to cover the body up.

The Doctor's gaze roamed over the entire room. It seemed to Beltempest that he was taking in every detail: every panel, every rivet, every bump in the walls.

'Very well,' he said finally. 'I've seen better, but this should do. For the moment.'

'Where do you want to start?' Beltempest prompted.

'How about a cup of lapsang souchong?'

Beltempest frowned. 'I don't think the cafeteria is set up to provide this "lapsang souchong".'

'I can't do anything without a decent cup of tea.' The Doctor folded his arms and stared up into the domed ceiling until Beltempest, with a muffled curse, started rooting around amongst the items of equipment lining the walls for something that could provide refreshments.

It took ten minutes for Beltempest to locate an old refreshment bot, patch it into the main computer and search the database for a reference to the chemical composition of 'lapsang souchong'. It seemed to Beltempest to be a tisane of some sort – an infusion of leaves in hot water. Intriguing. Beltempest thought he knew all the various tisanes used in the Empire. He would have to try this one himself.

Eventually he handed the Doctor a cup of steaming liquid that smelled of tar.

'Thank you,' the Doctor said. 'Now, how does one get these screens working?'

'Tell me what you want,' Beltempest replied, 'and I'll call it up for you.'

The Doctor hesitated for a moment, sipping at his tea. 'Can this computer of yours provide me with some kind of graphic display showing the locations of the various violent incidents that have occurred over the past few years? Just those with no obvious motive where the perpetrator was easily caught.'

'I'm sure it can,' Beltempest replied, and directed a list of instructions to the ever-attentive computer. Within moments, the dome above them lit up with a map of the galaxy. The Empire sectors were displayed in red. Beltempest felt his breathing quicken at the sight of fully half the galaxy under the dominion of the Divine Empress: an Empire upon which several thousand suns never set. He was almost convinced that if he increased the magnification enough he would be able to see the edges creeping forward as inferior races were persuaded of the economic advantages that would occur when they relinquished control of their own sectors to the Empire.

The Doctor turned away. Beltempest was surprised to see a bitter expression cross his face.

'A problem?' Beltempest asked.

'So many cultures,' the Doctor murmured, 'such a diversity of philosophies and ways of living, all lost in subservience to the Empire. Such a terrible waste.'

'You disapprove of the Empire?'

'I disapprove of all empires, anywhere,' the Doctor replied. 'And all federations, confederations, hegemonies, oligarchies, autarchies and whatever other weasel-words are used to disguise the fact that a small group of people have taken it into their heads to treat others as though their opinions weren't important.'

'Touchy, aren't we?' Beltempest said.

The Doctor looked bleakly up at him. 'Doesn't it bother you,' he asked, 'that the wealth of other races is being sucked away to make Earth richer?'

Beltempest frowned, the word 'No' on his lips, but he took a moment to think about the Doctor's question. He had developed a strange sort of respect for the Doctor's intellect, and didn't want to fob him off with an unconsidered answer.

'No,' he said finally, 'I'm sorry but I don't. Look at us. While other races stayed at home honing their philosophies, their religions and their artistic skills, we've spread out, developed and taken the universe by the scruff of the neck and shaken it. Other races are weaker than us: it's a fact of life. That means we have a responsibility to help them. We replace whatever archaic governmental system they have with the enlightened rule of the Empress and we give them education, technology, and protection from invasion.'

'Another invasion, you mean. And all you ask in return is unquestioning loyalty, and the chance to skim the wealth from their economies.'

Beltempest tried to see the Doctor's point of view, but couldn't. 'We impose taxation, of course, but only to pay for the help we give them.'

'Did you ask them whether they wanted your help?'

'If someone is ill, you don't ask whether they want to be cured or not,' Beltempest snorted, 'you cure them. If someone's flitter is malfunctioning, you don't wonder whether they want to keep it broken; you fix it. On a far vaster scale, the Empire is the same. If the Divine Empress sees a planet or a sector wasting its resources, or which could be run better, then she steps in. One of the responsibilities of power is that you should help those who aren't as powerful as yourself. Sometimes, races are too short-sighted, or too primitive, to recognize that they need help. In those cases, the imposition of help is necessary.'

'How right you are,' the Doctor said. 'Now, who was saying the same thing just the last time I saw them?' He put his hand to his forehead and mused theatrically for a moment. 'Oh yes. The Daleks.' Without allowing Beltempest to respond, he turned back to the display across the dome. 'Now, overlay the locations where these inexplicably violent occurrences have taken place,' he said.

The provost-major, smarting from the unwelcome comparison with mankind's oldest enemy, snapped an order to the computer. The display zoomed in on a particular portion of the Empire. One star in the centre of the dome glowed bright blue. 'As you can see,' he said, 'they are clustered heavily on Earth, although there have been a number of them scattered throughout the solar system, and one or two on other planets.'

'Like Purgatory,' the Doctor said brightly.

'Like Purgatory,' Beltempest agreed.

The Doctor thought for a moment. 'I presume that if there was any connection between the times or the places, it would have been noticed.'

'Yes,' Beltempest agreed.

'But we know that these events are caused by people – just like poor Fazakerli.' He patted the corpse's leg. 'People who may have been affected by icaron radiation.'

'I'd still like to have proof of this connection between icaron radiation and madness,' Beltempest growled, wondering how the Doctor could refer with such apparent pity to the man who had almost killed him and his companion.

'And I'd still like to know how you come to recognize the name of a very rare sub-subatomic particle,' the Doctor murmured. 'Can you arrange this so that the display shows us where the people who caused the events were at the time?'

'But the display will be almost exactly the same!' Beltempest protested, 'at this level of resolution, anyway.'

'Humour me,' said the Doctor.

Another command. The display flickered slightly, and one or two of the dots seemed to move sideways by a fraction, but otherwise it remained unchanged. 'As I said, if this is the sort of help you are supposed to be providing us with, Doctor, then – '

'And what I want now,' the Doctor interrupted, 'is to see the time-histories of all those people for . . . well, let's say the week before the events took place.'

'You what?'

The Doctor turned and raised an eyebrow. 'Don't tell me that your much-vaunted Landsknecht computer can't work out where these people have been? Surely you can tap into security files, or ships' records, or something?'

'If you think it will help,' Beltempest said with heavy-handed sarcasm. He snapped another set of orders. The blue dots were replaced with a set of wormlike lines. All of the lines converged on the Earth.

'Zoom in on the Earth,' the Doctor instructed.

Beltempest complied. The image on the dome blurred, shifted giddily, and became a globe of the Earth, cloud-covered and rotating as if seen from orbit. The globe was covered with blue lines, some coming from outside the screen, others starting from various points on the Earth's surface, but all of them passing at some stage through a particular area.

'That's where the answer lies,' the Doctor said. 'That's the source of all your problems. Zoom in again.'

They dropped through the atmosphere on a curving course, simulated clouds flashing past, until they were descending towards a cityscape.

'And where is this?' the Doctor asked.

Beltempest was about to give an instruction when the computer, as if tired of waiting for him to continually pass on instructions, flashed up a caption.

SPACEPORT FIVE OVERCITY.

It was early morning in Spaceport Five Overcity, but Bernice had lost all track of time. Ahead of her, the eerily empty moving walkway passed through a hole in the centre of a massive building. Other towers loomed all around like massive tree-trunks. She watched, while trying to overhear Forrester and Cwej's conversation behind her, as the three of them moved slowly towards the hole.

'Don't be so stupid,' Forrester was saying. 'We can't take her back to the lodge! Not after – you know.'

'So what's your suggestion?' Cwej asked. Bernice could hear the nervousness in his voice.

'I dunno,' Forrester sighed resignedly after a moment's thought. 'If you've got any bright ideas, don't keep them to yourself.'

There was silence for a moment, and Bernice watched the building slide over them. She didn't want to be back on Earth. She wanted to be with the Doctor, and she wanted both the Doctor and herself to be in the TARDIS, and she wanted the TARDIS to be somewhere nice and peaceful.

If wishes were fishes . . .

'Look,' Cwej said finally, 'if, and I repeat, if the Adjudicator Secular is involved in some kind of cover-up, then we go above her head. Talk to her boss, the Adjudicator Spiritual.'

'And tell her what?' Forrester snapped. 'We need proof. All we've got at the moment is suspicion.'

'We've got the mind probe recording.'

'Yeah, and what does it prove? That somebody tampered with it. We've got no real evidence that Adjudicators are involved. There's nothing to say that she and her friend didn't do it themselves.'

Bernice could almost feel the thumb being jabbed towards her back. 'Who's "she"?' she called back over her shoulder, 'the cat's mother?' It was a phrase she'd heard Ace use before, and she quite liked the sound of. God knew what it meant, but it seemed apt.

'Shut it,' Forrester growled.

'Yeah, shut it,' Cwej repeated dutifully.

Or not, as the case may be.

She turned to face them. The elliptical shape of the spaceport loomed behind them, set atop five spindly towers and surrounded by a cloud of small ships arriving and departing. Somewhere on its upper surface, the Imperial Landsknecht scout ship that Beltempest had lent them would be preparing to leap into the clear blue sky. Good luck to it. Bernice's journey from Purgatory to Earth, locked in the ship's hold, had been uncomfortable, but mercifully short, and if she never saw the inside of a military vessel again between now and the end of time it would be too soon.

The sun was in Bernice's eyes, and all she could see of the two Adjudicators was their silhouettes. Both of them were holding weapons. She wouldn't be able to make it more than a few steps without getting shot, and that wouldn't help her or the Doctor in the slightest.

'Can I ask a question?' she said, shading her eyes with

her hand. 'Does the concept "innocent until proven guilty" mean anything to you?'

Cwej looked at Forrester. 'Does it?' he asked her.

'Not to me,' she replied. 'Far as I'm concerned, some people are innocent and others are guilty. Innocent until proven guilty sounds like a dangerous philosophical concept. I hate ambiguity.'

The walkway had emerged from the other side of the building by now, and its edge sliced across the sun, casting a shadow over all of them. Bernice shivered at the sudden chill. 'So, where now?' she said.

Forrester hesitated for a moment. 'We have a problem,' she said finally.

'You surprise me.'

'Your friends in high places – '

'My *supposed* friends in high places. For the record, I haven't got a clue what you're talking about.'

'Your *supposed* friends in high places want us off this case. Unfortunately for you, we're not going to let ourselves be taken off. That means we can't go back to our lodge, so we're going to have to find somewhere else to interrogate you.'

'Interrogate? Do you have to use that word? Can't we just have a chat?'

'Whatever you want to call it, we're going to have to do it somewhere quiet and private.'

Bernice thought for a second. Something about what Forrester had said bothered her. 'Hang on a second. Am I right in thinking that you suspect your own superior officer – this Adjudicator Secular person – is implicated in this plot?'

Forrester grimaced. 'Yes,' she admitted.

'So does that mean that you went all the way to Purgatory to collect the Doctor and me without actually having official permission?'

'Er . . . yes,' Forrester said, abashed.

'Wow,' Bernice said. 'I'm impressed.'

The walkway began to curve to the left. Looking over her shoulder, Bernice could see that it diverged in a smooth arc around a spiky building – another of those oddities of architecture that Earth seemed to go in for in the thirtieth century.

'Hey!' Cwej said suddenly. Bernice turned back to face him and Forrester. 'I've got an idea!'

'Treat it gently,' Forrester murmured, 'it's in a strange place.'

Bernice tried to suppress a smile, but failed. Her eye caught Forrester's. The Adjudicator's lips twitched slightly, and she looked away. Bernice suddenly felt a laugh welling up within her. Great, she thought, here I am, sentenced to death for murder, light-years away from the Doctor, and I'm sharing private jokes with one of my captors. Life's odd sometimes.

Cwej looked from Forrester to Bernice, aware that something was going on but uncertain what it was. 'What's the big laugh?' he asked plaintively.

'Forget it, golden boy,' Forrester growled. 'What's your great idea then?'

'My family!' he said proudly.

'Your *what*?'

'We can hide out with my family. They'll be glad to see me.'

Forrester gazed at him.

'There's no way of breaking it to you gently, Cwej, but if I was your family and you turned up on my doorstep on the run from the Adjudicators with a prisoner you wanted to interrogate, I wouldn't be glad to see you.'

Cwej smiled sunnily.

'You don't know my family,' he said.

As she swallowed another sizzling piece of food, Voroneh Madillah tried to remember how she came to be sitting cross-legged in a square in the Undertown, overlooked by weathered gargoyles, her fingers and face smeared with hot fat.

'All right,' she remembered saying, in time-honoured Adjudicator tradition, as she had turned the corner and approached the knot of underlife, 'what's all this, then?'

At the sight of the stocky Adjudicator in her black hooded robes and iridescent blue and gold body armour, most of the underlife had scuttled away into the shadows on various sets of legs, tentacles and organic castors. She definitely remembered that. Three had remained: a bulky horned creature cowering against the wall and two small rodents with knives almost half their own body size. She recalled settling her hand on the butt of her judicial blaster and thinking that this one looked like trouble.

'Just a domestic dispute,' one of the rodents had squealed. No problem remembering that.

'And what's your story?' Madillah had asked the alien with the horns. Was that when her headache started? She tore off another piece of meat and chewed it reflectively. Yes, it probably was.

'They wanted my money!' the alien had hissed, nostril flaps flicking back and forth as it spoke. 'I asked them if . . .'

Madillah had missed the end of the sentence as a spike of sick pain suddenly blotted everything out. Had she raised a hand to her temple? She thought so.

'Hey,' one of the rats had said, 'the law's not feeling too well!'

'Scat,' the other one said.

Within seconds, they had vanished into the darkness of the Undertown. She could still picture their faces if she needed to pick them up later. So far, so good.

'Lucky you came along when you did,' the big alien had hissed. 'Thanks.'

The headache had intensified round about then, hadn't it?

'Aliens,' Madillah had said as she unholstered her blaster. 'You're all the same.'

That's where things started getting a little fuzzy. Had she fired her blaster? She seemed to remember playing the beam over something large and motionless. Well, more or less motionless, especially after a while.

She pulled another piece of meat off the carcass and licked the juices from it.

Did it matter what had happened, so long as she was happy?

Beltempest and the Doctor were perched on the edge of the trolley upon which Fazakerli's body lay.

'Very smart, Doctor,' Beltempest said. He held a cup of lapsang souchong in his trunk, which muffled his voice slightly. 'Whether or not you're right about the effects of icaron radiation – and I'm still reserving judgement on that – the probability that all those people were coincidentally in the same small area of Earth within seven days of the outrages they committed is so small that even the computer can't calculate it. What made you think of a time-based analysis rather than a space-based one?'

'I have a different perspective on these things,' the Doctor murmured, gazing moodily across the room. 'Of course, you realize that this just magnifies the scale of the problem.'

Beltempest contorted his trunk until he could sip from the cup. Thank God he'd allowed those two Adjudicators to persuade him to keep the Doctor alive. He'd originally thought that the Doctor and Bernice Summerfield were unwitting tools of whoever he was searching for, but it was beginning to look as if the Doctor could be of use after all. 'How so?' he said finally, savouring the oddly tarry taste of the liquid.

'Well, we know where the radiation contamination is occurring, but we still don't know why.'

'Why?'

'Is it an accident, or is there some malign intelligence behind it all?'

Beltempest frowned. 'An accident, surely. How could . . . I mean, who . . .?'

'Icaron radiation doesn't come free with packets of cornflakes, you know,' the Doctor said, still staring at the wall. 'It's produced under very special, very deliberate circumstances. Most civilized planets ban all research on icarons because of the dangers. No, I suspect that if there is a source on Earth, then it's been put there deliberately.'

He sighed. 'Still, there's a lot of work that needs to be done before we ascribe blame to anyone. I could be wrong. It might be accidental. I'm not the cosmos's greatest expert on icarons, after all. We really need to talk to someone who knows more about them.'

Beltempest thought for a moment. The Doctor, watching him intently, added: 'You know somebody who can help, don't you? That's how you come to know about icarons.'

Beltempest shook his head. He didn't want to think about this. He really didn't.

'Yes you do,' the Doctor insisted. 'Who is it?' When Beltempest failed to reply, he added, 'Look, people are dying as you sit there. Tell me the person's name.'

'Pryce,' Beltempest sighed. 'Professor Zebulon Pryce, of the University of Sallas. Famous case, ten years ago or so. He discovered how to produce icarons by smashing beams of blumons and zeccons together, published a number of papers on the basic mathematics, quantum states, and so on. The Landsknechte offered him facilities and a grant to study the weapons applications first hand –'

'Weapons applications?' the Doctor said darkly.

'Purely defensive, of course,' Beltempest said dismissively. 'We wanted to know whether icaron beams would be more powerful than the proton beams we're using now. Anyway, Zebulon came here to Purgatory to work. He had his own building, near the spaceport, with a cyclotron to produce the icarons. I was only a trooper at the time, but I remember the case . . .' He trailed off into silence.

'What happened?' the Doctor prompted.

'He went mad, of course,' Beltempest sighed. 'I suppose it's obvious to you, but we didn't know that icarons could cause people to go psychotic. Pryce was the first human researcher on them, and none of the alien races whose databases we'd examined –'

'Ransacked,' the Doctor whispered.

' – had discovered them either,' Beltempest continued. 'He fooled us all for three years. We thought Landsknechte were deserting into the training environments, living in the jungles and whatever. Turned out he was killing them off, one by one. He'd lurk in the ventilation ducts late at night, and leap out at them. Paralysed them with dermal patches, then took them back, still conscious, to his lab.' Beltempest took a deep breath. 'At the court martial it was said that he'd kept them alive for weeks, gradually dissolving the flesh from their bones with coronic acid but leaving their circulatory systems and their nerves still intact.'

'How was he caught?' The Doctor's voice seemed to be coming from a million miles away.

'Fuse blew on the cyclotron, causing a fire. He wouldn't evacuate the building, so they sent Landsknechte in to get him out. We found – we found . . .' His voice caught, and he stopped for a moment before continuing. 'Some of them were still alive when we broke down the door. Just skeletons wrapped in shreds of tissue. Skeletons with eyes. Staring, staring eyes. I'll never forget it. Never.'

The Doctor laid a hand on Beltempest's arm.

'They stopped the research and destroyed the building, of course,' Beltempest said finally in a voice that was just a shade too calm and too controlled, 'but they kept him alive. Justice had to be done. Justice had to be seen to be done. If you want an expert on icarons, Professor Zebulon Pryce is your man.'

'Where is he?' the Doctor asked.

'At the Imperial prison, on the planet Dis. The Landsknechte wanted him executed, but he's got the whole case tied up in knots with appeals and legalese. Something to do with the fact that although the Landsknechte employed him, he was still on the books of the University of Sallas and therefore under Imperial, rather than Landsknecht , law. It doesn't help that lawyers for both sides keep dying.'

'Will you take me there?'

'No.' Beltempest's eyes were bleak and dry. 'I might just be tempted to blow the planet to smithereens from orbit.'

'I need to see him,' the Doctor insisted, 'and I think you do too.'

'Oh I see him, believe me.' Beltempest turned his bleak gaze upon the Doctor. 'Every night, when I close my eyes, I see him.'

Powerless Friendless followed the smell of roasting fish until he found Olias's place.

He knew he was in the right area when he saw the fishing rods. They jutted from the roof of the massive edifice of cracked plasticrete, their lines trailing away into the surrounding waters. He could see shadowy figures behind them: fishermen or guards, nobody was sure. Could well be both. Olias's was not only the best, but the safest restaurant in the whole of the Spaceport Five Undertown. Everybody knew that. Olias had contacts. People up in the Overcity who dealt with her. Drugs, people, cheap technology: Olias could provide it. Olias more or less ran the whole of Spaceport Five Undertown. More powerful than the viscount who ran things up top, she was.

Powerless Friendless slid out along the catwalk that led to the building, aware of the eyes watching him from the roof. By the time he got to the door, he had been recognized and pronounced harmless. If he had looked like trouble, or if Olias had taken a sudden and unprompted dislike to him, he would never have made it.

As the door opened for him, one of the fishing lines nearby jerked and started to move. Powerless Friendless stopped to watch, his mouth already watering. There was a flurry of activity from the roof, and the line pulled taut. The water beneath the catwalk suddenly exploded into life as whatever had taken a fancy to the bait tried to escape. Too late. Whoever was working the line wasn't about to let their catch go. They reeled it in slowly, cautiously, letting the line out if it felt about to snap, but always reeling in more than they let out afterwards. Powerless Friendless caught a glimpse of a pale body lined with suckers as it was hoisted up, still jerking, to the roof. Might have been a mutated fish, might just as easily have been an alien underdweller out for a late night swim. Either way, within half an hour the creature would be gracing somebody's plate, roasted in its own juices, blackened with alien spices, served with a chilled Elysian wine.

People came from the Overcity for Olias's food. She was in off-world tourist guides. Bodyguards recommended.

Pangs of pain shot through his mouth as his glands went into overdrive. He hadn't eaten properly since – since he couldn't remember when.

Inside, Olias's restaurant was a huge, barnlike building of bars, winding stairways and tables tucked away in corners. Simcords of various planetary landscapes were scattered across the walls. Powerless Friendless recognised the ice forests of Zobeide and the towering fern-cities of Baucis, although he couldn't recall visiting the planets themselves. He felt faint at the smell of the food. His five linked stomachs were tying themselves in knots, and his mouth was so full of saliva that he had to keep swallowing to stop it from dribbling off his mouth-cilia and down his body. Retracting his pseudo-limbs to stop himself from inadvertently picking up food from people's plates, he slithered his way between the tables.

Dantalion was at the bar. He was smaller and fatter than Powerless Friendless remembered, and his skin was deeply furrowed, the Birastrop sign of old age. Something about his eye – his real eye – said that he hadn't got long to live, and he knew it. His other eye – the metal orb – reflected Powerless Friendless's face back at him.

He gazed blearily at Powerless Friendless over a frothing glass held in one of his lower limbs. 'Yes?' he said, thumping the glass down. It continued to froth, and something moved inside it.

'You – you don't remember me?' Powerless Friendless asked.

'People provide me with financial recompense in return for two services,' Dantalion said, and wiped the back of his hand across his upper lip. His voice had the careful precision of the very drunk. 'They pay me to stop them remembering something, and they pay me so that I don't remember who they are afterwards.'

'I think I remember you.'

'Then, my friend, you didn't pay enough.' Dantalion burped. 'Drink?' he asked.

'No. I . . .' Powerless Friendless couldn't force the words out.

'You want your memory back,' Dantalion said softly.

Powerless Friendless nodded.

'When did I excise the unwelcome remembrances?' Dantalion asked.

Powerless Friendless shook his head. 'I don't know. Perhaps a few years ago.'

'I was good then.' The Birastrop smiled mirthlessly. 'Better than I am now, at any rate. Have you been getting any breakthroughs? Any memories from your previous life?'

Powerless Friendless nodded. 'Some,' he admitted. 'Flashes. Faces and names. How did you know?'

Dantalion looked away, across the restaurant. Powerless Friendless waited, wondering whether the being had heard the question. Eventually Dantalion picked up his glass and sloshed the contents around for a moment.

'Long and painful experience,' he said finally. 'People come to me, and ask me to remove selected memories as if I were pulling a rotting tooth. Painful love affairs. Secrets. Tortures. Sometimes a few moments, sometimes a few years. They pay me, and I do my best. And then, years later, they find me again. "Give them back," they cry. "I'm incomplete! I can't live without them!" And I tell them what I'll tell you.' He took a swig from the glass, and Powerless Friendless could hear him gulp as he swallowed whatever had been swimming in the drink. 'I don't remove memories,' he said. 'I just hide them. I put them in places your mind won't think to look for them. Sometimes it rediscovers them by accident. Sometimes it searches so hard it finds them despite my best efforts.' He smiled. 'Sometimes they come crawling back into the light and announce their presence anyway.' He banged the glass down and signalled to the barman. 'What I am trying, in my long and roundabout way, to impart to you is that some memories I can get back for you, but others will have been recycled for dreams or overwritten by other experiences. It's a hit-and-miss affair. Are you still interested in taking advantage of my meagre skills?'

Powerless Friendless nodded.

Something sloshed against the side of Dantalion's glass, rocking it slightly on the table.

'Why do you drink that stuff?' Powerless Friendless asked, wincing.

'There are some things that even I don't want to remember,' Dantalion answered as the barman placed another inhabited drink before him. 'And, as I wouldn't let anybody like me anywhere near my mind, this is the next best solution.'

'Mom!'

'Christopher?'

The small woman in the doorway stared up at Cwej in astonishment. The smells of breakfast – irradiated animeat flesh – drifted out behind her.

Forrester turned to Bernice. 'Why did I let myself get talked into this?' she muttered, and gazed past Bernice, along the hallway. Nobody was around, but she still felt she was being watched.

'What's the matter?' Bernice asked.

'This just feels like a bad move.' Forrester let her gaze linger at each of the doorways along the hall. Unlike her level, where the entrances to the individual apartments were grey and anonymous, the ones down here on Level Fifty-three were brightly coloured, ever-changing rectangular kaleidoscopes with the names of the families, and in some cases, their smiling simcord images, appearing out of the coloured patterns.

'Christopher! It can't be you!' the woman exclaimed, clapping her hands to her cheeks. 'Oh, let me look at you!

We were so worried! We thought you might have been caught up in the riots!'

Riots? Forrester thought as Cwej grinned down at his mother. We've only been gone a few days. What's been happening?

'Mom, I brought some friends.'

'Any friends of yours are welcome,' she said, peering round him and gazing at Bernice and Forrester with warm curiosity. 'Come in, come in. You should have told me you were coming. The irradiator's playing up. I think the techbrain's gone again, but the cost of replacements these days . . .'

She ushered them all into a large room filled with furniture and decorated with simcord images of family and friends. A tall, elderly man who had been sitting watching a hand-held centcomp reader sprang to his feet, grinning. Forrester, uncomfortable at such effusive hospitality, studied the images intently as an alternative to joining in with the exclamations and introductions behind her. A large number of them seemed to be of Cwej: Cwej as a child, wide-eyed and two-headed; Cwej as a teenager, gangling and awkward, holding a small reptilian pet; Cwej looking uncomfortable in badly fitting Adjudicator's squire's robes; Cwej, bursting with pride at his graduation ceremony on Ponten IV. Forrester found it strange, seeing Cwej without his fur and his bearlike snout. He was so good-looking that he was almost a caricature.

'We were so proud of him,' a voice said from beside her. She turned. The elderly man was standing beside her. His face was deeply lined, and close up she could see that most of the left side of his face was artificial, but his eyes were as bright and as blue as Cwej's. 'I'm Christopher's father,' he added. 'His mother and I were there when he graduated. Pleased as punch. Pleased as punch. First time I'd been back to Ponten for seventy years, of course. Old place hadn't changed much. Reminded me of my own graduation, back in oh-five. I swear some of the lecturers were the same.'

'Roz Forrester,' she said, still ill at ease. 'You were an Adjudicator too?'

'Proud to meet you,' he said. 'Any partner of our son is a friend of ours. Yes, I was an Adjudicator, up till four years ago. It's a family tradition.'

Now that she knew, she could see it in his eyes: that searching, questioning, devil-may-care expression that could all too easily turn into world-weariness.

As hers had.

'My father, and his father before him,' Cwej senior added. 'Back as far as we care to look. There was a Cwej on the founding panel of Adjudicators, back when they were more like galactic sheriffs. Forrester. Now there's a familiar name. Could I have served with your dad?'

She shook her head.

'My father didn't – well, let's say I don't think you'd have met him.'

'No, I remember what it was,' he said, grinning. 'You were squired to Fenn Martle, weren't you?'

A fist tightened around Forrester's heart.

'Yes,' Cwej's father continued, oblivious to her expression, 'he squired me for his first few years on the job. Good lad. Very promising. Whatever happened to him?'

Forrester bit her lip to stop herself saying something she might regret. This was going to be a long day.

The rising sun shone through the window of the darkened office, casting the shadow of the figure across the translucent desk. Information flickered in the depths of the desk – financial, economic, military – but the figure did not react. Like a spider, the figure waited patiently for those faint, tell-tale vibrations of the web.

As the sun rose, its rosy glow slowly edged across the desk and onto the carpet, casting light into the shadowed recesses of the room. As the figure waited, the sunlight crept, inch by patient inch, further across the office, until it lapped against the foot of a large box.

A large, blue box.

The splash of bright colour attracted the figure's attention.

'I'll enjoy taking you apart, circuit by circuit,' it murmured.

Chapter 9

'I'm Shythe Shahid and this is The Empire Today, *on the spot, on and off the Earth. Today's headlines: Evan Claple, anchorman for* The Empire Today, *died last night in an incident at his home. Initial reports suggest that his long time partner, Cherri O'Halloran, has been taken into custody by the Order of Adjudicators. Also, as the Asian Undertown riots spill over into a new day, questions are asked at the Imperial Court. All this, and the latest news on the fighting on Murtaugh and Heaven, after this important message ...'*

'For Rassilon's sake!' the Doctor yelled as the Imperial Landsknecht scout vessel *Moorglade* emerged from hyperspace into a blazing inferno. 'You've put us in the centre of a star!' He clapped his hands over his eyes, shielding them from the glare of the bloated sun which filled the forward screens and washed out the stars and the velvet blackness of space. 'Quick,' he cried, 'get us out of here! We'll burn up!'

Beltempest just laughed. 'Don't worry! We're heavily shielded, didn't I tell you?'

Although the Doctor couldn't see anything, his sensitive Time Lord senses could make out the soft sounds of Provost-Major Beltempest's fingers caressing the controls, and the slight shift in local inertia as the ship came around on a curving path towards the sun.

'Sorry about the light,' Beltempest said, with no trace

163

of sincerity in his voice. 'Perhaps I should have warned you about that as well.'

Peering through the gaps in his fingers and squinting hard, the Doctor could just make out Beltempest's bulky, four-armed shape like a cardboard cut-out in front of the glowing white screen. It looked as if his ears were folded across his eyes.

'Yes,' the Doctor said 'perhaps you should.' Then, louder: 'Can't you polarize the screens or something?'

'I already have,' Beltempest rejoined. 'They're on maximum.'

Sniffing, the Doctor tried to tell if there was any burning insulation. That was usually the first sign that a ship's shields were failing. If only they'd travelled in the TARDIS. He wouldn't have worried then. Type 40s were rated for environments up to and including quasars.

If only he knew where the TARDIS was.

If only he knew where Bernice was.

He shoved the thoughts to the back of his mind and locked them up in a small cabinet that he reserved for stray worries. Time for that later. Concentrate on the here and now. He sniffed again, but the shields seemed to be holding. Beltempest had been right.

As the Doctor's eyes adjusted better to the light, he began to make out features on the surface of the sun: darker spots the size of planets and lighter cracks that broke the surface up into jigsaw piece areas. Typical stellar photosphere. He could still remember the droning voice of Lady Genniploritreludar, the Arcalian lecturer in stellar engineering back in the Academy. 'Theta Sigma, pay attention at the back there. Recite for me, if you will, the fifteen stages in the life cycle of the main sequence sun.' Odd, the things one could remember when one tried. He still had problems recalling the operating codes for the TARDIS, but trivial points of fact from nine hundred years ago were as sharp as a pin. It probably had something to do with the Time Lords mucking about in his mind before they regenerated him and exiled him to Earth. They liked to think they knew what they were doing, and they had assured him after that Omega business that they had repaired all the damage, but he was sure that his memories were still holed like a gruyère.

Outside the ship, a smaller, darker circle moved rapidly across the face of the sun. Ionized gas streamed behind it like veils.

'What's that?' the Doctor asked.

'What's what?'

'That object. It looks like it's orbiting.'

'You can see it?'

Beltempest turned and unfurled his ears a fraction so that he could squint at the Doctor.

'Only just,' the Doctor said. 'But it looks like a planet.'

'It is.' Beltempest gestured back over his shoulder. 'That's Dis.'

'A planet orbiting inside the photosphere of a *sun*?'

'What better place for a prison?'

The Doctor shrugged. 'A good question,' he said to himself. Man's ingenuity in finding uncomfortable places to imprison other men would never cease to amaze him.

The ship was engaged in a tail-chase with the planet now, and as their spiral path bottomed out, the edge of the simcord screen cut off the light from the sun. The streaming plasma still washed out all the details from the control room, but at least the Doctor could make out some of the details of Dis. The planet bristled like a hedgehog but, unlike the hedgehog, the bristles had an offensive as well as defensive capability. Mountainous laser turrets and plasma-gun emplacements, their sides melted and seared by the heat, tracked the ship as it approached. It wasn't a new experience for the Doctor, being the target of so many weapons, but he still didn't like it.

Beltempest guided the ship by intuition into a low orbit, travelling along a massive valley between the clifflike faces of energy collectors, under the watchful eyes of the guns. With an unexpected delicacy of touch, he guided it in to a small, crater-like landing pad, thick with the accumulated stellar dust of millennia.

'Welcome to Dis,' Beltempest said.

'Not a place I would wish to spend my holidays,' said the Doctor. 'I thought I'd been to some unpleasantly hot places in my time, but this one takes the entire packet of biscuits and the factory as well.'

'You were the one that wanted to come.'

'I hadn't seen the travel brochure then. How did this place get built?'

As Beltempest shut the ship's systems down, and a thick metal iris sealed off the landing pad from the relentless torrent of radiation and heat, he said: 'The empire appropriated it from a race called the Greld, centuries ago. They resisted our . . . advances, and so the Empire launched a quark bomb into their sun, forcing it from a white dwarf to a red giant. The outer layers of the sun exploded, sterilizing the solar system and annihilating the Greld. It struck the Empress at the time that the system would make a perfect prison, and so she ordered that one be built. And here it is.'

The dome finally closed above them. Everything was in darkness for a few moments while the Doctor's eyes adjusted to the lower level of illumination from the red-hot metal of the landing bay. The light altered, darkening and shifting through red down to infrared as the bay cooled, and smaller glow-globes around its edges flickered uncertainly into life. Figures in bulky thermal suits moved cautiously from recessed doorways towards the ship. They were armed, of course.

'Well,' said the Doctor, 'let's go and see whether Professor Zebulon Pryce is at home to visitors today.'

Light spilled around his body like water around a curved stone in a river bed. Green light, bright as a sun, washing out his thought, his personality, everything that he was, wearing him down, layer by layer, atom by atom, until it found the him he used to be . . .

. . . *and Daph Yilli Gar was lying along a padded bench in the navigator's cubicle, his eye-stalks inches above the gnarled, rootlike organic control nexus of the* Skel'Ske,

166

the new Hith fighter. His pseudo-limbs caressed the warm surface, leaving trails of light in their wake as he sensed his way through hyperspace. The vibration of the hyper-drive was an almost sexual thrill deep in his stomachs, and he blushed a dirty grey colour as he felt the skin along his flanks pucker into a row of small lumps, ready to fire impregnating darts at any passing female.

Thank the Gods of Hith that Captain Vap Oppat Pol was in a separate cubicle and had recently gone through the Change from female to male. The last thing they needed was an inadvertent coupling right here on the bridge. Even if the two of them were the only crew for this first flight, it would be so shameful that Daph would have to pay a scapegoat to kill itself for him.

In front of him, the simcord screen showed only the deep, featureless grey of hyperspace, but under his hands he could feel, through the nexus, currents and rapids, under-tows and reefs, and the occasional slippery touch of some-thing half alive sliding away from his touch. The way this new ship responded to hyperspace was like nothing he had ever experienced before. The tension was making his skin dry out and the underside of his basal foot knot up, but he had never been so proud. To think that a member of the Pir clan had been chosen as navigator of the Skel'Ske!

'Navigator,' growled Vap Oppat Pol from the command cubicle. 'Are we ready to emerge from hyperspace?' He sounded tense, and Daph Yilli Gar could imagine his eye-stalks standing erect upon his flat head and his flanks running with mucus. Perhaps it was the Change still affect-ing him, or perhaps it was the honour of being the first captain of this, the Hith's newest, finest, experimental spaceship.

'Ready, captain,' Daph Yilli Gar acknowledged. 'Cap-tain, may I ask – ?'

'You'll find out where we are when we emerge,' Vap Oppat Pol snapped. 'Until then, shut up!'

Daph Yilli Gar scrunched himself up in the command chair. The war against the pestilential humans was going *badly, but it didn't do anything for ship's morale to have a captain who kept things from them.*

'Prepare to emerge,' Vap Oppat Pol said. Daph Yilli Gar's tentacular fingers caressed the shivering nexus of the control panel, feeling for the granularity of hyperspace, ready to wrench it apart and drop them into real space.

'Now!' Vap Oppat Pol shouted.

Daph Yilli Gar wrenched at the fabric of unreality, and the grey of the simcord screen cleared to reveal a star-strewn black backdrop, against which stood fifteen Earth Empire heavy cruisers, weapons primed and aimed directly at the Skel'Ske.

'Captain!' he screamed, 'shall I . . . ?'

'No,' Vap Oppat Pol said calmly. 'No, you won't.'

A terrible realization swept over Daph Yilli Gar, but before he could make sense of it his eyes were filled with . . .

. . . Bright green light, washing away the barriers that had been built up, leaving him amid the wreckage of his mind, trying to piece the bits together.

'Come on,' Bernice drawled, 'you cannot be serious!' She threw the mind probe down on Cwej's bed. It hung, suspended in the repulsor field, a few inches above the surface. On the screen, Forrester could make out the frozen images of Bernice and her friend the Doctor. The Doctor's mouth was open, just as he was about to deliver the words that condemned both of them as murderers.

'What do you mean?' Forrester was affronted. Suspects weren't supposed to talk to investigating officers like that.

Then again, interrogations weren't supposed to take place in the bedroom of one of the interrogating officers. After Cwej's mother had more or less forced them to eat some breakfast, she had given them the free run of Cwej's old room for their 'meeting'. She and Cwej's father had apparently left it untouched since he had left home, apart from letting the cleaning bots go over it once a month. The walls were plastered with GALAXY'S MOST WANTED simcords mixed with a smattering of sim-stars and even a couple of semi-naked viy music singers in erotic poses.

Models of starships hovered on repulsor fields from the ceiling, some of them with a battery-operated short-distance warp capability.

All very telling, Forrester thought.

On entering the room, Bernice had immediately flung herself on the bed. Cwej, after a nostalgic and faintly embarrassed look around at the place where his childhood had been spent, had made for an auto-adjust chair beside a work surface. That left Forrester, much to her disgust, with a small floating armchair that fitted around her hips so tightly that it looked like a fashion accessory, and would only take her weight with a good deal of buzzing and quivering.

'I mean, just look at this!' Bernice waved the mind probe at Forrester. 'It makes no sense.'

Forrester cast a sour glance at Cwej, who was lounging around in his chair with his gun in his lap, flicking through a sim-book. 'Hey, hairball! Pay attention!'

Cwej looked up. 'Sorry,' he said, blushing.

'Yeah, you'd be sorry if she slit my throat while you were buried in kid's stuff.'

He looked sceptical. 'You think that's likely?'

'Well there's one way to find out for sure, isn't there?'

He threw the book onto the desk and picked up his gun. 'You win, as usual,' he muttered.

Forrester turned back to Bernice. 'That's very patently you in the memories of the underdweller. No ifs. No buts.'

'Look,' Bernice sighed as she hovered a few inches above the bed, 'let me get this right. Someone called Waiting For Justice, who lived down in the Undertown, was killed by someone called Annie, who also lived down in the Undertown. It originally looked like one of these motiveless murders that you've been getting, which the Doctor reckons are caused by some kind of radiation leak. You, however, think Annie's memory of the murder was implanted, and that Waiting For Justice was actually killed by the Doctor and me, on the basis that she saw us a few hours before you picked her up, even though I deny ever having seen her before. Is that a fair summary?'

'The phrase "condemned with your own words" springs readily to mind.'

'The phrase "faked evidence" springs to my mind. You've already admitted that the evidence has been faked once. Why can't it have been faked a second time?'

Forrester shrugged. 'What's the point?'

'The point is,' Bernice said in exasperation, 'that you were clever enough to penetrate one lot of false evidence, so the villains of the piece, whoever they are, concocted a second set to throw you off at a tangent. In the process, they decided to frame the Doctor and me for some reason which I have yet to fathom, but which probably has something to do with the theft of the TARDIS.'

'The what?' Cwej wanted to know.

'The . . . Never mind.'

'Once we start on that route,' Forrester said sceptically, 'there's no end to the levels of faked evidence we could assume. I've got a rule of thumb for this sort of thing. If there's any evidence that the evidence is faked, then I'll believe it. If not, I won't.'

'Fair enough.' Bernice stared at the image on the screen. 'There must be a clue here somewhere. Something out of place, some little thing . . .' She bit her lip. 'Did you say that we said something?'

'Yeah. Press the CONTINUE key.'

Bernice did so, and the images shifted slightly. A voice drifted out of the probe: 'Bernice, we make a fine pair of murderers.'

'Your friend's voice,' Forrester said.

'No, it's not,' Cwej said, beating Bernice to the punch.

Forrester stared at him. 'What do you mean?' she said.

He blushed. 'I mean, it's not the same voice as the man we saw on Purgatory.'

'Of course it is.'

Cwej shook his head stubbornly. 'No. We've got the wrong man.'

Forrester couldn't believe what she was hearing. She'd gone out on a limb for Cwej after he'd sprung that tale about faked mind probe records and mysterious calls to

Adjudicator Secular Rashid, and here he was, calmly telling her that he'd been wrong!

'It's not the Doctor's voice,' Bernice agreed. 'Listen to it.'

She fumbled with the controls, and managed to replay the sequence.

'The accent is missing, and the stress on the words is different,' she continued.

Forrester tried to remember the voice of the little man on Purgatory. Quite harsh, with an odd little roll on the R sounds. This voice, the voice on the mind probe record, was different: smoother, more tentative, with an odd little questioning lift at the end of the sentence.

'All right,' she said. 'I'm prepared to be convinced. How do you think this image got on here then?'

Bernice thought for a moment.

'I think somebody implanted this sequence in the memory of the mind probe. I think they used images of the Doctor and me they picked up from a camera somewhere, but I don't think they knew what our voices were like. For some reason, God knows why, they chose a voice for the Doctor, but it doesn't match the Doctor's real voice.'

There was a pause as Forrester thought through the implications of that.

'Hell,' she said finally, 'this is big. We need to send a message to Provost-Major Beltempest to make sure he doesn't do anything rash to the Doctor. It would also be useful if I could hear the Doctor's voice again, just to be sure.'

She looked at Cwej. Judging by his expression, he was still a few minutes behind on the conversation.

'How does your mother feel about long distance calls?' she asked.

'Terg Albert McConnel,' intoned the sombre voice of the judicial cyborg, 'I find you guilty of the murder of Anil Lymaner.'

The room was empty but for the two of them – McCon-

nel standing at one end and the cyborg suspended in a
null-grav harness at the other. A statue-like security bot
stood between them, it's heavy weaponry directed towards
McConnel. A desk, piled high with flimsy sheets of plastic,
was set behind the hovering cyborg. The walls were a
neutral grey.

'This judgement, in full accordance with Imperial Law,
is at a confidence level of point nine nine eight three six,
to five decimal places,' the cyborg continued. 'Do you
have anything to say in mitigation before I pass sentence?'

Terg McConnel had to close his eyes and to replay
the words in his head before he understood their true
significance. Guilty? Yes, of course he was guilty. He could
still feel the metal of the knife dig into the heel of his
hand as it ground against the back of Lymaner's skull. He
could still hear the ripples of shocked silence spread out
around the Undertown restaurant. He could still see the
blood well up like tears in Lymaner's eye, just before
the student fell forward into his plate of food. Guilty, but
– but blameless. He didn't know why he'd done it. He
could remember everything except the reason for his
actions.

How could he put that into words? Would it change
anything? He knew he was guilty.

He took a deep breath, and gazed into the judicial
cyborg's face. Beneath the burnished metal dome of the
cyborg's head – receptacle for the billions of laws, by-
laws, precedents, rules and regulations that governed the
Empire, as well as every single judgement ever made by
a judicial cyborg or an Adjudicator, on Earth or off, perti-
nent or not – a wizened face stared compassionately down
at him. The soft, fleshy cog in the legal machine. The
conscience. The remnants of an Adjudicator, too old now
to impose justice by force, content to sit and add a pinch
of humanity to cold, unyielding logic.

'No,' he said firmly, 'no, I have nothing to say.'

The judicial cyborg nodded, and took a sheet of plastic
from the pile, as it had done throughout the hearing,
referring to details of the case for and against McConnel.

Judicial cyborgs couldn't download their data from centcomp. No external links were allowed – the risk of undue influence, computer viruses and hacking were too high. All data had to be fed to them as hardcopy.

'Under normal circumstances,' the cyborg said, 'the penalty for your crime is mandatory brainwipe and indenture to a corporation for ten years. However – ' It looked up at McConnel with something approaching pity. ' – as a result of an increasing number of apparently motiveless crimes of violence, the Adjudicator In Extremis has introduced a new penalty, specifically for cases such as yours.'

It waved the piece of paper at him. Even before the words were spoken, McConnel felt his heart turn to ice.

'I withdraw your humanity,' the cyborg intoned, 'and reclassify you as alien. And, as alien, I sentence you to vivisection within the laboratories of the Surgeon Imperialis, so that your last moments may aid our understanding of this scourge of violence.' The wizened face beneath the metal grimaced. 'And may the Goddess have mercy upon your soul.'

As soon as they had landed, the Doctor and Provost-Major Beltempest had been escorted from their ship to a reception office whose walls were shielded with matt-white ceramic tiles.

Refrigeration units were humming at full capacity just to keep the room at a temperature where the Doctor could have fried an egg on the desk. A uniformed captain named Rhodd, whose dull, uncaring eyes looked over the authorizations that Beltempest had filled in before they left Purgatory, seemed to waver in the heat haze like a mirage. After checking the documents against the security clearances that Beltempest had also forwarded from Purgatory, he stamped the authorizations and gestured them towards a null-grav shaft in a corner of the office. All of this was accomplished without a word being said. The shaft – also lined with tiles and dripping with condensation – took them down into the bowels of the planet, down to a point where the reduced heat from the sun balanced out the increasing heat from the planet's core. The corridors sloshed with a thin layer of liquid, and grey, patchy fungus clung to the ceramic tiles.

Even thirty levels below the surface of Dis, the appalling heat was like a weight pressing the Doctor down. The stench of rot, mould and body odour was nauseating. Beltempest's blue skin had turned a dirty grey colour, and his ears flapped incessantly. The faces of the guards that accompanied them along the corridor, past the infinity of numbered metal doors, were glossy with sweat, probably because they were forced by regulations to wear their full uniforms at all times. And, of course, they were all human. Typical Imperial thinking, the Doctor mused. He knew that there were ten or eleven alien races subsumed within the Empire to whom this sort of environment was like a cold spring morning, but would it even occur to the Empire to use them as guards? Certainly not: aliens couldn't be trusted, so humans had to wreck their health doing the job.

'What sort of people are held here?' the Doctor asked as they walked past yet another heavy metal door.

'Two groups, Beltempest said. The Doctor could hear the strain in his voice. With his bulk, it was amazing that he had made it this far without collapsing. Military training, no doubt. It left you perfectly equipped to carry out all sorts of tasks you wouldn't dream of doing if you were in your right mind. 'Firstly there are the criminals who can't be brainwiped and recharactered. Some races just don't respond to wipes, for instance, and genetic criminals will reoffend no matter how many times you erase their personalities. Then there's the beings who have gone through a couple of wipes already, but still commit crimes due to circumstance. There's a limit to how many times personalities can be erased, and if another one would leave them mindless, they get sent here instead. And then there's Professor Pryce, who has managed to tie the legal system up for years in semantic and philosophical discussions.'

'There's no such thing as a genetic criminal,' the Doctor

growled, but Beltempest had fallen silent, brooding. 'And what about the second group?' he asked, trying to break through Beltempest's depression.

'Sorry? Oh, well there's those criminals who would be figureheads and foci for discontent if we let them back out into their own societies. Terrorists, primarily, although there's a fair number of discontented despots of one sort of another in here.' He mopped at his brow with his trunk. 'As you can appreciate, if the Empire takes over a planet against the wishes of the populace and after resistance from the rulers, we can't leave those rulers as a focus for bad feeling against us. Even if we wipe their minds and set them to work as street cleaners on Earth, they'll still be symbols of rebellion. No, the best thing to do is to incarcerate them here for the rest of their lives.'

The Doctor was speechless for a moment at the sheer inhumanity of the solution. 'Why not just kill them and get it over with?' he said eventually.

'We can't do that,' Beltempest said, missing the irony entirely. 'We're not barbarians, you know.'

The Doctor was still searching around for a reply when the guards stopped beside a metal door, no different from the rest apart from the number. One of them tapped out a security code on a keypad while another placed his forearm in the cavity of a biochip reader.

Beltempest took a deep, shuddering breath. 'There have been fifty-eight deaths here since Pryce arrived,' he said, his voice unsteady. 'Even though he's locked in a high security cell. They're listed as suicides in the official records, but nobody can explain how suicides could eat their own hearts.'

'Don't worry,' the Doctor said. 'We'll be safe.'

Beltempest nodded. 'And yea, though I walk through the valley of the shadow of death,' he quoted softly, 'I shall fear no evil.'

'That's all very well, but I doubt that Rhodd and his staff will do much comforting,' the Doctor said doubtfully, as the door slid slowly up into the ceiling.

The guards indicated that Beltempest and the Doctor

should enter the shadowed doorway. They did so, and the door dropped behind them so fast that the floor shook with the impact.

A cold, harsh light burst into life, illuminating a small room lined with the omnipresent damp white ceramic tiles and containing a bunk without a mattress and a rudimentary toilet.

And a naked man.

He stood a few feet from them, his eyes closed against the sudden glare. He was over seven feet tall, and painfully thin. His skull was hairless, his fingers long and thin. He looked like an animated skeleton.

Beltempest took an involuntary step back. The Doctor wondered whether he should join him, but there was something about the tiles on the walls that made him pause.

Of course. There was a barrier a few feet into the room. It was invisible, but there was a dry line on the tiles that marked its edges. Physical or energy? Almost certainly physical: probably transparicrete. The radiation from the sun even this far underground would mess up a force field to the point of uselessness.

One of the tiles on their side projected slightly from the wall, and the Doctor guessed the controls for the barrier were beneath it.

The Doctor looked back at the man, and this time he did take a step back. The man's eyelids were open, revealing matt-black eyes with no distinguishable pupil. An effect of the icaron radiation, or another example of genetic meddling? Whatever the reason, it was as if Pryce's eyes were just pits in his face, windows into the heart of a black hole. There was no feeling, no emotion, no character at all.

'Professor Zebulon Pryce?' asked the Doctor.

'I've been waiting for you,' Pryce said. His voice was oddly warm and comforting, like a favourite uncle.

'You knew we were coming?' the Doctor said.

'Of course. News filters through, even here. Even this

176

far from grace. When I heard your ship land, I knew it was you.'

The Doctor raised his eyebrows sceptically. There was no way a human could have heard the ship, not that far beneath the surface.

'Then you know why we're here,' he said.

The Professor slowly extended his hand towards the Doctor's face. His nails were almost as long as the fingers themselves.

'You want my help,' he said simply. 'You want my knowledge.'

'Very clever,' the Doctor said.

Pryce turned slowly towards Beltempest and took a step forwards.

'I don't believe we've been introduced,' he said, and extended his hand. Beltempest automatically reached out, then snatched his hand back, shuddering. Pryce smiled, and skittered his nails against the barrier, making a noise like a horde of cockroaches spilling down the walls. Beltempest flinched.

'Provost-Major Beltempest,' he said. 'I was ... I was one of the Landsknechte who arrested you on Dis.'

Pryce's dark eyes examined Beltempest from the top of his head to his large, circular feet.

'I remember Provost-Major Beltempest,' he said, frowning. 'You're not him.'

'Body-bepple,' Beltempest said, his voice trailing off as he looked away.

'No,' Pryce said, '*You* are not Provost-Major Beltempest. The you within the bepple.' He shrugged: a slow, almost balletic motion. 'Or perhaps you are. It doesn't matter. Memories escape in the darkness. I can hear them sometimes, laughing at me from the corners of this cell, breeding in the cracks in the walls.'

'They keep you in darkness?' The Doctor was scandalized.

'Only metaphorically. I don't believe we've met.'

'I am the Doctor.'

177

Pryce giggled. 'I don't need a doctor,' he said. 'There's nothing wrong with me.'

'I need your knowledge of icaron physics.'

Pryce frowned suddenly, and looked away. He wasn't completely hairless, the Doctor realized. A pure white pony-tail hung down his back like an electrical cable.

'There are some things,' Pryce whispered, 'that man was not meant to know. My mind has been opened to higher feelings, Doctor: the pure ethic of suffering, the clean absolution of death. The stunted subhumans that surrounded me didn't understand, of course. Transcendence is always stifled; prophets are never honoured in their own land. They could not see that I had been blessed by a vision of higher things. I tried to cleanse their minds with exquisite suffering, but they stopped me.'

His barren gaze swept across the Doctor and Beltempest.

'You want to know about icarons?' he said softly. 'But how much can you bear to understand?'

The figure in the darkened office was standing by the large blue box when the desk bleeped. It ran a hand lovingly over the box's surface: so rough to the eye, so smooth to the hand.

'Soon,' the figure said, 'soon I shall tease your secrets from you.'

It crossed to the desk and sat behind it, scanning the ceaseless flow of information. Ah! Yes, there! A fastline call placed from Earth to Purgatory, to Provost-Major Beltempest of the Imperial Landsknechte. Beltempest hadn't been present, so the message had been stored, awaiting his return. The figure passed a gloved hand across the sensitive surface of the desk, calling up the text of the transmission.

'Damn!'

Its hand slammed down on the translucent surface, sending ripples of disturbance across the information net. Certain blocks of shares were inadvertently sold for well below their face value, causing a handful of minor companies to go bankrupt and the economies of several distant planets to fluctuate alarmingly.

'Damn and blast!'

The figure considered for a moment. Things were slipping out of control. The fact that the Doctor's face had changed had been unexpected, but not completely beyond the realms of possibility. After all, had he not changed his own appearance? The voice, now ... that was unforgivable. He really should have anticipated that the Doctor's voice had also altered.

A deep breath, and a reconsideration. Was it such an avoidable mistake? After all, when the Doctor's marvellous travelling device had appeared on the walkway, the valet bot had been too far away to pick up his voice. The woman – Bernice – had spoken to the pursuer bot on the *Arachnae* when the figure was controlling it, so it had a record of her voice, but the Doctor ...

Hmm.

Time to bring this chapter to a close. Beltempest was unavailable – Landsknecht business, presumably – and so other methods would have to be employed. The figure's hands moved across the desk, placing a simcord call to the other end of the fastline transmission. An apartment somewhere in the local Overcity. Where the rats had gone to ground, so to speak.

Time to flush them out.

The null-grav lift deposited them in a cavernous flitterpark which took up the bottom five levels of a block some fifteen minutes by walkway from the apartment where Cwej's parents lived.

Looking around, Bernice was amazed how little multi-storey car parks had changed over the centuries. Call them what you liked, park whatever sort of vehicle you wanted in them, they were always drab, grey, urine-smelling affairs supported by stained pillars, flickering lights fitfully illuminating their depths, the sound of dripping water echoing through them. As an archaeological side visit on Earth back in the 1970s, while the Doctor had been trying to prevent the Vardan invasion, Bernice had visited one of the first of the species. Apart from the fact that the vehicles in this one floated a few feet above the ground, and the dates on the tax discs were different, she could have been back there again.

Near Ace.

Unwelcome memories tightened the back of her throat. Ace was gone. Like her or loathe her, and Bernice had done both in her time, she had left an Ace-shaped hole that would take a long time to fill. She supposed that the Doctor felt that way too, although typically he never showed it.

'So,' she said, her voice rebounding from the distant walls, 'what's the plan?'

'Whoever it was that simcorded told us to meet them here,' Forrester said. She had moved to one side, and her blaster was in her hand.

'And they didn't say who they were?' Cwej asked.

Forrester snapped, 'All they said was, if we wanted to know more about the murder of Waiting For Justice, we should meet them here. That's it. Nothing else. Zip. Zilch. *Nada. Echt.*'

'Okay, okay,' he protested, 'just checking.'

'I don't like the feel of this,' Bernice murmured. 'I've seen too many old films in the TARDIS cinema where the intrepid heroes are attacked in a car park.'

'What's a TARDIS?' Forrester asked.

'What's a car?' said Cwej.

Metal crunched on concrete.

The three froze, waiting for the noise to be repeated.

'Where did that come from?' Forrester hissed.

'Difficult to tell,' Cwej replied. 'The echoes – '

Again, the sound of concrete being ground beneath something metallic and heavy. Footsteps, getting louder.

A shape, moving in the shadows.

'It's a bot,' Cwej said.

'Be prepared,' Forrester said. 'Like Bernice, I've got a bad feeling.'

The bot walked into the light. It was tall and gangly, its

limbs like frozen mercury. There was some suggestion of concealed weaponry in its arms, and the sleek greyhound shape of its head barely concealed visual, IR, UV, kirlian and radar sensors.

Forrester frowned. She thought she'd seen all makes of bot in her time, but this one was new to her.

'Ever seen anything like that before?' she said to Cwej.

'New to me,' he said. 'Bernice?'

'Nope. But it's not designed to serve after-dinner mints, that's for sure.'

The bot's sensors moved to take in Forrester, Cwej and then Bernice.

'Three blind mice,' it said finally, it's plummy voice echoing and re-echoing through the flitterpark. 'See how they run.'

A shiver ran up Bernice's spine. There was something about that voice she recognized: not the sound, but the phrasing, the theatrical diction.

'Did you want to speak to us?' Forrester called out.

'No,' the bot said, sounding overly apologetic, and a trifle amused as well. 'I'm afraid that was just a ploy to lure you out of hiding.'

'Lure us out? Why?'

The bot's head searched Forrester out. Bernice could see the glint as it focused upon her.

'Because you have become an encumbrance. I had hoped that my various schemes to divert you would have worked, but you were more intelligent than I had given you credit for. A problem, but one easily solved. Please regard me as the farmer's wife, come to cut off your tails with a carving knife.'

It raised its arm gracefully.

'We've met before, haven't we?' Bernice shouted quickly, hoping to distract it.

'How very clever of you to remember,' it said.

'You were on the *Arachnae*. You were the purser bot.'

A chuckle, very unmechanical. 'I was indeed. The poor thing was so terribly confused to find half an hour missing from its memory, I believe it turned itself in for disassembly. I was also the valet who waved to you on the walkway when you arrived in your blue box, by the by. I am everywhere. I am everything.'

'And you've met the Doctor before, haven't you?'

A pause.

'Now that is *very* clever of you. How could you possibly know that?'

'Because the TARDIS went missing, and because you didn't get his voice right. You met him in a different body, didn't you?'

'Far too clever. I see I made the right decision.'

The bot swivelled quickly, targeting Bernice with its arms.

'As the sports commentators used to say when I was younger,' it said, 'it's goodnight, Vienna.'

It fired.

Chapter 10

'I'm Shythe Shahid and this is The Empire Today, *on the spot, on and off the Earth. Fighting has intensified on the planet Murtaugh. Rebel factions have taken control of the capital city, and the Imperial representative and his staff have been evacuated. Meanwhile, on Earth, five apartment towers are ablaze in the latest development in the Asian Undertown riots . . .'*

As soon as they boarded the *Moorglade*, Provost-Major Beltempest had locked himself in the control cabin. He had taken all of the weaponry on the ship with him, as well as the cutlery and anything else that had a sharp edge, and refused to come out.

'If anybody tries to get through that door between now and Purgatory,' he had said, 'I'll fry them until they're nothing more than a greasy blob on the floor. You can take your chances with Pryce, Doctor. I'm not letting him get to me. Oh, and Pryce? If you do anything to the Doctor, I'll depressurize the entire ship. Understand?'

To reinforce the point, he had taken all the spacesuits and evacuated the air from his cabin. The Doctor could picture him, sitting erect at the controls in his own personalized suit – the one that had been specially modified to take his paunch, his four arms and his trunk – screamer rifle in one hand and needler in the other, jumping at every noise.

'You're not human, are you?' Professor Zebulon Pryce asked as the engines wound themselves up for take-off. He had folded his tall, angular frame into a seat in the

183

ship's small lounge, still as naked as he had been in his cell. His milk-white pony-tail draped down the back of the chair. After a cursory glance around, he had shown no interest in his new surroundings. The Doctor couldn't fathom him out. Humans were usually so easy to understand, but Pryce ... a riddle wrapped in a mystery inside an enigma. The Doctor scratched his head. Now who had he said that to originally, and what about?

'No,' the Doctor admitted, settling himself into the Nauga-hide upholstery of a chair.

'Double circulatory system?'

The Doctor was impressed. 'Well spotted.'

Pryce's gaze was fixed on the Doctor's chest. 'I've had a lot of experience with hearts,' he said, then looked away, towards the sealed control cabin. 'Do I frighten Provost-Major Beltempest?'

'Of course you do,' the Doctor said, 'although, if you asked him, he would probably say that he was just being careful. Are you sure I can't get you some clothes?'

'No, thank you. I am ... accustomed to this state. Clothes would only irritate me now.' There was a flicker of genuine curiosity in Pryce's eyes. 'What is he frightened of?'

'He's frightened of dying,' the Doctor said in exasperation. 'You do have a reputation, you know.'

Pryce shrugged. 'He agreed to have me transferred into his custody,' he said. 'I didn't ask to be here, although the change of scenery is pleasant.'

'You said that you couldn't advise us on the icaron flux problem without access to the equipment in your old laboratory. He didn't want you back on Purgatory, and the prison authorities were very reluctant to release you, even temporarily, but I persevered. You should have seen the paperwork!'

Pryce gazed levelly up at the Doctor. 'Then he, and you, must think that the potential risk of my company is worth the possible benefit. That is your choice. I cannot be held responsible for what others think of me. I do what I must. We all do what we must.'

The temperature in the ship suddenly escalated. Tugging at his cravat, the Doctor supposed that the massive heat shield had been pulled back into its recess above them.

Scowling, he said, 'You cannot evade responsibility for your actions so easily.'

'I've never tried to evade responsibility,' Pryce replied, gazing at the Doctor with no expression in the black pits of his eyes. 'I killed people. Why should I evade that?'

'You don't think it was wrong?'

'No,' he said simply. 'I don't.'

The Doctor stood and busied himself in the small galley for a moment, making himself a cup of tea in a metal beaker. 'Can I get you anything?' he asked. 'A glass of wine, perhaps?'

'Thank you, but no. I don't drink ... wine.' As the Doctor re-entered the lounge, Pryce looked up at him. 'Do I frighten you?' he asked.

The Doctor hesitated, and sipped at his tea. He remembered a cave on Metebelis Three, and the way the radiation had sleeted through his body like rain through muslin.

'No,' he said. 'I have been frightened before, but I'm not frightened by you.'

Pryce smiled slightly. 'Good,' he said. 'But you are afraid of dying?'

Difficult questions. His mind flickered over a thousand human years of experience. For most Time Lords, death was nothing to worry about. Their minds were absorbed upon the moment of death into the APC, the Amplified Panatropic Computations Network that formed the repository of all Gallifreyan knowledge and experience, guiding the Time Lords in their philosophic enquiries and helping the President and the Celestial Intervention Agency decide upon their more mundane interferences in the affairs of the universe. The Doctor had lost that safety net when he fled his home world hundreds of years ago, and despite his subsequent elevation back to grace, his election as President of the Time Lords and his many adventures in the Matrix – the hinterland of the APC –

he had never bothered to formally connect his mind back to it. If he died – *when* he died – that would be it. No more Doctor.

A dark figure rose up before him in his thoughts: burning eyes raking him from beneath a black skull-cap. Perhaps there were some things worse than death.

And yet . . .

And yet he fought so hard against death's final embrace. He had endured agony, time and time again, rather than just lie down and give up. Sometimes, in his darkest moments, he suspected that more people died because of his interference than lived. But still he struggled. Still he fought.

'Yes,' he said, surprising himself. 'Yes, I *am* afraid of dying.'

He held that revelation up to the light and looked at it. Well, he thought, you learn something every day.

He drained his tea in one gulp and placed the metal beaker on a nearby table.

The ship lurched suddenly as Beltempest engaged the engines and took off from the pad. The environmental controls in the lounge were working flat out to combat the heat from Dis's sun. The Doctor imagined that he could sense it through the bulkhead: a malign, oppressive influence directly above their heads.

Perhaps Beltempest had the right idea, climbing into a spacesuit. At least he could filter out a lot of the heat that way.

'Death holds no fears for me,' Pryce said suddenly. 'She and I are on first name terms.' He reached out and picked the beaker off the table and started to turn it around in his hands.

'You said that you don't think it's wrong to kill people – or, at least, to have killed people,' the Doctor probed, peripherally aware that Pryce was displaying signs of nervous tension. 'Is that because you don't think that death is something to be frightened of?'

Pryce smiled. 'You are starting from the premise that murder is inherently wrong, and asking me to explain why

I feel differently,' he said. 'My position is that murder is right, and that it is your position that requires justification.'

'But you're the one...' The Doctor tailed off, unsure how far he could go in provoking Pryce.

'The one who was exposed to massive doses of icaron radiation?' Pryce finished the sentence for him. His hands still worked at the beaker. 'I dispute your allegation that icarons can drive people to psychosis – even if it is just those people who, like myself, have undergone the body-bepple process. I have seen no evidence, but even if you are right, I would argue that it merely opened my mind up to a larger truth: the inherent meaninglessness of moral systems.' He jerked his head slightly, and his pony-tail flicked up. 'I can see more clearly now.'

'But if I'm right about icaron radiation,' the Doctor said cautiously, 'you are the one who has been through an experience which could affect your thought processes adversely. You admit that?'

'Of course,' Pryce said easily. 'Have you never been in a situation which could have affected your thought processes adversely?'

Hanging onto Morbius's mind-bending equipment while his past lives were dragged from him, one by one... Letting the Zygons' bistronic radiation short-circuit through his body... Lying, squirming, while Davros's mind probe ripped his memories to shreds... Screaming soundlessly as Abaddon's tiny thought parasites worked their way through his neuronic pathways, burning as they went...

'Point taken,' he admitted. 'Nobody can argue from a privileged position.'

'Thank you. I repeat my question: why do you think that murder is wrong?'

The Doctor hesitated. This was a potential moral minefield. 'The state of being alive is intrinsically valuable,' he said eventually. 'And nobody has the right to take that away.'

'You disappoint me.' Pryce leaned back in his seat. He wasn't even sweating in the heat. 'That isn't an argument at all. You are merely saying that there is some value in what is being taken away. That fails to explain why taking it away is wrong.'

His hairless brows drew together, creating furrows in his broad forehead. He was holding something in his hand: something that had not been there before. The Doctor gazed down at it in surprise and dawning horror. Somehow, Pryce had managed to twist the metal of the beaker into a sharp-edged weapon.

'If you can't do better than that,' he said, 'I'm going to have to remove your eyes.'

The blast spread fire across the plasticrete where Bernice had been standing. She had instinctively dived to one side, feeling the hairs on the back of her neck shrivel in the heat. Gravel gouged at her skin as she hit the ground rolling sideways. The energy beam followed her, searing the plasticrete, spraying small splinters in all directions. Bernice felt them cut her face and neck as she kept rolling, trying to stay ahead of the ray.

Cwej dropped to a crouching position and fired. The beam from his blaster splashed harmlessly against the robot's burnished skin and reflected off in a distorted fountain of energy, blistering a nearby pillar. The bot didn't even seem to notice.

'It's armoured,' he yelled. 'That's unfair.' He shifted fire to the bot's body, concentrating on its joints, but that strategy was equally useless.

'No good,' Forrester shouted, scuttling into the cover of a pillar. 'Must be one of those assassin models the big corporations are supposed to use.'

'I thought they were outlawed?' Cwej exclaimed, holding fire for a moment.

'They are. Do you want to tell it or shall I?'

Bernice had rolled over and over until she was underneath a flitter. Her heart was pumping so fast she thought it would burst and there was blood in her eyes from multiple cuts on her forehead. The exposed flesh of her forearms and legs stung. Panic was a dead, cold weight in her chest. She knew that if that beam touched the flitter and ignited the atomic batteries, she'd be cooked like a lobster.

She scrambled to the other side of the flitter, preparing to make a dash for it but knowing that she would be cut down before she had taken three steps.

'Concentrate fire on the head!' Forrester cried, pumping off shots that missed the silver figure completely but blasted chunks of plasticrete loose from the ceiling. Bernice wondered for a brief, hysterical moment how Forrester had ever made it through Adjudicator training with an aim like that. Several chunks dropped on the bot's arm, knocking its aim off. The beam shot into the darkness and the bot's head swung around, its multi-sensored muzzle seeking out the source of the annoyance.

'How tiresome.' The strangely mellow, sardonic voice of the bot echoed around the flitterpark. It raised both of its lower arms and aimed them at Forrester. 'The Doctor's friends always were notoriously difficult to kill.'

The Doctor's friends. Bernice filed that one away for later consideration.

More metallic footsteps, like a metronome off in the shadows. Glinting highlights as the dim, scattered lights reflected off smooth metal.

Two more bots walked out of the darkness to flank the first.

'Fortunately,' said the one on the left in the same, relaxed voice, 'I've always preferred my own company . . .'

'. . . to that of anybody else,' the one on the right finished.

All three raised their gun arms simultaneously, each aiming at a different target. Two of them acquired Forrester and Bernice instantly. The third hesitated, trying to locate Cwej and failing. Bernice glanced around, but she couldn't find him. He'd obviously made a run for it – sensible man.

'Well,' Bernice sighed, 'it's been fun.'

'No it hasn't,' Forrester snarled, 'it's been a bitch.'

A gravimetric motor roared into life in the depths of

the flitterpark. Forrester and Bernice peered into the darkness, trying to locate the source, but failed.

'Cwej?' Forrester yelled. 'Is that you?'

The only answer was the sudden overload of the motor as the mag-brakes were abruptly taken off line.

'Cwej! What the hell are you doing?'

Something flashed out of the darkness towards the robots, something large and blunt: a flitter, cranked up to well over the recommended speed. Two of the bots tried to leap out of the way while the third attempted to fire, but the flitter struck all three before they could move, scattering them like ninepins. Metallic arms and legs flew off in all directions, trailing fibre-optic strands behind them. Lubricant splashed like black blood across the plasticrete.

'Way to go!' Forrester crowed, jumping up and punching the air with her fist. 'Score one to the kid.'

'The wall!' Bernice shouted, but it was too late. The pilot, a dark shadow through the flitter's canopy, tried to spin the vehicle around before it hit the approaching far wall of the flitterpark, but he was still travelling too fast. The flitter overturned and rolled. Bernice could just make out Cwej's silhouette fighting the controls, but he didn't have time.

The flitter hit the wall and exploded.

A wall of flame washed across the ground towards them. Bernice threw herself behind a pillar, but Forrester just covered her eyes and ran into the pall of greasy black smoke that erupted behind the fire. Cursing, Bernice followed.

The flitter was a blackened skeleton with a blazing heart when they got to it, and the heat was so fierce that Bernice could feel her skin blistering. Nobody could have survived the inferno. Nobody.

She had to drag Forrester away. Her face was contorted into a snarl of rage, and she struggled with Bernice, trying to get back to the burning vehicle.

'Don't be a fool!' Bernice yelled. 'You can't help him now!'

'I'm not losing another partner,' Forrester spat, 'I'm *not* losing another partner. Not now. Not like this.'

'Forrester, we need to get out of here. That explosion will bring everybody and their aunt Ada running.'

Forrester shook her head. 'I'm not leaving.'

'What?'

'You heard.' She took a deep breath. 'They've won. They've beaten us. We can't crack the conspiracy now, not with Chris gone.'

'Don't be stupid. We can – '

'We can't. I just don't care enough. Chris cared. He was the idealist. I'm just an old, tired woman, and I'm giving up.'

Blackened wreckage shifted a few feet away, and something tried to speak. Bernice's first thought was that it was the smashed remnants of one of the robots, still trying to kill them. She was just glancing around for something to use as a weapon when Forrester pushed her to the ground and went for her blaster.

'Help . . . me . . .' a voice whispered, full of pain.

Forrester's finger paused over the trigger. Her eyes were wide, disbelieving.

'Chris?' she cried.

Within moments, they were both crouching beside Cwej's body. His skin was blackened and cracked, revealing weeping red flesh beneath, and most of his fur had been burned off. One ear was missing.

'You stupid fool,' Forrester growled. Bernice glanced up at her, surprised by the vehemence of her reaction, and looked away again just as quickly. Tears were streaming down Forrester's face. 'I'm not losing another partner.' The Adjudicator repeated the words like a mantra. 'Whatever plans you might have had about dying, you'd better cancel them.'

'If you insist,' Cwej whispered.

'What happened?' Bernice asked. 'Can you talk about it?'

'Couldn't get the canopy open,' he murmured. His lips were bleeding. 'Saw the wall coming up. Managed to get

191

the emergency release to – ' He broke off, coughing. Forrester held his head tenderly. ' – got the release to work and jumped free. Got caught in the blast.' He tried to smile. The cracks in his lips opened wider, and the trickles of blood increased. 'Used to try that sort of . . . of stunt back in traffic control. Forgot I wasn't flying an Adjudication flitter. No stability, these civilian models.'

'For Goddess' sake, don't try to talk, you moron,' Forrester snapped.

'What happened to the bots?' he asked urgently.

'You got 'em,' she confirmed.

'Good,' he whispered, closing his eyes. 'Wouldn't want anything to happen to y . . .'

His voice trailed off into silence.

'Is he . . .?' Forrester's eyes were locked on Bernice's, as if she didn't dare look down at her squire.

Bernice quickly checked him over. 'No,' she said finally, 'but we need to get him to a medic, and quickly.'

Forrester bit her lip. 'We can't risk staying in the Overcity,' she said. 'It's too dangerous. We've got to go down into the Undertown. It's our only chance!'

'If that's our only chance,' Bernice said quietly, 'then we're in a pretty sorry state.'

The knife flashed in the half-light of Daph Yilli Gar's cell. A line of pain seared across his flesh.

'An old-fashioned device,' a human voice said, 'but then, I am an old-fashioned man. You may find this difficult to believe, but I am over a thousand years old.'

Flash. His scream tore at his throat as the tip of the blade drew a fiery line along his strapped-down tail, just above the point where they had burned the number in. It wasn't just the pain that made his mind squirm, it was the knowledge that there was another living creature near him and he could do nothing about it.

'I remember when there were no aliens . . .'

Flash. Great explosions of agony bloomed in his mind.

'. . . no Empires . . .'

Flash. There wasn't an inch of his skin that wasn't slicked

192

in blue blood. He tried to push the pain away, pretend that it was all happening to someone else, a long way away, but the human was too good. Too skilful with the sharp blade.

'... nothing but money, and pain. It's comforting to know that some things never change, isn't it? Now, shall we have another go at those questions?'

Daph Yilli Gar tried to nod, but the blessed green light spread like a salve across his body and he was elsewhere, another time, another memory.

'Okay,' the Doctor said hurriedly, 'I will admit that killing is sometimes justified. I've killed – I've been responsible for – the deaths of intelligent beings before. I regret that, but it was necessary.'

Pryce leaned forward, his bottomless eyes wide. 'How did you kill them?'

Sweat trickled down the Doctor's nose. 'Later, perhaps. The important thing is, I ... they died in order to save others.'

'What gave you the right to make that decision?'

Pulling the silk handkerchief from his jacket pocket, the Doctor mopped at his brow. He could say, 'The White Guardian,' but that wasn't a real answer. The Doctor hadn't realized that the Guardians were interested in him for a long while, and even then the White Guardian had been very careful not to actually condone what the Doctor did. He – it – just took advantage of it.

'I ... I suppose nobody did. I repeatedly found myself in the right position at the right time to make a difference. I balanced up the eventual outcomes, and decided that the death of one person, or a handful of people, was worth it if it kept more people alive.'

'In your opinion.'

'Yes. In my opinion.' He removed his jacket. Pryce's face seemed to shimmer in the heat. 'Backed up with experience.'

'But you didn't actually know, did you? You were just guessing. You might have been wrong.'

In his mind he was suddenly standing in a rubble-strewn

corridor, deep beneath the surface of Skaro. He held two wires in his hand, half an inch apart. *'Just touch these two strands together and the Daleks are finished. Have I that right? Some things might be better with the Daleks. Many future worlds will become allies just because of their fear...'*

'Do I have the right?'

'Yes,' the Doctor whispered into the silence of a million accusing ghosts, 'I might have been wrong.'

'And if I kill you now,' Pryce continued, fingering his impromptu blade, 'then all those people whose deaths you will go on to be responsible for will live. If the total number of people whose deaths you will cause outweighs the number whose lives you will save, does that mean that I have the right to kill you here and now?' His fingernails were making small scratching sounds on the plastic seat cover. 'By your logic, it does.'

He didn't appear to be sweating at all; the dome of his bald head was completely dry, even though the Doctor's silk shirt was wet against his skin.

'Everybody dies eventually.' Pryce's voice was hypnotically persuasive. 'What does it matter if I shorten their lives that little bit further? What do I rob them of? What do I rob you of if I kill you now?'

'But by shortening – ' The Doctor coughed to clear his throat. ' – by shortening somebody's life, you rob them of enjoyment, fun, and the pursuit of worthwhile activities.'

'Or the grief of bereavement, the pain of terminal illness, the misery and horror of war. Who are you to prejudge what might befall them?'

'I don't *know*!' the Doctor shouted suddenly, clenching his hands so tight that his fingernails dug into his palms. 'I don't *know*! Killing is wrong except when it's right, and I know the difference. That's all I can say. That's the only answer I can give.'

He raised his hands up in front of his face. Blood welled up into the crescents left by his fingernails and trickled down his palms.

'Yes,' Pryce murmured, leaning back in his seat. 'That's

the only answer I could give when they put me on trial. I hope it helps you more than it helped me.'

They entered hyperspace in silence.

Sandri Farrance woke with blood matting her hair and sticking her eyelids together. There was noise all around, shouting and screaming, and the acrid smell of pacifier gas was mingled with the stench of cooked flesh. She tried to open her eyes, but had to stop when a sickening spike of pain lanced through her skull.

Still, at least she was still alive. That was something. Wasn't it?

Eventually she forced her eyes open, wincing at the pain. The sun cast long shadows across the grassy parklands on top of the towers of Spaceport Nine Overcity. The riot appeared to have moved on past her. She listened for a moment, but couldn't hear anyone nearby. Taking a deliberate risk, she rolled over.

Flashes of light on top of the next tower suggested that the riot was still going on there but, in the distance, the harsh shapes of Adjudication flitters appeared to be retreating towards her through columns of smoke. The tide had obviously turned at least once since she had been hit.

She ran a hand across her scalp gingerly. It came away covered in sticky clots of blood. She hadn't been unconscious long, then. Looking around her immediate vicinity she couldn't see any of her comrades, although four underdwellers and a handful of Adjudicators lay contorted in death.

She looked back at the distant battle. The flitters were swooping low now, preparing to re-enter the fray. Squinting against the sun and the pain in her head, she thought she could make out helmeted and uniformed figures retreating back towards her across the bridges that linked the tower tops, firing backwards as they came.

Farrance glanced at the nearest Adjudicator. The man was still breathing, despite a massive wound in his neck. It was Gallion, her squire. She would have recognized his red hair anywhere. She crawled over to him, wondering if there was anything she could do to ease his pain.

'Gallion, it's Farrance, can you hear me?' She bent over him. His eyes opened, blearily focusing on her.

'Farra? Goddess, but it hurts.'

'Lie quiet,' she said. 'I'll call for help.'

She didn't even see his arm as he brought it up towards the back of her neck, and the touch of the knife was just a cold breath upon her skin. It was only the spreading warmth of her blood inside her body armour that attracted her attention.

It was the last thing she felt, apart from the cold hardness of his armour as she fell across him.

Daph Yilli Gar didn't even have enough energy to extrude his eye-stalks when the cell door hissed open. They had finally come for him, and he was ready. Past ready. He longed for the blessed amnesia of death, the deep and dreamless sleep which was all that could erase the humiliation he had been forced through.

'Daph!'

A familiar voice. He raised one eye-stalk a few inches and managed to rotate it. What he saw brought him to his basal foot despite the pain that throbbed through his body with the beating of his nodes.

'You traitor!' he hissed.

Vap Oppat Pol was standing just inside the cell door, holding a box with rough holes punched in the lid.

'Call me all the names you wish,' Vap said. 'Pull my eye-stalks out by the roots. Tear my shell from my tail. You cannot do worse than I would do myself. My shame could obliterate an entire Guild of sacrificial scapegoats.'

'Why?' Daph shook his head in disgust. 'Can you tell me? Do you know why you betrayed your own race?'

Vap Oppat Pol shrugged: a long shudder that ran the length of his body. 'Money, my friend. What else is there?'

'You did this for money!'

'We were losing the war. The Skel'Ske would have staved off the inevitable for a month, perhaps two. We would have

196

been wiped out. Hithis was lost, whatever I did.' Vap Oppat Pol looked away. 'I wanted to survive, so I offered the humans a deal. What was wrong with that?'

'And now? Have you come to watch me bleed for them too? Isn't the knowledge that you have betrayed Hithis enough?'

Vap glanced around, furtively. 'I've been betrayed too!'

'Really?' Daph ladled his voice with irony, but Vap didn't seem to notice.

'Yes! I overheard a conversation. They've just been stringing me along. They have no intention of paying me at all. They're going to torture me!'

'How terrible.' This time, even the thick-skinned Vap must have realized that he wasn't being taken seriously.

'I'm getting out,' he said. 'I've booked passage on a ship leaving Earth with the little money that they did pay me. I'll make a new life for myself, somewhere out in the galaxy. There's a planet named Oolis I've heard about. I could make a life there.'

Hope washed through Daph's body, washing away the pain and the weakness.

'And me . . . ?' he whispered, hardly daring to hope.

Vap Oppat Pol handed him the box.

'There's an electronic key here that will open all the doors between here and freedom, and a map of how to get from here to the Undertown. You'll be safe there.'

'I can't stay on Earth!' he said, shocked. 'They'll spot me instantly. I'm a Hith! We're at war!'

Vap shook his head sadly.

'The war's over, my friend,' he said. 'They don't like us, but they tolerate us.' He laughed mirthlessly. 'Humans are magnanimous in victory. They can afford to be.'

'Does that mean . . . I can go home? To Hithis?'

Vap Oppat Pol opened his mouth to answer, but his skin flushed grey with shame and he turned away.

'Good luck,' he said, and slithered towards the door. Before he reached it, he turned his eye-stalks to say: 'Three last things. Firstly, I've rescued the control nexus and put it in the box with the key and the map. They can't operate *the* Skel'Ske *properly without it. Keep it safe. Secondly, if I'm ever back on Earth, I'll leave a message for you written on the wall outside the Spaceport Five Off-world Zoo. Remember that: the Spaceport Five Off-world Zoo. Thirdly, I'm changing my name. Word has gone out that all Hith must do the same, to remind the humans of what they have done to us. I am going to call myself Homeless Forsaken Betrayed And Alone, because I am. If you ever need me, that's the name I'll be living under on Oolis.'*

He slithered away, leaving nothing behind him but bad memories and a box. Daph's pseudo-limb hovered indecisively over its lid before reaching out to flip it open. He gasped, and flinched as . . . the time tank hissed open and Dantalion's soggy face loomed over him.

'Powerless Friendless,' he said, 'my friend, how do you feel? Hold nothing back, describe every ache and every pain.'

'I . . .' He paused, thinking. So much information. So many memories. He extruded a fine pseudo-limb and traced the pattern of scars along his side, remembering every cut, every burn, every last inch of pain.

How stupid could he have been? All that time spent hiding down in the Undertown. All that money so carefully saved up so that Dantalion could rip out the memories of his humiliation like human dentists would remove a rotten tooth. All for nothing. Time and time again he'd busked outside the Spaceport Five Off-world Zoo, not knowing what residual memory drove him there. Time and time again he had crept into the INITEC building through the unlatched window in the lower level to clean himself, not knowing that it was from there that he had escaped in the first place. He had a score to settle. Oh yes, by the Gods of Hithis, he had a score to settle.

'My name isn't Powerless Friendless,' he said quietly. 'It's . . .' The knowledge welled up within him: familiar, yet new. 'It's Daph Yilli Gar!'

Dantalion nodded, unsurprised.

'I will have to ask you to remain quiescent for the nonce, whilst I perform numerous but painless checks

198

upon your newly restored psyche. However, I would be interested to ascertain what your intentions might be once you leave my humble abode?'

Powerless Friendless lay back, settling into his personality as he might slip on an old but much loved tunic.

'I have some unfinished business,' he said.

While Bernice tried to make Cwej more comfortable, Forrester hot-wired another flitter. Bernice could see she didn't have Cwej's skill at it, managing to lock the security systems on five of them before she hit on the right combination of wires, keys and brute force. The canopy on a dark grey company rental model sprang open.

'Come on,' she said eventually, 'let's get him in.'

Finding an area of unburned skin to pick Cwej up by was almost impossible. In the end Bernice slid her hands under his shoulders and Forrester grasped his half-melted boots. He groaned. His skin was feverishly hot and sticky, and smelled of roast pork. Bernice felt her stomach churn.

'Do you have any destination in mind?' she asked as they manoeuvred Cwej across to the flitter's open door, 'or are we just winging it from here?'

'There's a medic down in the Undertown. Dantalion's his name. He's an alien: a Birastrop. I've pulled him in on umpteen occasions for unauthorized brainwipes and unlicensed beppling, but he's under the wing of one of the crime lords so there's always plenty of witnesses to say he was somewhere other than where we say he was. He used to be Surgeon Imperialis, so the rumour goes, despite the fact that the Empress hates aliens. The rumours don't say why he's down here now. He's a juke addict, but he's good.'

They laid Cwej down in the back of the vehicle, accidentally smearing the covers with blood and flakes of burned skin.

'And we're going to him?'

'You have a better idea?'

'Loads,' Bernice muttered to herself, 'but this is your century.'

199

Forrester took the flitter up on a spiral path that would bring them out of the upper entrances. Daylight streamed in like the beam of a searchlight. Bernice shut her eyes against the glare, suddenly realizing how tired she was. She couldn't remember the last time she'd slept; even on the Imperial shuttle to Earth she had lain awake, staring at the ceiling, worrying about being separated from the Doctor and the TARDIS. The moment when she knew things were getting on top of her was when she realized she was missing Ace.

Whose stupid idea had it been to come to Earth in this era in the first place?

Oh yeah. Hers.

The flitter emerged into a rainstorm at the bottom of an immense inverted cone. Clouds diffused the sunlight into a pearly glow. Forrester angled their path to hug the block's sides as they headed downwards. Within moments they were clear of the block and heading down towards the darkness, the canals, bridges, old buildings and perpetual rain of the Undertown.

Forrester took them down as fast as she could, plummeting like a hawk after a mouse until she was barely ten metres from the surface of the canal. Just as Bernice was about to suggest that it might be a good idea if they levelled out *NOW!* thank you very much, she pulled them out of the dive and screamed left into an alley perpendicular to the one that they had been heading for.

'Should shake off anybody watching,' she shouted over her shoulder.

'Fooled me,' Bernice yelled back, 'and I was sitting here.'

The walls of the alleyway were buildings that Bernice dated to the late twenty-first century. It was a shame her first close-up view of the Undertown was under circumstances where she couldn't really stop to sightsee. A domed church that must have been seventeenth-century at the latest flashed past, followed by a stretch of transparicrete webbed with fine cracks. This place was an architectural archaeologist's vision of heaven.

'How's Chr– Cwej?'

Bernice forced herself to look down. His exposed skin was blistering almost as she watched, and the cracked areas were weeping a clear fluid. She didn't dare remove any of the ragged remnants of his robes or armour – they looked as if they'd melted into his flesh.

'I've seen worse,' she replied, and then, quieter, 'but not recently.'

'Not long now.'

The flitter was skimming so close to the surface of the water that it was throwing up arcs of silver spray. Privately Bernice wondered if that wasn't likely to draw attention to them, but Forrester seemed to know what she was doing. Of course, the Doctor always seemed to know what he was doing, but Bernice knew how deceptive that was.

The flitter slowed, settling onto the water. Forrester coasted up to a metal jetty that projected out from a brick walkway beneath an arched bridge. She opened the canopy. Keeping the engine running, she said, 'Quick, pull him out. I want to set this thing going as fast as possible.'

'Look, he's inju– '

'I know what he is, but if you don't get him out fast then we'll all be dead. Would that improve his condition?'

'It couldn't make it much worse,' Bernice muttered as she carefully lifted Cwej onto the jetty. Forrester ran her hands quickly over the controls, then leaped out to join Bernice.

'That should help,' she said as the flitter's engines roared, and it rose steadily into the sky. 'I've set it on a random flight plan. With luck, nobody will ever be able to track us back here.'

'Where's this Dantalion then?'

Forrester glanced around, orienting herself, and then pointed to a small side alley.

'Right now? Down there.'

Beltempest dreamed.

After entering the unreal realm of hyperspace and setting the controls to automatic, he had darkened the visor of his spacesuit and turned off the external audio sensors. The flickering lights, the little noises, they had all been bothering him. He'd lost count of the number of times he had whirled around, screamer rifle at the ready, just knowing that Pryce was behind him, long fingernails extended towards his eyes. Twice he had only just managed to stop himself blasting a hole in the door. He kept telling himself how stupid he was being – there was no way that Pryce could get through the bulkhead to him – but it did no good. He was so much on edge he was becoming a safety hazard.

Eventually he had realized that the only answer was to turn off every source of disturbance, and drift. Meditate. Relax.

For a while, as he sat listening to the rasp of his breathing and the intermittent beep of the life-support system, he had imagined he could hear a faint giggling in the distance, or feel thuds and crashes transmitted through the bulkhead as Pryce dismembered the Doctor, but gradually his fingers had relaxed their grip on the guns, and his mind had let go.

And he dreamed of a time before his name was Beltempest.

Sunset was a crimson slash across the soft underbelly of the clouds as he approached the cliff-faced rear of the laboratory.

'Ready?' he snapped.

'Ready, sir,' the under-sergeant said behind him. He turned. The troops were already in attack formation, spread out across the albino lawn with their weapons at the ready. Stunners only, of course. They wanted the professor alive.

He checked his chronometer. Perfect timing. The captain should be on the simcord to Pryce, keeping him occupied while the Landsknechte went in through the back. He didn't like sneaking around, but nobody knew what sort of weaponry Pryce had been working on in there.

'Okay, let's go.'

He had the only destructive weapon: an industrial blaster with a beam focus point six feet from the barrel. Quickly he made four precise cuts in the shape of a door. The adamantium wall glowed, and a rectangular section fell, towards him. Two Landsknechte ran in to catch it before it hit the lawn. A third took the blaster.

He led the way into the darkened building.

That was a mistake.

His bepple-enhanced infrared vision scanned the darkness, picking out hot spots. Human-shaped hot spots. He unholstered his stunner, but they weren't moving. There was something odd about them; they looked like bundles of spaghetti wrapped around narrow, rigid tubes. Moving closer, he switched his flashlight on.

Blood pumped through sagging arteries that were draped around human skeletons. Black nerve fibres like spiders' webs enveloped the bodies. Eyeballs rolled in soundless agony.

He didn't hear the sound of the stunners behind him, or realize until much, much later quite how close Professor Zebulon Pryce and his vibroknife had got to the back of his neck. All he did was scream as he realized what Professor Zebulon Pryce had done to his friends. And scream. And...

... Screaming an alert signal into his ear. Beltempest jerked awake, flailing his four arms for a moment, dropping his guns all over the floor. He whirled, expecting Pryce to be standing behind him, but the cabin was empty. The alarm shrilled on. His eyes scanned the controls, desperately searching for the problem. Life-support okay. Power levels okay. Hyperspace engines ... off line.

He raised his eyes to the simcord screen, dreading what he would find.

Black space, and stars.

They had left hyperspace.

And directly in front of them sat an old, battered warship of very alien design.

Beltempest flicked on the switch that patched him into the ship's communications net. 'Doctor?' he said. 'Prepare yourself. We have guests.'

Chapter 11

'—ease do not adjust your receiver. Normal service will be resumed as soon as possible. Please do not adjust your receiver. Normal service will be resumed as soon as possible. Please do not adj—'

Dantalion's lair was a sixteenth-century church sandwiched between two late twenty-seventh-century oxygen factories. Forrester didn't bother knocking. Instead she just kicked the rotting wooden door in. Or, at least, she tried to kick the rotting wooden door in. The door stayed where it was, while she rebounded, swearing.

Bernice watched with something between amusement and concern.

'Adamantium core,' Forrester gasped between curses. Her leg felt like it was on fire. 'He must have had it installed since the last time I was here.'

'Indeed I have, fair maiden,' a drink-slurred voice boomed at them from a hidden speaker. 'Indeed I have. These premises suffer from an infestation of Adjudicators in much the same way that other places have rats or ber hounds. Much as I enjoy watching the little creatures frolic and gambol, it does tend to be bad for business, and so I have, albeit reluctantly, been forced to take measures to prevent them from gaining access. The entire building is now sheathed in a substance that, I am assured by those in the know, will repel anything short of an attack by an Imperial Landsknechte frigate.'

'Does he always talk like that?' Bernice asked. She was

crouched over Cwej's body, trying to protect his extensive wounds from the ever-present rain.

'Only when he's drunk,' Forrester replied.

'How often is that?'

'Put it this way: I've never seen him sober.'

'An unfair slur,' the voice protested. 'I am not drunk. Merely affable. Congenial. Cordial, if you will.'

'As a newt,' Bernice murmured. 'Look, Forrester, we really need to get Cwej seen to. I'm not sure how much longer he can last.'

'Yeah, tell me about it,' Forrester growled as she surveyed the crumbling brickwork of Dantalion's domain. Now that she was looking closer, she could make out the signs of recent modification. The outer walls of the church looked like they had been stripped off and then reattached to the central adamantium box. Dantalion was right: she couldn't get in there with brute force and bludgeon him into treating Cwej. Only tact and diplomacy could save him now.

And she was honest enough to know that those weren't exactly her strong suits. 'Dantalion,' she began. 'I know we've never exactly seen eye to eye . . .'

'I seem to remember,' he said, 'that the last time we met, the last thing my eye saw was your fist.'

'That's because . . .' She took a deep breath. 'Dantalion, despite our . . . differences of opinion in the past, I need . . .' There was a lump in her throat. She swallowed it, and continued in a quieter voice. 'I need a favour.'

'Medical?'

'Of course,' she snapped, her patience almost worn out. 'If I wanted my apartment redesigned I'd have gone to a professional.'

Dantalion didn't answer for a while. When he did, he sounded a lot more reflective and a lot less drunk. 'It won't be the first time,' he said.

Forrester wondered what he meant by that. As far as she knew, their relationship had consisted entirely of her kicking in his door and arresting him, and him protesting about it and evading the charge. She shrugged. Who could tell what a juke-sodden alien meant by anything?

'I can pay,' she said.

'We'll sort that out later. For the moment, bring the patient in.'

With a click, the door swung open. Light spilled out around the edges. Forrester pushed it fully ajar, then helped Bernice with Cwej's unresisting body. His breath was coming in short gasps now, and his eyes were rolling wildly beneath closed lids. Forrester had seen plenty of death in her time, and Cwej looked about as close to it as anybody she'd ever seen. Something squirmed inside her, close to her heart. He couldn't die. Not Cwej. He was too young, too innocent.

An alien claw, slicing up into Fenn Martle's chest. His face as he looked down, surprise and confusion in his eyes. His mouth open, calling her name. The blood. The blood spilling down his chin and chest...

Down? But the claw had entered his back, hadn't it? She remembered...

Don't think about it, Roz. Just don't.

The door shut behind them. They were in the vestry; old stones with rounded corners and pillars formed arches above their heads. Dantalion had obviously decided to retain the inside as well as the outside.

Dantalion appeared in the doorway. He had put on weight since Forrester had last seen him, and the corrugations in his face had become more pronounced. Scuttling over to Cwej, he briefly examined him, running both sets of arms over his body and clucking in disapproval at what he found.

'Touch and go,' he murmured, the diagnostic tools in his cybernetic eye whirring as they extended themselves towards Cwej's body. 'His only chance is a time tank. Take him through into the narthex, and I'll deal with him there.'

'The what?'

'The big room through that door. Oh, and put your weapons in the font. Don't worry, it's dry.'

Forrester shrugged. If he wanted her blaster, he'd have

to prise it from her cold, dead fingers. Or ask politely. One or the other.

Forrester and Bernice half carried, half dragged Cwej through into the main body of the church. Buttressed arches soared above their heads, and the diffuse light from the stained glass windows – reinforced to blast-resistant standards, Forrester assumed – cast rainbows across the flagstones. Detouring around various items of medical equipment scattered across the floor, Dantalion led them to a number of large, black, coffin-like boxes from which pipes led away to three rounded machines squatting in a corner. Dantalion activated a control and the lid of the nearest coffin swung upwards.

'Place him in the receptacle,' he ordered.

They complied. The Birastrop lowered the lid and turned his attention to the other machines, caressing their controls and murmuring to them.

'Does he know what he's doing?' Bernice whispered.

'Better than we do,' Forrester replied.

Bright green light flooded out of the seams and interstices of the time tank. Forrester hated to think how bright it must be inside.

Beside her, Bernice was still worrying. 'How much is this likely to cost?'

Forrester shrugged. 'No idea.'

'Can we afford it?'

'Look, we'll rob a bank if we have to.'

Bernice raised her eyebrows. 'What's with this "we"?' she asked. Forrester was just about to explode when she noticed that Bernice was smiling.

'The slings and arrows of outrageous fortune have not quite penetrated the young man's thick hide,' Dantalion said, turning to them. The tools in his eyes were retracting like disturbed sea anemones. 'The burns are extensive, but not life-threatening in themselves. Shock is always the killer, of course. The tank will sustain his life functions, anaesthetize him, feed him, coddle him, comfort him and speed up the time that passes over his skin so that his burns heal more rapidly. We'll take him out in about an hour. Until then, we have things to discuss.'

He turned and walked away. Bernice watched him go.

'Bit more businesslike when he's working, isn't he?'

'Don't underestimate him. Stoned or sober, Dantalion is a force to be reckoned with.'

'A being after my own heart.'

'Don't say that,' Forrester cautioned. 'There've been rumours about illegal organ-trafficking in the Undertown for years.'

They followed Dantalion out of the church proper and into a side room that was lined with velvet curtains. Dantalion plumped himself into a chair of alien design and gestured them towards a rough pew. Forrester noted Bernice's quick appraisal.

'Genuine,' Bernice said appreciatively. 'Like the rest of the church.'

'St James Garlikhythe,' Dantalion said. 'Such poetry in the names you humans give to your places of worship. This building – or rather, the shell of this building – is over one and a half thousand Earth years in age. That's older than me!' He giggled, then, just as quickly, became serious again. 'And so to the sordid question of recompense.'

Forrester decided to forestall the hours of delicate negotiation that she could see looming on the horizon.

'We can pay whenever you ask,' she said.

Dantalion sighed.

'You will never make a good businesswoman,' he said. 'Just as you never made a good Adjudicator. Always too willing to hit when a hint might succeed. But no matter. I do not require your money. There are more important things you can give me.'

'Such as?' Forrester was wary.

'Two things I require of you. Just two. Merely two.'

'Such as?'

Unruffled, he continued: 'Firstly, information. Two Adjudicators, one of them badly injured, both of them on the run, correct?'

She hesitated, wondering how much information she could afford to give him. How much did he already know?

'Correct,' she said reluctantly.

'And they were running from an attack in a flitterpark in the Spaceport Five Overcity, above our heads, yes? An attack carried out by robots of unusual design?'

'Word travels fast.'

'And they cannot ask for help from the Order of Adjudicators. Why is that, I ask myself?'

Forrester looked helplessly at Bernice, who just shrugged. Thanks a lot, Forrester thought.

'Let me help,' Dantalion continued. 'Could it be because they believe that the Order of Adjudicators is itself implicated?'

Forrester just nodded mutely.

'The Adjudication service. Always so aloof. So secretive. So proud of its impartiality.' Dantalion took a sip at an oddly shaped glass of cloudy liquid. Forrester caught the sharp tang of juke. If he kept drinking that stuff, he would rot away from the inside, smiling all the time.

'And all this,' he continued, 'all *this* ... is because the two Adjudicators in question did not believe the "official" verdict that an old human female called Annie Falvoriss killed an old Hith male named Waiting for Justice?'

'You've got excellent sources.'

'Your warden – Lubineki, I believe his name is – in the Spaceport Five Undertown Lodge. An excellent man who commands my admiration in great quantities. And so inexpensive.'

Forrester felt a cold hand clutch at her guts. Was there a straight Adjudicator anywhere apart from her and Cwej?

'Waiting for Justice and Annie,' he mused. 'They were friends of mine. I don't make friends easily, you may be shocked to learn. Many people will not associate with an "alien", and those enlightened ones who will don't particularly like juke-drinkers. But they were different. I liked them. We used to talk.'

He sipped at his drink again, and Forrester thought

she could see something sloshing around inside the glass; something that kept moving when the drink stopped.

'Waiting for Justice didn't kill Annie,' he continued. 'Some kind of robot did. The same kind of robot that attacked you in the Overcity.'

'You saw it?' Forrester leaned forward.

'Somebody did. Somebody that owed Olias a favour, and I work for Olias. Sometimes.'

'But why?' Forrester smashed her fist into her palm. 'Why was an underdweller killed by an assassination robot? It just doesn't make sense.'

'Another assassination robot attacked an alien of my acquaintance: a member of the Hith race, named Powerless Friendless. The robot babbled about secret missions. My acquaintance didn't know what it was talking about – unsurprising, since I had wiped his mind of certain facts, some years ago. I spent a long while putting them back again today.'

'Putting them back?' Bernice raised an eyebrow. 'You make it sound so simple.'

'It is,' he said. 'Memories are often simple things to find. And hide.'

'Where is this alien now?' Forrester snapped.

'He left. He looked like a being with a mission. He had been tortured at some stage in the past, quite comprehensively tortured. He left here seeking vengeance for the sins that had been visited upon his body.' He sighed. 'I advised him not to, but he was insistent. I told him the memory viruses I inserted into his mind were delicate things. They were still uncovering memories when he left. Whatever he remembers is muddled, mixed up. He ought to allow it time to settle.' He looked up at Forrester with his good eye. 'As you should, later.'

'What's this about me?' Forrester's hand slipped unobtrusively onto the butt of her blaster.

If he had noticed the threatening gesture, Dantalion was ignoring it. 'There we come onto the second thing I require from you in payment.'

'And that is?'

'Do you remember coming here three years ago?'

She thought back. Three years. Shortly after Martle had been – Martle had died. Killed by the Falardi. There had been a raid . . .

'Yeah, we raided you for unlicensed gland removal from a Barrarian mating pair,' she said. 'Olias got you off the charge, as usual.'

'No,' he said, 'four weeks before that.'

She shook her head.

'No,' she said firmly, 'that was the first time I had seen you for almost a year.'

'You were here the month before.'

No, something in the back of her mind said, *no, you were somewhere else. You were somewhere else.*

'No,' she said, 'I was . . . I was . . .' That was odd. She couldn't remember. Where had she been? Martle's funeral was fresh in her mind, as was the raid, but the time in between was a blur.

'You were here,' Dantalion repeated. 'You were brought here. I was paid to remove a memory from your conscious mind and hide it where you would never find it.'

She shook her head wildly. 'No, it's not true.'

'It is true. And now I want to put it back again. That's the payment.'

The alien ship was closing rapidly on the *Moorglade*. A vast maw had opened up in its prow, ready to catch the ship. Beltempest guessed that the fringe of blunt appendages surrounding it like tentacles were part of whatever device had located them in hyperspace and pulled them back into the real universe.

'Better fasten your safety belts,' Provost-Major Beltempest called back to the compartment behind him. 'We're in for a bumpy ride!'

Beltempest uncoupled the controls from the autopilot and threw the shuttle hard to port, then dived beneath the approaching monster. The feel of the responsive controls beneath his fingers brought back memories of training sessions, many years ago. No simulators for the Landsknechte; they used and abused real ships. He'd stripped the spatial synchronets from more engines than he could count, pulling sharp turns in mock dog fights. It was all coming back to him now.

'What's happening?' a voice wailed from the loud-speakers in his suit.

'Doctor, glad to see you're still alive. We've been hijacked out of hyperspace.'

'By whom?'

'If I knew, I would tell you. But they appear to be aliens.'

'Well, try evasive manoeuvres!'

'Yes, thank you, Doctor. I'll do that.'

He shut off the connection in exasperation. Civilians! he thought, and concentrated on his screens. They appeared to be in clear space – no suns, no planets, no rogues – nothing but stars and the odd hydrogen atom. And the alien craft. It had turned slowly until it was facing him again, and was in the process of lumbering slowly up to speed. It would never catch him at that rate, and the pilot must know it. That meant –

He peeled sideways again, just as a pale violet beam transected the portion of space his ship had occupied only moments before. Gravity beam! These creatures, whoever they were, were heavily armed. He didn't recognize the design of the ship, and he'd been through all the military identification courses. Daleks, Sess, Scumble, Drahvins, Falardi: names, shapes and registration details of every ship in their fleets memorized. But this one was new. Damned aliens, always trying to put one over on the Empire. Slap them down hard, that was the only language they understood.

The craft had reorientated itself, and was coming after him again. The pilot was good, for an alien. Really quite good. Probably trained by humans. Yes, that would explain it.

Beltempest examined his options with finely honed tactical skill. If he tried to jump into hyperspace, the ship would just yank him out again. It had that capability.

However, if he destroyed that capability . . . All he had to do was to shoot off those tentacles and, as the old phrase had it, Robert would be his interlocutor's father's brother.

Except that Dis had strict rules about armed ships attempting to come within range of its laser turrets. The *Moorglade*'s weapons had been removed before it left Purgatory. Not just disarmed. Removed.

'Damn! Damn and blast! Damn and blast and – '

Instinctively he threw the ship into a corkscrew turn, just as the gravity beam flashed past. The beam spiralled with him, always a few hundred metres behind but in perfect synchronization. He counted seconds, anticipating the operator's reaction time, then, at the moment the operator manually dragged the beam across the spiral, he broke away and took the ship in a curving path away from the alien craft, downwards, under its belly and up towards its rear.

Where another gravity beam caught him in its violet grip. The *Moorglade* rang like a cracked and rather old bell.

Two gravity generators. That looked suspiciously like overkill to him.

'Imperial Landsknecht shuttle,' a voice boomed in his ears. He'd turned the communications systems off, so they were probably using some sort of modulation on their gravity beam. Smart. For aliens. 'Imperial Landsknecht shuttle, heave to. We are about to board.'

Standard Landsknecht message format as well. They must have been on the end of it themselves a few times. That gave him some clues. Obviously a race that had felt the sharp end of Imperial justice before. Not that it narrowed the field much.

The alien craft grew in his screens. He bent to retrieve his weapons from the floor. Try to board his shuttle, would they? He'd show them how the Landsknechte reacted to that kind of thing.

Chirell Tensen refastened the access plate and sat back on his heels. 'Never understood why they can't get a bot

213

to do this,' he grumbled, disengaging his heavy diagnostic unit and glancing around the room at the hulking but eerily silent null-grav generators. He didn't like being down in the lowest level of the towers. Too close to the Undertown for his liking, what with the riots and all.

'What?' his colleague Trav Chan shouted. He was still working on the other side of the unit, and the constant high-pitched whine of the generators made it difficult to hear.

'I said I don't know why they can't get a bot to do this,' he shouted.

'Accountability. If we screw up, we're responsible. If a bot screws up, there's nobody's butt in the sling.'

Chirell rubbed his temple. His head was throbbing fit to burst, and the strap of the diagnostic unit was biting into his shoulder. His wife had bought a cheap body-bepple kit as a surprise birthday present for him, and he couldn't stop thinking about the new softness of her skin and the fresh curves of her body. She was probably still asleep, curled up in the warmth of their bed. Goddess, he wished he were back there with her, running his fingernail up her back.

'If we screw up, this tower drops all the way down to the Undertown,' he snapped. 'They won't be able to find enough of our butts to put in a nutshell, let alone a sling.'

'No chance of that,' Chan said. 'These things are built with so much redundancy, you wouldn't believe.'

The pounding in Chirell's head was making it difficult to think. He turned to look at Chan, but something was wrong with his eyes. All he could see was a red blur.

'Screw it,' he snarled. 'I just want out!'

He stood up, but a sudden wave of nausea made him stagger. Something flashed into his mind: a picture of Chan's hands wandering across his wife's breasts and buttocks.

'Hey, you okay, man?' Chan asked in concern.

Chirell's head was pounding. He wanted to lash out, to smash something, to hear somebody scream. In his mind, Chan was holding his wife down while she bucked and moaned in pleasure. Chan was screwing his wife! How could he have been so stupid?

Chan caught hold of his shoulders. 'Hey, you want we should – '

His words were cut off as Chirell smashed the sharp corner of the diagnostic unit into his forehead.

Green light. Bright light.

Forrester crept closer to the doorway of the hotel room, vibroknife held tightly in her hand. From inside, Fenn Martle's voice snapped something short. He sounded angry. No, he sounded furious.

What in Goddess' name was the moron doing here, especially without backup? It had been obvious back at the lodge that he was on edge about something. It had also been obvious for some time that he was following up leads on a case but wasn't sure enough of himself to make it official – meetings at odd hours, mysterious actions while on cases, a general air of preoccupation. The big idiot. Couldn't he ever leave the job alone? He had to be the most dedicated Adjudicator that Forrester had ever come across.

Knowing how he could go off half-cocked sometimes, Forrester had followed him from the lodge in an unmarked flitter. She'd had to leave her judicial blaster behind; their use was tightly controlled, and Adjudicators weren't allowed to sign them out after work. Spiralling up in the wake of his expensive sportster model towards the Overcity, she had felt an unaccustomed excitement blossom within her. If Martle had discovered some kind of connection between the Undertown gangs and the Overcity crime bosses, this could make their careers. Even better, they might at last be able to get a handle on Olias and her sordid little dealings.

Martle's flitter had been heading for an access point halfway up one of the hotel towers in the eastern sector. This one was near the spaceport and overlooked the hole left in the Overcity by the Scumble ship that had crashed some years beforehand. She had recognized the one he was aiming for; it maintained suites of rooms with variable environmental controls for the various alien diplomatic delegations that regularly came, cap in hand, to the Empress. Forrester had a hard time keeping up with him; his flitter had a higher power rating than any she'd seen. Must have cost him a bomb.

Martle had brought his vehicle in for a smooth landing on the shelflike access point, and paid a valet bot to park it for him. It hadn't been hard to spot him: out of his robes he usually wore an expensive five-piece shrivenzale-skin suit and boots woven out of ditz hair. Circling high above like a hawk, Forrester had watched him enter the hotel, then swooped down and dashed in towards a slot just ahead of a large, black diplomatic flitter. The bot had tried to wave her away, but she had flashed her forearm at it. A laser had tickled her flesh, and the bot had backed away humbly.

'Park it!' she had snapped, jerking her thumb at her unmarked flitter, and then she had run into the hotel sub-lobby. The walls were lined with orange fur, and the floor was a mosaic of the shells of small turtle-like creatures. Opulent. Opulent to the point where it made Forrester feel physically sick. It reminded her too much of her family's mansion on Io: the same careless attitude towards wealth, the same impersonal feeling.

Martle had just been vanishing into a null-grav shaft. She had ducked back in case he had seen her, then, after his feet had vanished upwards, she jogged across the lobby, avoiding various human, beppled human and alien guests, and dived in after him.

And here she was, standing outside the open door of the hotel room, personal vibroknife in her hand, listening to him shouting. A tiny bud of worry was flowering inside her chest. The moron obviously needed backup, but had been too proud to ask Forrester to come with him. He'd be glad she was there.

Wouldn't he?

'You should be careful who you speak to like that,' a calm, sardonic voice said. 'I might just have you killed.'

'You wouldn't dare!' Martle snapped. 'I've been doing your dirty work for so long that you've forgotten what it's like to get your hands soiled. I've set everything up for you. If you kill me, who'll protect you from the Adjudicators?'

'What makes you think you're the only Adjudicator on my payroll?'

Forrester very deliberately tried not to think about what was being said. She didn't analyse the words for their meaning. She didn't dare think about Fenn Martle, fairest Adjudicator on the force, taking bribes.

She didn't succeed.

She had to see who Martle was talking to. Edging closer to the door, she tried to peer round the jamb.

'Someone else?' Martle sounded shaken. 'Who?'

'No harm in telling you, I suppose,' the voice drawled. 'Your Adjudicator Secular. Rashid, is that her name? Expensive, but she's worth every penny.'

'But – '

'Why? Because I needed the extra protection. We have the Hith ship, thanks to a pilot who was open to bribery, and we've shipped it here to Earth. A fascinating vessel. Exploitation will start any day now. We tortured the navigator for information, and we were about to do the same with the pilot until they both managed to escape. The pilot left Earth, but I've traced him to Oolis. No doubt if I pay enough money to the local militia, they'll kill him for me. The navigator is still on Earth, somewhere in the Undertown. I wouldn't be concerned about him, except that he took a vital control nexus from the ship before he went. We can't operate the engines properly without it. We need to find him.'

'I can do that for you.' Martle sounded as if he was pleading. Forrester couldn't believe it. Through the doorway, past Martle's expensively dressed figure, she could see a large picture window, overlooking the hole in the Overcity where the Scumble spacecraft had crashed. Far, far below, the fires of the Undertown glittered.

'But you're unreliable,' the other man said. 'And you are becoming increasingly expensive. Rashid can give us far better protection if we find this pilot and kill it. You, I'm afraid, are yesterday's news, Mr Martle.'

Forrester edged an inch further into the doorway, and saw the figure Martle was talking to. It glistened like metal, but it looked like a man. A man in an old-fashioned suit, with a round-collared shirt. Its head had been moulded to resemble a face: a middle-aged face with a stern frown, a supercilious droop to the eyes, a sneer. The sort of man you wouldn't want to cross in business. Or anything else.

A bot built to resemble a man? There were laws against that sort of thing. And why was it giving Martle orders?

It saw Forrester.

'My dear,' it said affably, gesturing her into the room, 'please join us.' It turned to Martle. 'You see,' it said. 'You're getting to be a liability, my boy. You were followed.'

'Please . . .'

'No, Mr Martle, I'm afraid my mind is made up.' It shook its head in mock sorrow, but Forrester could sense an undercurrent of dark humour in its voice.

'Fenn . . .' she said uncertainly. 'I don't understand. Why are you taking orders from a bot?'

Martle looked away, unable or unwilling to meet her gaze.

'I'm not a bot, my dear,' the bot said, striding forward surprisingly nimbly.

'Yeah, sure,' she said, 'and I'm the Draconian ambassador. Well, if you're for real, then I'm obliged to inform you that your words, gestures and postures will be recorded as soon as I can find a security bot to do it, and that they may form part of any legal action taken against you. Under the terms of the Data Protection Act 2820, as amended 2945, I am also obliged to inform you that you and any appointed legal representative will be able to purchase a copy of all recordings upon payment of the standard fee. Until recording starts I am obliged to warn you that you should say nothing.'

'Martle,' the bot said. 'You wish to redeem yourself in my eyes. Kill her.'

Forrester raised her eyebrows and looked over at her

218

partner, inviting him to share her amazement at the audacity of the bot. Her partner, who had saved her life five times that she could count. Her partner, with whom she had shared moments, memories, laughs and tears. Her partner, who was pulling a small but lethal needle out from a concealed holster.

'Roz, I'm sorry,' he murmured, raising the gun.

And the Falardi's claw carved its way up his spine with a thunk that she would hear for ever.

His hand, on the trigger.

The Falardi's claw carved its way –

The look in his eye.

Thunk!

She flicked her hand, sending the vibroknife spinning through the air towards Martle. It caught him in his right eye, sending him spinning backwards, screaming, the needle dropping from his spasming hand, falling to the floor just before his body hit the wall.

Thunk.

She stood, as still as a statue, seeing the blood but somehow not understanding it. A numb feeling crept over her body, as if she had been wrapped in cotton wool and insulated from the world. Shock? Was she in shock? She couldn't move her legs. She couldn't even blink.

The bot walked between her and Martle's body. It was holding a small stunner, and she suddenly recognized the feeling from training sessions on Ponten IV. She had been stunned, and shortly, she guessed, she would be dead.

'Thank you, my dear,' it said. 'You have done my dirty work for me, but provided me with a problem. One dead Adjudicator I could account for, with Adjudicator Secular Rashid's help, but two would raise eyebrows back on Ponten IV. No, I think that the easiest solution will be to wipe your memory of our meeting and implant a new version of events. An alien, I think, killing your partner and escaping while you tried to save his life. That way you all get to be heroes, and I remain safe.' It walked closer, its impassive metal face radiating sardonic good humour. 'There are people down in the Undertown who are experts

*at that sort of thing. It's the best course of action. I'm sure
that, given the choice, you would agree with me.'*

The bot raised the stunner.

*The last thing she could remember seeing was Martle's
blood pooling beneath his head* and the first thing she saw
when the lid of the time tank opened was Chris Cwej
smiling down at her. His skin was pink and new. And
furless, apart from a fuzz of golden hair across his scalp.

'Hey, Roz,' he said tenderly.

'Are you okay?' she asked.

'I'm fine,' he said, placing an arm beneath her shoulders
and easing her upright. 'I feel like I've slept for a month.
Probably have: all the beppled cells have been replaced.
I'm me again. But what about you? How do you . . . how
do you feel?'

Forrester turned her attention inwards. The memories
were there, as they always had been. She accepted them.
She knew they were true.

Oh, Fenn. I loved you. I loved you.

'Like shit,' she said. 'Nothing changes.'

Chapter 12

'I'm . . . ah, I'm Shythe Shahid, speaking to you live from the . . . the smouldering wreckage of the Empire Today *studio. Yesterday the riots that are slowly but surely engulfing the Earth claimed us: today it might be your turn. What is happening to this planet? Sources close to the Empress have told* The Empire Today *that she is close to declaring a state of emergency. We'll keep you posted. Keep watching . . .'*

Being inside the alien ship was like being inside the stomach of a living creature.

The walls of the hangar into which the *Moorglade* had been dragged seemed to have been formed from a moist, fleshlike material. As the Doctor walked down the ramp he could have sworn that they were even flexing slightly, as if the ship was breathing. The struts that supported the roof were white and bonelike, and the cables, pipes and ducts snaking around the walls looked more like a circulatory system. The floor even gave slightly beneath the Doctor's feet.

Except . . .

Except that elements of different technologies were apparent. In places the veined network covering the walls had been supplemented with fibre-optics, corrugated quark runs and even interstat wave tubes with their distinctive cryogenic sheathing. Areas of the rounded ceiling had been reinforced with metal plates, and some of the bonelike ceiling supports had been replaced with a mixture of simple metal I-beams, intricate Gothic buttresses and plasticrete spars.

Even the few other craft scattered around the hangar were of wildly differing design. A sleek fighter with hyperspace capability sat next to a battered old garbage scow whose engines were of almost outmoded P-shift design; two guppy-like cargo craft with bulging stomachs had been parked side by side, but the hydrogen baffles of one of them had been replaced with a quantum engine designed by a different race for a different class of ship. There was even a long, viper-like Sess-chaser over by the wall. The entire place looked as if it had been assembled with loving care from the bric-a-brac of a thousand interstellar jumble sales.

Behind the Doctor, Professor Zebulon Pryce emerged, stark naked, from the Imperial naval shuttle. Pryce paused for a moment, and glanced towards the far end of the hangar – the end through which the shuttle had been dragged. The Doctor followed his gaze, and gulped in alarm. The gap had been sealed by a force field that strobed alarmingly, and the pressure of the air in the hangar was causing it to bulge out into space. Around the lip of the gap, the protrusions of the gravitational beam generator stuck outwards. It was like being inside a gigantic mouth.

Glancing down at the Doctor, Pryce's lips twitched slightly, but he said nothing.

'Hardly the cutting edge of astro-engineering, is it?' the Doctor said.

Pryce looked as if he might have responded, but he suddenly stumbled forward as Provost-Major Beltempest prodded him from behind with the barrel of a screamer rifle.

'I still say we should have stayed in the ship,' Beltempest growled, glancing round the empty interior.

'To what end?' the Doctor asked. 'If they could locate us in hyperspace, drag us into the real universe and then reel us in with a gravity beam like a gumblejack on the end of a piece of twine, I don't suppose a couple of layers of adamantium would keep them out.' He glanced around again. 'Whoever they are.'

'An interesting mix of cultures,' Pryce said from beside the Doctor. The Doctor jumped. He hadn't noticed that the professor had got that close. 'I count fifteen disparate technologies in this room alone, although biological systems predominate. Do you concur?'

'That's exactly what I thought,' the Doctor bluffed.

Beltempest suddenly cried out and dropped his screamer. The barrel was glowing red-hot. Bending, he tried to pick it up, but couldn't. A pocket on his space suit abruptly burst into flame. Fumbling, he managed to prise a small blaster out and let it fall to join the screamer, whose barrel was now nothing more than a puddle of molten metal. He turned and made to dash back into the shuttle, but the door slid shut in his face.

'Come out,' he shouted, blowing on his burned hands. 'Come on out and show yourselves, if you dare.'

Pryce glanced back at him. 'I would advise caution where our friend Beltempest is concerned,' he said quietly. 'He is not who he appears.'

'So you said back on Dis, but how can you tell? You last saw him years ago, and he's been through a body-bepple since then.'

Pryce shook his head. His white pony-tail waved gently behind him. 'No,' he said firmly. 'He is *not* the Provost-Major Beltempest I remember.'

'He certainly remembers you,' the Doctor said grimly. 'You made quite an impression on him.'

'His voice is familiar. Perhaps he was one of the other Landsknechte with whom I had . . . contact on Purgatory.'

The Doctor frowned. 'But why would – ' As he spoke, a section of the wall irised open, revealing a stretch of pristine corridor beyond. Three heavily armed creatures stood in the doorway. The Doctor recognized the columnar form, the stalked eyes, the boneless limbs, the vestigial shells. They were Hith, just like Homeless Forsaken and Powerless Friendless. 'Oops,' he said. 'I think we have company.'

* * *

'Hey, slug!'

Powerless Friendless kept slithering along the corridor.

'I'm talking to you, mucus brain.'

He stopped and turned around. The uniformed man standing at the door of the room he had just passed was glaring at him.

'Yes, sir?' he said.

'I got a mess in here. Come and clean it up. That's your job, isn't it?'

Powerless Friendless glanced down at the mop and bucket in his pseudo-limb as if he had never seen them before. He had only taken them from the janitorbot as protective coloration, enabling him to slip along the corridors of the INITEC building without being spotted, but it looked as if he should have chosen something else. Something less demeaning for a Hith warrior.

'Yes, sir,' he sighed, dreaming momentarily of ripping the man's head off. Instead he swallowed his pride and followed the man into the room. There was nothing in it except for a desk and chair on one side, a metal vault door set into the far wall, a window beside the door that looked out across the void of the next Overcity block, and a coffee stain on the floor.

'Where's the janitorbot?' the man said, slumping into the chair and putting on a set of centcomp goggles. The desk in front of him was clear, apart from a keypad which probably controlled access to whatever was behind the door. The INITEC building was full of sealed doors and security guards. It was making Powerless Friendless's search hell. It was lucky he already knew a way into the building.

'Malfunction,' Powerless Friendless said. It was true. The janitorbot had malfunctioned quite dramatically when Powerless Friendless had pushed it out of the window. 'I'm filling in for it.'

'Goddessdamned slugs,' the man muttered, 'taking up good bot jobs. Well, clean the spill up if you're going to.' He pointed to it, as if he didn't expect Powerless Friendless to spot it without his help.

'Yes sir.' Powerless Friendless quickly ran the mop over it, hoping that the man wouldn't look too closely at the mop itself. He hadn't been able to wrench it out of the bot's shoulder without leaving trailing wires and a bulbous universal joint at the end. 'Is that okay, sir?'

The man grunted, absorbed in his centcomp goggles, and Powerless Friendless quickly slid out of the room, making an insulting gesture as he went. He added the room to his list of places to investigate if he couldn't find any trace of the man he was looking for. The man who had tortured him.

As he slithered along the corridor, he heard the door open behind him. Powerless Friendless angled an eye-stalk to check whether the guard had followed him. Perhaps the mop had attracted his suspicion. There was something emerging from the room, a bot of a design that Powerless Friendless hadn't seen before: small and multi-legged. It must have been in the room behind the sealed door.

As the bot scuttled off down the corridor away from him, Powerless Friendless suddenly came to a halt. There was something bothering him. Something about that room. Something about its position. His mind had been mucked around with so much, he wasn't absolutely sure of any of his thoughts any more, but alarm bells were definitely ringing. He ran his pseudo-limbs along the corridor walls. They vibrated slightly, as if there was a power source behind them. Odd. Very odd.

He started moving again, making for the little cupboard he had discovered earlier on. Looking both ways along the corridor to check that the bot had gone, he slipped inside. He consulted the map he had detached from the wall by the null-grav shaft. Extruding a pseudo-limb, he traced his path along the corridor. Yes, there was the corner, there was the cupboard, there was the room, but there was no door marked on the other side of it, no sign of any generators or power conduits. Whatever was going on in that area, it was secret.

A shiver ran through him. Not only was the door not marked, but all of the rooms on that side of the corridor were on the outside of the building. If that sealed metal door led anywhere, it should be into empty air. Thousands of metres above the Undertown.

That window. He hadn't really taken it in at the time, but the window showed a view across to the next block. And yet there was a door beside it ...

And why have a guard on it?

Powerless Friendless ran his pseudo-limb up his eye-stalks in confusion. He knew enough about the INITEC building to know that the map wasn't wrong. From the outside it was a smooth, featureless block with no protrusions and no flitter access ports. He couldn't understand where that door might lead.

Perhaps ...

Perhaps it led to the man. The man with the soft, smooth voice.

The man with the knife.

He had to get inside.

Powerless Friendless rummaged amongst the shelves of the cupboard until he found the rucksack that he had left there earlier, and slid a pseudo-limb into it. Something sharp closed on his fingers, and he quickly jerked the limb out.

'Ungrateful little bastard,' he hissed at the gelatinous creature that was attached to the end of his limb, its eye-stalks glowering sulkily at him. 'I've got a job for you.'

Krohg relinquished its grip and allowed Powerless Friendless to stroke its back.

'You're going to distract somebody's attention,' Powerless Friendless cooed to it, 'while I creep in somewhere. It'll be just like old times.'

The door suddenly crashed open, flooding the tiny cupboard with light. Powerless Friendless whirled around, pseudo-limbs extruded for action.

A shadow fell over him.

'Well,' said a familiar voice, 'so we meet again.'

Rachel Trethewi, Surgeon Imperialis, leaned against the control console and stared through the transparisteel barrier at her latest subject. He was suspended like a puppet from the ceiling of the chamber by a complicated web of monofilaments. He was awake, of course, but immobilized. The room was illuminated by the light from Rachel's side of the barrier and by the winking green and red tell-tale lights of the medical machines.

And by the vein of fire that throbbed in the tissue of the subject's exposed brain.

As far as Rachel could see, he was doing fine. His vital signs hung in the air beside him: pulse rate, blood pressure, various neurological traces, a complete kirilian scan. Just above them was his name. Some of her staff didn't like names, saying that they detracted from the professionalism of the job, but Rachel felt more comfortable using them. The subjects needed reassurance, and using their names seemed to help.

'Well, Terg McConnel,' she said, emphasizing her lip movements so that the subject could lip-read. His eyes – wide with panic and with pain – flickered slightly, and his neurological traces peaked. Yes, he was reassured. 'Terg, we're going to do some more tests. Do you understand? I know they hurt, but we need to know the answers. We need to know why you went mad and killed your student. You do remember doing that, don't you?'

The skin around the subject's eyes tightened, as if he was trying to close them. It did him no good – his eyelids and tear-ducts had been removed to facilitate observations of his pupillary reactions at the same time the top of his head had been removed to expedite access to his brain – but Rachel had noticed that autonomic reactions such as blinking couldn't be suppressed very easily. Perhaps she should extend the level of immobilization to minor as well as major muscle groups. The results of her tests might be affected otherwise.

It was so difficult to tell what might be important.

Rachel's gaze was drawn back to the line of brightness that throbbed within the subject's naked cerebellum: a physical change in the soft tissue, cause unknown. Always the same place, subject after subject. Always giving off the same spectra. Always indicative of sudden, unpredictable fits of psychosis followed by instant remission. Always unrelated to any physical changes that the Surgeon Imperialis and her staff could find.

Still, they kept trying.

'Try to relax, Terg,' she mouthed as she manipulated the control board, manoeuvring skeletal metal arms with laser scalpel tips down from their nest in the ceiling. 'We're only going to remove a small sample this time.'

Provost-Major Beltempest stared at the flap of the tent. Through it he could see a wide expanse of blue grassland and a green sky, and the bulky shape of the Hith ship, draped now in camouflage netting. Freedom, just a few steps away.

'Release us immediately,' he growled at the two slugs who stood upright by the open flap of the tent. They were standing about as far apart as they could while still guarding the opening. 'Abduction of a Landsknechte provost-major is an act of war. The Empress will take a dim view of your actions.'

The left-hand slug – a muscular female – jerked her weapon towards him.

'Shut up,' she said. 'You're unimportant.'

Beltempest felt a surge of anger and resentment. How dare these jumped up invertebrates talk to him that way, a man who had personally seen the Empress five times! His fingers tightened on the edge of the table as he tried to control himself. Mind racing, he considered and rejected plan after plan of escape. It was no good. The Hith had them cold, and had done for the five hours between their capture and their landing some ten minutes ago on the blue savannah of this unidentified and yet oddly familiar planet. He wished he'd been able to see it from space as they landed. There was something about its smell, and the colour of its sky, that he recognized.

Slumping back as best he could into the S-shaped chair, he turned to see how the other two were taking the humiliation. The Doctor was sniffing at the cool, scented air, while Professor Zebulon Pryce was sitting calmly with his eyes closed and his hands folded on the table. Damned civilians. Didn't they realize what a disgrace it was for a Landsknecht to be captured in battle?

'Kill them,' Pryce whispered.

Beltempest tried not to jerk in his seat. 'What?' he said.

'Kill them.' Pryce's eyes were still closed, but his fingernails were tapping lightly on the wooden table. 'Ripping off the small vestigial shells on their tails will cause systemic nervous shock and kill them or send them into an irreversible coma. A blow to the base of their eye-stalks will make them writhe in agony for hours before expiring. Kill them, Provost-Major. It's your duty as a human.'

'Why not just sprinkle salt on their tails?' the Doctor asked sourly. 'Alternatively, why not just leave them alone until we find out what they want with us?'

'Why don't the two of you just shut up while I work out a means of escape?' Beltempest hissed. 'We're dead meat here. We destroyed their home world during the Wars of Acquisition, remember? The Hith have no reason to love the Empire.'

'Yes, and whose fault is that?' the Doctor asked with a petulant tone in his voice.

Beltempest rubbed his hands over his eyes. The waiting was getting to him. He was just about to leap to his feet and protest at their treatment again when the tent flap was pulled open and two more slugs slid into the room, leaving a trail of mucus on the blue sward. One of them was old: wrinkled and pink. It seemed to be in the androgynous transition between male and female stages, if the lectures on enemy physiology that he'd attended during the Wars of Acquisition were anything to go by. Some kind of metal symbol had been implanted into its head between its eye-stalks. The Hith beside it was a smaller male with moist, unlined flesh. He carried a metal box in a pseudo-limb. As he put the box down, Beltempest noticed that air holes had been punched in the lid.

The elder Hith surveyed them for a moment.

'Which human is the important one?' it asked in a wavery voice.

Beltempest stood up. 'Beltempest, Montmorency,' he snapped. 'Provost-Major third class, nine oh one five seven. And that's all you're getting.'

'Sit down.' The female Hith with the gun squelched forward. 'I told you before: you're unimportant.'

The Doctor put a hand on Beltempest's arm. 'I think it's me they want,' he said quietly, standing as Beltempest slumped back into his seat. 'I am the Doctor,' he announced to the elderly Hith. 'You've gone to a lot of trouble to find me. I hope it's worth your while.'

The female Hith guard sighed. 'The arrogance of you humans appals us,' she said. 'Sit down, will you?'

The elderly Hith turned to Pryce. 'Then you must be Professor Zebulon Pryce,' it said.

He nodded slightly. 'I am.'

'I am Hater of Humans And Leader Of Hith. This unworthy one – ' It indicated the younger male Hith by its side, the one that stood beside the box. ' – is my scapegoat, Hopeless Itinerant Taking The Blame. May we talk?'

As Beltempest and the Doctor gazed on, open-mouthed, Pryce smiled. 'Nothing would please me more,' he said. Turning to the Doctor, he murmured, 'I really should start charging for my time.'

'Well?' Bernice said, 'what have you found?'

Powerless Friendless looked around the cupboard. It was getting a little tight, what with him, Bernice and the two Adjudicators. He wasn't very good at reading human expressions, but the dark woman with the close-cropped grey hair didn't look happy about being in close proximity with him. Shame. Her companion – the one who had been covered in golden hair the last time Powerless Friendless had seen him, assuming that wasn't another spurious memory – was playing with Krohg: tickling him around the cilia while the little bastard rolled around as if he was enjoying it.

For a moment, after the dark-skinned Adjudicator had kicked the door of the cupboard in, he had thought he was finished. A feeling of relief had washed over him. No more struggle. No more pain.

And then he had seen Bernice's face, heard her voice, and had known that the struggle was going on.

'Well,' he said, 'let's start with what I've remembered.' He took a deep breath, trying to sort the memories out. At the moment it was rather as if somebody had dropped them all and scooped them up into a pile, like dead leaves. 'I was a navigator, during the Great Patriotic War – '

'He means the Hith Annexation during the Wars of Acquisition,' Forrester murmured.

'I know what I mean,' he hissed angrily. 'You took our planet and poisoned it so that we couldn't live there any longer. You – '

'You were a navigator,' Bernice prompted.

'Yes,' he sighed, 'I was a navigator. We had a ship – an experimental ship. Two-Hith crew. We knew that we could devastate the Empire's fleets with it. It was our last great defence against humanity.' He shook his head sadly. 'What we didn't know was, our captain had sold out. We made a jump through hyperspace on our first flight and ended up in the wrong spot. The traitor must have fed the wrong coordinates into the navigation computer. We emerged surrounded by Landsknecht ships.' He shivered. 'The ship and I were taken to a planet named Purgatory. They started to disassemble the ship, and torture me. They were going to torture him as well, just in case he had been holding back on them. Humans – ' He looked at the three warily. ' – just can't be trusted. For some reason, we were both moved here to Earth. To this building. I don't know why, but they brought the ship with us. The captain and I escaped with the control nexus for the ship. He managed to get off Earth while I hid out in the Undertown. I knew the people who had tortured me would still be searching. I had Dantalion make a new identity for me, and erase the memories of my old life. That way, I could never give myself away accidentally. That way, I didn't have to wake up screaming every night, remembering the way they sliced strips from my flesh.' Powerless Friendless hung his eye-stalks ashamedly. 'I lost the nexus, of course. With my memory gone, I didn't know what it was. I still can't remember where I left it.'

Bernice had a strange expression on her face. Strange for a human, anyway.

'Your pilot,' she said, 'the one who turned traitor. What was his full name?'

Powerless Friendless thought for a moment, feeling his way through the shards of memory. 'His Hith name was Vap Oppat Pol, but all Hith changed their names after we lost Hithis. The name he chose was Homeless Forsaken Betrayed And Alone.'

Bernice's face tightened, and she glanced away. Powerless Friendless thought he heard her say, 'Bastard,' but he might have been wrong.

Beltempest watched impotently as Hater Of Humans And Leader of Hith rotated an eye-stalk to face one of the two Hith guards. The guard immediately pushed a chair over from the side of the tent. Hater of Humans sank into its curves. The Hith referred to as its scapegoat stood erect by its side, next to the metal box with the air holes in the lid.

Hater Of Humans's eye-stalks turned towards Zebulon Pryce.

'We have been waiting for years, hoping that you would find a way off Dis,' it said. 'We debated whether to attempt to rescue you, but we could find no gaps in security, no weaknesses, nothing that we could use. Finally, you are here. If you can help us, we will set you free. You will never have to return to Dis.'

'What makes you think I want to go free?' Pryce asked. 'I had everything on Dis that I needed.' Somewhere, deep inside his dark eyes, a small red spark seemed to glow.

Hater Of Humans's eye-stalks drooped. 'Whatever you want will be provided,' it said.

'I need victims. Lots of them.'

'Then they will be provided.'

Beltempest could see that Pryce was ignoring the Doctor's appalled expression. 'You must need my help badly,' he said.

'The future of the Hith race depends upon it,' Hater Of Humans replied with heavy dignity.

Beltempest couldn't contain himself any longer. 'The Hith race hasn't got a future,' he shouted. 'You're just a ragged bunch of scavengers skulking around the universe, finding homes wherever you can, and yet you dare –'

The stunner beam caught him without warning as he was breathing out. He tried to catch his breath, but couldn't. A red haze settled over his vision and pins and needles tingled through his limbs. He slumped back into his chair, trying desperately to breathe.

'One more sound from you,' the female Hith said, reholstering her weapon, 'and I'll kill you.'

Beltempest listened against his will as Hater Of Humans continued speaking.

'Yes,' it said in apparent sadness, 'our race is scattered around the universe. Our warriors serve in restaurants on half a hundred planets; our diplomats clean urinals; our scientists and industrialists beg on the streets. Our most sublime artists clean shoes for a living. We are forced to congregate together, even though we hate company. Even here, in our most secret base, we have to hide. We are destroyed as a civilization. And yet –' The Hith sighed deeply. ' – we still have our pride.'

'The technology on this ship,' the Doctor's voice prompted, from outside Beltempest's field of view.

'Ah.' Hater Of Humans nodded, its eye-stalks bobbing. 'Yes. Without recourse to our factories and stockpiles, with our home world taken from us, we have found other ways to keep our race intact. The Hith who are scattered across the accursed human Empire pay a proportion of whatever they can earn or beg to us in taxes. These taxes – paid in various ways, in various currencies – are being used to rebuild our fleets, our weapons, our pride. We will

233

buy from anybody – humanity, the Draconians, the Daleks, the Usurians, the Ook. Even the Cimliss.'

'To what end?' the Doctor asked.

'To regain our world,' Hater Of Humans said simply.

'By war?'

Beltempest managed to shift his head slightly so that he could see along the table, past the Doctor's head to where Pryce was sitting.

'By whatever means necessary,' Hater Of Humans said, and glanced at Pryce. 'And that is why we need your help.'

'You realize,' the Doctor persisted, 'that this man is a murderer?'

'He killed other humans?' Hater Of Humans sounded amused. 'And you think that we should disapprove of that?'

'He would kill you, if you gave him a chance.' The Doctor scowled at Pryce, who smiled slightly and closed his eyes.

'Indeed I would,' he murmured.

The guards shifted slightly by the tent flap.

The Doctor sighed in exasperation. 'Professor Pryce has been driven mad by icaron radiation. Whatever you want from him, he isn't in any condition to provide it.'

'You are mistaken.' Hater Of Humans's voice held the unmistakable tone of command. 'It is Professor Pryce's knowledge of icaron radiation that we need. That is why we have been waiting for him.'

Pryce's interest was aroused. Beltempest watched as his fingers began to scratch the surface of the table. 'Please explain,' he said.

Hater Of Humans continued: 'In the dark days towards the end of the War, as the Empire sent in its terraforming ships while we were still on our planet's surface, our scientists made a breakthrough. They learned how to harness the power of icaron radiation, and how to use it in a new generation of ships that could outrun and outgun anything the Imperial Landsknechte had got.'

Beltempest felt a tension growing in his chest. Nothing could outgun the Imperial Landsknechte.

'But icaron radiation is extremely dangerous!' the Doctor protested. 'There are laws prohibiting its use! The Fourteenth Resolution of the Armageddon Convention clearly states – '

'Icaron radiation is only dangerous to life-forms whose body chemistry is based upon carbon,' Hater Of Humans snapped, 'and even then, there have to be certain specific modifications. I suspect it is this degenerate human habit of "body-bepple" that has made them vulnerable; but, to be frank, we didn't care about any risk to humans.'

The Doctor's expression was thunderous as he prepared a verbal broadside, but Hater Of Humans interrupted him.

'Save your misplaced concern, Doctor,' Hater Of Humans said, shaking its head in sorrow. 'Before we could build a fleet capable of defeating humanity, Hithis was destroyed for us, and we were dispersed. We were a race without a home, but we still had our pride. We had to rebuild our fleets, regroup our forces, reclaim our heritage. Apart from a few old cargo ships, all we salvaged from Hithis was one craft with the new power source: the *Skel'-Ske*. It was to be the flagship of our new fleet. Sleek, fast, armed and armoured, it was to spearhead our attempts to regain our home and defeat the Empire.'

'What happened?' the Doctor asked.

'It was stolen,' Hater of Humans spat, a grey flush spreading across its skin. The male Hith beside it, the one who had been introduced as its scapegoat, suddenly extruded a pseudo-limb and began to tug upon one of its eye-stalks in penance. 'On its test flight, it was hijacked. The captain – one of my most trusted aides – and the navigator vanished along with it. Perhaps they were paid to take it and are now living in luxury somewhere. Perhaps they were killed. It took years for my people, scattered the length and breadth of the galaxy, to determine who was responsible.'

'The Earth Empire,' Pryce murmured.

'As you well know,' Hater Of Humans said, drawing itself up. The Hith scapegoat, sensing the change in emotion, ceased its self-flagellation and subsided, panting, to the floor. It curled up around the metal box, inside which something shifted slightly.

Pryce nodded. 'Yes, I know,' he said.

'I don't,' the Doctor piped up.

Pryce gazed at the Doctor, the black wells of his eyes reflecting nothing. 'It was when I was at the University of Sallas,' he said finally. 'I was approached by the Landsknechte. They offered me a job. They told me that they had . . . found an alien spacecraft, drifting through human space. They thought that it was powered by an icaron generator, and they wanted me to help them take it apart. After all, if they could get icaron technology working safely, it would mean a vast leap in human technology. I agreed, and they took me to Purgatory, where they had taken the craft for analysis.'

A cold hand seemed to be squeezing Beltempest's heart. He hadn't known anything about this! There was nothing on the files about it. Nothing. Could this be the break in the case he had been waiting for?

'The cover story,' Pryce continued, 'was that I was working on icaron weapon systems.' He smiled. 'They gave me a laboratory, an inflated budget and all the attention an overinflated ego could require. All they wanted was results. I was young, naive. I took risks.'

'You went mad,' the Doctor said.

'I'll always regret that I didn't get the chance to finish what I started,' Pryce continued. 'Others, no doubt, will try, but not as well as I would have done.'

'Others *have* tried,' Hater Of Humans said. 'The ship was taken from Purgatory after you . . . you failed to find out its secrets. It was moved elsewhere. Our agents all over the galaxy have been searching for it with no success. Until now.'

It was all becoming clear to Beltempest now. There *was* a conspiracy at the heart of the Landsknechte, and it involved this ship. What else? He remembered the message that had been sent to – to the man who had been

Provost-Major Beltempest. 'Earth,' he mumbled, trying to get his lips to work. 'It's on Earth, isn't it?'

The guard stepped forward, but Hater Of Humans waved her back.

'Yes,' it said, 'the ship is on Earth, but we don't know where. Our agents can find no trace of it.'

'That's why people are being driven mad,' the Doctor said. 'Whoever has it is slowly dismantling it to get at the power source. The fools! They probably don't even know the risks! We desperately need to get to that ship.'

'We agree,' Hater of Humans said.

Beltempest was surprised. 'Why?' he asked.

'Because, after so many years, the Empress has finally deigned – ' It almost spat the word. ' – to receive a Hith diplomatic mission. Dweller In Sorrow Abandoned And Lost – one of our most persuasive diplomats who, until now, has been working in a fast food restaurant on Alpha Centauri – is currently on Earth awaiting an audience with the Empress. We believe that the Empress is sympathetic to our cause. It is possible that we may get our home world back again. However, if it became public knowledge that a Hith device was driving humans mad . . .'

'I see the problem,' the Doctor said. 'May I ask a completely unrelated question?'

Hater Of Humans nodded.

'I've been examining the landscape outside the tent,' the Doctor continued. 'And I must admit, I'm confused. If your world was destroyed by the Earth Empire, where are we now? This world distinctly resembles the description of Hithis given to me by another member of your race.'

Hater Of Humans's answer was directed at the Doctor, but it was looking at Beltempest as it spoke.

'We have established a secret base in the midst of the only remnant of Hithis left to us: a sanctuary in the midst of our enemies. We are in one of their training areas on the Imperial Landsknecht planet Purgatory.'

* * *

Forrester paused in the doorway. Cwej could tell that she wasn't happy, but she flicked the switch anyway.

'Good luck!' he hissed, and gave her a quick thumbs up. She shot him a dirty glance, then the door opened and she stepped inside the room.

'She's in,' he told Bernice and Powerless Friendless, who were standing behind him.

'We know,' Bernice said. 'We saw.'

He was just about to explain that he *knew* that they knew but was just making conversation when a voice snarled, 'Whaddya want?' from inside the room.

'I hear you've been abusing one of my staff,' Forrester snarled louder.

'Whaddya mean?' The guard sounded suspicious. Cwej reached for the reassurance of his gun.

'I mean that I've had a complaint from one of my cleaners. He said you verbally abused him.'

Beside Cwej, Bernice shook her head. 'Not trying very hard, is she?'

'Give her time,' Cwej said defensively, 'she's not trained in undercover work.' He remembered the incomprehension on Forrester's face when Powerless Friendless suggested the plan. 'But you're an alien!' she had said. 'You should expect abuse. And why should a human supervisor be concerned? The guard'll never buy it.'

'All you have to do,' Bernice had explained patiently for the third time, 'is get the guard where Cwej here can come in and lay him out from behind.'

An explosion of anger from inside the room snapped him back to reality.

'He said what? The dirty scummy slug!'

'I know, I know.' Forrester's voice was world-weary. 'But the shift supervisor's a fraggin' alien-lover. Me, I get caught in the middle. Do us both a favour: show me the stain. If I say it's still there, then we've got grounds to get rid of the slug. Nothing but a troublemaker, that one.'

Powerless Friendless shifted slightly beside Cwej, and frowned.

'It's all right,' Cwej said soothingly. 'She doesn't mean it.'

'I suspect she does,' Bernice said softly.

There was a scuffle of movement inside the room, then the guard said, 'There, look at it. What kind of job do you call that?'

'Hmm.' Forrester was silent for a moment, then she said, 'Hey, look at this.'

'What?'

'No, down here.'

'Where?'

'Look, right down here . . .'

Cwej risked a look around the edge of the door. The guard was kneeling down, his eyes a few inches from the floor and Forrester's pointing finger. Forrester looked up at the doorway, saw Cwej and nodded towards the nape of the guard's neck. A few quiet steps brought Cwej up behind the kneeling man's back.

'Can't see nothing,' the guard said.

'What about this?' Forrester said as Cwej's hand sliced through the air, impacting on the guard's temple with a meaty *chunk*! He shook his head slowly, and tried to turn around. By the time his eyes locked with Cwej's, there was nobody home. He slumped gracelessly to the floor.

'Brilliant,' Bernice said as she and Powerless Friendless entered the room. 'If ever I want some heavy hitting done, I'll be in touch.'

'Thanks,' Cwej said, pleased at the unexpected praise. He looked around, taking in the details of the room for the first time. Apart from a desk and chair on one side and a metal vault door and a window set into the far wall, the room was empty. Like Powerless Friendless had said, the window showed a view across to the next block, but the door in the wall next to it was security rated. He moved across and looked out of the window. It was no simcord, that was for sure.

Bernice walked across his side and stared at the vault door. As far as Cwej could see it was made of solid alutrium. A small but sophisticated security lock on the desk presumably controlled access to whatever lay beyond.

'I don't suppose . . .' Bernice started to say, then looked back at Forrester, Cwej and Powerless Friendless. 'No,' she finished, 'I don't suppose any of you do.'

'Wait a moment,' the Hith said, and slid forward. 'I think I might be able to help.'

'You?' Forrester said. 'How?'

Powerless Friendless's eye-stalks rotated to look at her. 'Krohg,' he said. 'My pet. He's good with locks.' He started rummaging around in his rucksack.

'This isn't just a lock,' Bernice said. 'It's a computer-controlled access system. No budgie, however smart, is going to get in.'

'He's very clever,' Powerless Friendless said, still rummaging. 'But I can't seem to – '

'He's here,' Cwej said, reaching into his pocket and closing his hand around the small, soft form of the creature named Krohg. At Forrester and Powerless Friendless's accusing glares, he shrugged and said, 'Well, he's cute.'

'Cute?' Forrester said. 'Cwej, you're sick.'

Cwej tickled the little orange creature under the chin – at least, he assumed it was the chin – and handed it to Powerless Friendless. The Hith slithered across to the desk and placed Krogh against the access panel, murmuring something to it as he did so. The little creature flattened itself against the keys, and quivered slightly.

'We're wasting time,' Forrester said. 'We need to get through that door, and this isn't doing us any – '

With a beep and a faint rumble of machinery, the door opened.

'I don't believe it,' Forrester murmured.

Cwej rushed across and picked Krohg up before Powerless Friendless could retrieve it.

'Well done,' he said. Turning to Bernice he said, 'Don't you think that was well done?'

She didn't answer. She was just staring through the

opening that the vault door had revealed. A strange grey light was playing across her face.

Cwej turned to follow her gaze. Through the doorway, a catwalk extended for a hundred or so metres. At the end of the catwalk was a spacecraft of a strange design, rounded and spiked, like some alien insect. Everything else through the opening apart from the catwalk and the ship was a pearly, shifting grey that looked as if it was simultaneously infinitely distant and close enough to touch.

'Isn't that . . .?' Cwej started to say, but Bernice beat him to it.

'Yes,' she said quietly, 'it's hyperspace.'

Chapter 13

'I'm Shythe Shahid and this is The Empire Today, *on the spot, on and off the Earth. Reports from the Imperial Palace in orbit around Saturn suggest the Empress is on the verge of imposing martial law in selected Overcity areas in an attempt to contain the rioting that is slowly but surely eating its way like a cancer across the heart of the Empire. The first measure to be announced will almost certainly be a curfew, with death as the penalty for non-compliance. Meanwhile, it is rumoured that Professor Zebulon Pryce, noted scientist and mass murderer, has escaped from the Landsknechte Penal Institution on Dis. We go live now to . . .'*

The Doctor's eyebrows rose in surprise and amusement, partly at what Hater Of Humans had said and partly at Provost-Major Beltempest's open-mouthed astonishment.

'You've built an encampment on *Purgatory*?' he said.

Hater Of Humans nodded.

'Before terraforming Hithis,' it said, 'the Landsknechte preserved a portion of its surface and transplanted it to their own world. They did this not in remembrance of our planet, but as a trophy, and as an example of territory on which their tactics had been tested, and found to be lacking.' Hater Of Humans sighed heavily. 'It was all that was left of Hithis as we remembered it. After the War, some Hith were allowed to take menial jobs on Purgatory. Dedicated agents managed to work out a way to disable the Landsknechte's sensors. Our ships can slip in and out of

242

Landsknecht space at will, without being detected. This encampment was built for myself and the Hith government in exile. Our agents – cleaners for the most part – alert us if an exercise is to be carried out, and we pack up the tents and leave the planet for the duration. Given the number of planetary environments on Purgatory, it happens very rarely.'

Beltempest was making spluttering noises through his trunk.

'Good for you,' the Doctor said, grinning. 'I can, however, appreciate your desire to regain your own world, and presumably your plan is to use this sample of Hithis as a template with which to "Hithisform" your own world again.' As Hater Of Humans nodded, he continued: 'I do, however, have a question concerning this lost ship of yours.'

Hater Of Humans sighed. 'Yes, human?'

'I'm not ... Oh, never mind. What was so special about it? How exactly did icaron technology help you to construct a better warship?'

Hater Of Humans shrugged. 'I am not a technician,' it said loftily, 'I am a ruler.'

The Doctor scowled. 'Indulge me. What can you remember?'

The guard started forward, but Hater Of Humans waved her back with a languid pseudo-limb.

'My advisors informed me,' it continued, 'that the main problem with our warships was the immense power they need to generate in order to enter ... hyperspace? and thus move between the stars. With so much power dedicated to that task, there was less to use for weaponry and manoeuvring in ordinary space. It seemed at the time a plausible argument.'

'So?'

'Somehow,' Hater Of Humans said, 'icarons helped solve this problem. I know not how. My only interest was in preventing the Earth Empire from raping our glorious planet. I would have grasped at any passing opportunity.'

The Doctor turned to Professor Pryce, whose eyes were

closed and whose body was relaxed. 'Professor? Perhaps you can help us out here.'

Pryce's eyes opened slowly, and he turned his black gaze on the Doctor.

'Icarons are elementary particles that exist in their rest state in hyperspace,' he whispered. 'As their energy levels increase, they slip from hyperspace into the real universe. In this regard they are the opposite of normal matter, which requires energy to take it from the real universe into hyperspace. It is that extra energy, over and above the rest-state energy of particles of normal matter, that makes them so dangerous to the human mind.' He smiled slightly. 'You appreciate that I use the term "real" with some distaste. Nothing is real. All is illusion.'

'And so,' the Doctor added, 'by building a spaceship around a low-energy icaron particle accelerator, you ensure that it actually prefers being in hyperspace – which is, if you like, its natural habitat. The low-energy icarons act as an anchor in hyperspace, whereas, if they are given energy, they pull it into real space. Most of its power can then be diverted to weapons and manoeuvrability.' He raised his eyebrows as the implications of the thought unrolled before him. In a strange sort of way, the Hith had done with a spaceship what the Time Lords had done with a time craft. After all, TARDISes 'lived' in the time vortex, and only emerged into reality under protest and with much encouragement.

Beside him, Provost-Major Beltempest caught his breath. 'Incredible,' he said. 'A ship like that could have changed the course of the war if it hadn't been captured!'

Hater Of Humans shifted in its seat. Beside it, Hopeless Itinerant curled a pseudo-limb around the vestigial shell at the base of its tail and yanked hard.

'You have no idea how pleased I am to hear it,' Hater Of Humans murmured over Hopeless Itinerant's squeal. 'But you distract me.' It turned to Pryce. 'Professor Pryce, where *is* our ship? Where is the *Skel'Ske*?'

Pryce shook his head.

'I do not know,' he said simply.

'But . . . ?' Hater Of Humans jerked upright in its seat. The guard grabbed for her gun.

'After my mind was opened to higher possibilities,' Pryce whispered, low and compulsively, 'after the sacrament of pain and degradation was revealed to me, the Imperial Landsknechte took your ship away. I believe it was given to an independent company with experience in subatomic particles. They were contracted to take it apart, on the basis that they could patent any spin-off technology. I don't know which company it was.' He smiled. 'By then, I was past caring about such mundane things as finance. Only death interested me. Death, and the prolonging of the moment of death, the stretching of pain until it became like a fine, taut wire that, when plucked, rang out in a scream of pure agony.'

Pryce closed his eyes and leaned back in his seat. All eyes and eye-stalks turned from him to Provost-Major Beltempest.

'Don't look at me,' he protested. 'Even if I knew, I wouldn't tell you.' He turned to look at the Doctor.

'Who would be likely to get such a contract?' the Doctor said.

'Doctor, I will not discuss classified information with aliens!'

The Doctor removed a gold Hunter watch from his waistcoat pocket and opened the face. As Beltempest, Pryce and Hater Of Humans watched, fascinated, he counted off ten seconds, then put the watch away.

'Based upon my earlier calculations in your laboratory,' he said, 'fifteen people have just gone mad on Earth as a result of the release of icaron radiation from the *Skel'Ske*. How many more will you allow to die? What proportion of humanity will have to be sacrificed before you change your mind? Who knows what the effects will be on the Empire? We have to make them realize the dangers of dealing with icarons!'

Beltempest took a deep breath. 'You have an unerring knack of reducing everything to a simple choice between two unpleasant alternatives,' he said through clenched

245

teeth. 'If I wanted robotic workers for something, I would choose INITEC. Their experience in cybernetics and robotics is unparalleled.'

'INITEC?' the Doctor queried. 'I thought I'd come across most of the major corporations in my time, but that's a new one on me.'

'It stands for Interstellar Nanoatomic ITEC,' Beltempest replied.

'If I knew what ITEC stood for it might help,' grumbled the Doctor.

Beltempest sighed. 'Where have you been? ITEC is an acronym for Independent Terran Empire Corporation.'

A bit like the words 'limited' or 'incorporated' back in the time of his exile on Earth, the Doctor reflected. Interstellar Nanoatomic ITEC. Something about that name caused a shiver to run up his spine. Not the name itself, but its component parts. He'd heard them before, in a different order, and not in a pleasant context.

'Interstellar Nanoatomic ITEC is the only major corporation whose headquarters are still on Earth,' Beltempest continued as the Doctor rolled various alternatives around in his mind. 'Every other one has moved to the outer Rim planets, but INITEC stayed. Their building is in Spaceport Five Overcity, but – '

Now *that* name rang a bell, as Quasimodo once said.

'Spaceport Five Overcity,' the Doctor said grimly. 'The area of Earth that everybody who went mad had passed through, if you remember our calculations on Purgatory.'

It fell to Beltempest to sum up what they were all thinking. All except Pryce, whose thoughts were of a colour and texture that nobody else could understand.

'So the *Skel'Ske* is on Earth,' Beltempest whispered, 'and the radiation from its engines is driving people mad.'

The null-grav lift shaft was only large enough to carry one normal-sized person, and Viscount Henson Farlander, aide-in-chief to the Empress, could feel its curved walls scraping his sides. He rose gently away from the vast ballroom with its teeming flocks of the aristocracy toward the Imperial Presence. The walls were cold – cold enough that ice was forming on them – and he tried his best to pull his flesh away to avoid blisters. Still, it was a miracle of engineering. Not six inches away was the hard, cold vacuum of space. Here in the shaft it was just a trifle uncomfortable.

The shaft deposited him at the base of the spherical Imperial Throne Room. He looked around, stunned as always by the view. The transparisteel walls were polished so well that he couldn't even see them. All that he could see was Saturn's majestic bulk, and the rainbow of its rings arcing away from him, front and back, as if the Imperial Throne Room were a transparent bubble sliding gracefully along an endless road of ice.

The Divine Empress's naked body hovered above him: a warty excrescence of flesh with stumps for limbs, bloated by the incurable, inoperable tumours and diseases of extreme old age. Thin wires haloed her asymmetric head, leading to the machines that boosted her intelligence and sent it flying across space. She had ruled for so long that generations had lived and died without realizing that she was centcomp; that she was the controlling intelligence that ran the solar system. And yet . . . and yet . . .

There were some problems that even she couldn't solve.

'NEWS?' her voice boomed. Farlander knew that only a fraction of her attention was directed at him. The rest was shunting information for hundreds of trillions of people across billions of miles.

'Most Supreme and Puissant Majesty . . .' Farlander began in his most humble voice.

'NEWS?'

Henson clapped his hands across his ears. 'It's *protocol*,' he snapped. 'Whether you like it or not, it's the way an Empress is addressed.'

'NEWS?'

'Oh, very well.' Farlander sighed. 'Where do you want to start?'

'MEMORY PROBLEMS.'

'Well . . .' Farlander hesitated. The Empress was direct,

247

brutal even when it came to plain facts, but Farlander was uneasy about discussing her frailties. Even in the Imperial Court, rumours spread fast.

Even in the Imperial Court? *Especially* in the Imperial Court.

'The technicians believe that someone else has gained access to centcomp,' he said finally, taking a deep breath. 'To you. They believe that this person has the ability to alter your memories. They think that – '

'FIND THEM,' the Empress said. 'KILL THEM.'

'Find them?' Farlander raised his eyes to the inhuman form that hung above him. 'How, if we can't trust centcomp?'

'ISOLATE MEMORIES. COMPARE WITH MONTHLY BACKUPS FOR PAST TEN YEARS. LOOK FOR ALTERATIONS. PUT RIGHT.'

When the Divine Empress had to speak at that length to the man who was supposed to be able to take one word of hers and translate it into complex actions, Farlander knew that she wasn't happy.

'Yes, your most Supreme and Puiss–'

'NEXT.'

'Your Surgeon Imperialis seems to have discovered that the violence and the riots sweeping the Empire are connected to body-bepple. Apparently every violent event can be traced back to a person who has undergone the process.'

'STATISTICALLY INSIGNIFICANT,' the Empress scoffed.

'A message has been passed on by the Imperial Landsknechte. One of their provost-majors has intelligence that seems to back up the theory. He claims to have discovered a connection between the violence, body-bepple and some obscure form of radiation.'

'REWARD. CROSS-REFER TO SURGEON IMPERIALIS. NEXT.'

'The Hith delegation are down in an anteroom. They've been waiting for three days to see you.'

'KEEP ALIENS WAITING. NEXT.'

Farlander felt sweat beading his forehead. There were five hundred points on the agenda. He might be there for some time.

The ship wasn't in any condition to fly; Cwej could see that from the other end of the catwalk. The distorting effects of hyperspace, and the lack of any referents to aid perspective, meant that the ship alternated between being a huge shape millions of miles away and a small object hanging just in front of him. Despite the tricks his eyes were playing on him he could see that large areas of its almost organic hull plating had been removed to reveal its skeletal frame, leaving it like a gutted fish. Small bots were crawling over it, dismantling the plates with bright plasma lances. The area at the front – the cockpit, judging by the bulbous transparent canopy – was almost complete, as was the engine compartment at the rear. The ship's middle – the cargo area and weapon emplacements – had been stripped away, leaving only the central backbone-like main spar. The catwalk led to an open hatch in the cockpit area.

'I hope those bots aren't watching out for intruders,' Forrester muttered.

Cwej nodded absently. He'd seen something like it before, he was sure of it. The smooth, spavined surfaces were terribly familiar. Was it a Dravidian design? Shlangian? Antonine?

'Of course!' He slapped his forehead with the palm of his hand as the memory came to him. Forrester whirled around, gun at the ready, then cast him a dirty look as she gradually relaxed. 'It's a Hith ship!'

Beside him, Powerless Friendless bobbed his eye-stalks in agreement. 'The *Skel'Ske*,' he said, awed.

'*Skel'Ske*?' Cwej tried out the unfamiliar syllables.

'Skel'Ske is the sound made by the wings of Jakkat-Kajjat, the twin-headed Goddess of Justified Retribution, as she passes overhead at dawn, tearing the souls of her enemies from their bodies.'

'What's wrong with *Rosebud*?' Bernice muttered.

'I used to have a model of a Hith battleship,' Cwej said. 'I made it myself. Big thing, it was, with these spike things jutting out of the front.' He waved his arms around, trying to convey to Powerless Friendless some impression of the size and sheer spikiness of the ship as if the Hith didn't already know. 'Big, *big* hyperdrive motors in a ring around its middle. I had it hanging above my bed for years. The cleaning bots used to hate dusting it.'

Powerless Friendless just nodded sadly.

'The *Gex*,' he sighed. 'Flagship of the Hith Cosmic Fleet. Destroyed by the Imperial Landsknecht Fleet while defending Hithis during the Great Patriotic War. Fifteen thousand Hith dead. Less than twenty survivors.'

Cwej could almost feel the weight of the model in his hands. It had taken him almost a week to paint the concentric yellow and red Hith battle colours on the complex curves of the hull. He'd been so proud of that ship. 'And what about the little things,' he said excitedly, 'the ones that looked like needles with hyperdrive engines? I always loved those ones.'

'The flickerships?' Powerless Friendless said. 'Our front-line fighters? I trained on one of those.'

'They were brilliant! They looked like they could run rings around anything.'

'That's what we thought,' Powerless Friendless said bitterly, and slid off along the catwalk towards the ship.

Cwej watched him go, wondering what he had said to depress the Hith.

'Ever considered a career in the diplomatic service?' Forrester asked as she walked past Cwej, clapping him on the shoulder.

Cwej felt a flicker of anger, and bit down on it before he said something he might regret. Shaking his head, he followed Forrester along the catwalk. He didn't usually get annoyed at her banter. He must have been more tired than he had thought, despite his subjectively long rest in the time tank.

Bernice's long stride brought her up to his side as he walked. She was looking around at their surroundings.

Cwej, after his initial wide-eyed reaction to hyperspace, had been trying to ignore it. There was something about it that reminded him of a large blind spot; he felt that if he looked at it for too long, he would want to throw himself off the catwalk.

He looked backwards, but that was worse. The entrance doorway hung unsupported in hyperspace at the end of the catwalk. What would happen if it closed? Would it vanish? Leave them stranded?

He shuddered, and gazed resolutely back at the approaching ship, trying not to wonder how he was managing to breathe in hyperspace.

'I wonder how they keep this tunnel from drifting off,' Bernice said. 'I mean, anchoring something to one spot in hyperspace must be quite an engineering feat. There are tides, whirlpools and all sorts of things. Presumably the air just hangs around here on the basis that it hasn't got anywhere else to go.'

'Haven't got a clue,' he said, gulping.

'I prefer you without the fur and the pointy ears, by the way.'

He smiled at her. 'Thanks,' he said, touched. He could feel a blush spreading up from his neck, and walked faster, hoping that Bernice would mistake it for signs of his exertion. Joining Forrester and Powerless Friendless by the knobbly hull of the ship, he gazed up in wonder at the brightly coloured spikes and spines and the smooth curves of its hull.

'It's incredible,' he murmured.

Powerless Friendless extruded a pseudo-limb and caressed the ship's skin. It seemed to bend slightly under the pressure of his tentacular fingers.

'No sign of any power,' he said. 'I was half afraid that they might have found a way to turn the engines on, but without the nexus – '

'The nexus?' Bernice asked, but Powerless Friendless turned away.

Cwej ran his hand over the hull as well. Turning to Powerless Friendless, he asked, 'What was it armed with?'

'Klypstrømic warheads,' the Hith said softly, 'quark projectors, high-power masers and long-range transdyne impellers. All the energy we saved by using the new power source was diverted to weapon systems. It was our last, best hope.'

Cwej's breath hissed out in a long impressed exhalation.

'Incredible,' he murmured. 'This ship could've won the war.'

'Tell me about it,' the Hith murmured.

'Powerless Friendless,' Bernice said, 'you mentioned that this ship had a new power source. What was it?'

'Something called an icaron ring,' he said. 'That's what the engineers called it. Apparently these icarons are particles that prefer to be in hyperspace. That's their natural habitat. The icaron ring kept them circulating inside a magnetic Klein bottle. The theory was that if enough energy was pumped in, they started to slip into the real universe.'

Icarons. That word was familiar. Cwej scratched his head, trying to recall what it meant. He could see from the puzzled expression on Forrester's face that it was familiar to her as well.

'Icarons,' Bernice mused. 'The Doctor mentioned them.' Her face suddenly brightened at the same time that Cwej remembered where he had heard the word before.

'Purgatory!' they exclaimed together.

'The things that drive people mad,' Forrester added.

They all gazed up at the jester-coloured bulk of the *Skel'Ske* with something approaching dread.

'Look,' Bernice said eventually, 'offhand, I can't think of any good reason to go in there.'

With no warning, fire suddenly bloomed across the hull of the ship. The three of them recoiled in the sudden heat.

'What the . . . ?' Bernice started to say as she turned, but the words dried in her mouth at the sight of the three bots pounding along the walkway towards them. They were tall, sleek, four-armed and terribly familiar.

'I can,' said Forrester, and dived through the hatch.

* * *

Hater Of Humans's eye-stalks perked up, then dropped slowly.

'No, Doctor,' it said. 'I appreciate your efforts to help, but our agents work as cleaners in every major corporation on Earth, including INITEC. If the *Skel'Ske* was there, we would have known about it.'

'Not,' the Doctor said, 'if it was held in hyperspace.'

There was silence around the table as they all digested the idea. Even Zebulon Pryce's eyes opened in interest.

'Explain,' Hater Of Humans snapped.

'Unlike ordinary ships, the *Skel'Ske* was designed to be able to stay in hyperspace with a zero power output.' The Doctor waved his hands in the air as if clutching at passing thoughts with which he was building his theory. 'All the Interstellar Nanoatomic ITEC had to do was to leave it there, and build some kind of hyperspace portal in their building. That way, they could get to the ship easily while still keeping it isolated from Hith space. That's why your predictions were wrong about the levels of madness that should have swept the Earth by now. The particles only emerge, beaming like a searchlight across Spaceport Five, when the door is opened.'

'A ship in hyperspace on Earth!' Beltempest said, stunned. 'It's never even been attempted before. The amount of power required to keep it there, so close to a planetary core, would destroy the planet entirely!'

'Not with this ship,' the Doctor said. 'Remember: it likes being in hyperspace. It *prefers* it. With the engines off, it's almost impossible for it to be anywhere else.'

'But the icaron radiation is still escaping,' Hater Of Humans said. 'Our predictions may have been wrong, but humans are still going mad. If the ship was in hyperspace . . .'

'Whoever is in charge of taking it apart has to get to it,' the Doctor persisted. 'The portal has to be opened in order to get the workers to and from it, and to get components back and forth. If they'd known about icarons driving people mad they could have fitted a double door at least, but they obviously haven't, despite – ' He glanced over at Pryce. ' – despite the evidence. If your ship is in the INITEC building on Earth, then the urgent thing is to switch the icaron power source off. Can you do it?'

In reply, Hater Of Humans beckoned to Hopeless Itinerant, who picked up the box at his feet and slithered forward, placing it on the table in front of Hater Of Humans, who said: 'In this box is a control nexus for the *Skel'Ske*. As with much of our technology, it is a living being, genetically engineered for its task.'

'Is it intelligent?' the Doctor asked, intrigued.

'To a certain extent,' Hater of Humans replied. 'These mechanisms require some measure of self-determination in order to carry out their tasks. This one is more intelligent than most, as it has to control the functions of our most advanced craft.'

'A spare, I presume?'

'The original was on board the *Skel'Ske*,' Hater of Humans admitted, dipping its head. 'We must presume that either the pilot or the navigator stole it.'

'And their names were Homeless Forsaken Betrayed And Alone and Powerless Friendless And Scattered Through Space,' the Doctor said quietly.

'How did you know?' Hater Of Humans was incredulous.

The Doctor just shook his head. 'It's a small universe,' he said. 'I met one of them on – '

He was interrupted by Zebulon Pryce, who calmly leaned forward and picked up the box.

'Put the nexus down!' Hater Of Humans screamed.

'Am I right in thinking,' Pryce said casually, 'that this organic device is the only thing that can switch the icaron generator off?'

'Put it *down*!'

Pryce's long fingers flicked the lid of the box up. Something shifted inside, and he reached in. A thin, piercing shriek filled the room, making Hater Of Humans, Hopeless Itinerant and the two guards flinch.

'Am I right?' he repeated, his voice calm and level.

'Yes,' Hater Of Humans said tightly. 'It is our last hope. Put it –'

'And if it is destroyed, then thousands, if not millions of people will go mad and kill each other?' He withdrew his hand from the box. He was holding a small creature shaped rather like an Earth cuttlefish. Its skin was slimy and orange, and its three stalked eyes had a nasty gleam in them. It twisted in Pryce's hand and sank its cogwheel teeth into his palm. He smiled slightly as the blood trickled down his arm.

With a sickening realization, the Doctor could see where the conversation was leading. If he hadn't spent so long talking to Pryce on board Beltempest's spacecraft he wouldn't have believed it himself, but he knew what the man was going to do. The Hith, with limited knowledge of the limits to which the human mind could be driven, had no chance. He opened his mouth to warn Hater Of Humans, but he was too late.

'Yes,' said Hater Of Humans. 'As the shielding around the icaron ring is removed and the radiation builds, more and more people will be affected every time the door into hyperspace is opened. According to the fastline reports we have been receiving, there are already riots on Earth and insurrections on some of the colony planets. Murder rates are rising steadily. Earth is on the verge of collapse. If you value the lives of your fellow humans, put the nexus down! It's your only chance!'

Pryce suddenly clenched his hand. The nexus screamed shrilly for a brief moment before it ruptured and a pink liquid splattered up and across the table. Pryce smiled at the other six people in the room.

'My only regret,' he said licking at the gelatinous remains that slid down his wrist and forearm, 'is that I will not be around to watch it.'

'Kill him,' said Hater Of Humans.

Pryce made no attempt to escape as the female guard aimed her weapon at him and pulled the trigger. His face creased into a smile as the beam of pure, unsullied energy burned its way through his forehead, blackening and blistering his flesh. Amazingly, he stood up and stretched his arms wide. For a split second, light shone from his eyes and mouth as he was consumed from within. The Doctor wasn't sure, but he thought that Pryce said something just before his head imploded and his body slumped to the floor. Whatever words he said, the Doctor couldn't make them out, and he was glad that he couldn't. Whatever message Pryce had sent back from the edge of death, it wasn't one the Doctor wanted to hear.

Pryce's death took just under three seconds, but the Doctor felt as though he had been sitting watching the man die for an eternity. When he turned back to Hater Of Humans, he felt older than he ever had before.

Hater Of Humans was ashen and shivering. Beside it, Hopeless Itinerant reached down towards its tail.

'No!' the Doctor shouted, but before he could stop it, Hopeless Itinerant curled a pseudo-limb around its vestigial shell and, without a moment's hesitation, pulled it right off.

It screamed, and died before its blood could hit the walls.

The Doctor shook his head sadly. There were moments in his life when he felt as if he was in the last act of a Jacobean tragedy.

Chapter 14

'Please listen carefully. This is an announcement by the Imperial Landsknechte. By order of Her Highness the Divine Empress, Glory of the Empire, Ruler of the High Court, Lord of the Inner and Outer Worlds, High Admiral of the Galactic Fleets, Lord General of the Six Armies and Defender of the Earth, a state of martial law has been declared across the planet. From this moment forward until further notice, a twenty-four-hour curfew is in effect. This is purely for your own protection, and law-abiding citizens have nothing to fear. The punishment for rioting is immediate death. The punishment for looting is immediate death. The punishment for sabotage is immediate death. The punishment for breaking the curfew is immediate death. The punishment . . . '

'Powerless Friendless?' Bernice hissed. 'Where the hell are you?' The spongy walls of the *Skel'Ske* absorbed the sound of her voice, deadening it, stripping it of the tension that she felt and leaving it sounding flat and almost bored.

There was no answer. Bernice moved farther down the corridor, sweat cooling her brow, continually swivelling her head to check that none of the sleek bots were creeping up on her or lurking around the curve ahead. Everything was curved in this ship; there wasn't an angle or a flat surface anywhere in sight. Question: why did the Romans build straight roads? Answer: so that the Saxons couldn't hide around corners. She wished she had a gun. Cancel that; she wished she had a *big* gun, one of those ones that took two hands and a shoulder strap to carry, and was linked by a big curly cable to a power supply so huge that it had to follow along behind on caterpillar tracks. Alternatively, she wished she had the Doctor there. Better than any gun. Not quite as impressive to the casual glance, but far more effective, and didn't need reloading. Just shutting up occasionally.

She stopped for a moment and took a deep breath. The tension was getting to her. Even her thoughts were babbling. Think calm, Bernice. Gently lapping waters. Birdsong. Chocolate mousse.

As her heartbeat slowed to a level where she could actually distinguish the separate beats, she sank against the wall, resting her back and her hands against its moistness. It gave slightly beneath her weight. Perhaps it was her imagination, or perhaps she was just picking up her own pulse, but she could have sworn the wall throbbed slightly beneath her palms.

Like huge, bloated flies, her thoughts kept circling around a particular notion. What if, somewhere deep inside her brain, a, vein of fire was beginning to glow? What if she was already being driven mad by the icaron radiation from the *Skel'Ske*'s engines? What if it was already too late?

Then again, what if she'd just stayed on Earth and joined Spacefleet? What if she'd never gone to Heaven and met the Doctor? To think of all the things she would have missed, all the glorious sights she never would have seen . . .

She shook her head slightly. Never say die, that's what the Doctor had told her the last time she had thought about giving up. Never say die.

She remembered finding a book of poems in the TARDIS library, during her period of moping after Ace had left. The poems had been written by a man named Dylan Thomas. According to the introduction, he had been something of a drinker. That's what made her read on. A man after her own heart. A phrase still echoed in her mind from one of those poems, a gauntlet flung in the face of the universe.

'Rage, rage against the dying of the light.'

Never say die.

She pushed herself away from the wall. If she was going to go as mad as a Dalek in the middle of a universal battery shortage she'd do it standing up and cursing, thank you very much. She had a job to do, and she'd better get on with it.

They had split up on entering the ship. They had agreed that, with hunter-killer robots on the case, the important thing was to search the ship to ensure that nobody else was aboard, and then try and find some way of taking off and getting the hell out of there. Forrester and Cwej had headed towards the engine room; Bernice had volunteered to make for the control room with Powerless Friendless.

But by the time this had all been agreed, Powerless Friendless had vanished.

'Powerless Friendless?' she hissed again, just in case he was around.

'Bernice?' The voice was loud, and came from just above her head. Bernice remembered to clap a hand over her mouth before screaming against her clammy palm.

'Did I startle you?' Powerless Friendless asked. She looked up. His mollusc body was attached to the ceiling with mucus and his eye-stalks were almost on a level with her eyes.

'No!' she exclaimed, her voice so high that even the sound-deadening walls of the corridor couldn't disguise her surprise.

'I've found something interesting,' Powerless Friendless said. 'Follow me.' He slithered off around the bend in the corridor, his course taking him across the ceiling and halfway down the wall before he vanished from sight. Bernice ran a hand across her forehead, and followed, keeping to what she thought of as the floor.

There was an open doorway just around the bend, and through the doorway was a room lined with organic control panels. The whole thing looked suspiciously to Bernice like a garden centre.

'Communications room,' Powerless Friendless said succinctly as he reached the floor. 'I've checked over the controls. They're still operative. INITEC obviously started their deconstruction in the middle of the ship, at the weapons bays, and are working their way in both directions. They haven't got here yet.'

'And this helps us how?' Bernice asked.

'It doesn't help you,' he said, 'it helps me.' He extruded a trio of pseudo-limbs and began caressing the controls. They bloomed and sprouted beneath his touch. 'I'm sending a distress call.'

'To whom?'

He rotated an eye-stalk to face her. His gaze was thunderous.

'To whatever remains of the Hith,' he said.

The Doctor was standing outside the Hith encampment, enjoying the cool breeze and the sight of Purgatory's sun poised above the distant horizon. If this replica was anything to go by, he thought that he would have liked Hithis. It had a certain calmness about it, a rightness that reminded him of Florana and Metebelis in the good old days. The feeling of a planet at peace with itself.

Now Florana was a dumping ground for the waste products of thirty-six races, Metebelis was a desert wasteland and Hithis had been terraformed into a suburb of Earth. All that remained was a hexagonal section some three hundred kilometres across on somebody else's planet. Sometimes he despaired.

'Doctor?' Provost-Major Beltempest emerged from the tent behind him, past the Hith guards who were watching the Doctor and studiously ignoring each other.

'Over here.'

Beltempest lumbered over, wheezing asthmatically at the effort of moving his elephantine bulk. For a moment, he too watched the sun slide down beneath the edge of the world.

'Beautiful, isn't it?' the Doctor said rhetorically.

'No,' Beltempest said, and shivered. 'It reminds me too much of spilled blood. And spilled blood reminds me of – '

'He's gone,' the Doctor murmured without turning away from the thin sliver of light that showed above the skyline. 'He won't come back.'

Beltempest shook his head, his trunk swinging from side to side as he did so. 'No,' he sighed. 'He'll be back every time I go to sleep.' He caught his breath. 'Why does he bother me so much? Why can't I get him out of my mind?'

The Doctor watched as the sun finally slid from sight, leaving a crimson stain behind it that faded as he watched to a deep, meditative blue.

'Because you could have done the same,' he said finally, 'and that knowledge scares you. In the end, Pryce was right. There is no reason why one person should not kill another. No argument against murder stands up to scrutiny.' He sighed. 'For every religious prohibition saying, "Thou shalt not kill", there's another one that allows killing under certain special circumstances – sinners are fair game, "Thou shalt not suffer a witch to live", and so on. Moral codes are no better; they're just formalized opinions, without any logical backup.' He was aware that his voice was getting louder and louder, but he couldn't seem to help himself. 'The sociological history of almost every race,' he continued, 'is riddled with examples of laws against murder standing beside legalized examples of murder, be they executions, wars or euthanasia. Ultimately, every single argument that we can come up with, stripped of its pretty words, boils down to a fundamental truth: we disagree with murder because *we don't want to be murdered*. No more and no less than that.' He closed his eyes for a second. 'Does that help?' he said finally.

'No,' Beltempest said sadly. 'But thanks for trying.'

There was silence for a few moments as darkness spread across the sky. High above, moving stars denoted watchful Vanguard laser satellites and the comings and goings of

Landsknechte ships. Odd, the Doctor thought, that the Hith should choose to live under the noses of their enemies, conducting their affairs of government from hiding. Odd, and rather courageous. That seemed to be the Hith way.

'Did you come out for anything in particular, or just fresh air?' he said finally.

'There's some sort of flap going on,' Beltempest replied. 'I think a message has come in. The slug in charge wanted me to come and fetch you.'

The Doctor sighed. 'The slug?' he said, raising his eyebrows. 'You mean the Hith.' The Doctor's tone was dark with foreboding, but Beltempest either didn't or wouldn't take any notice.

'If you like.'

'It's got nothing to do with what I do or do not like,' the Doctor explained as if talking to a small child. 'How would you like it if the Hith referred to you like that?'

'They wouldn't dare.' Beltempest walked away. The Doctor watched him for a few seconds, then shrugged and followed. There was no hope for some people.

Together, they re-entered the tent. Hater Of Humans was slumped in its chair. There was a feeling of suppressed excitement in the air.

'Good news?' the Doctor asked brightly.

'We have received a message from Daph Yilli Gar, the navigator of the Skel'Ske!' Hater Of Humans said, quivering slightly. 'He is calling himself Powerless Friendless And Scattered Through Space now. He has found the ship! You were right, Doctor, it is in hyperspace, occupying the same coordinates as the INITEC building.' Hater Of Humans's eye-stalks gleamed with pride. 'To think that after all this time, the Skel'Ske still works as it was intended to!' Hater Of Humans was ecstatic. 'We are preparing our fleet now.'

'Fleet?'

Beside the Doctor, Beltempest frowned. 'Yes,' he said. 'What do you need a fleet for? I thought you were worried in case the radiation from this ship of yours interfered with the efforts of your diplomats?'

Hater Of Humans shifted slightly in its chair. 'To help Daph Yilli Gar,' it said. 'He is under attack, and cannot get into the control room. He requests our aid.'

'Don't you think,' the Doctor interposed, 'that a Hith fleet in hyperspace near the Earth might be counter-productive?'

Hater Of Humans gazed at him for a moment, then slid away. The Doctor drummed his fingers against his lips. Much as he wanted to return to Earth, to Bernice and to the TARDIS, he didn't particularly want to do it at the head of what might seem to be – or might actually turn out to be – an invasion fleet.

The figures for profit and loss that flickered deep in the desk indicated that the riots were spreading. Insurance claims were climbing steeply, weapon sales were going through the roof, tickets for off-world flights were changing hands at vastly inflated prices. Accordingly, the artificial intelligence that controlled INITEC's financial affairs made various decisions in the absence of its master. Property was obviously a bad investment at the moment, on the basis that it might not be there for much longer, so various buildings and prime sites on Earth were placed on the market – or rather, on markets far enough away that the news of the riots probably hadn't reached them yet. Shares were purchased in construction and repair companies. All funds were transferred to financial systems off-world, just in case.

The flickering financial information in the desk reflected off the metal skin of INITEC's chairman and major shareholder. Its only shareholder. Columns of blue and red figures scrolled in reverse across his gleaming chest. He did not notice. His attention was elsewhere, flitting back and forth between fifty sleek killer robots as they hunted their prey through the corridors of the Hith ship. His ship.

For the first time in a millennium, he was enjoying himself.

* * *

In the Doctor's almost unparalleled experience of the various forms of space travel, most of the time spent journeying from planet to planet was taken up by the manoeuvring through the solar system at either end. Comparatively little time was spent in hyperspace. Because the Hith didn't intend leaving hyperspace at all when they arrived in the vicinity of Earth, the journey time was cut to less than an hour.

The Doctor watched from the oval, mazelike control deck of the Hith flagship as they made their approach. He and Beltempest were standing beside Hater Of Humans in a central hub of the maze, obviously making the Hith leader uneasy by their proximity. Above the walls of the maze, the ceiling was one vast screen upon which the Earth showed up as a vast distortion, a gigantic twist in the grey, swirling non-realm of hyperspace.

'We have a homing signal,' one of the Hith crew announced. It, like its compadres, was out of sight around a bend in the maze, sitting at its own set of controls, unable to see anybody else. Given the Hith dislike of company, it probably made them feel better if they could each imagine that they were the only Hith on the ship.

'Daph Yilli Gar has left the transmitter on,' Hater Of Humans announced. 'Head directly for it.'

Beltempest, standing beside the Doctor, said, 'Has it occurred to them that this might be a trap?'

'And what would they do differently?' the Doctor asked.

Beltempest shook his head. 'I don't know,' he said finally. 'I've lost track of who's doing what to whom, and why. If somebody had told me a week ago that I'd be standing on the flight deck of an armed slug battle cruiser heading for Earth I wouldn't have believed them. I keep having to stop myself from trying to sabotage the controls.'

'And why don't you?' the Doctor asked, interested.

'Because I have the sneaking suspicion that I might be doing more harm than good that way,' Beltempest said.

'Ship sighted!' a Hith crew member shouted jubilantly. 'Positive identification: it's the *Skel'Ske*!'

A cheer broke out through the maze as a small, thorny shape appeared on the main screen. The hyperspatial distortion made it shimmer, as if it was being viewed through water, but it was apparent that large parts of it had been dismantled already.

'Bring us up close,' Hater Of Humans ordered.

As they drew nearer to the *Skel'Ske*, the Doctor could make out the walkway that led away from the ship. At the other end there was a doorway, hanging in the void without visible means of support.

'See,' the Doctor said, pointing it out to Beltempest. 'That's how the radiation from the ship got to Earth.'

'That's a doorway to the real world?' Beltempest stuttered. 'I don't believe it!'

'That's human ingenuity for you,' the Doctor said.

He glanced over to where Hater Of Humans sat in its S-shaped chair. The Gatherer of the Scattered Shards of Hithis was poised eagerly, watching with bright eyes and erect eye-stalks as they drew alongside the sleek, spiked ship.

'Glorious,' it murmured. 'Absolutely glorious.'

'The weapon bays have been removed,' the Doctor murmured.

'We can replace them,' Hater Of Humans said. Its eye-stalks suddenly whipped around towards the Doctor. 'Not that we want to,' it added. 'We're merely trying to turn the icaron ring off.'

'Of course,' the Doctor said. 'I believe you.'

'Look!' a Hith shouted. On the screen a squad of ten tall, angular robots were running along it towards the *Skel'Ske*. As they watched, the bots disappeared inside the hatchway at the front of the ship.

'So,' the Doctor mused, 'that part of Powerless Friendless's story was true, at least.'

'Bring us alongside that walkway,' Hater Of Humans ordered. 'Order a squad of my personal honour guard to prevent further incursions through the doorway. Two more squads to enter the ship and find Daph Yilli Gar!'

The ship slowed to a halt under the expert pseudo-limb

of the pilot, and rotated until it lay parallel to the walkway. A tube extruded from the ship's side towards the walkway. Lasers flared as the tubes joined. Robotic grapples pulled them close, to form an airtight seal.

'Doctor,' Hater Of Humans snapped, 'you will aid me in . . . Doctor?'

But neither the Doctor nor Provost-Major Beltempest were there.

Adjudicator in Extremis Bij Kakrell stood on the highest point of the Adjudication lodge, watching the towers burn.

'I can't believe it,' she said, the flames casting her shadow back across the roof like a huge, flapping cape. 'After all we worked for. To see it all like this. In flames . . .' Lost for words, she just shook her head.

'The Divine Empress has declared martial law,' Duke Marmion, Lord Protector of the Solar System, murmured. His thin, emaciated face seemed to glow in the light from below. Behind him, a small knot of peers – the Marquesa of Earth and her retinue of counts and countesses, viscounts and viscountesses, barons and baronesses – milled in a panic. 'Crowds are gathering on the approaches to the lodge. Under the authority vested in me by the Divine Empress's proclamation, I've taken the precaution of ordering all of your Adjudicators to shoot to kill.'

Kakrell whirled around.

'Shoot to kill?' she snapped. 'Isn't that a little . . . premature?'

Marmion's face was slicked with sweat, and there was a wild, uncontrolled look in his eyes that Kakrell didn't like one bit.

'It seemed a prudent course of action,' he said, ignoring her accusing gaze. 'The Surgeon Imperialis is no nearer discovering the cause of this plague of violence. She believes that it might only affect those people who have seen the inside of a body-bepple tank, but . . .'

Kakrell could have finished the sentence for him. Over sixty per cent of humans on Earth had beppled themselves in major or minor ways. This could mean the apocalypse had finally arrived.

A distant explosion distracted her. She turned her head towards the source of the sound. For a moment the world was as it had been, as it had always been, with the tops of the towers stretched out below the lodge, the forests, lakes and sculpted gardens linked by walkways and bridges.

And then one of the towers slowly sank from view, pulling its bridges after it. She could clearly hear the terrible tearing noise as they snapped, one by one, echoing like the crack of doom across the burning cityscape.

'I don't – I don't believe it!' she sobbed, as the slow, remorseless crash of the tower hitting the Undertown reached her ears. 'The null-grav engines are failing!'

'Not failing,' Marmion murmured. 'They're being sabotaged.'

'Then this is the end,' she breathed. 'The end for the Earth Empire.'

'Yes,' he breathed, and she glanced over at him, unwilling to believe that she could hear excitement in his voice.

'How did you do that?' Beltempest asked as the airlock of the Hith ship opened to the Doctor's touch, revealing the translucent tunnel of the boarding tube extending ahead of them.

'It's a gift,' the Doctor said. 'We'd better move fast. Hater Of Humans's troops will be right behind us.'

'Remind me,' Beltempest said as they ran along towards the walkway that linked the *Skel'Ske* to Earth. 'Why exactly are we in the vanguard of an alien invasion, rather than bringing up the rear?'

'If Powerless Friendless is aboard that craft,' the Doctor panted, 'then Bernice is probably with him. Knowing Bernice, there's no knowing what trouble she's getting herself into.'

'Fair enough,' Beltempest said, his trunk swinging as he ran. 'Just so I know.'

They reached the end of the boarding tube, where it

had been melted into the substance of the walkway. The Doctor's head turned right, as if he intended to swing into the walkway and run on towards the *Skel'Ske*, but his entire body turned left and took him off towards the doorway to Earth. An expression of comical amazement twisted his features.

'Doctor?' Beltempest shouted, coming to a halt. 'I thought . . . ?'

The Doctor slowed to a halt just inside the doorway, and frowned. 'The TARDIS?' he said in puzzlement and dawning joy. 'The TARDIS! I've found her!'

'What's a TARDIS?' Beltempest asked.

'She's . . . Never mind. Go and find Bernice. Keep her out of trouble. Tell her – tell her I have another engagement. Tell her . . .' he paused, thinking. How to pass a message on without attracting suspicion? Pig Latin, perhaps? He knew that Bernice was familiar with it. The question was, was Beltempest? 'Tell her, "Ashtray the ipshay," ' he said finally.

Beltempest frowned.

'Ashtray the ipshay? Will she understand that?'

'It's vital to us all that she does,' the Doctor said, and with that he was gone.

Beltempest glanced back along the boarding tube. A solid phalanx of Hith warriors was sliding towards him.

'Come on, lads,' he yelled, and ran towards the *Skel'Ske*.

'Yes,' the man behind the desk said. 'Come to me, Doctor. I've opened the way for you. I've made it easy. Don't disappoint me now.'

Through the eyes of a security camera above the door to hyperspace, he watched the Doctor's hesitant footsteps, and whispered: 'Come into my parlour.'

'Said the spider to the fly,' the Doctor said and wondered why the thought had popped into his head. Then again, this had all the signs of a classic trap. Beltempest had wondered why the Hith hadn't suspected one, and now the Doctor was in a similar quandary. Well, *he* was there, and that was the only sign he needed. He and traps seemed to have a natural affinity for each other.

The room through the doorway was plain, apart from a desk and a door in the far wall. The Doctor paused for a moment to inspect the dry coffee stain on the floor, then quickly dived behind a desk at the sound of pounding footsteps. In the metal wall he saw the reflections of a horde of sleek, four-armed bots running past. He counted to ten, then climbed to his feet and left the room through the other door.

The corridor outside was deserted. Left or right? He closed his eyes and sniffed with his mind. Right. Right, and up a number of levels.

There was a null-grav shaft at the end of the corridor. He climbed into it and let it carry him upwards. Carry the battle to the enemy, that was his motto. Walk blithely into the arms of danger, that was another one. Sheer stupidity usually carried the day, that was a third.

The shaft kept going up, and so did he. The TARDIS was getting slowly and surely closer. Bernice would be all right for a little while longer. She would understand that his present priority was to ensure that the TARDIS was safe. Wouldn't she?

He kept checking up and down the shaft's length, but nobody else was using it. Was that an ominous sign?

Flashing past one of the upper levels, the Doctor thought he saw a sleek metal form standing watching him from the opening. It made no attempt to step into the shaft after him. Perhaps he had been mistaken. Perhaps it hadn't noticed him.

Another, standing in an opening. Its head twisted to watch him hurtle past, ever upward. He watched it diminish below him. He was expected: that much was obvious. And he thought he knew by whom. The Interstellar Nanoatomic ITEC – that was an unforgivably obvious clue, a real cock pheasant of a clue, as Holmes would have said.

The null-grav field began to slow him down as he approached the top of the shaft, and the TARDIS. He

269

slowed to a halt, and waited nervously in the shaft, gazing into the shadowed room that lay through the only exit.

The director's office. Under normal circumstances, there was no way that he should have been allowed to get that far. *Ergo*, he was expected.

Nothing. No sound. No movement.

Cautiously he stepped into the room.

The carpet was deep and soft. A desk stood over to one side, lights flickering in its depths. His deep-seated empathic connection with the TARDIS told him that his time craft was over to one side, but for the moment he was more concerned with the way the lights from the desk played over a metal shape sitting behind it: a bot whose surface had been formed into the creases and folds of an old fashioned, high-collared suit. He couldn't quite see the face, but he didn't need to. He knew who was sitting behind the desk; or rather, who was sitting inside the machine that was sitting behind the desk.

The Doctor stepped forward into the room. 'I should have guessed,' he said. 'Interstellar Nanoatomic ITEC. An obvious anagram of International Electromatics. Your Freudian slip is showing.'

Tobias Vaughn stood up, the multicoloured light from the desk reflecting from his metal body, casting rainbow highlights across the room and onto the side of the TARDIS. Behind him a red glow filtered in from the wall-wide window.

'You've no idea how refreshing it is to see a familiar face, Doctor,' he drawled in that plummy, affected, once-heard-never-forgotten voice. 'Even if it won't be around for very much longer.'

Chapter 15

'I'm Shythe Shahid and this is The Empire Today, *on the spot, on and off the Earth. Martial law is in effect across the Earth. Initial reports are that the Imperial Landsknechte and the Order of Adjudicators are deploying in force to ensure that the provisions of the Imperial Proclamation are enforced. And as the riots spread further, and damage to property tops thirty trillion Imperial schillings, we ask: are we listening to the death knell for humanity?'*

Bernice slammed her fist into the control console. It sank in up to the wrist.

'It's no good,' she said, fighting to extract her hand from the spongy surface. 'I can't get any of these controls to operate.'

'Not like that you can't,' Powerless Friendless snapped.

It occurred to Bernice that the Hith navigator had become a great deal less willing to tolerate other people since he had regained his memory. He reminded her more and more of Homeless Forsaken Betrayed And Alone, and the resemblance kept sending small pangs of memory through her heart. Homeless Forsaken was dead, and she didn't want the same thing to happen to Powerless Friendless – or Daph Yilli Gar, as she supposed she ought to call him.

'We've been in and out of these control cells for the past hour,' she said. 'One step ahead of the bots and several steps behind any idea of how to turn the engines on. You were the navigator, Powerless Friendless. Can't you remember anything about this vessel?'

'I told you,' Powerless Friendless snarled, 'my memories are still in pieces. Dantalion did a good job. He's managed to put most of them back together again, but there are still a lot of holes. The most important one is: I can't remember how to turn the engines on.'

'But you operated the comm system.'

'The comm system is different!' he shouted, and immediately flushed grey in shame. 'I'm sorry, Bernice. What I meant was, I have no problem remembering how to operate the comm system. My memories in that area are intact.'

Bernice frowned. 'Hang on,' she said, 'if the engines are off, and emitting icarons, how come the comm system and the gravity generators still work?'

'Organic capacitors,' Powerless Friendless said. 'It meant we could still call for help if there was a power failure.'

'Makes sense,' Bernice said. 'It was an experimental ship, after all.' She sighed, and glanced around the tiny room. 'But that doesn't explain why there are so many control rooms.'

'So we don't have to see each other,' Powerless Friendless explained. 'Hith are solitary creatures.'

She nodded. Something moved in the corner of her vision. She turned, ready to run, but it was only Krohg wandering across the floor.

'This is like doing a jigsaw puzzle without the picture on the box,' she said, turning back to Powerless Friendless. 'Let's try again. How much *can* you remember about the engines?'

Powerless Friendless rippled in the Hith equivalent of a shrug. 'Only that the control nexus goes over there.' He pointed to a puckered area of panel.

Bernice walked over and examined the area. Tiny veins seemed to terminate in cilia that jutted upright like stalagmites.

'Like all good jigsaws,' Bernice sighed, 'there's a piece

missing. Come on: let's check some of the other control cells for this nexus thing. I don't suppose you can remember what it looks like?'

As she spoke, she touched the area of wall that operated the door. The muscle-like sheet swept back, revealing a large expanse of burnished metal.

A bot.

Its outstretched gun arms were aimed at her head.

'Ms Summerfield,' it drawled, 'I believe we have already met.'

She slammed the door shut again and leaned against it. 'Then again,' she said, 'perhaps there's a couple of nooks and crannies here we overlooked.'

A section of the door suddenly bulged inwards in the shape of a large fist. She ducked as the flesh-covered arm punched through the air next to her head.

'Is this the only door?' she shouted at Powerless Friendless.

The Hith nodded. 'I'm afraid so,' it said.

The flesh of the door stretched and distorted as the bot outside pushed against it. Bernice could make out the seams and rivets in its surface. Its blind, blank head swivelled to face her, a bizarre parody of humanity.

'I'm going to kill you, my dear,' it said, voice muffled by the skin of the door. 'I *am* going to kill you.'

Vaughn's attention appeared to be momentarily distracted; his eyes, despite being metal, had a dreamy, abstracted quality, and his lips were moving. The Doctor thought he caught Bernice's name being mentioned, but he couldn't be sure. He took the opportunity to study the figure standing behind the desk, its skin gleaming in the reddish light of the window. Vaughn's body was obviously robotic, more robotic than the last time they had met, but designed more as an acknowledgement that he had once been human than as a facsimile of one. How long had it been since they had last stood facing one another: another office, another time? A thousand years for Vaughn; five hundred or so for the Doctor. They were both older, but were they any wiser?

Vaughn's attention suddenly focused back on the Doctor. He was frowning slightly, as if he had received some unwelcome news.

'Tea?' he offered in that hatefully familiar voice. Even half a millennium couldn't erase the Doctor's instinctive reaction to Vaughn's patronizing tone. 'Forgive me, but I can't remember whether you take sugar and milk.' Vaughn smiled sleepily. 'Tell me, Doctor, do your tastes change when your body does, or do your likes and dislikes remain constant?'

'I still abhor evil,' the Doctor snarled, filing away for the moment the fact that Vaughn knew about his regenerative ability. How had he found that out? From the Cybermen, perhaps? 'I still fight the guilty on behalf of the innocent.' He felt rather petty, reacting so extravagantly to Vaughn's hospitality, but the man had always brought out the worst in the Doctor. That smooth, cultured façade concealed a mind as amoral and as calculating as any machine. The only difference between Vaughn in the twentieth century and Vaughn now was that his outside was now as hard as his inside.

'Doctor, I wouldn't have you any other way,' Vaughn said, and ran a gleaming finger across the surface of the desk. Lights rippled in response. 'It will take my butlerbot a few moments to prepare the tea; I hope you don't object.' The glow from the window flickered, making his shadow shimmer across the desk.

Despite himself, the Doctor remembered.

He stood beside Vaughn, watching with horror as the flimsy double doors at the International Electromatics factory burst open, and three Cybermen strode forward. The sunlight glinted off skin like mercury. Vaughn – once their ally but now their enemy – struggled with the ungainly shape of Professor Watkins' cerebrotron mentor, dropping two of the invaders to the concrete floor, but the third Cyberman fired its X-ray laser and Vaughn's chest

274

exploded. He fell forwards onto an iron railing, trailing smoke behind him . . .

Soon after that, UNIT had arrived. The Doctor hadn't bothered looking for Vaughn's body after the battle had ended, and before long he and his companions had moved on to the Collection and that nasty business with the Bookworms. Obviously UNIT hadn't bothered either, and the question of the precise whereabouts of Vaughn's cadaver had got lost in the overall cover-up.

'It's been a long time,' he said.

For a second, Vaughn did not react, as if his attention was elsewhere. The Doctor had noticed that it happened every ten seconds or so.

'Longer for me, or for you, Doctor?' Vaughn finally replied, his normally benevolent voice suddenly sharp, betraying an underlying tension. 'I've lived through a millennium waiting for this moment.'

'Lived through? I would query that. You were killed. I saw you fall. Nobody could live through that. Nobody.'

'Ah, but you forget,' that hated voice said, oozing false comradeship, 'I had a Cyber-body, and a Cyber-augmented brain. They built me well, you know.'

'They built you for a purpose. They were using you.'

'Of course.' Vaughn smiled. 'I knew that, but to use me they had to rebuild me. I took what they offered – the immortality, the power, the vast increase in memory and processing power – and played them along.'

'How did you survive?'

Vaughn shrugged, as if the information was of little concern, but the Doctor knew that he wanted to talk, *had* to talk, and if the Doctor could keep him talking for long enough then something might happen.

'I had other bodies, hidden away,' Vaughn replied. 'Copies I had made without the knowledge of the Cyberplanner in my office. Spares, if you like. I never trusted the Cybermen. I knew that they would betray me eventually.' A flicker of transient information in the desk cast highlights across his burnished metal face, his drooping eyelid, his sardonic smile.

275

'That's not the way I remember it,' the Doctor sneered in provocation. 'Perhaps your much vaunted memory increase is failing you. As I recall, you were shocked when the Cybermen showed their true colours. You had been completely sucked in by their pathetic offer of power.'

Vaughn looked away. 'Perhaps,' he said casually. 'It was a long time ago. I ... I disremember, in the words of a long-dead American president. I have moved on to other projects since then, and I have done it by myself. I don't need any help. You taught me that, Doctor.'

'If I had thought that anything of you might have survived the Cybermen's guns,' the Doctor said venomously, 'then I would have hunted down every last nut and bolt of you and melted them down for scrap.'

'I was cleverer than you, even then,' Vaughn said calmly. 'When the Cybermen destroyed one body, my mind – my personality, my essence – was transmitted to an International Electronics communications satellite in geostationary orbit, then downloaded into another robot body in our New York office. From there I regained control over the company using a different identity. Share prices had crashed, of course, but they picked up again. It was not difficult. Unbeknownst to the Cybermen, I had already established fifteen separate identities around the world. Within three years, the entire board of Directors of International Electromatics consisted of various versions of myself.'

'That must have made board meetings interesting,' the Doctor said, amused despite himself.

'Especially considering the fact that I was the secretary as well,' Vaughn chuckled.

A sudden yellow flare outside the window reflected from Vaughn's metal skin and momentarily illuminated the office.

'Bonfire night?' the Doctor ventured. 'I'm afraid I didn't bring any sparklers.'

'Riots,' Vaughn said casually. 'Certain portions of the Overcity and Undertown are ablaze.'

'Riots?' The Doctor's brain raced through facts,

assumptions and theories. 'Vaughn,' he said, leaning forward earnestly, 'I have to tell you something. About these riots – '

'They're due to the icaron radiation emitted by my Hith ship,' Vaughn said. 'I know.'

The Doctor felt a sudden wave of black anger welling up within him. 'You know,' he hissed, 'and you don't *care*?'

Vaughn shrugged. 'I take the long-term view, Doctor,' he said. 'And if that means a few million people have to die so that I get what I want, then so be it. I consider it to be a large-scale research project on the effects of icarons on the general populace.'

The Doctor was about to say something he would probably have regretted for the short time that it would have taken Vaughn to kill him, but just then Vaughn's butlerbot entered the office. Its face was a black ovoid, and numerous pairs of spindly arms radiated from its chest, each terminating in pincer-like hands sheathed in white gloves. It was carrying a teapot, two cups, two saucers, a jug of milk, a sugar bowl, two teaspoons and a plate of lemon slices.

'Ah,' said Vaughn. 'Shall I be mother?'

Doc Dantalion passed a comblike front limb through his antennae. If he didn't get out of there soon, he was going to boil in his exoskeleton. The Spaceport Nineteen departure lounge was so full of humans that the air above them was rippling in the heat, and their exuded sweat was condensing on the walls and ceiling. The place stank of them: a greasy, dirty, meaty stench that, most off-world races agreed, was one of those things that distinguished humanity from most other bipedal humanoids.

Queues were snaking across the room, crossing and recrossing each other, joining ticket booths to baggage check-in areas, drinks dispensers to insurance bots, quicksleep booths to fastline booths. Dantalion could have sworn that the front ends of some of the queues had joined up to their own rear ends, and that the people standing so patiently in them had been shuffling in circles for hours.

Not that it seemed to matter. Nobody was going anywhere.

Olias was standing some twenty metres ahead of Dantalion, in front of the off-world ticket booth. Behind her, her retinue of mainly off-world, mainly Undertown friends, colleagues and servants was attracting glowers and barbed comments from the mass. Her Ogron bodyguards had created a space around her which moved through the fetid atmosphere like a bubble of air through the stagnant waters of the Undertown canals. The bodyguards loomed over the harassed ticket clerk like a mountain range of grey flesh. His face was drenched in sweat, and it wasn't just from the heat.

'I keep tellin' you, they're all booked solid for the next six months. Every scheduled flight is full!'

Olias's skin rippled in barely concealed anger. 'I don't care what it costs,' she boomed, her voice cutting through conversations across the other side of the cavernous hall and echoing back like thunder. 'I am leaving this miserable planet, and I am leaving it now!'

'On what?' the clerk suddenly screamed, his eyes bulging and his face flushed. Dantalion took a step backwards. He recognized the signs of sudden, irrational anger. ''Less you off-worlders can fly through hard vacuum by yourselves, you ain't goin' nowhere!'

The Ogrons also recognized the man's state. Their hands swung to their weapons: battered blasters as long as their arms and almost as thick.

The clerk's fists clenched. Slowly, he stood up, face to chest with the leading Ogron. Shaking with anger, he gazed up into its small, bloodshot eyes for a long, silent moment.

And then he reached up and hit it on the nose so hard that Dantalion could hear the sound of cartilage grind against bone.

The Ogrons didn't shoot him. They just pulled him to pieces and watched him bleed to death.

* * *

'Forrester?'

Cwej looked around, but the dead-end corridor was empty. Forrester had vanished. Ahead of him the corridor twisted to the left and rose slightly before disappearing. As far as Cwej and Forrester had been able to ascertain, it corkscrewed around the backbone of the ship for about five hundred yards, providing access to the weapons rooms, which were now stripped voids open to hyperspace. The corridor linked the forward compartments and the control room to the engine room in the rear. Except that the engine room was presumably behind this veined, spongy dead end.

'Stop playing games!' he yelled, his voice slightly shriller than he would have liked. This cat and mouse game was getting on his nerves.

The wall beside Cwej suddenly screamed and flinched. Instinctively he dived to the ground as the blaster bolt seared its way across the fleshy substance toward him, blistering and burning as it went. The beam passed over his head; he rolled sideways and returned fire. The beam from his judicial weapon hit the spindly four-armed bot squarely in the chest. It staggered, but it didn't fall.

Another two bots appeared around the curve of the corridor. Their greyhound-like snouts jerked from side to side until the multi-spectral sensors on either side pinpointed his position. They raised their lower sets of arms: the ones with the built-in weapons. He might be able to put one of them off its aim with a well-placed blaster bolt, but not all three. He could swear that he could see the red sparks of the nascent beams, deep in the barrels of the bots' arms. This was it: curtains, *finito*, *s'vetch*!

He tried to climb to his feet and run, but there were two bots coming up behind him. No sign of Forrester: looked like she'd got away, thank Goddess. He'd hate for anything to happen to her.

The bots advanced on him. They moved slowly, enjoying their moment of victory. He tried to raise his blaster for one last, despairing volley, but he couldn't even decide which of the machines to shoot at. In the end, it didn't matter. They had him cold. It had never occurred to him that it might end this way, but then, until the flitter crash, it had never occurred to him that it might end at all. Dying in the line of duty was about as good as it could get.

The bots stopped a few metres away, their smooth metal bodies reflecting his drawn face back at him. He sank back against the resilient warmth of the wall and tried to think of something smart to say, something they could etch on his gravestone, but all he could come up with was: 'Order of Adjudicators! Freeze, scumsuckers!'

It wasn't much of an epitaph.

As Vaughn poured tea for himself and the Doctor, the diminutive Time Lord gazed across the office at the comforting yet unreachable form of the TARDIS. So near, as the phrase went, and yet so far.

From the corner of his eye he saw a movement behind him. Turning slightly, he found that the butlerbot was poised a few feet away, its sensors twitching with his every move.

'I can't drink tea myself,' Vaughn said as he placed the Doctor's cup on the corner of the desk. Walking around to the other side of the desk with his own cup, he sat and sniffed at the steaming liquid. 'But there is something about holding a steaming cup that I find therapeutic. The Cybermen conferred so many advantages on me when they gave me the choice of abandoning the flesh, but there are times when I wish I were human again, and could enjoy a lobster thermidor, or a *crème brûlée*, or a fine Armagnac.'

The Doctor sniffed cautiously at his tea. There was something lurking beneath Vaughn's words, something worth probing for. 'Yes, that's something I was going to ask,' he said. 'The body that you had the last time we met could have passed for human. Did pass for human, in fact. This present one – ' He gestured at Vaughn's gleaming metal form. ' – is hardly comparable, now is it? Aren't you slumming it rather?'

Vaughn smiled slightly, and looked away, but the Doctor could tell from the way his drooping eyelid twitched and the way his hand clenched upon his cup that the question bothered him.

'The Cybermen are an old race,' Vaughn said, 'and, even when I first met them, they had forgotten more about bionic technology than humanity ever knew. Even with all the resources of INITEC and a thousand years of research, it is a source of some regret that I have not been able to build myself as good a body as they did. This is the best I have been able to do, and even this ... inadequate ... simulacrum represents a triumph of engineering, Doctor.'

'But you can't eat a *crème brûlée*.'

Vaughn closed his eyes and leaned back in his chair.

'No,' said a voice behind the Doctor's head, 'but there are advantages.'

A pair of white-gloved steel pincers bit into the Doctor's shoulder. Dropping his cup and spilling tea over Vaughn's deep carpet, he gasped at the agony that spread like wildfire along his nerve fibres.

'I am every bot built by INITEC,' Vaughn's voice said from the butlerbot's bland face, 'I am every bot that contains a component built by INITEC. I am every bot that runs software designed by INITEC. I am everywhere. I am everything.'

'Yes,' the Doctor gasped, 'but you're not human, are you? You aren't the Tobias Vaughn that I met in London in the nineteen seventies. That Vaughn died when the Cybermen copied his mind and placed it in one of their metal shells. It thought it was Vaughn, but it was a bad reproduction. And you? You're another generation down the line: a copy of a copy. Or has it gone further than that, Vaughn? How much of yourself has been lost along the way?'

The claws dug deeper into the Doctor's flesh, sending pain radiating outwards through his chest and down his arms.

'I am Tobias Vaughn,' Vaughn said from his own mouth. 'I have his memories. I have his experiences.'

' "His"?' the Doctor cried, squirming in his seat as he tried to prise the pincers from his shoulders. 'How thinly have you spread yourself, Vaughn? How many pint pots is your quart divided between?'

'I was in the bot who waved to you when you first arrived in your time machine,' Vaughn said, ignoring the Doctor's words. 'Do you remember? I had been waiting for you, Doctor. I discovered from the Cybermen that you were a traveller in time and space, and with a thousand years at my disposal, I have searched every database, every video recording, every simularity, every holovid, every simcord for you. I know more about your adventures on Earth than you do, Doctor.'

'And what exactly do you need me for, if I might make so bold?' the Doctor hissed through clenched teeth. He was on the verge of blacking out; the world had turned fuzzy around the edges and the fuzziness was encroaching further and further upon his vision.

Vaughn gestured languidly towards the TARDIS. 'Time travel, of course,' he said.

Chapter 16

'I'm Shythe Shahid and this is The Empire Today, *on the spot, on and off the Earth. The buildings are falling. Thirty towers in Overcities around the globe have fallen onto the Undertown following acts of sabotage. Insurance claims are estimated at five hundred trillion Imperial schillings, a sum which will effectively bankrupt the First Galactic Bank, assuming that anybody remains alive to make a claim . . . '*

Forrester hit the wall twice in rapid succession on the puckered spot that had to be a door control. The door itself, an almost invisible slit, opened instantly. Before it could close she reached through the opening, grabbed hold of Cwej's hair with her left hand and pulled him toward her.

'I can't take you anywhere,' she snapped. She caught a quick glimpse of three gleaming forms moving towards them. Her right hand came up, finger pumping the trigger of her blaster. A cone of hard radiation filled the opening: an opaque wall of light too bright to look at directly. The bots staggered back, their surfaces blistering, as the fleshy door pulled itself shut behind Cwej.

'How did you – ?' he breathed.

' – end up with a partner like you? Goddess knows.' She scowled at him, then seemed to catch herself and ruffled his hair instead. 'The door's pressure-sensitive. I leaned against it and fell through. It must have shut behind me. Don't worry, golden boy, I wasn't trying to escape your adolescent charms.' She gazed at the now blank wall through which she had dragged him. 'A wide-beam blaster will blind them temporarily, but it won't stop them for long. They'll figure out the door trick pretty soon. We need to think, and quickly. I know that's not your strong suit, but give it a try, will you?'

'I don't think . . .' he started, but trailed off as he realized where they were. 'The engine room?'

'The engine room.'

He gazed around in awe. The icaron ring – at least, that's what Cwej presumed it was – lay like a quiescent animal, taking up most of the space in the oval room. Its smoothly contoured lines suggested tension and reined-in power. Great knobbly cables linked it to nodes in the ceiling.

'That's what's been causing all the trouble?' Cwej breathed. 'That's what's driving people loopy with these icaron things?'

'Yep,' Forrester said. 'The icaron ring.'

He looked at her dubiously. 'Are we safe?' he asked.

'Are we ever?' she replied snappily, then sighed. She was riding the kid pretty hard. 'Look, if the Doc's right, then it takes a frequent exposure plus possibly body-bepple as well to make someone susceptible. So long as we don't end up living here, we should be all right.' She looked levelly at him. 'But if I see your blaster turning my way, I'll fry your head till your eyeballs pop, understand?'

He swallowed. 'I understand.'

The door suddenly bulged toward them as one of the bots leaned against it. Forrester could see its hands, fingers splayed, stretching the thin but resilient flesh. Another pair of hands appeared, then another. For a moment they hesitated, then they pulled in different directions, straining the material almost to transparency. A gap appeared between the folds of the door: small, but growing.

A metal face moved close to the door, gazing through it, its sensors meeting her eyes.

'There's no hope for you,' the bot said, its voice muffled but still comprehensible. She recognized that voice now, although she hadn't in the flitterpark. It was the same voice that the bot in the hotel had talked in, the bot who had – even now she had trouble believing it – who had made her kill Martle. 'Even if you escape this ship,' it continued smoothly, reasonably, 'where can you go? You must know that your Adjudicator Secular is in my pay. You're criminals now, she's made sure of that. The Order of Adjudicators will hunt you down like rabid ber hounds. There's nowhere you can run. There's nowhere you can go. Why not just give in and let me end it for you now? I'll make it easy, I promise.'

'Like you made it easy for Fenn Martle?' she yelled. 'Screw you! If you want us so bad, come in here and get us!'

'So,' it said, 'you have regained your memory, Ms Forrester. How very unpleasant it must be, knowing that you killed your friend, your partner and, had he lived, perhaps even your lover.'

Cwej glanced over at Forrester, frowning. She closed her eyes for a moment, remembering, then took a deep breath and consigned her newly recovered memories to the large area of her mind labelled JUST TOO BAD.

'Not as unpleasant as what I'm going to do to you,' she snapped.

'What's it talking about?' Cwej asked, looking at her but keeping his blaster trained on the door.

'Dunno.' She grimaced. 'But I think this is the end, kid.'

He smiled. 'Couldn't be in better company.'

Didn't the kid ever give up? Forrester tried to come up with a snappy comeback, but there was nothing left to say. She had run out of words, run out of time, run out of life.

The bot hands pulled at the flesh of the wall. The gap in the door gaped wide. A metal arm reached into the engine room towards them, its hand a multi-barrelled plasma cannon.

She took up first pressure on the trigger. Make every shot count.

A series of explosions rent the air beyond the door-wall, coming so close together that they almost sounded like one long detonation. Quiet reigned for a second or two.

And then the door irised open.

Forrester's blaster was up and tracking before Cwej could even blink. She had time to take in the entire panorama outside the door – the bots sprawled on the floor with huge, smoking holes in their backs, the group of aliens who looked like Powerless Friendless but wore blast-resistant battle armour and were attached to floor, walls and ceiling, and the guns that were pointed at her and Cwej. Especially the guns.

She saw Cwej's knuckle whiten on his trigger.

A blue, four-armed shape with big ears moved behind the Hith warriors.

The next thing Forrester knew she was standing beside Cwej and knocking the barrel of his blaster upwards. It discharged into the ceiling, just missing a Hith warrior. Cwej's expression was confused as he turned towards her.

'It's all right,' Roslyn Forrester and Provost-Major Montmorency Beltempest said in unison to their respective companions, 'I think they're on our side.'

The pain in the Doctor's shoulder suddenly ceased. He gasped great ragged breaths as the butlerbot's pincers withdrew and Tobias Vaughn suddenly jerked in his seat.

'I can't do it,' he said, and tensed his neck, awaiting the claws of the bot again, but Vaughn didn't seem to hear him.

'Whether you believe me or not, Doctor,' Vaughn continued as if nothing had happened, 'my only aim has always been the protection of humanity. I believed that my alliance with the Cybermen could bring great benefits for the Earth. I was wrong, I know that now, but in the thousand years since then I have worked to ensure the success and the technological advancement of first the Alliance, then the Empire. INITEC has been in the forefront of weapons development as well as robotic and genetic research. I had to ensure that humanity was safe

– safe from Daleks, Jullatii, Cybermen, Draconians, Che-
lonians, Ice Warriors, Sess, Kraals, Nestenes, Greld,
Zygons and every other one of the many races that have
tried to invade this small but oh-so-important planet of
ours. Sometimes you have been here to help us, or so I
have later found out from the records and the reports of
those involved. Sometimes you haven't, but we coped
anyway. Whether you were here or not, I took it upon
myself to help.'

'Tobias Vaughn: Defender of the Earth?' the Doctor
asked, tongue very much in cheek.

'And why not?' Vaughn abruptly stood up and gazed
out of the wall-wide window, stained crimson now by the
fires outside. 'My weapons, my spaceships, my warbots –
they have all contributed to making the Empire what it is.'

'A monolithic force for oppression and misery!' the
Doctor snarled.

'Yes,' Vaughn said, nodding, 'but a stable one. A safe
one.'

'You really claim to have saved the Earth?'

'If it wasn't for the invention of the boson cannon – a
development of the INITEC laboratories – the Jullatii
would have overrun the Earth in 2350. If my researchers
had not already built the first of the Vigilant laser defence
satellites, then the Zygons would have melted the ice-caps
and flooded the world in 2765. And who do you think
designed the glitterguns that won the Second Cyberwar?'

'You must have enjoyed that.'

'I confess that I derived a certain pleasure from the act,
but my primary aim was to ensure the safety of the Earth.
After all,' and Vaughn turned and bestowed a superior
smile upon the Doctor, 'we couldn't always rely on you
to turn up in time, could we?'

The Doctor grimaced, and Vaughn continued: 'When
the chance came to capture the new Hith battleship, I
grabbed it with both hands. After all, to be able to exploit
such a radically different piece of technology . . . Just think
of the years of research that we could forgo!'

'And how far have you got in five years?'

Vaughn pursed his lips into a little moue of resignation.

'These things take time, Doctor. The Hith had developed their science along a parallel course to ours, one based on biological systems rather than mechanical ones. With that they overcame fundamental problems that we had wrestled with for years. It takes time to analyse such a radically different technology, but we are succeeding, by taking that ship apart, piece by piece, plate by plate, vein by vein, cell by cell.'

The Doctor waved a hand at the window. 'But look at the result: riots, madness and death. Is it worth it? Is this the stability that you were so proud of achieving?'

Vaughn shook his head. 'You don't understand, do you Doctor? You're stuck in the short-term view, whereas I, with the whole sweep of history behind me, can appreciate the long-term one. Yes, there are riots. Yes, there is madness. Yes, there will be some deaths. The Empire will survive, however. Earth will go on, stronger than before, backed by the knowledge of icaron manipulation. This is just a blip in the upward graph of human progress.'

'The end justifies the means?' The Doctor was livid. 'Don't tell me it all comes down to that discredited philosophy, Vaughn? Even you cannot be so unimaginative. Icarons are fantastically dangerous.'

Vaughn shrugged, and looked away. 'Perhaps you are right,' he said finally. 'Perhaps, as the years have passed, my moral sense has become eroded.'

'You didn't have much moral sense back when you were helping the Cybermen.'

'You think not?' Vaughn asked. 'You examined my micromonolithic circuits, Doctor. You know how easily they could have been modified to kill people, rather than render them unconscious. I had to fight the Cybermen over that. They would have preferred a clean sweep.' He paused momentarily. 'It worries me that I stand between mankind and the darkness, and if I . . . fail, then mankind is lost. That is why you must help me, before it is too late.'

'I don't understand,' the Doctor said quietly. 'What are you so scared of?'

Vaughn's full metal lips pursed slightly. 'Doctor,' he said carefully, 'I am not . . . what I was. I have paid a galaxy's ransom over the years to fund research into biological engineering, genetics, bionics, robotics and data storage. Do you remember the Biomorphic Organizational Systems Supervisor, Doctor? I built BOSS, although, looking back, I see that it was a mistake. And Professor Kettlewell – remember him? I funded Think Tank's research into robotics so that they could build a body for me. I have ransacked the bodies of Cybermen left behind in the snows of the south pole, the rotting brickwork of London's sewers, the sterile surface of the moon and the metal corridors of Space Station W3, and I have learned many lessons from them, but I have found no way of placing my mind back into a human body again, nor building a robot body as good as the one that Cybermen built for me. You are right about me, as you were right about the Cybermen a millennium ago. Each time I decant my mind from one body to another, I lose a little bit more. My memories are beginning to become – '

'Corrupted?' suggested the Doctor.

'A thousand years . . .' Vaughn looked away, 'and I have lived every second of them. How many different methods of data storage has my mind passed through? With every conversion from magnetic media to optical crystal, from optical crystal to positronic lattice, from positronic lattice to hyper-cache, information is lost. Entropy, nibbling at the edges of my thoughts. I can no longer remember the names of my parents, the taste of fresh strawberries, the feel of a woman's skin. I have lost so much.'

'Well,' the Doctor said, slapping his hands upon his legs, 'this has been nice, Vaughn, but – ' He got up from the chair. ' – I must be going. Things to see and people to do. Thank you for looking after the TARDIS for me, and all that, but – '

'Sit down.'

The Doctor sat down again.

'I need you,' Vaughn said. 'I thought that I just needed your time machine, but I cannot even open the door.'

'Isomorphic controls,' the Doctor murmured, glad that he had managed to lock the TARDIS's door when he left. He had been known to leave it open for the entire duration of his stay upon a planet.

'I need you to operate it for me. I want you to take me back to before the time we first met and help me rescue the body I once had, the body the Cybermen built for me. Or take me into the future to a time where humanity can build me an equivalent. I . . . I need to touch and to taste again, Doctor. Not for me. Not *just* for me, but for the Empire. I am its last defence. If I die, humanity is lost. I had hoped that the Hith ship, and that remarkable organic technology of theirs, could help me in my bid to build a new body, but their body chemistry bears no relationship to anything we understand. You are my only hope.'

'No, Vaughn.' The Doctor's voice was less of a negation and more of a warning, but Vaughn didn't pay it any heed. 'You don't understand the way that time works. I can't change what has already occurred, or influence what will be.'

'But you have, Doctor. I've seen the evidence. You continually interfere with history. I've tried to catch you, time and time again, but by the time I discovered that you had appeared, you had already left. I planned different methods of intercepting you, but they all failed.'

'Until now,' the Doctor said sourly.

'Until now,' Vaughn concurred. 'Earth demography has finally developed to a point where robots almost outnumber humans. Every few hours I would send my attention skipping from one bot to another, all over the Earth. When I finally saw your machine arrive, I had it taken away before you could return to it, and hidden in hyperspace so that you could not locate it. I tried to have you taken into custody by the Adjudicators knowing that my agent could have you brainwiped, but you were too fast again, and you had left Earth for Purgatory before the Adjudicators could find you.'

'Cwej and Forrester?' the Doctor said, raising his eyebrows. 'They're your agents?'

'No,' Vaughn said, 'they are just as they appear to be: foolish humans. I should have taken charge myself, but I left it up to them. More evidence of my growing ... problems. I moved your TARDIS – my TARDIS now – back into this building and sent a message to my agent on Purgatory to have you killed there, but I was too late; you and Provost-Major Beltempest had already left for Dis. Always one step ahead, eh, Doctor? The Adjudicators and that tiresome companion of yours – such a disappointment after the keen mind of Miss Herriot, by the way – returned to Earth and started to make a nuisance of themselves, so I determined to put them out of my misery. Even that failed. They took refuge in the Undertown, and now they are causing trouble in hyperspace.' Vaughn's metal eyes took on their dreamy look again, as if he was looking at something a long distance away. 'I see you still choose your assistants for their persistence,' he said eventually.

'More often than not, they choose me,' the Doctor pointed out.

'The woman – Summerfield – is currently causing quite a disturbance aboard by Hith ship. She and her friends are systematically destroying some of my most sophisticated bots.'

'Bernice does have a habit of getting into trouble.' The Doctor grimaced. 'Of what interest is that ship to you, Vaughn? Just a plaything, a bauble to amuse yourself with?'

'Just think how secure humanity would be if the Earth Empire had such vessels.' Vaughn frowned, and turned to look out of the window. 'We are safe from attacks from space, I have made sure of that. The INITEC ships and the INITEC weapons that the Landsknechte use are an almost impenetrable shield. But attacks through time ...' His metal fist clenched impotently at his side. 'I sometimes sit here, dreading the first signs that I am being unwritten, Doctor. Do you understand that?'

His froglike features swung back towards the Doctor, crimson light coating his skin. The Doctor just looked back without any expression on his face, apart from what he hoped was a tinge of loathing but probably, knowing his luck, looked more like worry.

'Are you familiar with W. B. Yeats?' Vaughn asked suddenly, apropos of nothing. 'He wrote: "Never to have lived is best, ancient writers say; never to have drawn the breath of life, never to have looked into the eye of day; the second best's a gay goodnight and quickly turn away." ' Vaughn shook his head. 'He was wrong. The knowledge that I – I, Tobias Vaughn, might never have existed, gnaws at me constantly. Your time machine can not only preserve me, but also preserve the Empire. Two birds with one stone.'

'In the same poem,' the Doctor said quietly, 'Yeats also wrote: "Endure what life God gives and ask no longer span." You might do well to think on that, Vaughn.'

Vaughn wasn't listening. 'The Daleks have time travel, I know that,' he said, scowling. 'I saw their time ship at the 1995 Earth Fair in Ghana, but it left before I could capture it. Cybermen from the future came back in time to the sewers of London, so I know that they will develop it too, and they still hate me for what I did to them . . .'

Paranoia, thought the Doctor as he watched Vaughn's histrionics. The man is insane. Truly insane. Identifying his best interests with those of humanity. Such hubris.

'. . . and even those moronic Sontarans can travel through time, albeit in a crude fashion. Despite all my best attempts, despite my financial support of Whittaker, Blinovitch and the rest, I have not been able to get hold of a workable time machine. Until now.'

The Doctor shook his head. 'Time is fragile, Vaughn. It's a connected net of delicate threads, each one under tension, each one pulling on uncountable others. Nobody can predict the changes that they might cause if they break one of the threads.'

'Not even you?' Vaughn said, lightly but dangerously.

'Not even me,' the Doctor said. 'I'm playing with a fire so dangerous that I could scorch eternity.'

'And what gives you the right?' Vaughn asked.

292

The Doctor thought back to his conversation with Professor Zebulon Pryce.

'Nothing,' he said. 'Nothing gives me the right, but having got it, I will not relinquish it. I am time's champion, Vaughn, in the same way that you claim to be Earth's champion, and it is my responsibility to protect history. Humanity doesn't even come close to developing usable time travel until –' He bit his tongue, thinking about the Crystal Bucephalus. Best not to give Vaughn too much help. 'Well, for quite some time yet.'

'Then you will not help me?'

'I would rather die first.' The Doctor folded his arms and tried to look firm, while wishing that his words hadn't sounded quite so much like a dare.

Vaughn watched the Doctor for a long moment, smiling slightly.

'I promise you,' he said quietly, 'by the time you have screamed out your knowledge, one agonized fact at a time, you *would* rather have died first.'

A gloved metal claw scratched oh-so-lightly at the Doctor's temple.

'Where's the Doctor?' Forrester shouted as they pounded through the twisting, turning labyrinth of corridors that made up the *Skel'Ske*. Hith warriors paralleled their course, sliding along the walls and the ceiling, regardless of gravity. Cwej brought up the rear.

'We went our different ways,' Beltempest panted. 'Not still interested in arresting him, are you?'

A bot leaped out of a side passage and skewered three Hith on a beam of light. Even before their charred bodies had fallen to the floor, the combined firepower of four more had sent it staggering backwards in a spray of molten metal.

'Not at the moment.' Forrester gasped and wiped a quick hand across her face.

'But I might think of something.' Her gaze flickered over Beltempest's face. 'You've been using him, haven't you?'

Beltempest nodded. 'We've known for some time that there's been corruption in the highest levels of the Landsknechte,' he puffed. 'Blackmail, bribery, undue influence, you name it. What we didn't know was who was doing the corrupting and why they were doing it. I was put in charge of a special team trying to track down the top dog.' He broke off to fire shots down another side corridor. 'Damn, thought I saw something. Never mind. Where was I? Oh yes, I'd set up a special monitoring team checking all incoming messages. When one of our provost-majors received an anonymous order to arrest and kill two people who were about to arrive on Purgatory, I got suspicious.'

'The Doctor and Bernice?'

'Indeed. The provost-major was arrested and I substituted for him.' He looked down at himself. 'This was a rush bepple job. Used a time tank. Bit of a shock when I woke up, I can tell you.'

'So you're not the real Provost-Major Beltempest?'

Beltempest shrugged. 'I had a partial brainwipe. I can't remember who I used to be. As far as I'm concerned, I am Beltempest.'

'Why, for Goddess' sake?' Forrester was appalled.

'You know. It's in case I'm captured and interrogated. All that a mind probe session would reveal is that I am Provost-Major Beltempest. We couldn't afford to tip off Mr Big, whoever that turned out to be.'

'But you were going to let the Doctor and Bernice die,' Cwej protested from behind.

'They had to,' Beltempest said without any hint of remorse. His trunk shook as he ran, making his voice quaver. 'The top dog would have got suspicious otherwise, and we had to assume that he had other agents who would have notified him if their bodies didn't turn up. The intention was to track back the movements of the Doctor and Bernice and find out who they had offended enough to get themselves killed.'

'That's very calculating,' Forrester said. She wasn't sure whether she approved of amorality on that scale or not.

'Perhaps,' Beltempest said, shrugging.

'What about the provost-major you arrested?' Cwej persisted.

The Provost-Major didn't reply for a moment, concentrating instead on catching up with the Hith warriors. 'He died,' he said finally. 'Someone had set up a mental booby-trap. The minute we arrested him, he pulled a gun and killed himself. No choice – it was an implanted reaction. We suppressed the news, brainwiped the Landsknechte who saw the body, and I took over. We couldn't trace the Doctor or Bernice back more than a few hours, so the only course left was for me to go along with the Doctor and hope he would lead me to the person behind the conspiracy. We couldn't risk questioning the Doctor, for obvious reasons.'

'Good thing we forced you to keep him alive,' Forrester muttered *sotto voce*.

A sudden volley of blaster fire ahead, down a side corridor, made the leading Hith slow to a halt. Extruding a pseudo-limb, she waved the rest of them back.

'Wonder what's going on,' Cwej said as they all flattened themselves against the wall.

'Well, there's one way to find out,' Forrester replied as another outbreak of firing made them all flinch. 'Just stick your head around that corner. If it comes back black and crispy, we'll know there's a problem.'

'Thanks,' Cwej said.

Ahead of them, the Hith were having a conference. Eventually one of them split off and slithered back towards them.

'There's one of us and one of you up ahead,' it said. 'They're under fire. Any ideas?'

'It must be Bernice and Powerless Friendless,' Forrester said grimly.

'Rescue them!' Cwej exclaimed.

The Hith just looked at him.

'Good idea,' it said finally. 'I'll pass that one back.'

It slid away.

'Goddess!'

Adjudicator Secular Gerrial Rashid shifted her position, trying to ease the ache of her piles as reports of the riots fought for attention on her centcomp screen. With her centcomp glasses on she couldn't see the flames outside, but she knew that they were getting closer. Much closer.

She should be concerned about the spread of violence, she knew that. She should be deploying her forces, rounding up ringleaders, protecting the innocent majority who were squirrelled away in their homes and their shelters, waiting for peace to be restored. The riots, although violent and apparently spontaneous, only involved a minority of people. She should be thinking about moving the lodge.

She should be concerned about others, not herself.

And yet . . .

Forrester and Cwej had left Earth on the trail of two suspects without telling her. That meant they suspected something. They suspected that the official conclusion of the case was wrong, and if they suspected that, then they suspected her, because she had warned them off.

And they had come back. Again, they hadn't told her.

She reached out with a fat finger and touched a virtual button that hung in mid-air. A menu appeared before her. She navigated through several nested menus until she found the one she wanted: a list of known and suspected rioters and killers still at large. Faces of people seen running away from sabotaged walkways, recorded by nearby securitybots. Descriptions given by victims of acts of random and senseless violence. Names mentioned in the dying breaths of relatives and friends who had been murdered over lunch, or in bed, or during casual conversation. People who were to be shot on sight under the new emergency powers that the Adjudicator in Extremis had brought into effect by order of the Empress. Every Adjudicator had immediate access to the list through centcomp, wherever they were.

Rashid ran a hand over her oiled quiff, smoothing it back to perfection. Her puffy face creased into a smile as she typed two more names into the list.

If there was one thing that an Adjudicator hated more than anything else, it was an Adjudicator gone bad. The Creed demanded only one penance for that: the penance of death. They wouldn't last long enough to tell what – if anything – they knew.

She sighed, pleased with herself. She hated loose ends. Now she was safe, and the mysterious man who paid her wages – her *other* wages – would be grateful.

Perhaps she would even get a bonus.

Something warm trickled down the Doctor's cheek. He didn't know whether it was perspiration or blood. He'd lost a lot of both in the past ten minutes.

Ten minutes? It felt more like half a lifetime. The years he had spent on Pella Satyrnis during his fifth incarnation seemed like a snap of the fingers compared with the time he had spent held down in Tobias Vaughn's chair while the metal claws of the butlerbot went to work on him. Pain had a way of stretching time like warm toffee, until every second was a year and every year a millennium.

If the something that he had been waiting for didn't happen soon, it was going to be too late.

Red light flooded in from the window, making the office look like an anteroom of hell. How very apt, the Doctor thought. He shifted slightly in the chair, and suppressed a cry as he tried to find some part of his body that was untouched, a few square inches of flesh upon which he could rest, but the butlerbot had done its work well. Under Vaughn's expert tutelage it had inflicted so much pain upon him, abused his nerve endings to such an extent, that he had felt the dark shadow of his eighth incarnation hovering over him, awaiting the signal to take over. Not that it would have done him much good. Vaughn would quite happily have tortured his way through the Doctor's remaining bodies, one by one, in his obsessive and so far fruitless quest for the secret of temporal control.

Concentrating on each part of his body in turn, the

Doctor tried to assess the damage. Sad to say, there wasn't very much: some bruising and painful but superficial lacerations, a little internal bleeding, a snapped ligament or two. After all the agony, he felt strangely cheated. The least Vaughn could have done was to break a couple of bones. How was he ever going to get any sympathy from Bernice if there wasn't a mark on him?

Assuming, of course, that he was going to see Bernice again. Numerous times during the questioning session he had noticed Vaughn break off and look away, staring through another set of eyes at events occurring elsewhere, issuing orders perhaps, or just monitoring the actions of his bots. He was doing it again now. Unfortunately, the Doctor hadn't been able to take advantage of the man's distraction. The bot's claws had dug just as deeply, held him just as tightly, in the temporary absence of any controlling authority.

And yet . . .

Something was biting at the back of the Doctor's mind: something that Vaughn had said earlier. He flicked back through the memories of the last twenty minutes, picking over the words that Vaughn had spoken, trying to spot meanings or implications that he had missed at the time.

'Well, Doctor?' Vaughn said, coming back to life, 'are you ready to cooperate yet?' His metal face was so close to the Doctor that the Time Lord could see every detail: the fake pores, the metal jowls, the artificial bristle that would never need shaving.

'Give me a moment to catch my breath,' the Doctor whispered, still trying to rediscover the words that he thought might be important. His mind was like a lumber room, full of odd memories, cross-linked in the strangest ways. He would have to have a clear-out at some time.

'Doctor,' Vaughn said in his silk-soft tone, the one that meant he was at his most dangerous. 'Doctor, I'm impatient.'

There! He could see Vaughn's lips moving. What was he saying? *I am every bot built by INITEC.* That was fairly unambiguous; Vaughn could operate every single robot built by the company that International Electromatics had become. And yet, a few seconds later: '*I was in the bot who waved to you when you first arrived in your time machine . . . Every few minutes I would send my attention skipping from one bot to another, all over the Earth . . . *' The Doctor went carefully over the words. '*Send my attention skipping . . . *' Did that mean that Vaughn could only be in one bot at a time? Did it imply that Vaughn's consciousness flitted about from one bot to another but was always in one *and only one* bot at a time?

Hmm . . .

A flare of white light beside him made the Doctor turn, and quickly turn away as the cold light from the plasma scalpel seared at his eyes. The butlerbot's claw held it steady a few inches away from the side of the Doctor's head.

'I will ask you one last time,' Vaughn said in the same tone of voice with which he had offered the Doctor a cigar earlier on, 'and then I shall start causing permanent damage. A heart, I think. After all, you have two of them, or so my infrared eyesight tells me. Given your amazing physiological capabilities, you may even be able to regrow it, but I suspect that the process will hurt more than a little.'

Vaughn's sleepy eyes continued to stare at the Doctor while the bot moved the plasma blade closer. On a hunch, he shifted sideways in the chair, wincing at the pain in his limbs. Vaughn's eyes didn't track him; they stared at the position he *had* been sitting in. Point proven.

The plasma blade was so close that he could see it as a bright pink glow if he closed his eyes.

'You win, Vaughn,' he said, trying to put as much defeated resignation into his voice as possible. 'I'll let you into the TARDIS.'

'No, Doctor,' Vaughn purred. 'Your treachery is legendary. *Tell* me how to get in.'

'Isomorphic controls,' the Doctor sighed, hanging his head in an attempt to convey utter humiliation. 'Only I can operate them.'

Vaughn was silent for a moment. Casting a glance at him from the corner of his eyes, the Doctor assumed that he was scanning his database of knowledge about the Doctor's various adventures on Earth in the past thousand years, looking for confirmation of the statement. The Doctor did the same, hoping that he hadn't actually contradicted them himself. The controls were isomorphic, but only when he bothered setting them up that way.

'Very well,' Vaughn said. 'But remember, the pain you have endured so far has been a mere headache compared to what I can put you through. I've learned a great deal in the past thousand years.'

The clamps on the Doctor's shoulders released. He staggered upright using the arms of the chair as support, unsure if his legs would take his weight. The butlerbot waved the plasma blade towards him, and he retreated towards the comforting blue shape of the TARDIS. The surface was cool, and he rested his cheek against it for a moment.

'I'm waiting,' Vaughn prompted.

Chapter 17

'I'm Shythe Shahid and this is The Empire Today, *on the spot, on and off the Earth. Spaceports around the planet are being besieged by people desperate to leave the planet, despite the fact that no ships have landed since last night. The skies above the Earth are reported to be full of ships whose captains are unwilling to attempt a landing in case somebody shoots them down . . .'*

The bot had ripped the muscular door into shreds of bloody flesh and was reaching towards Bernice's face with its gun arms when its head exploded.

To Bernice, crouching in the control cell, it seemed that a great number of things suddenly happened at once, and most of them were noisy. The cacophony lasted for what seemed like hours, but could only have been a few minutes. Thinking about it later, over a drink in a seedy bar on a backwater planet, she found that her memory was good enough for her to be able to classify the noise into various categories: blaster fire of three different types, explosions, screams, war cries, shouts of 'Damn you, Cwej, get out of the way!' and 'Look, if you were shooting straight, I wouldn't *be* in the way!' – but at the time it was just noise.

At one point she looked down, to find that Krohg was cowering in her arms, its eye-stalks retracted so far into its slimy body that they made three dimples in its head. She looked around for Powerless Friendless, worried that if Krohg was seeking safety in her arms then he must be dead. She saw him flattened to the ceiling, his pseudo-limbs extruded and twitching as if he was returning fire. In his mind, perhaps he was.

As a stray blaster bolt turned the air above her head to ozone, she scrunched up in the corner. Her hand passed across Krohg's flat underside. Terrified by the noise, the light and her proximity to death, her mind retreated, finding solace in details. She became very aware of the way that Krogh's underside wasn't flat at all, but contained countless small pits, like a very fine sponge.

And something went click in her mind as two separate ideas collided.

Fascinated by the conclusion that her mind had accidentally sidled up to, it took her a few moments to realize that the firing had stopped

'Hi, Bernie!' a voice said from the ruins of the doorway. She glanced up. The bits of Cwej's face that weren't covered with soot looked as if they'd been badly sunburned.

'Unless you want that blaster inserted rectally,' she said, 'don't call me Bernie. Benny, if anything. Bernice, at a pinch. Not Bernie.'

'I thought you'd be pleased to see me,' he said, hurt.

She climbed unsteadily to her feet, grabbed hold of the top of his chest plate, pulled him halfway through the doorway and kissed him, long and hard.

'I'm pleased,' she said finally, pushing him away. 'All right?'

'All *right*!' he said. It was difficult to tell through the blaster burn, but she thought that he was blushing.

'What's the sitrep?' Forrester said, approaching the door. Behind her, Bernice could see a number of Hith warriors and a number of half-melted or half-exploded bots. Provost-Major Beltempest was sifting through the robotic remains. A great knot of tension seemed to unwind in her chest. If Beltempest was there, the Doctor couldn't be too far behind. Assuming, of course, that he was still alive.

'The what?' she asked, distracted.

'The sitrep. Situation report.'

'You mean, "What's happening?"?'

Forrester frowned, and nodded. 'That's what I said,' she growled. 'Don't waste my time.'

'Well,' Bernice said, glancing across to where Powerless Friendless was uncurling himself, 'I'm sure you'll be pleased to hear that we're all in one piece. How about you?'

'Fine for the moment,' Forrester replied, 'but I'm not counting on the condition remaining permanent.' She glanced out into the corridor. 'Whoever's controlling those bots will know they've been destroyed. Reinforcements will be on the way.'

Cwej nodded. 'We need to get this show on the walkway. Have you discovered how to turn the engines on yet?'

Bernice walked across to the puckered area of panel into which, according to Powerless Friendless, the nexus was supposed to fit. Without really thinking about what she was doing, she hefted Krohg in her hand for a moment, then placed the creature gently in the recess. It gazed up at her with its three stalked eyes, its lipless mouth seeming to her to stretch into a smile, and then it was gone, melted into the panel until it was just a knob of flesh with three small nub-like switches on top.

The walls of the control room began to throb and, all around, panels blossomed with fleshy controls. In the pit of her stomach Bernice could feel a slow, subsonic thump, like the beat of some gigantic heart. 'Well,' she said brightly, 'Geniuses-R-Us strike again.'

Powerless Friendless's eye-stalks dipped in acknowledgement. 'I had forgotten so much,' he said. 'How did you know that Krohg was the nexus?'

She shrugged. 'Little details and a massive amount of guesswork.'

He nodded. 'Then you guess well.'

'I had a good teacher.' And that reminded her. 'Beltempest!' she called, 'is the Doctor all right?'

Out in the corridor, Beltempest glanced up from his investigation of one of the bots and gave a thumbs-up.

'He's out looking for something called the TARDIS,' he said. 'But he asked me to pass on a message.' It looked to Bernice as if he was frowning. 'I think he said, "Ashtray the ipshay." Does that mean anything to you?'

She thought for a moment. Ashtray the ipshay. Pig latin. Take the ays off, then move the last letter or two to the front of the word.

Trash the ship.

Bernice took a deep breath, then nodded slowly. 'Yeah,' she said. 'Thanks.' She let her gaze roam over the corridor, and the armed Hith troops. They were setting up blaster emplacements, preparing to dig in for a siege. One of them, in an ornate body-sleeve, was glancing over towards her. Although he was engaged in conversation with a number of his troops, he looked as if he might be heading over at any moment.

'Powerless Friendless,' she said, 'what will your people do if they get this ship back?'

'With the engines on, the icarons are getting more energy, aren't they?' Cwej interrupted. 'I mean, that was the point. The Hith can take the ship away and junk it. I mean, it's dangerous.'

'Don't be a fool,' Forrester snapped.

Powerless Friendless sighed. 'It's a weapon,' he said, 'and my people have been wronged. Grievously wronged. If somebody kills your friends and family, and takes your planet away from you, and then you find a weapon, what do you do with it?'

'You use it,' Forrester said levelly.

'But we can't let them.' Cwej sounded outraged.

'No,' Powerless Friendless agreed. Forrester and Cwej both looked surprised. 'There's been too much killing. Too much hurting. Too much pain. If the Hith are going to get anywhere, it has to be through talking. Diplomacy is the only solution.'

Bernice nodded. 'Right on,' she said, ' "Jaw-jaw," as the Doctor once told some fat old man who smoked cigars

and tried to pinch my bottom, "is better than war-war."
As I see it, our priorities are: firstly, to destroy this ship;
secondly, to defeat whatever evil bastard has been trying
to kill us; and thirdly, to get out alive.'

'But not necessarily in that order,' Forrester added.

'And,' Bernice continued, shooting Forrester a dark
glance, 'we can do it all in one fell swoop.' She turned to
Powerless Friendless. 'Can you set the controls so that
this ship appears in real space?'

'In real space?' Powerless Friendless looked stunned. 'I
thought you wanted to fly it away in hyperspace?'

Bernice shook her head. 'We've got a whole load of
your people on board. They'd just take the ship off our
hands. And even if we could defeat them, or lock
ourselves in here, they must have arrived in something.
All they have to do is follow us through hyperspace. No,
the best course of action is destroy it here and now;
bring the whole thing crashing down, and the INITEC
building with it.'

Powerless Friendless shrugged. 'I have bad memories
of this building,' he said. 'I'm game.'

Cwej opened his mouth to protest, but Forrester
elbowed him in the stomach. 'Sign me up for it,' she said
as he bent double in pain. 'I'd like to shove this ship right
up the arse of the person who runs INITEC. After what
he did to me ...' She paused, and swallowed. 'After
what he did to Martle.'

Cwej nodded. 'Fine,' he said, still trying to catch his
breath. 'Whatever you say. But what about the people in
the building?'

Glancing out into the corridor, Bernice could see the
Hith commander slithering towards them.

'If the congruities are preserved,' she said, 'then the
ship will appear in mid-air outside the building. I think. I
hope. It'll drop down to the Undertown. Is there anything
in particular underneath us here?'

'Mostly deserted buildings and water,' Powerless
Friendless said, moving over to the controls. 'The INITEC
building is above the area where the old Scumble ship

crashed, years ago. It's a wasteland. And, let's face it, if we can stop the icaron radiation, we'll save more lives than we squander.'

'I see you've got the *Skel'Ske* working,' the commander said, addressing them all from the doorway. 'Good work. How long before the ship is ready to go?'

'Five minutes,' said Powerless Friendless, without turning. 'But it's only going in one direction.'

'What do you mean?' the commander hissed. 'Which direction?'

'Lingerie, stationery and kitchen utensils,' Bernice said with a smile.

The Doctor slipped a hand into his right trouser pocket, frowned, and brought it out empty. He repeated the process with his left pocket. Still nothing. Pulling them out like an elephant's ears to check their depths, he shrugged. Next he checked his jacket pockets, one by one, but they were empty too.

'Doctor, your juvenile sense of humour is proving to be a little wearing.'

'You've waited this long,' the Doctor snapped, slipping his shoe off and upending it. 'Impatience doesn't suit you.' The key dropped into his palm, and he grinned. 'Obvious place!' he cried, and slipped it into the lock. The TARDIS door swung open, revealing a dark interior.

'Follow me,' the Doctor said, limping towards the darkness.

Vaughn hesitated for a moment, then reached out with a chunky metal hand and took the Doctor by the scruff of the neck. The Doctor winced as the fingers tore open one of his rapidly healing wounds.

'I'll keep you by my side, I think,' he said. 'I am not unaware of the trick you pulled on Planet 14.' Dragging the Doctor along beside him, he stepped through the vulnerably open door and into the sterile white light of the console room. His gaze passed across the roundelled walls, the central console, the scanner screen and the enormous object embedded in the ceiling. 'Doctor,' he said, gazing around in avuncular fashion, 'you have no idea how impressed I am by the achievements of your race. Even the Cybermen could not construct a vessel such as this.' He tightened his grip on the Doctor's neck.

'Thanks a bunch,' the Doctor muttered. 'As I recall, they once stole one from us.' He squirmed slightly, trying to ease his way out of Vaughn's grip. He had hoped to shut the huge time doors, cutting Vaughn off from the outside world, but he hadn't anticipated Vaughn wanting to keep him quite so close.

'Doctor?' Vaughn's voice was sharp, as if he could read the Doctor's thoughts. 'Don't think you can betray me. I can kill you faster than you can move!'

Judging by the way that Vaughn's metal fingers cut into the tender flesh of his neck, the Doctor believed him.

The high-pitched scream of the *Skel'Ske*'s engines powering up followed Bernice and the others as they pounded and slithered their way along the twisting, turning corridors of the Hith ship. The Hith troops were sliding along the walls and ceiling in Powerless Friendless's wake, blasting any bot that dared show its face. Provost-Major Beltempest had retrieved two laser cannons from fallen Hith and was cheerfully laying down covering fire with one cannon in each pair of arms. They'd left quite a trail of wrecked metal behind them, but they'd lost a lot of troops in the process.

Chris Cwej suddenly appeared beside Bernice. His arm slid around her back and beneath her arm, taking some of her weight. She rested gratefully against the mass of his body. 'Thanks,' she said.

'Don't mention it,' he said, grinning.

Forrester, who was running beside Cwej, growled, 'Nothing personal, we just don't want you holding us up.'

Bernice turned to make sure that Powerless Friendless was keeping up with them, and felt a sudden pain stab through her. Powerless Friendless wasn't with them. Powerless Friendless had stayed behind.

He had tried to explain, in what little time they had before the Hith commander would have got suspicious.

'There's no remote timer,' he had said. 'And besides, Homeless Forsaken Betrayed And Alone and I caused the problem. He's dead, and so it's up to me to sort it out once and for all.'

'But . . .' Bernice had stammered, desperately trying to think of ways out of the situation.

'No buts,' Powerless Friendless had said gently. 'I don't want to survive. I can't live with the memories of what was done to me by INITEC, and I can't live without them either. I hid in the Undertown for too long. I have to . . . to atone for my cowardice.'

And he had pushed her gently towards the doorway with a pseudo-limb.

Impulsively, she had returned and embraced him. 'Goodbye,' she had said, kissing him softly between his eye-stalks.

And she had left, taking Cwej and Forrester with her.

Bernice's mind suddenly jerked back into the present as they all rounded a corner, and found the hatch into hyperspace ahead of them. Two bots were standing guard over it. Beltempest dropped both of them with withering blasts of radiation.

'Out!' he yelled, 'and quickly!'

As Bernice passed through the doorway and onto the walkway across hyperspace, she momentarily wondered how Beltempest felt, defending a group of Hith against human-built robots. Perhaps he didn't see the incongruity. Perhaps he'd go back to hating aliens the minute they were all safe. People, as the prophet said, were strange.

Ahead of them, another ship, presumably the Hith ship, was attached to the walkway by a long boarding tube.

The whine of the *Skel'Ske*'s engines had spiralled up and out of the range of human hearing, to the point where it was giving Bernice a headache. Casting a glance over her shoulder as she ran, she saw the ship phasing in and out of unreality. She could see the non-stuff of hyperspace through it. They only had seconds.

They passed the point where the boarding tube connected to the walkway. The Hith troops turned off and slithered along it without any farewells, while Bernice, Cwej, Forrester and Beltempest kept going towards the door out of the void. The Hith obviously knew as well as Bernice that the particular area of hyperspace they were located in was the second most dangerous place in the area at the moment, and that they should vacate it immediately.

Bernice, on the other hand, was heading straight for the first most dangerous place.

She turned as they reached the doorway. Forrester, Cwej and Beltempest ran past her, but she stayed for a moment, desperately looking at the *Skel'Ske*. It had almost vanished, but she thought that she could see a movement at the front, through the transparent screen of the control room. Someone waving. Someone waving goodbye.

Forrester grabbed her elbow and pulled her through the massive door into the INITEC building, just as the *Skel'Ske* vanished. The room was full of people and bots, but Bernice had only a split second to register the fact before she was deafened by a huge boom. As they all collapsed to the ground, clutching their ears, she realized that she couldn't tell whether it was the sound of the door slamming, the *Skel'Ske* vanishing from hyperspace or the shock wave of its arrival in real space, just outside the INITEC building. Perhaps it was all three.

Kaii Derrim and Londi Gav stood face to face on the walkway. Like all the others in the area, it had jammed shortly after the fires started. They didn't care. They didn't care about the way the sky glowed orange, either, or the bodies that littered the walkway's surface. They just stood there, face to face, hatred in their eyes, knives in their hands, each waiting for the other to make a move.

When the Hith ship appeared in the sky above them, the thunderclap of displaced air making the walkway tremble beneath their feet, they didn't even notice. It hung, poised above them, for a timeless moment, like some ancient god made manifest upon Earth, then began to fall. It fell gracefully, it fell slowly, but it fell.

It took out three walkways, smashing through each one and sending the broken halves curling away like suddenly cut ribbons, before it reached the one that Derrim and Gav were standing on. The blood-tinted, smoke-dappled sky was occluded by its dark and growing bulk, until there was nothing above them but a rounded, spavined expanse of metal. It was only then, when it was too late to do anything but watch in awe and fear, that Derrim's gaze flickered upwards, and Gav, seeing his chance, sent his knife spinning through the air towards him.

Less than a second later, nothing mattered to either of them.

Vaughn's face suddenly blanked over again. He'd been doing it every few seconds for as long as the Doctor had been there, but this was different. It was as if whatever he was watching was so dramatic that it absorbed all his attention and kept him elsewhere, out of his own body. The Doctor didn't know what it was, but he did know that this was the only chance he was going to get. He'd been waiting for something to happen, and if this wasn't it then it was close enough.

The Doctor twisted in Vaughn's lifeless grip, tearing the skin that was pinched between Vaughn's fingers in his frantic efforts to get free. With a last despairing wrench, he finally prised himself loose, and went staggering across the TARDIS console room, ending up leaning on the console itself. He turned towards Vaughn just as Vaughn's consciousness returned to his body.

'My ship!' he snarled, his normally calm voice clogged with hatred and anger. 'They have destroyed my ship!'

He turned to leave.

The Doctor slammed the red lever that operated the huge time doors. They swung shut in Vaughn's face with a muffled thud.

'You meddling fool,' Vaughn cried. 'Do you think you

can trap me here?' His brow suddenly creased, the flexible metal skin furrowing into a broad V-shape as he tried to contact his subsidiary bodies outside.

And failed.

'I've severed your connection,' the Doctor said with a smile. 'We're in a separate universe here. Once I closed those doors you became unable to communicate with anything outside. Any *thing*, Vaughn. You're separated from your little metal army. You're on your own.'

The Doctor suddenly realized that he was shouting, and took a deep breath. Time for vituperation later. One immensely powerful robot body was all that Vaughn needed to kill the Doctor and open the doors.

The same thought had occurred to Vaughn. He stepped forward menacingly.

'Then either you will open the door or I will rip your arms and legs off,' he growled, opening his arms wide to prevent the Doctor from running past.

'Catch as catch can!' the Doctor said. As Vaughn reached out for him, he leaped across the control room to the other door, the one that led deeper into the TARDIS. He was counting on two things: firstly that Vaughn wouldn't dare follow him into the unfathomable depths of the machine, and secondly that Vaughn's overweening arrogance would lead him to examine the console, sure that he could decipher its operation. Which he probably could. After all, if Tegan could do it, anybody could.

The Doctor knew he had about a minute before Vaughn found the door control and re-emerged into his office. Once he had done that, he could shift his mind into any bot on the planet and the Doctor would never be able to find him.

Bernice watched through the window in the otherwise bare sentry room as the *Skel'Ske* hung for a moment, stationary in mid-air. Its harlequin colours and spiky, organic texture were out of place against the wet, grey surface of the towers. Her heart missed a beat as she thought that it might never drop, that Powerless Friendless had changed his mind and turned the engines on. Finally, as if it had committed itself to a difficult decision, it dropped: slowly at first, but gathering an unstoppable speed, and she breathed again.

Bernice winced as the ship smashed straight through a section of walkway with two people on it. They didn't even seem to notice.

Behind her, Forrester and Cwej were browbeating the INITEC security guards. Beltempest was lending his considerable weight. The guards were trying to refer back to their superiors, but there seemed to be a vacancy at the top. Nobody seemed to know what to do.

Bernice knew how they felt.

The ship started to tumble as its irregular vanes and spines caught the air. It fell away like a leaf falling in the breeze. The rain-clouds swallowed it up within a few moments, and then it was as if nothing had happened. The towers and the slice of rose-tinted sky above were the same as they had always been.

The explosion, when it came, was distant and quiet. Quieter than Powerless Friendless And Scattered Through Space deserved. He should have had fireworks, symphonies and a vast cosmic thunderclap.

Bernice closed her eyes and leaned against the window. The surface was cool against her forehead. What was it about her that meant that her friends and acquaintances had to die? Homeless Forsaken and Powerless Friendless were only the most recent. Behind them, the queue stretched so far that she couldn't see its beginning.

On the other side of the window, the sky glowed with the distant fires.

Sixty seconds.

He pelted along the white, roundel-lined corridor that led away from the console room, ignoring the screams of pain from every limb, every muscle, skidding at the next junction and heading left past the boot cupboard, the rose garden and the swimming pool.

312

Fifty seconds.

A right and a sudden left led him through the library, past rows and rows of dust-covered tomes and a very surprised tabby cat.

Forty seconds.

To save time when he came to the spiral staircase in the centre of the library he slid down the bannister, hopping off two floors lower and limping as fast as he could across the echoing vault of the wine cellar.

Thirty seconds.

A broad white avenue led past paintings and statues from myriad worlds, myriad centuries, and terminated in a roundelled white wall which the Doctor flung himself against, panting, frantically searching for a small white button.

Twenty seconds.

The wall slid open, and five steps took the Doctor across the TARDIS airlock – a large room lined with hooks upon which quilted spacesuits with clear helmets hung – to the TARDIS's back door.

Ten seconds.

Emerging from behind the TARDIS, in the small gap between it and the wall of Vaughn's office, the Doctor discovered the butlerbot desperately attempting to collect the tea crockery with its plasma blade still lit.

Zero.

The room was shaking. Bernice had obviously come up with the goods, and the Doctor had to do the same. He used every last iota of his strength to wrench the arm holding the blade from its socket. The bot tried to resist, but he pushed it out of the way. It fell onto Vaughn's desk in a shower of broken crockery, cracking the translucent surface. Holding its arm like a spear in one hand, its blade of pure energy pointing straight ahead, the Doctor shoved his key into the TARDIS lock for the second time in five minutes and kicked the door open.

Tobias Vaughn stood at the console, his hand closed around the knob of the door control. His head snapped around as the TARDIS doors opened.

'Make the most of that dramatic entrance, Doctor,' he said, 'because it will be your last. This machine is childishly simple to operate.'

The Doctor took three steps into the centre of the console room and swung the butlerbot's arm like an axe, turning the plasma blade into an arc of eye-numbing white that sliced through the air and Tobias Vaughn's neck with equal ease. Coolant fluid sprayed into the air as his head tumbled from his shoulders, trailing wires and jagged blue sparks. In the few seconds before it hit the floor, the expression on it changed from triumph to surprise, and then to utter fury. It bounced twice, then came to rest lying on one ear. Bereft of a power source, the metal muscles surrounding the mouth and eyes drooped.

Vaughn's body stood for a moment by the console, its hand still clutching at the door lever. Without Vaughn's mind to control it, sub-systems and failsafes came into effect. The stocky metal body carefully sat, cross-legged, on the floor of the TARDIS and placed its hands, palms up, on its knees.

The Doctor moved slowly across to the console. He felt old. Old and tired. His hands moved to the twin nubs of the telepathic circuits. As they tingled beneath his palms he reached out with his mind, seeking the heart of the TARDIS.

There! She surged up to greet him, glad, as always, of his company but reproachful that he had not communed with her for so long. He soothed, he apologized, he explained. She understood, and gladly lent him her energy.

The lights in the console room dimmed as the pure artron energy flowed into the Doctor's body. He straightened up, feeling his pain, his tiredness and the dregs of despair that he had not been able to admit to having washed away.

'You were taking a bit of a risk, weren't you, Doctor?' he murmured to himself. 'Assuming that Vaughn kept his mind somewhere in his head. The logical place would have been in his chest, where he could protect it better. Still: once a Cyberman, always a Cyberman, I suppose.'

He bent down and picked Vaughn's head up. Striking a pose, he proclaimed, 'Alas, poor Tobias. I knew him, Horatio: a fellow of infinite . . .' He grimaced sadly. 'A fellow of infinite arrogance, in point of fact.' He patted the console. 'Don't worry, old girl, I wouldn't have let him have you.'

The Doctor paused, as if listening.

'I don't know,' he admitted. 'I should dispose of him completely, I suppose, but . . .'

Another pause. The Doctor smiled and shook his head.

'No, I can't do that. I . . . I owe it to the memory of a man named Zebulon Pryce to keep Vaughn alive.'

He turned the head over and delved around inside the neck. His hand came away covered in coolant and lubricant fluid, but clutching a small crystal.

'Delight becomes death-longing if all longing else be vain,' he quoted softly, then slipped the crystal into his pocket, threw Vaughn's head away and walked towards the doors.

'Let's see how Bernice is getting on with that Hith ship,' he said, then paused in the doorway. 'And you'd better prepare two guest rooms,' he added. 'We may be playing host to a few more passengers.'

The TARDIS seemed to make a soft, contented sound.

'Yes,' he agreed. 'It will be just like the old days.'

Bernice was still staring out of the window into the red darkness when she realized that the Doctor was standing beside her. Behind him, Cwej and Forrester seemed to be arresting security guards wholesale.

'It's all falling apart,' she said dully.

The Doctor nodded. 'Entropy gets to us all, in the end,' he said. 'People and computers and empires. Nothing survives. Nothing goes on for ever.'

'Except for death and injustice,' she said without looking at him.

'But,' he added, 'we can rage against the dying of the light.'

She nodded towards the scarlet sky and the scattered fires outside.

'I thought that once we'd turned the ship's engines on, everything would be all right. I thought we could just turn off all the madness, like we had a switch or something. I thought Powerless Friendless's death would matter!'

'No,' he said. 'It had all gone too far. The riots have their own momentum now. And there are still people out there whose madness hasn't emerged yet. They're just time bombs, walking around, waiting to explode. When they do, they may take someone with them. They may take a lot of someones.'

'Then what have we accomplished?' she whispered.

He thought for a moment. 'We've stopped more people going mad,' he said finally. 'Lanced the boil, if you like. The riots will die away, instead of leading to full anarchy. The Earth Empire will still fall – there's a lot of pain here that wasn't caused by the icarons, a lot of planets that want to secede – but it will fall more gracefully and slowly than it would have done had we not been here. Fewer people will die. A lot fewer people. And what replaces the Empire will grow out of stability, rather than destruction. In the end, the scales are tipped a little bit towards the light.'

'But not by much.'

'But not by much,' he agreed. 'And there are other things that won't happen, because we've been here.'

She turned to face him. He was looking shifty. 'Other things?' she challenged.

'I've faced some of my own personal demons,' he said, 'and prevailed. Earth will be a better place. For a while.'

Now it was her turn to nod. 'We did good?'

He thought for a moment. 'We're not the score-keepers,' he said finally. 'But, in the end, when the points are tallied, I think they'll say we did good.'

She smiled at him, and he smiled back at her.

'I keep meaning to ask,' she said. 'Do we get a salary for doing this?'

Epilogue

'More tea, Roslyn?'

'It's *Roz*,' Forrester said to Cwej's mother, trying not to snap. The poor woman would probably have a heart attack. 'No. No thanks.'

Mrs Cwej wandered off, not looking at all hurt. Forrester silently cursed. She did not want to be there.

Then again, where did she want to be? Her empty apartment? The Adjudication lodge which, if it hadn't been destroyed in the riots, would be staffed by colleagues she couldn't trust? Her family estate on Io? Where could she go where she would feel welcome?

'Something stronger?' Cwej's father said, coming in from the kitchen. He was carrying a bottle.

'Yeah,' she said, 'why not?'

'My thoughts exactly,' he said, handing her a glass and pouring a generous measure. 'Three hundred years old. Got it on Gallavax Prime. Brewed from the fermented pollen of mutant space bees.'

'Lovely,' Forrester said. 'There's nothing better than mutant space bee pollen when you're looking for something to ferment.'

'I've had it ever since I was Chris's age,' Cwej's father continued, oblivious to Forrester's sarcasm. 'Saving it for a special occasion. Last night, while we were barricaded in, I thought, if we ever get through this, I'll drink it.'

'Moments don't get much more special than living when you thought you were going to die,' Forrester agreed. She glanced over to where Cwej stood talking to Bernice beside a large blue box that belonged to the Doctor. 'Or

317

seeing it happen to someone else,' she added, and took a sip. It tasted of honey and sunlight. Not bad. Not bad at all.

Then again, anything would taste nice after what they had been through.

The simcord was on in the corner, and she tuned in to the voice of the newscaster saying: 'I'm Shythe Shahid and this is *The Empire Today*, on the spot, on and off the Earth. Martial law was rescinded this morning as the Imperial Landsknechte and the Order of Adjudicators reported that their attempts to get the riots under control were succeeding. Fires still rage throughout the Undertown, but reports of violent incidents are dropping and flights have resumed from most major spaceports. Damage is estimated at up to nine hundred trillion Imperial schillings, most of which is expected to be raised by taxation of off-world dominions, but the questions now being asked are: why did it happen, and will it happen again? Meanwhile, news just in from the planet Solos ...'

'We're thinking of moving off Earth,' Cwej's father confided. 'It will happen again. Bound to. People just aren't happy.'

'Off Earth?' Forrester was taken aback. Despite the riots, she couldn't imagine living anywhere else.

Except, a cold voice within her said, you'll have to. Adjudicator Secular Rashid is on the INITEC payroll. You'll never be able to forgive her for that, and for Martle's – Martle's death – but you'll never make anything stick. Never.

'Yep,' Cwej's dad continued, 'but we're still trying to work out where. I mean, the galaxy's so big, and the Empire extends so far.'

'Why not try Hithis?' the Doctor said, emerging from the kitchen. He was carrying his jacket slung over his arm, and he had his shirt sleeves rolled up as if he'd just been doing some work.

'Hithis?' Cwej's dad said.

'A lovely world, soon to be returned to its rightful owners, I hope. Provost-Major Beltempest – or whatever

318

his real name is – has promised to intercede directly with the Empress. You'll be welcomed there.' He turned to Cwej's mother. 'Oh, by the way, I think I've managed to fix your irradiator, Mrs Cwej.'

'Was it the techbrain?' she trilled.

'Indeed it was,' he replied. 'Fortunately I had a replacement with me. It might be a tad more intelligent than your irradiator actually needs to be, but it should work perfectly.' He smiled to himself. 'Just promise me that you won't go connecting it up to a radio transmitter.'

Mrs Cwej smiled vaguely, and moved off towards Bernice.

'If you're operating a travel agency,' Forrester murmured to the Doctor, 'then I'd like a chat.'

'Of course,' he replied. 'Thinking of emigrating?'

She sighed. 'We can't stay here,' she said, glancing over at Cwej. 'I don't know if the boy wonder's realized yet, but there's a lot of angry people out there. Conspiracies always run deep, and Rashid knows that we know. We can't touch her for it – there's no evidence – but she'll always be worried. We'll have to start over, somewhere else.'

The Doctor nodded, and was about to say something when Cwej walked over.

'Doc, there's something I need to ask you,' he said.

'Ask away,' the Doctor replied. 'Advice is free.'

'It's – well . . .'

'It's about this friend of yours,' the Doctor prompted.

'Yeah. Right. He's got a problem.'

'Friends always do.'

Cwej was blushing now; Forrester was amazed to see it extend all the way up to the top of his ears.

'You see, my friend had a lot of body-bepple done, some time ago, and he got exposed pretty heavily to the radiation from that icaron thing.'

'Hmm,' the Doctor said, non-committally.

'And I – my friend – was a bit worried that he might be, you know . . .'

'At risk?'

'Yeah. At risk.' Cwej's face was heavy with expectant dread. 'Should he be?' he asked.

The Doctor glanced over at Forrester and smiled a warm smile that made his face crease up in unexpected ways. She was suddenly taken with the vast and caring humanity that shone out of his eyes. The sight made something well up inside her, something she hadn't felt in years. Hope? Perhaps it was too early to tell, but she welcomed it cautiously, like an old but irresponsible friend.

'I have some equipment that could pinpoint any deep-seated effects,' the Doctor said, turning back to Cwej, 'and eradicate them easily. Perhaps your friend would like a quick examination. Just to be on the safe side.'

'Yeah,' Cwej said softly. 'Yeah, he would.'

The Doctor's smile encompassed everyone in the room. Like a showman, he gestured towards the blue box that stood in the corner.

'The Doctor will see you now,' he said.

Masero 94

most wanted criminal in the galaxy, believes he has found it. The Doctor and Bernice must battle to stop him on a planet where chance and coincidence have become far too powerful.

ISBN 0 426 20377 1

THE PIT
Neil Penswick
One of the Seven Planets is a nameless giant, quarantined against all intruders. But when the TARDIS materializes, it becomes clear that the planet is far from empty – and the Doctor begins to realize that the planet hides a terrible secret from the Time Lords' past.

ISBN 0 426 20378 X

DECEIT
Peter Darvill-Evans
Ace – three years older, wiser and tougher – is back. She is part of a group of Irregular Auxiliaries on an expedition to the planet Arcadia. They think they are hunting Daleks, but the Doctor knows better. He knows that the paradise planet hides a being far more powerful than the Daleks – and much more dangerous.

ISBN 0 426 20362 3

LUCIFER RISING
Jim Mortimore & Andy Lane
Reunited, the Doctor, Ace and Bernice travel to Lucifer, the site of a scientific expedition that they know will shortly cease to exist. Discovering why involves them in sabotage, murder and the resurrection of eons-old alien powers. Are there Angels on Lucifer? And what does it all have to do with Ace?

ISBN 0 426 20338 7

WHITE DARKNESS
David McIntee
The TARDIS crew, hoping for a rest, come to Haiti in 1915. But they find that the island is far from peaceful: revolution is brewing in the city; the dead are walking from the cemeteries; and, far underground, the ancient rulers of the galaxy are stirring in their sleep.

ISBN 0 426 20395 X

SHADOWMIND
Christopher Bulis
On the colony world of Arden, something dangerous is growing stronger. Something that steals minds and memories. Something that can reach

out to another planet, Tairgire, where the newest exhibit in the sculpture park is a blue box surmounted by a flashing light.

ISBN 0 426 20394 1

BIRTHRIGHT
Nigel Robinson
Stranded in Edwardian London with a dying TARDIS, Bernice investigates a series of grisly murders. In the far future, Ace leads a group of guerrillas against their insect-like, alien oppressors. Why has the Doctor left them, just when they need him most?

ISBN 0 426 20393 3

ICEBERG
David Banks
In 2006, an ecological disaster threatens the Earth; only the FLIPback team, working in an Antarctic base, can avert the catastrophe. But hidden beneath the ice, sinister forces have gathered to sabotage humanity's last hope. The Cybermen have returned and the Doctor must face them alone.

ISBN 0 426 20392 5

BLOOD HEAT
Jim Mortimore
The TARDIS is attacked by an alien force; Bernice is flung into the vortex; and the Doctor and Ace crash-land on Earth. There they find dinosaurs roaming the derelict London streets, and Brigadier Lethbridge-Stewart leading the remnants of UNIT in a desperate fight against the Silurians who have taken over and changed his world.

ISBN 0 426 20399 2

THE DIMENSION RIDERS
Daniel Blythe
A holiday in Oxford is cut short when the Doctor is summoned to Space Station Q4, where ghostly soldiers from the future watch from the shadows among the dead. Soon, the Doctor is trapped in the past, Ace is accused of treason and Bernice is uncovering deceit among the college cloisters.

ISBN 0 426 20397 6

THE LEFT-HANDED HUMMINGBIRD
Kate Orman
Someone has been playing with time. The Doctor, Ace and Bernice must travel to the Aztec Empire in 1487, to London in the Swinging

Sixties and to the sinking of the *Titanic* as they attempt to rectify the temporal faults – and survive the attacks of the living god Huitzilin.

ISBN 0 426 20404 2

CONUNDRUM
Steve Lyons

A killer is stalking the streets of the village of Arandale. The victims are found each day, drained of blood. Someone has interfered with the Doctor's past again, and he's landed in a place he knows he once destroyed, from which it seems there can be no escape.

ISBN 0 426 20408 5

NO FUTURE
Paul Cornell

At last the Doctor comes face-to-face with the enemy who has been threatening him, leading him on a chase that has brought the TARDIS to London in 1976. There he finds that reality has been subtly changed and the country he once knew is rapidly descending into anarchy as an alien invasion force prepares to land . . .

ISBN 0 426 20409 3

TRAGEDY DAY
Gareth Roberts

When the TARDIS crew arrive on Olleril, they soon realize that all is not well. Assassins arrive to carry out a killing that may endanger the entire universe. A being known as the Supreme One tests horrific weapons. And a secret order of monks observes the growing chaos.

ISBN 0 426 20410 7

LEGACY
Gary Russell

The Doctor returns to Peladon, on the trail of a master criminal. Ace pursues intergalactic mercenaries who have stolen the galaxy's most evil artifact while Bernice strikes up a dangerous friendship with a Martian Ice Lord. The players are making the final moves in a devious and lethal plan – but for once it isn't the Doctor's.

ISBN 0 426 20412 3

THEATRE OF WAR
Justin Richards

Menaxus is a barren world on the front line of an interstellar war, home to a ruined theatre which hides sinister secrets. When the TARDIS crew land on the planet, they find themselves trapped in a deadly reenactment of an ancient theatrical tragedy.

ISBN 0 426 20414 X

ALL-CONSUMING FIRE
Andy Lane

The secret library of St John the Beheaded has been robbed. The thief has taken forbidden books which tell of gateways to other worlds. Only one team can be trusted to solve the crime: Sherlock Holmes, Doctor Watson – and a mysterious stranger who claims he travels in time and space.

ISBN 0 426 20415 8

BLOOD HARVEST
Terrance Dicks

While the Doctor and Ace are selling illegal booze in a town full of murderous gangsters, Bernice has been abandoned on a vampire-infested planet outside normal space. This story sets in motion events which are continued in *Goth Opera*, the first in a new series of Missing Adventures.

ISBN 0 426 20417 4

STRANGE ENGLAND
Simon Messingham

In the idyllic gardens of a Victorian country house, the TARDIS crew discover a young girl whose body has been possessed by a beautiful but lethal insect. And they find that the rural paradise is turning into a world of nightmare ruled by the sinister Quack.

ISBN 0 426 20419 0

FIRST FRONTIER
David A. McIntee

When Bernice asks to see the dawn of the space age, the Doctor takes the TARDIS to Cold War America, which is facing a threat far more deadly than Communist Russia. The militaristic Tzun Confederacy have made Earth their next target for conquest – and the aliens have already landed.

ISBN 0 426 20421 2

ST ANTHONY'S FIRE
Mark Gatiss

The TARDIS crew visit Betrushia, a planet in terrible turmoil. A vicious, genocidal war is raging between the lizard-like natives. With time